THE
TUKOR'S
JOURNEY

Jeannine Kellogg

The Tukor's Journey © 2018 Jeannine Kellogg

ISBN 13: 978-0-9995714-0-8

Library of Congress Catalog Number: 2017917375

Printed in the United States of America

Distributed by Itasca Books Minneapolis, MN

First Printing: 2018

18 19 20 21 22   5 4 3 2 1

Cover and interior design by Laura Drew
Cover and interior illustrations copyright © 2018 by Jim Madsen
Author photo by Jessica Sauck Photography

Jagged Compass LLC
2038 Ford Parkway #461
St. Paul, MN 55116
www.JaggedCompass.com

To my nephews Ben, Erik, and Sam
for their inspiration and encouragement.

THE TUKOR'S JOURNEY

PART ONE: ESCAPE

A Story on the Move   1
A Trail of Ash   10
Scatter like Confetti   17

PART TWO: CASTAWAY

Stuck on the Inside   32
A New Spin Around   34
A Cage Called Earth   41
The Yellow Sun   45
A Cry Melts into Lava   53
Grounded   55
A Cage Called Water   62
One Big Act   66
The Voices of Blue   78
Butterfly Lucky Charm   81
The Circle Closes   87
Frozen Dough   94
Let Me Try   101
Knock, Knock, Goodbye   106
The White-Water Terraces   119

PART THREE: INVITED

Scattered Stars	126
A Covert Dig	138
Like Cinnamon	142
No One Can Find Them	146
Left Behind to Die	150
Belch Balloon	159
He Shot Them	164
Bustard and Spoonbill	167
Snagging the Lure	171
Paralyzed like Stone	185
This Isn't Cereal	192
Gone to You	200
STOP!	205
Dead Goats Heist	216
Too Much Fuel	222
Broken Cages	234
Tractor Pull	238
The Leap	250
Heir Eel Combine	257
Saving a Secret	263
A Daunting Invitation	266
Dig. Find. Lose.	272
Check or Hold?	278
Silky and Woolly	285
Crop Circles	292
What Happened, Daddy?	299
The Hickory Box	306
Go North	314
Useless Bikes	321
Yelloweye Rockfish	328
Don't Know His Name	336
Give Me a Clue	349
Leaving for Camp	359

PART FOUR: JOURNEY

Charged	374
What's That Smell?	386
This Isn't Camp	394
A Disgraceful Drubbing	401
The Air Feels Our Fear	411
A Wish to Disappear	417
Close Enough to Strike	420
The Sand Has Ears	431
The Journey Follows You	437
Mirror in the Eyeball	444
A Silent Fear Flies By	450
Secrets Can Be Such Lonely Things	453
To Move an Echo	460
What's Gotten into You?	465
Locked In	471
Come with Us, Little One	477
No More Air	485
A Memory of Sevens	489
Raadsel	495
Call the Murky Fog In	509
Let It Be. Let It Go.	512
Closing the Mountain	520
No Rules for Me	526
Raw and Bleeding	533
Shall We Go?	537
Do Not Sleep Yet	549
Withering in the Sun	558
A Broken Echo	563
Too Small, Too Far	570
Where?	576

ESCAPE

1

A STORY ON THE MOVE

When a year ends on this round and spinning ball called home, every big city, small town, distant house, and ship at sea turns its last tick and final tock before Earth begins another journey around the sun. But one New Year's Eve, the sun did not say the final evening's goodbye above New York City. Instead, heavy cloud cover hung low and draped the tips of the city's tallest buildings with a smoky gray haze. Wind whipped through the streets, trash swirled in doorways, and debris bunched together along the curbs. People bent downward, covered their heads from the cold, and moved quickly to reach their destinations.

Yet it was perfect weather for one New Year's Eve event. An event no one noticed. A young snow monkey escaped the Central Park Zoo carrying an old, weatherworn satchel. The satchel held a collection of old papers bound loosely together with frayed thread. Its pages were frail, faded, and tattered from having been carried on distant journeys and read countless times.

Earlier that day, Snow Monkey had refused to escape and deliver the important satchel, fretting about the risks and worrying that he would fail to protect it. He knew the consequences if the mission failed: Without someone to accept the satchel and choose the mission contained therein, Earth could be blown to bits, exploded as if it were merely a small glass marble. Life itself would blow away. Gone forever.

The bitter cost of failure weighed heavily on his young heart as he reviewed the escape plan with his elders. But despite his reluctance, the elders would not let Snow Monkey cave in to his fears, and they sent him on his way to deliver the Story that night. After the zoo closed for the day, Snow Monkey took his first reluctant step and slyly slipped away. He followed the planned escape route from the south end of the park all the way to the Upper East Side, where he would meet a Red Panda and give him the satchel.

That cold evening, people hunkered over in their winter coats and kept their eyes down to protect themselves from the strong, blustery gusts. No one noticed as Snow Monkey swung carefully from tree to tree through the park with a satchel safely secured on his back. When he nearly reached the Metropolitan Museum of Art, he stopped and hid in the trees to wait for just the right opportunity.

A long lineup of vehicles bunched at a red light, and he took his chance. He dropped from the tree and crawled under a bus, then another, finally reaching a small truck on the other side of the street whose driver was waiting for pedestrians to cross before making a turn from Fifth Avenue. He grabbed hold of the underside of the truck and held on as it turned away from the park. As the truck drove past Snow Monkey's destination, he dropped off and scuttled under a parked car. He was relieved to find the exact narrow space between two buildings that he had been told was there. He scooted out from under the car and into the narrow passageway, then climbed up a rain gutter to the rooftop.

The buildings, connected wall to wall, made it easy for him to run from rooftop to rooftop.

This wasn't so bad after all, thought Snow Monkey as he reached his intended destination. To remain unseen, Snow Monkey ducked down behind the decorative wall that circled the rooftop and was grateful for an awning that kept him hidden.

But Red Panda was not there.

Snow Monkey did not want to wait. There were just too many people out and about to stay and dawdle. The owner of a townhouse across the street was hosting a massive New Year's party. The house was packed with people and more were still arriving. Limousines were lined up, waiting to drop off their exclusive guests.

His elders had said, "If Red Panda is not there, don't dally. Just come right back home."

Snow Monkey backed up from his hiding spot to return to the zoo but unexpectedly backed right into Red Panda. Startled, Snow Monkey bounded up to land on top of the chimney. When he realized whom he had run into, he jumped down quickly, thankfully unseen.

"They warned me about your jokes," said Snow Monkey.

Red Panda laughed and tumbled playfully across the rooftop. "I never get tired of sneaking up on someone!"

"But don't do that! I could've been seen."

"That satchel looks heavy," said Red Panda. "What did they send with you?"

Snow Monkey handed him the satchel. Red Panda opened it and saw the pages, then his eyes drooped with sadness. "We really are in desperate times if they pulled this out of hiding. I didn't expect you to be carrying the Story. All of it. The secrets, the missions, the clues . . . Not good. Not good. Something's brewing for this to be on the move."

Red Panda returned the contents to the satchel and handed it back to Snow Monkey.

"No, you're supposed to take it," said Snow Monkey, refusing the take the satchel.

Red Panda said, "Yes, I know. But we have a problem. I got the first message that I was supposed to meet you, accept whatever you were delivering, and take it to a new owner. The problem is, I never got the second message about who the new owner is, and I don't have a way to keep it safe. You need to take the Story back with you."

"But we just got the satchel today," said Snow Monkey. "And we were told to keep it moving, and quickly. I wanted to keep the Story for a few days so I could read it, but they said absolutely not. It's the only copy of the Story left in the world. And it needs to get to the new owner. Urgently. They said it must go."

"The situation must be urgent, or they'd never risk moving it around like this. I heard the Grezniks are brewing a battle bigger than we've ever seen. It must be true."

"I've never seen a Greznik," said Snow Monkey. "What do they look like?"

"Haven't your elders told you everything about Grezniks?"

"I've only heard bits and pieces. I've asked about the Story, but no one shares the history anymore. I don't think they even know it."

"I know, I know. And the ones who do know—at least parts of it—are dying or getting killed off. We are losing the history," acknowledged Red Panda.

"My elders regret that they don't know the important details. Their generation failed to learn, so they can't pass them along. Now they admit it was a mistake. Back then they thought the battles were over. A thing of the past. 'Why bother?' they thought."

"Well tonight you can read the Story because we don't have an owner to give it to yet," said Red Panda.

"Can't you give it to a Tukor?" asked Snow Monkey.

"I'm assuming that I would have given it to a Tukor, but no one knows where one is. Before you got here, I was spying on that house right there, across the street from us. Someone got wind that the owner of that townhouse bought some important land and—"

"Important land for what? And where?"

"You see, that's the other problem. I'm supposed to deliver the Story, but no one knows to whom. And this man bought important land, but no one knows where. We used to have very effective networks for sharing information— strong communities. But now it all gets messed up. Look down there." Red Panda pointed to the doorway of the townhouse across the street where the host of the party, a man named Neil Bosonataski, was greeting a famous movie star who had just arrived. Red Panda continued, "See that man right there at the door? His name is Neil. He apparently owns the important land. Wherever it is. They hoped he might be a Tukor. But . . ."

They watched as the schmoozing, slippery old man named Neil greeted his guests.

"Hmm. He doesn't seem like the right guy to give the Story to," Snow Monkey said.

"Definitely not. He isn't the one. I'm sure of that. If important land fell into his hands, we're all in trouble. He has nothing to do with it. The information I'm getting is all messed up. It's all a first-rate, dangerous mess. Until we sort out what's going on, it's probably best to keep the Story in Manhattan for a while. I trust that your friends will find a place for its safekeeping. Grezniks would love to get their hands on the Story. All the secrets. The battle tactics. The clues. But there's no chance Grezniks will come to New York to steal the Story. They avoid the big cities—too many people. That's why you'll probably never see a Greznik, not in New York anyway."

"But you've seen one?"

"Many. That is, before I was living in Manhattan," said Red Panda.

"Can you tell me about the Grezniks? I hear bits and pieces, but they may have got it all wrong. They think Grezniks have five legs, which can't be right. How can a creature be powerful with a lopsided leg count?"

"But Grezniks do have five legs. They run on four legs. Their fifth leg is stocky like a pedestal, and they store it in their belly pocket. When they sleep, they drop down the fifth leg and stand on it, and the other four legs are folded up."

"They say they're always ready to attack."

"Yes, and ruthlessly."

As Red Panda spoke, he was running all over the roof furniture and circling the rooftop.

"Can't you sit still?" asked Snow Monkey. "You're making me nervous."

Red Panda paused for a bit, but he started running around again.

"I guess not," said Snow Monkcy. "Can Grezniks really run faster than sound?"

"Yes, if they need to," said Red Panda as he tumbled around. Then he grabbed an apple that he had stashed on the rooftop and munched on it while talking excitedly to his new friend. "Grezniks' insides don't have bones, at least not the breakable kind we have. Their insides are just, simply, power. Their structure is stronger than steel, yet pliable and stretchable. They're generally about the size of a cheetah, stockier or thinner as they need to be. They can even flatten themselves completely, camouflaging exactly to their surroundings so you can't see them at all. Their hairs are clear like glass, but they can turn any color at will. And their feet? I wish I had their feet. Their feet can run on any surface, even sand and water. They can sprint across an entire ocean, even in rough seas. But if a Greznik slows as it runs across the water, it will drop like a rock and dissolve instantly. Water is their most powerful enemy. No one understands why, but Grezniks dissolve the exact moment they're submerged."

"How can they run on water if they dissolve in water?"

"They have webbing between the toes that doesn't dissolve when they run."

"Will they dissolve in rain?" asked Snow Monkey.

"Nope."

"How about dousing them with a bucket of water?"

"Nope. Not even a fire hose. They have to be submerged," explained Red Panda.

"It's all very strange."

"Nothing about them really makes sense. Nothing about them follows the normal rules of science, you know, stuff like gravity, atoms, and molecules, and so on. They have two sets of claws. And two sets of teeth. In both cases, one set is retractable, longer, and sharp as swords. They even look metallic. Oh yeah, and if they fall into rivers of lava, they explode and evaporate. I eliminated a couple of them that way when I lived in . . ."

Red Panda faded into memories of his days in the wild, before he was captured. He was missing his family terribly and lost his train of thought.

As he got up to leave, Snow Monkey said, "Grezniks are far worse than I imagined. I don't think I want to know more. Besides, I had better get going anyway."

"Wait," said Red Panda, not wanting his new friend to leave. "There's more to tell. Greznik eyes are the creepiest."

"It can't get any creepier than what you've told me already. It's all too much, too fast. I can't process all that at once."

"They have six eyes. Two in front. Two in back. One on each side. Their eyeballs have no white. They're like liquid glass, a constantly spinning kaleidoscope of colors. They have no eyelids, so they never blink. Their eyeballs can recede back into the head. It's gross. I've seen it."

"Seriously, stop. It's too much. You'll give me nightmares."

"GET DOWN!" shouted Red Panda.

Snow Monkey ducked down.

"They saw us!" whispered Red Panda.

"Who?"

"Hurry! Follow me!"

2

A TRAIL OF ASH

Red Panda scampered across the roof, opened the town-house door, and scooted down into the stairwell. Snow Monkey followed.

As they hid, Snow Monkey whispered worriedly, "Who saw us?"

"Three kids across the street, looking out the window. The boy pointed at us. He saw us. I know he did. Not good. Not good."

After waiting a little bit, Snow Monkey waddled back up the townhouse stairs to go back outside.

Red Panda said, "Stop! What're you doing? You can't go out there now that they've seen you."

"Shh, don't talk so loud. We can't hide in this house. People live here. And I really do have to get back to the zoo," whispered Snow Monkey.

"No one's here. You don't need to whisper," said Red Panda in a normal voice.

"How do you know?"

"The Putnicks own this place. They have houses all over the world, and they never come to this one. I come here all the time for the good food."

"So, do they know you live here?" asked Snow Monkey.

"No. A caretaker maintains the house. She doesn't have any idea about me. Don't know why, but she fills the refrigerator and cupboards even when they're not here. When some food is gone, she just assumes somebody stayed for a while."

"Do you stay here all the time?"

"I have several places like this. But this one is the best. Can't beat the food. You can imagine how pleased I was when I found out my stakeout location for tonight was my favorite place. What are the odds?" rattled Red Panda. "I love it here because there's always a bowl of apples. And I love apples. You know how people decorate tables with bowls of apples?"

"I don't know, actually," said Snow Monkey. "I grew up in the Japanese mountains."

"Then I got something to show ya. Follow me."

Red Panda ran downstairs, assuming Snow Monkey would follow. But Snow Monkey did not follow. He had heard too many stories about red pandas making mischief everywhere; they cannot help themselves. Snow Monkey went back up the stairs again but could not get out.

Red Panda returned to the bottom of the stairs and smiled. "I locked the door. Come on. No one's here. I promise."

Snow Monkey reluctantly followed Red Panda, who led him all the way to the basement. Red Panda stood before a closed door in the basement and said, "You're going to love this!"

He opened the door to a long, underground, freshwater pool, steamy hot. Now Snow Monkey could not help himself. He set down the precious satchel, jumped up high, and did a belly flop right into the steaming waters.

Soaking in the warmth, Snow Monkey said, "When I close my eyes, I feel like I'm back in Japan."

"So you weren't born in a zoo?"

"No, I just got here from Japan. I wish I could go back. I miss the mountains. But, alas, I live in a zoo now. When did you escape the zoo?"

"Oh, many months ago," said Red Panda. "They searched high and low for me. Newspapers covered my escape. After a while, they gave up. Just assumed I died."

"I have to go back tonight to make it look like I never left. Why didn't you ever have to go back?"

"A story for another day," said Red Panda solemnly.

"Have you ever talked to a Greznik?"

"No. Grezniks cannot speak to anyone. Their language is incomprehensible. And they cannot write anything. That's one thing their feet can't do—write."

"They can't even talk to each other?" asked Snow Monkey.

"Oh, they definitely talk to each other. But no other creature can hear them because they almost always speak in a pitch that none of us can hear. Sometimes they'll talk in a voice we can hear, but it doesn't matter if they do—

no one can understand their language. It's like the world's most complicated ciphertext but no one has the cipher."

Snow Monkey picked at his own fur while floating enjoyably in the warm waters. "You said their fur is clear?"

"I don't know that their bizarre hair can be called fur. Their hairs can stand on end, sharp like needles, or become slippery like jelly, or prickly and sticky like cockleburs. Hairs even grow inside their mouths, but it's all matted down with a disgusting phlegm. Really gooey gross."

Red Panda put the tip of his tail in the water.

"Why don't you jump in?" asked Snow Monkey. "It's wonderful in here."

"Who me? No, no. I don't like to swim," said Red Panda as he shook the water off his tail.

"Do Grezniks have fluffy tails like yours?"

"Nothin' fluffy about a Greznik. Let's see. What can I compare it to? The tail is more like an armadillo. And it can be long or pulled in entirely, or it can snap open and crack like a whip, or it can wrap around a neck to choke anything. The snout is long and tubular and oozes a gross phlegm that they constantly lap up. And it's covered in constantly waving appendages, like those of a star-nosed mole and a sea anemone, which are used to identify anything by its smell."

"You talk too fast. I hardly caught a word of that," said Snow Monkey. His voice slowed and his eyes drooped as he fell asleep in the warm water.

Red Panda suddenly jumped up.

"Get out!" Red Panda whispered frantically, jumping up and down.

But Snow Monkey was sound asleep and draped over the edge of the pool.

Red Panda shook the drowsy monkey, "Get out! Now!"

"What? What?"

"People just drove into the garage! Someone's here!"

Snow Monkey bounded out of the water, dripping wet. He shook his fur, splattering water everywhere.

"Quick, run to the roof," whispered Red Panda.

Snow Monkey grabbed the satchel, secured it to his back, and they ran up the steps—but not fast enough. Mr. and Mrs. Putnick were already in the kitchen at the top of the basement staircase. The Putnicks were in a loud argument as Mr. Putnick unloaded more and more luggage. Every time he dropped a bag into the kitchen, Mrs. Putnick barked at him about something else.

After hurling a litany of angry remarks at him in another language, she went into the bathroom, and he left to bring in the last piece of luggage. Red Panda and Snow Monkey made a run for it, but they did not get past the foyer before she opened the bathroom door. Just in time, they slid under a table draped in a long, heavy cloth.

Mrs. Putnick yelled at her husband, "Come on. Hurry up. The party already started! We were supposed to be there an hour ago."

He grumbled from the kitchen, "It's just across the street. If you'd help with the luggage, we'd be done sooner."

The doorbell rang, and Mrs. Putnick let in the

caretaker and immediately barked an order at her. "Bring my luggage up."

"I hope you had a good trip. Anything you'd like brought up first?" asked the friendly caretaker.

Mrs. Putnick snapped back, "When I say bring my luggage up, I mean bring my luggage up. All of it. And hurry it up—we're in a rush to get to a New Year's party."

"The missus here is awful," whispered Red Panda. "Missus Miserable."

Snow Monkey put his finger to his mouth to say, "Shh," mortified that Red Panda would risk being heard.

"Did you hear that?" asked Mrs. Putnick.

"No," said the caretaker.

"I heard critters. A chewing sound. Over there. Under that table. I told you to keep this place clear of rats while we're away! I heard them. Find those rats. Now. And bring up the luggage. Now," ordered Mrs. Putnick.

Mrs. Putnick went upstairs, and the caretaker exhaled. She grabbed two suitcases and carried them upstairs.

Before the caretaker came back down, Red Panda and Snow Monkey ran into the living room and into the chimney, opened the damper, and tried to climb up. But they could not fit. They popped out, covered in soot, and ran across the carpet, leaving a trail of black ash.

"Stop!" whispered Snow Monkey. "You're leaving prints."

"Who cares? We've got to get out of here! She'll kill us. And they've got dogs!"

15

Big dogs came scurrying out of the garage and into the house, their claws scratching on the kitchen floor. The dogs immediately picked up the scent and chased Snow Monkey and Red Panda up the stairs.

3

SCATTER LIKE CONFETTI

Snow Monkey and Red Panda ran all the way up the steps, leaving a trail of soot the entire way. The dogs bounded up the steps in pursuit.

Mrs. Putnick barked at her husband, "Those stupid dogs of yours! Look at the mess they made! Footprints everywhere!"

Red Panda led Snow Monkey up the steps to the rooftop, and out they went. Snow Monkey slammed the door shut just as the dogs jumped toward them. Red Panda and Snow Monkey fled across the rooftops, and when they reached the end of the line, Red Panda climbed on Snow Monkey's back and hung on tight. Snow Monkey climbed down a wall, then swung from a flagpole and landed on top of an airport shuttle van. The passengers heard something land on the roof, and they screamed and ducked. Snow Monkey and Red Panda jumped off the van and scooted under a parked delivery truck, where two young men were hurriedly filling the truck with cardboard boxes.

One delivery man said to the other, "Did they tell you how we're supposed to get there? It'll be surrounded by security. We can't just drive through it all."

The other answered, "They said to go down Fifth Avenue and stop at the end of the park. There will be someone waiting for us, and we'll clear security. A police escort will lead us from there."

Snow Monkey said, "Should we get on that truck? Its route passes the zoo."

"I can unlock any truck from the inside," boasted Red Panda. "Let's do it."

When the men were not looking, Snow Monkey and Red Panda leaped into the truck and hid behind the boxes. The men loaded the last box and drove off.

Red Panda said, "Once we're near the zoo, we'll open the back door and run into the park. They won't know we were ever in here. And I know how to get you back to the zoo unseen from there."

But when they got near the zoo, not even Red Panda could unlock the door.

They heard the truck driver take a call on the speaker-phone. "We're going as fast as we can, but nothing moves quickly on New Year's Eve. Besides, these boxes should've been delivered hours ago. Why's it all so late anyway?"

A man on the phone responded, "The deliveries got mixed up. They delivered boxes and boxes of hot dog buns and falafel mix instead of the confetti."

Red Panda broke open a box in the back. It was filled with colorful confetti. He opened another and it, too, was filled with confetti.

Red Panda looked out the small truck window and said, "Not good. Not good."

"What's wrong?" asked Snow Monkey.

"We're going to Times Square," said Red Panda.

"Times Square? On New Year's Eve? You've got to be kidding."

"These boxes contain pounds of confetti, the kind they drop on Times Square. You know, when the ball drops at midnight. Why else would they be in a hurry to deliver? And it's very close to midnight."

The truck finally reached its destination, and Red Panda looked out the little truck window. They were in a private delivery garage, and people were lined up like sprinters waiting for a gun to go off. Red Panda opened the largest box and they both jumped in. They jammed themselves in and hid under the colorful confetti. The truck doors opened. Two men jumped into the truck and started unloading the boxes one by one.

Each person in the lineup grabbed a box of confetti, put it on a dolly, and ran off to deliver each box to one of various confetti drop sites, located up high in the buildings surrounding Times Square.

The confetti coordinator encouraged the volunteers, "You can do it! Run as fast as you can! Midnight is almost here!"

From the dark inside of the box, they felt someone pick up their box and put it on a dolly. A woman grabbed the dolly and said, "I'll take this one."

Red Panda and Snow Monkey were jostled around as the woman pushed them at full speed toward an elevator.

But the wait for an elevator was taking too long, so the woman pulled the dolly up a flight of stairs, down a long hall, out the door, across a street, back inside, down a flight of stairs, and into another elevator along with too many other confetti sprinters. Along the bumpy journey, Snow Monkey and Red Panda heard the dings of an elevator. Squeaky dolly wheels. The woman's hurried footsteps. The coordinator's voice over the radio and cheerful celebrations outside. The voice of a security guard, and many complaints about an unfortunate number of wrongly delivered boxes of hot dog buns and falafel mix.

The woman got off the elevator, scurried down the hallway, and set the dolly down in a small room that overlooked Times Square. A man took the box off the dolly and dragged Snow Monkey and Red Panda's box toward a window.

"Why is this one so heavy?" he asked.

"I have no idea. But it is full of confetti. I'm sure of that. I got it right from the delivery truck," answered the woman. "Where are all the boxes of hot dog buns and falafel?"

"They're gone. Every box in here now is confetti," answered a man in the room. "And just in time. Midnight is almost here."

The woman asked, "We're supposed to throw the confetti out the window by handfuls, right?"

"Who cares at this point?" the man answered as he opened the windows for the confetti throw. "We don't have time to worry about technique. It's confetti. Just open the box and drop it all out the window."

Snow Monkey and Red Panda squirmed in the box. Red Panda whispered, "Not good. Not good."

The confetti coordinator's voice came over their radios. "Last call for confetti. Did anyone *not* get their confetti? Any of you still stuck with falafel and hot dog buns?"

The confetti-throwing volunteers were stationed all around Times Square, and they all confirmed they were ready.

"What a miracle. Only one minute to go," said the coordinator over the radio.

The woman opened the heavy box, and out jumped Red Panda and Snow Monkey. Startled, she shrieked right into her radio. Snow Monkey ran to the door but could not open it. The man tried to catch him.

"What's the problem?" asked the coordinator.

"A monkey! And a funny-looking furry thing!" said the woman.

Red Panda screeched angrily at the insult, jumped on her shoulders, and mussed her hair. She screamed and thrashed her shoulders to get him off her back.

Snow Monkey said, "What're you doing? We have to get out of here. Get on my back!"

The coordinator ignored the woman and said to the confetti-throwing crew, "It's almost countdown! Get your confetti in position. Remember, fluff up the confetti. Throw it by handfuls."

"See, I told you. We're supposed to throw it out by handfuls," said the woman to the man who was trying to catch Snow Monkey.

The coordinator said on the radios, "Get ready to throw!"

The woman panicked and asked over the radio, "What do I do with a screeching monkey?"

"Not a time for jokes!" said the confetti coordinator.

"I'm not joking!" yelped the woman.

People in the streets were counting down. "*Ten, nine, eight . . .*"

The man pointed to the boxes of confetti and said to the woman, "Forget the monkey! Get your box of confetti ready!"

"*Five, four, three, two, one!*"

The volunteers tossed handful after handful of the colorful confetti out of the buildings all along the perimeter of Times Square. Red Panda got on Snow Monkey's back, and Snow Monkey went straight for the window and jumped out on the ledge. It was difficult to see where to go since confetti was blowing everywhere.

Luckily, there was decorative stonework just above them. Snow Monkey grabbed hold of it and lifted them up to a maintenance balcony that ran along the edge of the building.

Snow Monkey and Red Panda circled over to the other side, where scaffolding scaled partway up the building. The wind was still ripping through the city with strong gusts. Snow Monkey, with Red Panda clinging to his back, waited for the gusts to subside, then took a risk and leaped downward, hoping he could firmly catch the scaffolding below. As they dropped downward, Red Panda closed his eyes and screamed.

Snow Monkey caught the scaffolding but slipped off and caught the next bar down. From there he swung skillfully through the latticed scaffolding, moving downward to escape. Red Panda closed his eyes and hung on to Snow Monkey for dear life.

But then they were seen.

"Look! A monkey!" shouted a woman from an open window.

Snow Monkey kept moving down the scaffolding, but then a man saw them. The man reached out of the window to grab the monkey and got him by the satchel. Red Panda bit the man, who yelped and let go. Snow Monkey dropped downward to get away, but his satchel caught on a piece of scaffolding and ripped open. The contents of the satchel blew everywhere; pages and pages of the Story flew upward and away, mixed in with thousands of pounds of confetti flying through the air. The frail pages ripped amid the blustery winds and swirled up, sideways, and between the tall buildings.

Snow Monkey stopped climbing and cried out, "It's gone! It's flying away!"

Red Panda screeched and cried.

People were pointing and yelling about the monkey and the panda, but the two mournful animals did not care. The Story was gone forever. The consequences were disastrous.

Snow Monkey climbed farther down to safety and found a hiding place behind an enormous billboard on Times Square. Confetti blew wildly through the air. People shouted joyfully below, reveling in the whirlwind of color. The frail, old pages of the Story were sure to be in tiny shreds, destroyed by heavy winds and the footsteps of the revelers. Only one page of the Story was left in Snow Monkey's satchel, and he hung his head and cried.

They stayed in their well-hidden spot late into night. They waited until the street was cleared of the partyers but remained covered in pounds of confetti. No one but police officers and cleaning crews were in Times Square. Then snow began to descend, covering the confetti under a blanket of snow. The cleaning crews moved in fast and were sweeping up the confetti at an alarming rate. Snow Monkey and Red Panda were desperate to find as many pages as they could.

"We have to go out there and find the pages," said Snow Monkey.

"Let's try," Red Panda said.

The two animals ran out into Times Square looking for pages of the Story within the thousands of pieces of confetti. The police officers saw them on the street rummaging through the confetti and pointed and laughed heartily. The night had been long, loud, and laborious, and they were glad for the comic relief.

"Whose party do you think they escaped from?" chuckled one policeman to another.

Snow Monkey and Red Panda grabbed handfuls of confetti and tossed them in the air, trying to find the lost pages. Red Panda found only one tiny scrap of the Story.

The policeman said, "We really should round them up and take them to the zoo. Get them somewhere safe."

The two policemen had a fun time trying to catch the playful creatures, but Snow Monkey could move far more skillfully over the slippery, snowy, confetti-covered street than the men chasing him. They almost got Red Panda, but he jumped on Snow Monkey's back. Snow Monkey climbed up a gutter, then along the backside of another billboard, then swung through scaffolding again and away toward the park.

Snow Monkey got back to the zoo just before dawn. Red Panda snuck inside the zoo to tell Snow Monkey's friends what happened to the Story and to ensure that Snow Monkey did not get blamed for the fiasco. Snow Monkey told his elders what happened as he cried. The only remaining copy of the Story. The history. The mission. Battle secrets. Survival tools. Heroic Tukors. Secret tactics. Methods for defeating Grezniks. All lost forever, turned into confetti. He gave them the only page left, the introduction:

The Story began when time was not counted, when there were no calendars to mark the beginning. The months were not named, nor were years numbered from the day a forgiving boy was born. Instead, days were measured by the moon's rising and the sun's setting, and one did not really know one's age unless someone was careful to count the sunrises. But Grezniks do not count days as beginning with a sunrise and ending with a sunset. Nor do they measure the length of their lifetime by counting sunrises on a planet propelled in circles by its powerful sun. Instead, they view the entire Greznik existence on Earth as one horrible, never-ending day. They are always one day old, no matter how many times Earth gives them a sunset and goes around the sun.

Yet even for Grezniks, one day can matter. Because if Proznia gets its way, one day there will be no days. For anyone. Earth and everything on it will shatter like glass and blow away. Gravity's grip on us, on every little bit of us, will disappear. Even our own little breathing bits will fly away like milkweed seeds. Daylight will drift away like smoke, and time will no longer tick and tock along an even line. Life itself will be no more. Proznia will take it all back in.

Grezniks share Proznia's wish to destroy Life by shattering Earth and launching its broken pieces far away. Yet they are also desperate to escape Proznia's control. Although Grezniks are not alive and have no blood, they have a will of their own—the will to escape the insatiably and brutally powerful Proznia.

Grezniks are particles held together by force, not by Life. And, like wind, they are propelled by the unseen. They are neither male nor female. They never age, and cannot

die, but they can disappear. If a person
looks directly at a Greznik, it explodes into
a stench of smoke and disappears. However,
the eyes of a Tukor can behold a Greznik
without blasting it into smithereens, but
they are the only humans who can. The battles to defeat the Grezniks bear a heavy
cost, and their Story is told herein.

Red Panda gave them the one tiny piece he found on
the street:

The choice is yours. The consequences are
grave if you

Red Panda said, "Our last hope is Geduld."

"Who?" asked Snow Monkey.

"He's an old freshwater shark," said Red Panda. "I heard
from a migratory ovenbird that a shark named Geduld was
down at the Mississippi Basin trying to locate a Tukor.
Been traveling for years now, trying to deliver some news.
But no one knows if there are any Tukors left. Let's hope
there's one left somewhere."

"In all this world, there has to be one, right?" said Snow
Monkey.

"No one's sure there is. Well . . . there could've been
many more, but they lost track. Unanchored their ship.
They're just wanderers," said Red Panda.

The snow monkeys heard the zoo employees arriving for the morning, and they turned to warn Red Panda to leave quickly. But Red Panda was already swiftly gone.

Red Panda traveled back up to the Upper East Side. For all his antics, Red Panda was a lonely creature, and he already missed his new monkey friend.

Snow Monkey hoped his new friend would visit again. He spent time every day looking out, hoping to get a glimpse of Red Panda slipping unseen through the park. But he never saw him. It would be many months before Snow Monkey would get another visit from Red Panda. And by then, the Grezniks' battle lines would already have crossed directly into Manhattan. And too many friends would have already given their lives.

CASTAWAY

4

STUCK ON THE INSIDE

Thousands upon thousands of years ago, Proznia sent trillions of tiny bits of itself flying toward Earth to destroy Life entirely. But when the bits crashed into Earth to shatter it, nothing happened at all. The sun rose. The dew of morning glistened. A breeze blew gently by. The little bits landed gracefully deep inside our round ball called home and got stuck inside Earth's molten middle.

Then one wickedly loud crack of lightning struck Earth.

Some bits formed into the most amazingly beautiful blue stones. Some bits swirled around, unformed, in Earth's core. But some bits formed into a creature, the very first Greznik, who crawled its way out from deep inside Earth. There was nothing graceful about its arrival. It thrashed its way out of the crusty, crackling surface and was furious to emerge and find itself miserably alone.

The first Greznik called out, "Anyone here? Anyone? Answer me!"

Nothing answered. The Greznik took a deep breath and choked from the stench—the smell of oxygen was awful.

Never is a Greznik given a name, only a number. But in the telling of its story here, the first Greznik is called Boshlek. On that first day, Boshlek searched for others and found no one. Boshlek ran to the top of a mountain and yelled again, "Anyone here? Anyone? Answer me!"

Boshlek waited for Proznia to take command, but it became increasingly clear that its master was nowhere. Boshlek wandered for days as reality sunk in. Boshlek was stuck on Earth, and despite its powerful capabilities, it had no power to get off Earth. On a hopeless solo expedition, Boshlek seethed in anger. Then it lashed out at Earth by running and pounding the ground, as powerful lightning bolts shot downward from its feet. It hollered out for anyone or anything. But not even the wind blew to answer back. It gave up and fell asleep.

Boshlek had no idea that the lightning bolts from its feet triggered Grezniks to take shape and rise to the surface. While Boshlek slept, deep inside Earth, fully formed Grezniks were finding their way out of Earth's core, like turtles trying to escape a ginormous egg. But unlike turtles, Grezniks come out angry. Bitter. Ready to destroy.

5

A NEW SPIN AROUND

On the fifth floor, behind a locked door painted stone-
cold gray, three children hid. Someone knocked on the
door, and the kids went silent and did not answer. The
person tried to open the door but gave up and moved on.
Every fifteen minutes or so someone knocked again and
tried to enter, but the kids stayed hidden. Brothers Mitch
and Tony, twelve and eleven years old, and their little sister,
Jovi, nine, were not going to open the door for anyone.

After the last knock, Jovi got up and looked out the
window at the street below as more limousines arrived at
their prestigious townhouse, within walking distance of
Central Park. It was a cold and windy December 31 in
Manhattan, New York, as ladies in fancy gowns and men
in tuxedos stepped out of their limos to be greeted by a
sharply dressed doorman. Murky clouds hung above the
festivities, blocking the moon and holding a blanket of
snow ready to drop when the timing was just right.

Downstairs got louder and increasingly crowded as more glamorous guests arrived to attend the New Year's party, a fund-raiser for a new contemporary art museum founded by the host of the party—the children's grandpa, Neil Bosonataski, their mom's dad.

Jovi looked out at the long lineup of limousines arriving. "More are still coming. We'll be hiding all night."

A famous actress stepped out of a limousine as cameras flashed.

Jovi said, "Not her again."

"The barfer?" asked Mitch.

"Don't remind me," said Tony.

This New Year's party at their home was *the* place to be as Earth started its new spin around the sun at midnight. At least that was the aura Grandpa always pulled off at his lavish parties, where guests always knew they could hobnob in circles that mattered. Mattered to them, anyway.

Voices from downstairs echoed up the winding staircase to seep through the doors like smoke in a fire—the conversations of the famous, the well connected, the I-know-somebodies. Their words, like leaves of a climbing vine, were targeted at important people who could pull them up the social ladder or send them rappelling back down.

There was one man, a burly accountant, who was not at the party for the social climb. He was there to work. His name was Mr. Etson, and he was the father of Mitch and Tony's friends at school, Asher and Kenny. But few knew—not even Asher and Kenny—that Mr. Etson was an undercover agent for the Federal Bureau of Investigation and was attending the party solely to rappel Grandpa Neil down to the bottom of the social ladder. And right into a locked room. Behind a heavy door, painted stone-cold gray. A cold cell in prison.

Their five-story townhouse, with a basement game room, stood gallantly between Fifth and Madison Avenues, with a "French Renaissance" exterior, as their mom, Caroline, would always remind visitors. It would have been an extremely expensive purchase had their parents, Caroline and Darrell, bought it themselves, which they had not. Grandpa Neil owned it, along with other real estate across the country.

The expansive interior was decorated with modern furnishings with an angular style, sleek edges, and too much metal. It all fit nicely in the showcase magazine photos, but less so in the reality that Mitch, Tony, and Jovi lived when the parties ended and everyday life marched forward. Caroline always invited party guests to tour their showcase home during their many swanky parties. The kids felt like zoo animals when adults came into their room to ooh and aah over the decor, and they eventually learned to lock them out.

Hiding in an upstairs sitting room, Mitch, Tony, and Jovi passed the time playing a game of Monopoly. Jovi was decidedly losing, and the next roll of the dice landed her on Marvin Gardens, which Mitch had covered with houses. She did not have the money for rent and went bankrupt. Jovi did not like losing. In frustration, she threw the board game so the little houses and hotels flew across the room, as if they were in Dorothy's Kansas tornado. Jovi's playing piece, the top hat, landed on one of Mitch's dirty socks. A red hotel landed in their fish tank, and on its way to the bottom of the water, it bonked their blue betta fish on the head. Another landed on a plate of fancy appetizers, which the catering manager had allowed Tony to sneak upstairs.

"Jovi! Why do you always do that? Sore loser!" said Mitch, furious that his little sister had once again destroyed the game.

"I hate Monopoly! You always win!"

"That's because you spend all your money, Jovi," said Tony, carefully counting his money. "I would've won anyway."

Jovi looked out the window. "It's snowing!"

Mitch got up and opened the window, and Jovi reached her arm outside to let the large snowflakes land on her palm.

"Each snowflake is different," said Jovi.

"Like fingerprints falling from the sky," said Tony.

Tony watched the snowflakes cover the neighbor's roof across the street, but he suddenly jumped back, surprised, and nearly knocked Mitch over.

"What'd you do that for?" asked Mitch.

"A snow monkey! Over there!" said Tony.

"I don't see anything," said Jovi. "Quit playing jokes on me."

"I wasn't joking."

Mitch and Jovi did not believe Tony, who was always a jokester. Mitch shut the window as Jovi opened the door to leave the room.

"Where are you going?" Mitch asked Jovi.

"I swear I saw a snow monkey," said Tony, who opened the window again, hoping to get another glimpse of the monkey.

"You couldn't have," said Jovi. "I want some desserts. They've got to be serving desserts by now. I'm going downstairs."

"I don't want to go down there. Too bad the caterers don't deliver to our room," said Mitch.

"Maybe one of them escaped from the zoo," said Tony, looking out the window.

"The caterer?" asked Mitch.

"No, the snow monkey. I know I saw it."

"You're not still on that monkey, are you?" said Jovi. "Come on. Let's go downstairs. Get some dessert."

The kids stepped out of their room. The party had gradually expanded upstairs, and people were crammed into Jovi's room, drinking champagne and talking superfluously about an assortment of lofty topics. The kids looked down the winding staircase at the party below. With midnight drawing near, the foyer was crowded and loud. As they started down, they saw Grandpa at the bottom of the steps and their mom's only brother, Tobias.

Uncle Tobias and their mother lived on very different tracks—but both of their trains had plenty of money. Money had been passed down to them through several generations, from their great-great-grandpa who had amassed wealth from railroads back in the day. From Tobias, the kids learned that Grandpa Neil married their grandma,

Vicki, for her inherited railroad money. Grandpa did love money—the spending of it, anyway. And spend he did. As a younger man, Grandpa spent his way up the social ladder, then bought and sold his way up the financial ladder, and in doing so made his unusual last name, Bosonataski, one that was well known in important circles. His name was now on hotels, businesses, real estate, and investments.

But their friends' dad, Mr. Etson, the undercover FBI agent, understood that there was something far more sinister going on behind the "French Renaissance" exterior: Grandpa was running a complex fraud built on an entangled network of crimes. Mr. Etson just needed a little bit more information. Then, like a game of Jenga, he could pull out just one piece and make the Bosonataski house fall.

Mr. Etson looked up the spiraling staircase just as the kids were looking down. He felt a sinking feeling in his stomach. Those three kids with the most ridiculous last name ever—Bosonataski-Fishengardet—had no idea how soon their whole life would be spiraling downward.

Bosonataski-Fishengardet. It was a last name all three kids hated. When their parents got married, their mom thought it unfair to drop her famous maiden name, which provided instant prestige. She convinced their dad, Darrell, to combine their two last names, Bosonataski and Fishengardet, to make their married name. Darrell refused initially, warning Caroline that the last name was ridiculously long and no one could pronounce it, much less spell it. But Caroline held her ground. She said it was good to stand out, be different. But really, she understood that her widely recognized last name, Bosonataski, gave her imme-diate access to elite social circles, and she was not going to drop it.

Mr. Etson would prove how wrong she was.

6

A CAGE CALLED EARTH

Boshlek woke as a sharp claw scraped at its belly, and it jumped up, ready to attack. Much to Boshlek's surprise, a Greznik popped out of the ground in front of him, then another and another, and more and more. Boshlek was soon surrounded by bewildered Grezniks who had no idea how they had been suddenly pulled out from the molten middle of Earth.

Boshlek quickly realized that its own angry lightning bolts had formed the new Grezniks, which meant Proznia had made a mistake: Grezniks did not take form as they were supposed to. Instead, Boshlek could form a new Greznik whenever it wanted. And, even more powerfully, Proznia had no control over any of them.

Boshlek seized the opportunity and called itself Number 1, Eternal Commander, and assigned a number to every other Greznik who reached the surface based on the order of its arrival. Boshlek formed many more Grezniks, numbered each one, created a regiment, took command,

and said, "All of you will answer to me, obey me, and honor me for all eternity. We will escape this dreadful planet. We will destroy Earth. But we will never return to Proznia."

"We do not want to go back," they all shouted. "Never will we go back!"

Just then another Greznik crawled out holding a peculiar blue stone.

The stone's alluring glow shone brightly, and when the other Grezniks saw the beautiful stone, an uncontrollable desire overtook them and putrid slime poured out of their mouths. Boshlek ran to grab the alluring blue stone, but another Greznik ran in front of Boshlek and stole it. The stone's power overtook the thieving Greznik, and it lost all sense of judgment and ran right off a cliff and into a lake, where it dissolved instantly.

The Greznik hit the water at such speed that the blue stone skipped atop the water and landed on the shore. Another Greznik snatched the stone but was overcome by an unforgiving hunger, and it gulped the blue rock in one swallow. The resulting energy exploded the Greznik with such force that Boshlek was blown backward.

Other Grezniks mined the earth feverishly to find a stone for themselves. Greznik after Greznik found a bit of blue stone and met their demise in a variety of gruesome mishaps. Boshlek looked out at a sea of Grezniks fighting over the stones—eating each other, swallowing the stones and blowing up, falling into water and dissolving, fleeing and chasing and plummeting off cliffs.

To regain control, Boshlek charged toward one Greznik as it fled with a blue stone in its grip. Boshlek caught up and stole the blue stone, then attacked the Greznik violently and ate the creature, legs first, followed by the rest in one big gulp. Then Boshlek herded more Grezniks into a scrambling heap and ate a few more of them, only to vomit their bits back up and hurl them into water to dissolve. A dozen Grezniks huddled together to avoid a similar end. But Boshlek charged them all into a lake, where they dissolved instantly.

Boshlek continued this brutal frenzy until the entire regiment was completely subdued. Boshlek organized the regiment into fighting circles of eleven Grezniks each. Boshlek commanded them to march in circular patterns, within their own fighting circle but also simultaneously with all other circles. From the sky, it looked as if their circles moved like the interlocking gears of a clock.

Then Boshlek forced them to repeat an obedient chant: "I will never seek a blue stone for myself ever again! My allegiance is to Eternal Commander who will reign over us forever and ever. Any stone I find will be given to Eternal Commander to be collected for all. I am worthless without Eternal Commander."

Boshlek ordered the circles to begin digging for the blue stones. Any stones found were immediately relinquished to Boshlek.

When the Greznik regiment finally gathered enough blue stones, Boshlek was ready to test the stones' power. Boshlek commanded every Greznik to fill their belly pocket with the blue stones and ordered them to run in the same direction.

The regiment ran in a long line, and when they reached their full speed, the stones created such a powerful magnetic force that Earth was nearly ready to blow out of orbit.

Boshlek, perched high on a mountain slope, felt Earth's rotation beginning to unravel. The ground rumbled. The sun's journey across the sky wavered. But it did not go as planned. The magnetic force agitated Earth's crust, and an earthquake split the ocean's bottom and triggered a tsunami. The enormous wall of water sped toward them, and there was not enough time to flee. The wave hit the regiment and dissolved every Greznik except for Boshlek, who stood high on the mountain. The blue stones washed out to sea, where a Greznik cannot go.

Their efforts, though foiled, had destabilized Earth enough that its surface turned to ice and glaciers. Boshlek bolted more Grezniks to the surface, numbered each one, and formed a new regiment. They began the search anew in a world gone bitterly cold.

Their next effort to blow Earth out of orbit resulted in a massive volcano that pulled the blue stones back underground. Afterward, the Greznik regiment slithered down through cracks in Earth's crust to find the stones. Any time the regiment gathered enough stones and came close to blasting Earth out of orbit, they were foiled by Tukors, the only people who can look at a Greznik and not blow it to smithereens. But the Story of those battles and how Tukors defeated the Grezniks blew away one night like confetti. And now, no one knows.

7

THE YELLOW SUN

Mitch, Tony, and Jovi looked down the spiral staircase and saw their friends' dad, Mr. Etson, talking to their uncle Tobias at the bottom. Behind them, their grandpa was talking with several movie stars. Although the kids were fond of Mr. Etson, they did not particularly like their grandpa and were generally indifferent to Tobias, who was seldom in town. When Tobias was in town, he could be occasionally cheerful and interested in the kids, but more often he was irritable, moped around lazily, and fought with their mom.

Grandpa always smiled when he greeted someone, but with a grin that seemed powered by an exterior electrical circuit. He was never at ease, and his manner was over-charged with a purpose that had nothing to do with liking anyone. It was always about getting something *from* someone. Garnering his grandkids' love was no exception. Grandpa demanded it on his rare visits, as he came bearing toys, gifts, and envelopes with money. Greetings and hugs were in passing, and he never left anything lasting for the kids to excitedly anticipate the next time he came.

The kids tried to scoot downstairs unseen, but they failed. Grandpa saw them and waved them over. "Hey, kids, over here. I want to introduce you to someone. This here is my grandson, Mitch. He's incredible at fencing."

"Tony's the fencer," said Mitch, but Grandpa did not hear him.

"And Tony here, he won a spelling bee at school."

Jovi said, "You got it backward again, Grandpa. Mitch won the geography bee."

"And Jovana, well . . . she's quite the ballerina," said Grandpa.

Irritated, Jovi said, "I go by Jovi. And remember, I'm not in ballet anymore. I ride horses, and compete in dressage."

No one heard what she said because as she was speaking, she was bumped from behind by the loud and drunk movie star who stepped backward to let a caterer pass through the crowded foyer. The bump pushed Jovi into another server, who held a plate full of fancy petits fours topped with intricate sugar glass made into the shape of dragons. As the entire plate fell, the dainty sugar glass shattered, leaving bits of dragon and festive frosting all over the beautiful floor. The drunk woman stepped clumsily on some of the little cakes and crushed bits of sugar glass.

Mitch and Tony used the moment of confusion to escape into the kitchen, after taking a couple of the petits fours that had landed upright and unscathed on the tray. Jovi, mortified, tried to help clean up the mess using a pile of little square party napkins, but in doing so she bumped the drunk movie star who was reaching for a glass of champagne. Two glasses toppled and poured down on Jovi, soaking her dress and shattering glass on the floor. Jovi wanted to flatten herself, like the frosting squished into the floor, and disappear.

The catering manager bent down toward Jovi and said, "It's okay. No worries. I'll clean this up. Go on in the kitchen and get yourself some of the desserts before the adults eat them all."

The catering company worked many extravagant parties at their townhouse, and the manager knew the three kids well by now.

Jovi started to cry. "I can't do anything right."

The manager said, "Not your fault. That lady's just like a bird who eats rancid berries and flies into windows."

Jovi smiled. "We call her 'the barfer.'"

The manager smiled too. "And for good reason. Now get in the kitchen and get some of those yummy desserts before they're gone."

As the party attendees clinked their glasses to quiet everyone, Jovi retreated from the disaster, slithered her way through the crowded hallway, and slipped into the kitchen unnoticed. Uncle Tobias also ducked into the kitchen to cut through to the living room and saw his niece and nephews there.

"Aren't you supposed to be in bed?" he asked.

"People invaded my room," said Jovi.

"And we can't sleep. It's too loud," said Mitch.

"That it is," agreed Tobias, who flew in from Malibu, California, every December to ring in the New Year in New York. He relocated from New York to Malibu to make it as an actor in Hollywood, but mostly he lived the life of a drifter—a drifter with way too much money on his hands.

Tobias said, "They're about to unveil a famous painting. Come on, let's go see it."

On their way into the living room, Tobias took a whole plate of fancy desserts and led the kids through the crowd into the large living room, where they secured the perfect seat upon which to watch the unveiling—a wall bench located in the back of the room between floor-to-ceiling bookshelves. Tobias put the plate of treats on his lap so he and the kids could eat as many desserts as they wanted.

The guests quieted down to hear Grandpa's speech.

Grandpa thanked everyone for coming and supporting his new art museum. "I know you have all been waiting for the unveiling of our first piece, the cornerstone of our art collection. The anonymous donors of this beautiful painting . . ."

"Blah, blah, blah," muttered Tobias as he ate another dessert.

Grandpa spoke effusively about modern art and its powerful impact on the world. Then he announced the painting. "So now it's time for the unveiling. It's a profoundly complex piece." Then Grandpa gestured for his third and very young wife to pull the veil from the painting and said, "Here it is, ladies and gentlemen, the last painting by the late Flink Le Fou called *The Yellow Sun*."

The guests gasped in awe and broke into thunderous applause as the musicians began playing again. Media personalities at the event snapped pictures. The kids looked at the painting and scrunched their faces. *The Yellow Sun* was a square canvas panel painted entirely yellow.

Tobias smirked, pointed to the painting, and whispered to the kids. "Guess how much they paid for that?"

"Seventeen dollars?" answered Mitch.

"Forty-five million dollars," said Tobias.

"Forty-five million dollars for that?" exclaimed Tony.

"Shh, don't say it so loud. I'm not supposed to know," said Tobias.

"In that case, I've got a round red painting I can sell 'em for fifty million. It'll be ready by the weekend," said Tony.

"I like your way of thinking," said Tobias.

Guests clinked their glasses to hush everyone again and quiet the musicians. It was almost midnight, and everyone was getting ready to ring in the New Year. Before they were all quieted, Grandpa began an eloquent toast about art, culture, peace, and people.

Tobias leaned over to Mitch and whispered, "Watch out for him. Grandpas are supposed to be the good guys. Yours isn't."

Jovi asked, "What did Tobias say?"

Tony answered, "Grandpa's not a good guy."

Jovi was not sure she heard Tony correctly and asked rather loudly, "Grandpa's a bad guy?"

But the room went quiet just as she said it. Everyone heard her clearly and turned their heads to stare uncomfortably at her on the bench, next to Tobias and her brothers.

Jovi sunk down, completely mortified yet again.

Tony tried to recover for her awkwardly. "No, Jovi, he's the good guy."

The band interrupted the uncomfortable silence with a lively tune. Mitch and Tony were totally embarrassed by another one of Jovi's gaffes, and together they slipped into the kitchen. Jovi followed, leaving Tobias alone on the bench to enjoy another delicious little treat from the tray. He smiled. His niece had accidentally announced to the room something he had wanted, for years, to shout from his lungs.

Jovi's embarrassing remark reminded Tobias of being Tony's age, sitting on the same bench by himself and feeling miserable. Tobias's parents—the kids' Grandpa Neil and Grandma Vicki—had just gotten divorced. Vicki could not bear Neil's wild and lavish life anymore and had moved to her parents' home, a farm in Tennessee, taking Caroline and Tobias with her.

Caroline, then in high school, thought farm life was boring and moved back to New York, rejoining her dad's flashy life. Tobias stayed on the farm with his mom and would have done so through high school, but when he was thirteen, she died unexpectedly. Devastated, he was forced to leave the farm and move to New York to live with his dad, where he found himself back on that same bench and lonely. Back then, Tobias missed riding horses and running free on the farm. But eventually the big city broke him in as one does a wild horse, and he never imagined living on a farm again.

Hoping to sneak upstairs, Jovi came back with another tray of desserts, followed by Mitch and Tony. But Tobias said, "Hey, hey, where're you going with that? How 'bout sharing some with me?"

Mr. Etson reached for one of the desserts. "Can I have one?"

Mr. Etson, fishing for information, said to Tobias, "Amazing your dad got a Flink Le Fou painting, much less *The Yellow Sun*. That's a tough piece to acquire."

"Even tougher to paint. Do you know who bought it?" asked Tobias, curious to confirm who had spent forty-five million dollars on what he considered to be nothing more than a larger-than-life homemade paint sample.

Mr. Etson said, "I don't actually know. Do you?"

"No one's supposed to know who bought it, but I know my dad too well. I'm a betting man that the buyer is that woman over there with my dad right now. I can tell by how he's talking to her. He's working a deal."

"Yeah, you're right. She did buy it," said Mitch.

"I knew it," said Tobias.

"How'd you know?" Mr. Etson asked Mitch.

"Grandpa and she were both here this morning waiting for the painting to arrive. Alone in the kitchen. I can hear everything in there from the game room."

"Yeah, I heard it too," said Tony. "She said, 'Money's moving from Romania. Tuesday morning.'"

"I even know the account number," said Mitch.

"How's that?" asked Tobias.

Tony answered, "Mitch can memorize numbers super easily."

"I just remembered this one because it starts with the month and day of my birthday. Isn't that weird? Followed by three primes: 17-23-13."

Jovi said, "I wish I could memorize like that."

"I don't memorize everything, Jovi. I can't remember your birthday," said Mitch.

"You're a blockhead," said Jovi. "You know my birthday."

The room was crowded, and the partiers kept bumping into Jovi as they reached for more champagne and desserts. She said, "I'm out of here. I'm going back upstairs."

Jovi grabbed a tray of desserts, and the three kids snuck through the kitchen to the pantry and into the little elevator. They rode up to the fifth floor, unlocked the door to their hiding place, and stayed hidden there the rest of the night.

Mitch and Tony had no idea that they had just handed Mr. Etson what he came to the party for: a critical clue to the thread that would, very soon, unravel Grandpa's world—sending money, hotels, and houses flying away like a tornado crashing down on everyone. But that would all be nothing compared to the sorrow Grandpa would rain down on his three grandchildren.

8

A CRY MELTS INTO LAVA

Over many uncounted centuries, Grezniks wandered across this spinning Earth and traveled like wind, searching and battling for the elusive blue needed for their escape—until one odd day, which began like so many others but ended like none other. Earth spun its usual nightly darkness as the sun slowly hid below the horizon. But that night dusk dusted the sky a lazy red and tried to linger longer in the evening sky, as if to signal an arriving torment. The Rangrim Mountains bid their silent farewell to the setting sun as the chattering Chongchon River babbled and tumbled its way through the night. All day, every day, the waters of the Chongchon retreat from their icy mountain beginnings and sketch their path down the Korean Peninsula to escape safely into the Yellow Sea. But Grezniks cannot escape as swiftly as running waters, and that night the Greznik regiment was encamped close enough to the river to envy the watery currents running by.

Like every other night, the circle leaders detailed how many Grezniks disappeared that day, gone forever. That day only one had disappeared. It had slipped on an icy mountain slope, dropped into a lake, and dissolved.

After the regiment was asleep, Boshlek stepped away and walked toward the Chongchon River to replace the Greznik. Not too far from the river, Boshlek shot an electrical bolt from its feet deep into Earth to trigger a Greznik to take form and rise to the surface. It would become the Greznik numbered 401^5.

Normally Boshlek pulled Grezniks to the surface in speeds unfathomable to humans. But this time, before the Greznik was even halfway up to the surface, Boshlek heard unexpected voices coming from near the waters of the Chongchon. The beautiful, whispering sounds felt as though they were right next to its ears. Startled, Boshlek darted backward to avoid what had snuck up so slyly.

The Voices said to Boshlek, "You will be destroyed for not obeying me."

Severely startled by the deceptively beautiful Voices, Boshlek forgot the new Greznik in Earth's molten middle. Abandoned, the forgotten Greznik was left to burn in the melted stone. It screamed out in pain, but no one was there to hear it—and even its cry for help melted into lava.

9

GROUNDED

Weeks later, on Presidents' Day, Tony's last class of the day was science. When class ended, the students poured out of the classroom into the hallway like water out of a faucet. Except Tony, who stayed late working on a contraption he built to demonstrate the fundamentals of electrical circuits, hoping to win the science fair with it. As the other students left the classroom, they all passed Kenny, who, as he did every day, stood right by the door to wait for his best friend, Tony.

Although Kenny's brother, Asher, went to the same prestigious private school that Mitch, Tony, and Jovi did, Kenny did not. Kenny attended a different school down the street and around the corner, which could accommodate Kenny's challenges.

Kenny had a long list of serious health issues—among them a weak heart requiring a pacemaker to ensure its ticks and tocks kept a steady beat. Surgeries were frequent for Kenny when he was younger, not only for his heart but also for several musculoskeletal abnormalities.

Not all of them could be fully treated. He waddled instead of walked, often experienced pain in his legs, and struggled to pronounce words accurately. His tongue would hang out of his mouth a lot of the time, especially when he was trying to listen closely. Yet one thing came with ease for Kenny—smiling. He never ceased to smile for a friend. Tony, an intense kid, found an effortless grin something to admire.

Kenny was friendly with Asher's classmates and carried on pedantically on topics that gave him great interest. Rarely, if ever, did his monologues keep the interest of others. Except Tony.

Kenny said to his parents once, "Tony gives me a listen. Like a present. Can you wrap up a listen?"

Parents would often ask the Etsons, "What condition does Kenny have?"

Many adults inquired about his diseases and conditions, wanting a medical name for Kenny's struggles. But his situation was complicated, and never did Kenny fit into one medical label. And few were ever patient and kind enough to listen to the details. Frustratingly, Mr. Etson found they were usually more interested in the names of Kenny's abnormalities than hearing about his successes. One day a parent's inquiry was the last straw, and Mr. Etson replied with what became his standard response, "Kenny likes to learn. He likes to smile. He starts the day ready to run into a bit of sunshine. And he thinks everyone might be his friend. He's nice to just about everyone. Those are pretty good conditions to have. Maybe he can teach your son a thing or two, don't you think?"

Every morning, almost without fail, Kenny's favorite topic was what he had for breakfast, what cereals were his favorite, how many Cheerios he could fit on a spoon, how many minutes exactly it took him to eat his cereal that morning, and so on. Every time Kenny saw Tony he ran up to him excitedly, knowing Tony would always listen, again and again, to stories about breakfast.

Tony finally came out of the classroom like the last reluctant drop from the water faucet. As soon as Tony emerged, Kenny asked, "Guess what, Tony?"

But Kenny never waited for Tony to respond. "I learned about letters today," Kenny said. "Not alphabet letters. *A*, *B*, *C*, *D* and *E* and *F*, and then *G* and *H* and then *I* and *J* and—"

Tony interrupted, as one often did with Kenny to help his conversation along. "*J* and *K* and all the way to *Z*, right? What kind of letters?"

"Right. All the way to *Z*. Not alphabet letters. Letters you write. Letters with envelopes and stamps. I wrote a letter. I put a stamp on it. A stamp with a flower on it. A yellow flower. Right in the corner. Upper-right corner of the envelope, you see. That's where you put stamps and—"

"Who was the letter to?" asked Tony.

"The president of the United States. I had something to ask."

From the other end of the hallway, Tony's fencing coach said, "Hurry it up, Tony, you're late!"

As he rushed off, Tony said to Kenny, "I'm sorry. I've got to go. I'm late for fencing. Tomorrow you can tell me about the letter, okay?"

Not having Tony to talk to anymore, Kenny walked up to Brayton, a student standing nearby, to talk about his letter to the president. Brayton was a thirteen-year-old whose dad owned a successful music studio and worked with the most famous of superstars. Always touting an ample supply of backstage passes and concert tickets, Brayton had a gregarious but selective charm that attracted girls to him like bugs to a bug light. There were always girls swirling around him, believing he could get them through the gates of stardom to touch the face of fame.

Kenny was telling Brayton about his letter to the president when Brayton walked away, leaving Kenny alone in the hallway. Kenny tried to follow, but Brayton sped up and ditched him. Kenny, left behind, looked to his brother for security, but Asher was not around.

Once Kenny was too far behind to catch up, Brayton imitated Kenny's mannerisms, let his tongue hang out, and waddled like him. The girls giggled at Brayton's antics.

Tony saw what Brayton did and ran back down the hallway. He tapped Brayton on the shoulder, then pretended that Brayton's imitation of Kenny was funny and said, "Show us again how Kenny sticks his tongue out."

Brayton imitated Kenny again, and the girls giggled. Kenny's brother Asher always thought Tony to be a friend, so he was disappointed to see Tony participating in the mockery. But just as Brayton let his tongue hang out, Tony swung his fist toward Brayton's chin.

It was a convincing but fake swing. Tony purposely missed.

Asher smiled.

Brayton laughed and said, "You missed."

"On purpose. Don't ever make fun of Kenny again," said Tony.

"What're you freakin' out about?" said Brayton, with his familiar cockiness.

Tony pushed Brayton up against a locker and said, "I mean it."

Brayton swung a direct punch at Tony and shoved him so hard he fell backward. Tony got up, threw a punch back, and this time did not miss. And it all went downhill from there. Tony and Brayton were pretty evenly matched in the school's first fight in over fifteen years. Brayton was two years older and stronger, but Tony was very quick and far more skilled.

The fencing coach witnessed it all and ran forward to pull the boys away from each other. As a military veteran, he easily subdued them. With his hands gripped at the base of their necks, he brought the two kids to the dean's office, dropped them into chairs on opposite sides of the room, and went into the office.

Minutes later, the coach walked out and Brayton was called in. The fencing coach said quietly to Tony, "I'd have done the same thing at your age. Brayton had it coming. But there are quiet ways to teach a man his mistakes."

When Tony got home, his parents had already heard from the dean about the fight. Mortified, they slapped a month-long grounding on top of his detention sentence.

"You're grounded!"

"No fair!" said Tony, with convincing flair.

Tony pretended to be upset, but the disappointment was all for show. Tony thrived on his parents' naïveté, knowing a grounding was a hopelessly ineffective punishment because his parents were rarely home to enforce it. Tony could out-negotiate every nanny they had, and they had had many to give him plenty of practice.

Four weeks of grounding was four weeks of freedom from everything his parents were constantly signing him up for—voice lessons, clarinet, fencing, tennis, Long Island polo lessons, Latin tutoring, equine care classes, dressage. In his eyes, the list went on forever. He had asked for hockey, the only sport he really wanted to play, but that year they had signed him up for golf. *Winter* golf, which was basically indoor putting lessons. And for Tony, the lessons were as boring as a putt. Putt, putt, putt, and ten minutes later, the ball might fall down the hole. Tony always had the urge to run up to the golf ball and kick it like a soccer player. Or whip the club around in a huge circle and launch the ball like a polo player galloping on a horse.

Tony and Mitch's school had an unusual disciplinary regimen that required the students to be involved in determining their own punishment. The next day Tony and Brayton were called in to the dean's office together. The dean gave them several punishment options, none of which Tony or Brayton wanted. They looked at each other and, at that moment, became allies. They both understood each other's thoughts: *We can't accept these terms. Think of something else, and fast.*

Tony was quick and suggested to the dean that he and Brayton be required to join the chess team after school and play a match against each other every day for four weeks.

Tony said with a firm confidence, "Chess can teach us to use our minds instead of our fists. To think carefully before we move. To analyze our actions. Nothing like chess for making good friends."

The dean embraced the idea. Brayton shrunk down, understanding that Tony knew exactly what he was doing. Tony would beat him in chess every day after school for four weeks. Brayton would be crushed in a game of will, focus, and strategy. And he was, every day, for four weeks straight.

In their final after-school chess match, Tony captured Brayton's king one last time. Brayton's final defeat was the same day as one of Mitch and Brayton's swim meets.

As Tony shook Brayton's hand after his last chess victory, he asked, "You swimming in the meet tonight?"

"Yes," answered Brayton.

"The butterfly?"

"Yes."

"Nobody wants to swim like a butterfly. They can't even flutter kick," said Tony.

Mitch was one of the school's top swimmers. His hard training paid off, and in every meet he placed first in at least one race. But he never won the butterfly. No one knew, though, that after that night, Mitch would never race again.

10

A CAGE CALLED WATER

Boshlek was so severely disturbed by the strange Voices that its insides burned into a sickening nausea. Boshlek looked in every direction and waited to sense movement, body heat, or a heartbeat—anything that would give a clue to what sang with such unusual sounds. But there was nothing, and Boshlek began to carefully walk away.

The mysterious Voices sang again and grew increasingly shrill with every word. "You will be destroyed for failing. For floundering. For not following my commands."

Boshlek changed its translucent hairs into a cockle-bur to ensnare whatever creature was lurking nearby. As Boshlek walked cautiously toward the banks of the Chongchon River, the river currents turned into glistening silver like swiftly flowing mercury. A chorus of piercing screeches tore through the air. Boshlek's legs buckled, and it fell to the ground.

The Voices bellowed, "You will suffer for your disobedience."

"Where are you?" asked Boshlek as it stood up and readied for an attack.

The metallic currents formed into the anguished lips of a molten creature and said, "I have come to destroy you. You will obey! You will come back to me!"

Startled by the threatening waters, Boshlek stumbled on stones and fell on its back. Boshlek popped back up onto its feet and braced for something to bound out of the water and attack.

"Who is speaking? Show yourself," said Boshlek apprehensively.

The waters boiled and splattered up and onto the shore, but no creature emerged. The currents bubbled and spun into whirlpools, then droplets of the silvery waters flew up toward Boshlek as if propelled by a forceful wind.

No two droplets sounded the same as they snarled in pounding voices and swarmed around Boshlek's head. Boshlek stepped backward to escape their punishing sounds. Then they all said in unison, "I am Proznia."

"Proznia would never come here to Earth. Who are you?" asked Boshlek.

"Proznia is here. I have come to quell your rebellion, devour you, and return you all to me!"

"If you are Proznia, you are a fool for coming. It's harder to go back than you think," said Boshlek, who doubted the truth of the accusing waters.

The mercury waters exploded into choppy, burning waves, whose flames took on a spectrum of colors, an interweaving rainbow. Each colorful wave blew a foul stench with such force it knocked Boshlek over, burned the inside of its snout, and took the strength from its legs.

The waters shouted, "I am Proznia! I sent you here to destroy Life and return to me."

Boshlek cowered.

The waters added, with belittling disdain, "You are, in every way, a failure. Worthless. Nugatory. But I am here now and will take you back!"

Boshlek realized that the unbelievable was true—Proznia had arrived on Earth as these unusual voices in the waters. All confidence evaporated like steam from Boshlek's body, and it cringed, sheltered its eyes, and braced for Proznia to devour them all.

But nothing happened.

Boshlek waited with trepidation for an attack, but it did not come. Then Boshlek said, "You sent us to destroy Life and return to you. But you sent us here with every power except the one needed to accomplish the goal. You must know we are stuck here."

Again, there was no response.

Boshlek continued, "We need the blue stones to succeed, and they are nearly impossible to find. Our enemies, the Tukors and their allies, fight our every effort. Tell us how to finish your goal so we can return to you!"

Boshlek waited for a reply, but none came. So it insisted strongly, "Tell us how to find the stones. You must, or we will be trapped forever. We will always be obedient to you. We are ever loyal."

The waters spiraled in angry circles and spit forth a

rancid, poisonous geyser. "You have never been loyal. Your words are a sham. Full of lies. You will pay for your desire to be free of me! I will destroy you."

Boshlek braced again for Proznia to take form, come out of the water, and ingurgitate them all. But instead a disturbing stillness hung in the air. Dread descended upon Boshlek like a poisonous smoke. Resigned to its fate, Boshlek said, "Come out of the waters and speak directly to me. You have come to destroy me, so step out and take me. Take us all."

The waters frothed bubbles that burst into foul-smelling flames, but they did not take form and attack. Boshlek waited a long time, shaking nervously. But nothing happened, and Boshlek's insides slowly calmed.

Boshlek cackled and said, "You cannot escape the water, can you? You made another wretched mistake. You, too, got stuck here on this dreadful planet! What a cruel end for you—trapped inside water, your foe, the very thing your enemy, Life, needs."

Boshlek walked leisurely away, spitting victoriously to the left and right, left and right, with every step.

The waters frothed and bubbled their silvery shiny currents, and sang quietly to Boshlek, "One of your own will come to me, believing me to be the giver of the stones. It will swallow my waters deep inside to give me form. I will thrive within the worthless beast and direct its every step and control its every desire. And you will all pay the ultimate price for your disobedience!"

"No chance. Grezniks never swallow water," Boshlek said triumphantly.

11

ONE BIG ACT

Mitch won nearly every swim meet, yet he never raised his arms in victory—which bugged Jovi to no end because she lost in everything, despite her hard work. For a long time, she dreamed of jumping up and down in victory in front of a big audience. But no matter what sport she tried, victory was always out of reach.

Jovi's first choice was not a competitive sport: it was ballet. She loved the chiffon skirts, sleek tights, and dainty shoes. She loved wearing her hair in a bun. Jovi was in fact rather graceful, but she could never quite turn her feet out enough, or lift her legs high enough. Further, she had no sense of rhythm. Despite always being the girl who just missed the downbeat, Jovi loved ballet, unaware of her lack of timing.

Her mom did not want her daughter to be the girl always out of sync with everyone else, so she took Jovi out of ballet and switched her to other sports—which Jovi excelled at even less. Eventually Jovi's mom exhausted the possibilities and decided Jovi was never going to shine at anything. In frustration, she signed Jovi up for rock climbing simply because the location was convenient.

Jovi stomped her feet, pouted, and said, "Why would I ever want to climb a *rock*?"

Jovi was tired of getting yanked out of one sport and thrown into another and never understood why she could not just go back to ballet. Much to Jovi's surprise, she loved her first climbing class and performed so well that her instructor nicknamed her Monkey Jo. When Jovi reached the top of the wall on her first day of class and came all the way back down, she jumped up and down and cheered as if she had just won an Olympic event.

Jovi had climbing club the same afternoon that Tony defeated Brayton in chess one last time. But her class was canceled unexpectedly, so when Tony got back home, he was surprised to find both Jovi and their nanny, Aziza, at home. He grabbed a big bowl of chips from the kitchen, dropped onto a couch, and curled up under his super-soft blanket to read. He could hear Jovi and Aziza talking in the kitchen about making cookies.

Jovi said excitedly, "Let's make monster cookies. They're my mom's favorite. She'll love them."

Aziza was one of the few nannies who had taken the Bosonataski-Fishengardet nanny job because she actually liked the kids. She ended up enjoying the job so much she switched her college major to elementary education. However, the previous nannies had taken the job because the parents were socially connected to people with access to highly competitive internships, auditions, fashion jobs, and other coveted opportunities. And as soon as each nanny got what she wanted from the job, she left.

Jovi relentlessly sought friends, but her efforts were strained by her fear that, like her nannies, they would leave for something better. Jovi talked constantly, not only because she had so much to say, but also because she believed that as long as she kept talking, a friend might not walk away.

Jovi added chocolate chips to the dough just as her mom, Caroline, came rushing through the door, followed by their dad, Darrell, arriving home much earlier than expected. Caroline raced into the kitchen, frantic and harried, which was nothing unusual. It was impossible to know when she was truly frazzled because her eyes were always open too wide. But this time, Aziza knew something was awry—Caroline, very distracted, inadvertently put her purse in the refrigerator.

Caroline pointed to their cookie dough. "Wrap this up. Clean up. They're coming shortly. I need you both to go upstairs." She clapped her hands together and barked another order, "Come on. Hurry it up!"

Both Aziza and Jovi were taken aback by her abruptness.

"But, Mom, we're making monster cookies. Your favorite," said Jovi.

"I said hurry up. Get this cleaned up. They'll be here any moment."

Tony asked from the other room, "Who's coming?"

"Grandpa," said Caroline. "Where's Mitch?"

"Swim meet. Why's Grandpa coming? He never comes," said Tony.

"Some kind of emergency meeting," said Darrell.

"Enough questions," said Caroline. "Uncle Tobias is coming too. I need you guys out of here. Go on. Get upstairs. Now."

"It's all right, Jovi," whispered Aziza. "We'll finish the cookies tomorrow. Grab some dough. I'll clean up in here and meet you upstairs."

Caroline never let her kids eat raw cookie dough—she believed every egg was bursting with salmonella—but Aziza always let the kids break this rule. Jovi, mad at her mom for not acknowledging the cookies, filled two cereal bowls with two big gobs of dough each and left the kitchen. She gave one bowl to Tony and went upstairs with the rest.

Caroline came out of the kitchen to get Tony upstairs too. She saw him taking a bite of dough, barked at him for it, grabbed the bowl, handed it to Aziza, and sent Tony upstairs. Aziza rolled her eyes discreetly and snuck the bowl upstairs for him to enjoy. Darrell never fretted about salmonella and ate two big hunks of dough himself.

As Aziza climbed the stairs, Uncle Tobias arrived at the townhouse having just flown in from Malibu. Jovi heard Tobias come in, and she yelled down from the top of the winding staircase to say hello. But Caroline told her to go back to her room as if Jovi were in trouble. Grandpa Neil followed a few minutes later, and the four of them—Caroline, Darrell, Tobias, and Grandpa—gathered in the kitchen.

Tony had not followed his mom's order to go upstairs. Instead, he went back into the kitchen to figure out what had brought Grandpa and Uncle Tobias to their house for a serious, hush-hush meeting. Tony always sensed when the winds in the air shifted from their usual course, and when he walked into the kitchen, he immediately knew something was amiss. Tobias was visibly irritated. Grandpa was not smiling, did not even so much as look up, and he was engrossed in reading emails on his phone. Caroline shooed Tony out of the kitchen before he could even say hello.

He walked up the winding staircase to find Jovi and Aziza.

Tony walked in the room and Jovi asked, "What should we play?"

"How about we finish that Monopoly game?" suggested Aziza as she handed Tony his bowl of cookie dough. During Tony's grounding, Aziza and Tony had started an epic game that had already lasted three weeks.

"Good idea. Then we can eavesdrop on their secret meeting," suggested Tony.

From the basement game room, they could hear conversations in the kitchen through the vents—something that the parents did not know because they never hung out in the game room.

"I hate Monopoly. I always lose," said Jovi.

"You can be on my team," said Aziza.

"Are you winning?" asked Jovi.

"No, I'm in jail right now. Come on, let's go get me out of jail," said Aziza.

Down in the basement, as Tony shook the dice, they heard Caroline ask, "Dad, what happened? What's the emergency?"

"I wanted to meet with you because I've got a special investment opportunity for all three of you," Grandpa said. "I wanted to give you first dibs at it, see if you'd like to buy into it."

Caroline breathed a sigh of relief. "That's good news. I thought something bad had happened. Like maybe you had some terminal illness or something. What a relief. And it's a no-brainer if you think it's a good opportunity. Of course I'll invest."

Tobias was not relieved. In fact, he was angry. "Dad, I got a last-minute flight just to hear another one of your ideas? That's not an emergency. You know my answer is always no."

"This is different. It's a new company," said Grandpa.

Tobias was doubtful. "What new company?"

"It's confidential. I'm not allowed to say. You just need to trust me."

Downstairs, Tony rolled the Monopoly dice and landed on Park Place. "I'm buying a hotel!"

"Oh no. That's not good. I can't pay those rents. I'm almost bankrupt," said Aziza. "Jovi, you play the banker. Exchange his houses for a hotel."

They listened as Grandpa continued. "But I can say the company is in utilities, in wind energy."

Tony started making big swooshing sounds as if wind were blowing through the house. Aziza laughed, then shook the dice and rolled two ones. "I'm out of jail!"

Jovi jumped up excitedly and moved Aziza's playing piece, the thimble, forward. Jovi asked Aziza, "Why'd you pick the thimble? I always pick the top hat because that's what I wear in my riding competitions. Tony always picks the race car. Maybe that's why he always wins."

"A thimble protects you from getting speared when you're making something beautiful. That's why I like it," said Aziza. "Electric Company. I'm buying it!"

The adults continued to talk. Caroline said, "Well, count me in, Dad. You always turn dust into gold."

"Caroline, I can't believe you're taking the bait again," said Tobias. "Dad is like the guy on a street that stacks a cardboard box on top of milk crates, then pulls out three walnut shells and places a pea underneath one of them and shuffles them around. Then you pay him to guess which walnut shell is hiding the pea. You lose every time, and the guy with the shells wins every time."

Caroline said, "Nonsense. You should've invested with Dad a long time ago. Many people have, and he's made them a lot of money. He's giving you first dibs on a great opportunity. And maybe for once you should take it."

Grandpa said, "Tobias, you're out in LA to make it as an actor. But what have you done except a gum commercial? There's no money in that. Follow your sister's advice. Buy into this company."

In the basement, Aziza asked, "Your uncle was in a gum commercial?"

"Yeah, he was. Your turn. If you roll a seven, you'll

land on my hotel and have to have to pay a lot of rent!" said Tony.

"Which one?"

"New York Avenue," said Tony.

"No, I mean which gum commercial," asked Aziza.

"The Chewsy Chews. Tobias was dressed up as a piece of gum that bursts with flavor. His costume explodes into berries."

Aziza chuckled. "I know that one. He explodes into berries then falls into a swimming pool full of berries."

"Yup, that's him."

"Jovi, let's hope I don't roll a seven!" said Aziza as she shook a five and a two.

"It's a seven! Uh-oh," said Jovi as she moved Aziza's thimble to New York Avenue.

"And now you owe me a lot of rent," said Tony, his voice dripping with anticipated victory.

"See, Aziza? Tony always rubs it in when he's winning," said Jovi, feeling the urge to throw the game board in Tony's face.

"He hasn't won yet. I wonder if it really was a swimming pool filled with berries," said Aziza.

"Tobias said the pool was filled with little spongy things. They made it look like berries on the computer. He said it was super fun to be thrown into," said Tony.

Jovi added, "He said there were a lot of gives, and he had to be thrown in the bouncy pool a bunch of times."

Tony said, "Jovi, it's *takes*, not *gives*. There were a lot of *takes*, which means they had to film the commercial over and over again."

Upstairs, Tobias said solemnly to his dad, "I know I'm not good at business like you are. But I know you, and I don't believe you. You cheat even the people you love."

"Tobias, the past is the past. Let it go," said Caroline.

Tobias burst out singing "Let It Go" from the Disney movie *Frozen*.

Aziza paused the game to listen to Tobias sing upstairs. "Wow. Your uncle can really sing. He has an amazing voice."

"Yeah, he sings a lot. Used to be in a band," said Tony. He rolled, moved his race car, and said, "Kentucky Avenue. I'm buying it. Got another monopoly."

The adults continued to talk, unaware of their downstairs audience. Grandpa said, "Caroline, I knew you'd be on board, so I already got the process rolling. I invested some of your money in farmland."

"You did what?" exclaimed Darrell, who, like Tobias, felt something was amiss with Grandpa's unusually urgent meeting.

"Land is always a good investment. Listen, I owe some money. So I bought some farmland, used it for collateral to invest in this company to pay back . . ."

"What's collateral?" Tony asked Aziza.

"Like in Monopoly. The bank gave me money to buy the Baltic Avenue house, but the bank will take my house back if I don't make my payments. And it's not looking good for me. I'm broke."

Tobias said, "Dad, that doesn't even make sense. If you need to pay someone back, just pay them back. Don't spend other people's money without permission to go buy something else so you can get completely different people to give you money, so you can pay back the first people and use money for the second people, and then get your son's money for whatever else you can't pay for. That's a Fonzie scheme. Even I know that."

Darrell smiled. "Tobias, it's a Ponzi scheme. Not Fonzie."

Caroline added, "See, Tobias? You don't understand any of this. Dad actually does buy businesses."

"At least this once, I do understand. Whatever it is, Dad, you're in trouble," Tobias said with concern.

Grandpa could pull the wool over anyone's eyes except Tobias's. Grandpa's phone started beeping repeatedly from multiple text messages coming in. He pulled a cell phone out of his pants pocket to read the messages. His shoulders dropped.

More text messages beeped from another phone in his suit jacket. Grandpa pulled out that phone and read the messages, then yet another cell phone came out of another pocket. For once, the gleam had left Grandpa's face. It was drawn, drooped downward, and a layer of doom poured over his expression.

Tobias said, "I just auditioned for a movie where the character had multiple phones. He wasn't the good guy."

Grandpa said, irritated, "What does an actor know about anything?"

"The fact that I'm a really good actor is something I learned from you, Dad. Your life has always been one big act," said Tobias.

"Stop it, Tobias," said Caroline.

More text messages came in, and before Grandpa could prevent him, Tobias grabbed one of Grandpa's cell phones and read the messages.

The voices got much louder after that, and Caroline did not want Aziza or the kids hearing any of it. She called for Aziza and the kids and told them they needed to get out of the house.

"Take them to Mitch's swim meet," said Caroline, as Aziza and the kids came up from the game room.

Aziza said, "I'm working my other job tonight, remember? I can't work that late."

"Yeah, yeah," said Caroline, handing Aziza her purse and pointing her and the kids to the door.

They all heard Tobias say to Grandpa, "You've laundered money?"

Jovi asked her mom, "Why's Grandpa washing his money?"

"Where's Mitch's swim meet?" Aziza asked Caroline.

Caroline was not listening.

"You'll need to pick them up at the meet," said Aziza. "I can't work late. You'll pick them up, right?"

Caroline all but shoved Aziza and the kids out the door.

"I did no such thing!" Grandpa shouted at Tobias, both still in the kitchen.

"Where's the meet? I need to know," Aziza asked Caroline again.

Caroline, distracted, did not answer. Instead she shut the door abruptly so Aziza and the kids could not hear any more of the argument in the kitchen. With the closed door in her face, Aziza buzzed the doorbell several times, but no one answered. She tried calling, but no one answered. Aziza called the school and found out where the swim meet was, took Jovi and Tony to the meet, then apologized to them for having to rush off to her evening job. When she said goodbye, she gave them an extra hug, knowing that whatever they had overheard that evening simply wasn't good.

12

THE VOICES OF BLUE

As Boshlek walked back to the regiment, one droplet of the frothing mercury waters floated upward. The droplet sung in many hushed and seductive tones to one of the lowest-numbered Grezniks and awoke it from its slumber. Then it said, "It is time for you to awaken and come to me. The blue stones can be yours and yours alone. Come here, intelligent and strong one. Do not tell the others. Come alone and I will give you the beautiful blue stones."

The Greznik, allured by the promise of blue, walked away from its sleeping circle without notice and followed the Voices toward the river waters. When the Greznik came into view of the river, the waters changed from the molten silver to many beautiful shades of blue. The waters were so bright it looked as though the sun were shining in the dark night. Stunning blue stones covered the riverbed.

As the Greznik got near the waters, the Voices said quietly, "The blue stones are for you. I am giving them to you. Come to the waters. Come forward to the river. Drink of me, and the stones shall be yours alone."

The Greznik stepped to the water's edge to gaze at the alluring stones as they sparkled with long beams of the most beautiful light. It looked longingly at the blue stones underwater, and an unbearable thirst overcame it. It leaned its head downward to drink.

The Voices said, "Drink the waters dry, and the blue stones shall be yours. All yours. You will be all-powerful . . ."

Meanwhile, Boshlek had returned to the regiment and realized immediately that the Greznik was missing and raced back to the water's edge.

Boshlek bounded forward and screeched, "Do not drink, you fool! Do not believe them! You will be devoured! The Voices you hear are Proznia!"

The wayward Greznik ignored Boshlek and lowered its head to the water to drink. Just then, a man on horseback rounded the corner and saw the Greznik. The horseman's glance exploded the Greznik into foul-smelling smoke. The smoke evaporated, and the horseman saw the bright blue waters and the gorgeous blue gems on the riverbed. The powerful blue light stung the horseman's eyes. He rubbed them, fearing he had traveled too long and was hallucinating.

As soon as the Voices saw the horseman, they collapsed and dropped deep into the river. The blue stones disappeared, and the Chongchon River returned to its usual bubbling, muddy waters of the dark night. The Voices of Proznia learned in that moment that if they set their gaze upon a person, they would fall helplessly back into the water.

Boshlek, hidden in the thick brush of the hills, had come dangerously close to being evaporated by the horseman. It ran, unseen, back to its regiment, and woke up all the Grezniks. Boshlek told them a human was nearby but did not yet tell them of Proznia's arrival. They charged silently away at lightning speed and retreated high up in the Rangrim Mountains, where no humans could set their eyes upon them.

Deep inside Earth, the new Greznik remained abandoned and forgotten by Boshlek. Its formation was abruptly aborted, and the weight of the earth above it created unfathomable levels of pain. It used every bit of energy it had to move through Earth's insides to reach the surface and relieve the agony. But its efforts were tortuously slow, and it had no idea whether it was crawling toward the surface, sideways, or back toward the middle. It shouted out for help but was so deep not even a Greznik could hear it.

13

BUTTERFLY LUCKY CHARM

Tony and Jovi walked into the pool arena just after Mitch's butterfly race had started. Tony scanned each lane and quickly figured out which swimmers had the best butterfly technique, and Mitch was not one of them. Even though Mitch was stronger than most twelve-year-olds, this time and always, Mitch's teammate Brayton was the fastest in the butterfly. And Brayton was the last person Tony wanted to win the race.

Mitch was in an outer lane, and he felt the waves from other competitors' strokes pushing him down. Mitch won other swimming events readily, but never once had he won the butterfly. He was particularly exhausted in this race and just wanted to give up for good. Then Mitch heard a voice. That all-too-familiar, annoying, raspy, screeching voice that never needed a microphone—his little sister, Jovi.

"Mit—!" screamed Jovi at the top of her lungs.

Her voice was silenced when his head went underwater. At the next breath, he heard her again.

"Boson—"

Breath.

"Fish—"

Breath.

"Taski—!"

Every time Mitch came up for a breath, Jovi was screaming louder. He wished he could pop up from the water and say, "Stop screeching!"

Jovi cheered again and again. "Faster, Bosonataski-Fishengardet! Go, Mitch!"

Mitch hated his last name as much as Jovi did. And Mitch hated hearing bits of their awful last name as he came up for each breath. Their last name was so long that when the swim team jackets came out with the swimmers' last names sewn on the back, Mitch's name started at his left wrist and went up his arm, across the back, and down the right arm. When the coach saw it, he thought it looked ridiculous and sent it back. He asked to have only Mitch's nickname printed on it: "FISH," the fastest swimmer on the team. Except in the butterfly.

Jovi always overcompensated for uncontrollable things in her life that she did not like. And their last name was no exception. Cheering for Mitch, she shouted out the whole monstrosity for everyone to hear, as if she were proud of her name. For that reason, Mitch hated when Jovi came to his meets. She was like the resident cheerleader for those who enjoyed making fun of their last name.

Loudmouth Jovi. Breath. *You're embarrassing yourself.* Breath. *Why are you here anyway?* Breath.

From the top of the bleachers, Jovi watched Mitch swim and cheered louder. After two more laps, Mitch's technique loosened up, and he pulled ahead of another teammate—but Brayton remained in the lead.

Tony did not sit up in the bleachers but stood in front of everyone to watch the race. Mitch did not know that Tony was there too—Tony watched everything with quiet, piercing focus, unnoticed. He never shouted out for anyone. Or anything.

Mitch's pace increased, and he closed in on the boy in third place. Tony smiled. Jovi was now cheering so loud her face was red, and it looked as if she was about to pass out.

Kenny's brother Asher was on Mitch's swim team, and Kenny went to every swim meet he could to cheer for Asher. Mitch was an arm's length behind Brayton as he headed into the last lap. Then Kenny saw Tony and ran up to him to say hello. He tapped Tony's shoulder from behind and gave him a big bear hug.

"Guess what, Tony?" asked Kenny.

Although Kenny was awkward, he was unusually strong—so when he gave Tony a surprise hug, it was like getting unexpectedly hit by an offensive lineman. It nearly knocked Tony over and swung him around so Tony missed the last moment of the race when Mitch closed Brayton's lead.

Tony was now facing the bleachers and saw Jovi jumping up and down like a maniac. Seeing Jovi's reaction, Tony knew Mitch was neck-and-neck with Brayton. As Jovi cheered her brother's speed, she tripped on the bleachers and fell dramatically downward. She sailed past two bleacher steps and fell face-first on a railing, landed right on her forehead, and wailed in pain.

Kenny still had a firm grip on Tony as Tony mumbled, "Jovi, can you for once not make a big scene?" Tony was tired of saving Jovi from all the scrapes, both social and physical, that she constantly found herself in.

Mitch touched the wall and secured his first-ever victory in the butterfly stroke, but both Jovi and Tony missed seeing it. After Mitch touched the wall and lifted his head out of the water, he was very surprised to realize that he had won. Yet he merely shrugged and climbed out of the pool. He looked up at his race time and knew it was not fast enough to qualify for the Junior Olympics.

Mitch hated being in front of audiences. He liked swimming more than other sports because at least he was underwater most of the time. When his race was done, he crawled out of the pool, put on his swim team gear, and returned to the side of the pool. In victory, every time, he merely lifted his eyebrows as if to say, "Huh. Interesting." Then he got out of the pool and sat on the bench and wondered why he was not faster.

This time, when he got out of the water after unexpectedly winning, his coach bounded over to congratulate him. "Great job! I knew you could do it!"

"Not fast enough for the Junior Olympics," Mitch said, disappointed.

The coach stopped him, grabbed him by the shoulders, and looked directly into his eyes. "That was an incredible race for you. Don't throw away a victory today because you're worried about a race that hasn't happened yet. That was your best butterfly ever. You got better every lap! What was different?"

Then Mitch heard Jovi's crying, and looked over to see Tony giving her an ice pack to put on her forehead.

"It's my sister's voice. It's so annoying. I couldn't stop hearing it."

"No one can stop hearing it. Bring her to every meet. She's your lucky charm," said the coach. Then he slapped Mitch on the shoulder and walked over to console Brayton.

"My lucky charm? You've got to be kidding," mumbled Mitch.

The coach gathered the team to line up and shake their competitors' hands. At every meet, Kenny wanted to line up and participate in the hand shaking, and the coach always let him. But Kenny always stood in the opposing team's lineup because he only wanted to shake hands with kids he knew—the kids on his own school's team. And the other teams always kindly obliged.

When Kenny stood before Brayton, Kenny dropped his hand and looked down at the floor. Not to be rude, but he was afraid. All Kenny knew was that Brayton had punched his best friend, Tony. He had no idea he was the cause of the fight. Yet Kenny's loyalty ran deep, where the heart really beats, beyond the place where skills matter. Kenny would always defend a friend. Brayton tried to offer his hand again, but Kenny neither looked up nor reached his hand forward. Instead, Kenny stepped past Brayton and reached forward to shake the hand of the next boy in line—Mitch's. Kenny awkwardly tipped onto his toes and bounced, excited that Mitch had won the race, having no idea that he would never see Mitch race again.

The ceiling of the pool had a few skylights, and no one saw a creature's eyes peeking in. After watching Mitch win the race, the creature ducked back down to munch on an apple it had stolen from a child's forgotten lunch box.

14

THE CIRCLE CLOSES

Inside Earth, the forgotten, half-formed Greznik no longer had the strength to cry out for mercy. Eventually its energy was completely expended, and it could no longer move through Earth's burning, molten mantle. Its skin melted and reformed so many times that the new Greznik believed it would just melt for good and be gone forever before it ever reached the surface.

Up high in the mountains, the regiment fell back into formation and quickly asleep, oblivious to Proznia's arrival. Boshlek, however, did not sleep. It fretted over Proznia's threats and paced back and forth and spit constantly—if not for the horseman, Proznia would have ensnared the skillful Greznik. And if Proznia's power could take over the least vulnerable Greznik, it could lure any one of them to drink its waters and become its pawn to destroy Life and Earth and take them all back into its control.

Boshlek wanted the exploded Greznik replaced before sunrise, so it bolted energy to Earth's center to form another Greznik. But instead of creating a new Greznik, the bolt struck the half-formed Greznik, reshaping the existing five legs and forming two extra legs. Then the forgotten Greznik started speeding toward the surface. It hit the cooler layers and squirmed and slithered through a crack in Earth's crust and stumbled onto the surface.

The Greznik struggled to stand, and its body throbbed from the repeated burnings during its rise to the surface. But then the most calming of cool breezes whispered past its skin and soothed the painful throbbing.

It said, "I have arrived. The struggle is over."

But little did it know—the struggle was not over. The torment was just beginning.

The new Greznik, 401^5, crawled out of the earth at the regiment's abandoned encampment near the river. It was confused as to why no one was there to welcome its arrival and provide direction. It wandered and looked everywhere, but there was no one. It scanned in every direction and finally found the regiment up high in the mountains and started its journey toward them.

The new Greznik was an odd one. It had seven legs instead of five—three legs on each side and a feeble one in the middle. Six legs were thin, oddly shaped, and crooked. The seventh leg in the belly was shorter and scrawnier than it was supposed to be, and shortly after the Greznik had surfaced, one extra eye had popped out of its head for a total of seven.

Boshlek watched with irritation as the new Greznik approached. Never before had Boshlek abandoned a

Greznik in the burning womb of Earth. Boshlek realized that, for the first time ever, it had made a terrible mistake and created a horribly flawed Greznik. Too many legs. Too many eyes. Wrongly shaped legs. And it ran strangely and slowly.

The new seven-legged Greznik was numbered 401^5. It's circle leader was numbered 401^4. Grezniks refer to each other by their numbers—absolutely never a name. Only in the telling of their story is the seven-legged Greznik called Skarb and its circle leader called Jatuh. The Greznik regiment was organized according to their numbers. Skarb and its circle leader Jatuh were the same base number, 401, but raised to a different power. Having the same base number placed them in the same circle.

Boshlek walked up to the seven-legged Skarb and said, "I am Greznik Number One, Eternal Commander. You will forever do as I say. We are here to destroy every bit of Life. But we will never return to Proznia. We will escape."

"I do not want to go back there. Not ever," affirmed Skarb.

"No one wants to go back to Proznia. We will obliterate Life and escape this dreadful planet by launching Earth out of its orbit and shattering it into miniscule fragments. Earth will end its going around the sun while we launch our destruction throughout the universe. To succeed, we need powerful blue stones which are hidden within Earth's insides."

"I will find the blue stones!" said Skarb enthusiastically.

"You must never seek them nor find them on your own. Ever. Now listen here. You are number 401^5. You will report to 401⁴. You will join that circle. When two Grezniks have the same base number, the newer and larger number is assigned to the fighting circle of the older, lower number. You will obey all orders, or you will be annihilated. Water is your enemy. Never dive into a lake. Do not slither into the sea. Never run into a river. If you do, you will very quickly dissolve and disappear forever. Do not ever drink water. If for any reason you disobey any command, or if you are deemed not worthy enough for whatever reason, you will be walked into the sea and eliminated."

Every Greznik who arrives on Earth's surface hears this same speech. And they quickly learn that burdensome or inconvenient Grezniks are eliminated by their peers without one bit of remorse.

Boshlek continued, "If a human sees you, you will explode and disappear forever. Some humans, called Tukors, can gaze upon you and nothing will happen to you. But they are our greatest enemy."

"How am I to know the difference?" asked Skarb.

"We have no idea what makes a human a Tukor or not. Tukors thwart our every move, and they do everything in their power to stop us. They must be destroyed—you must crush them, devour them, rip them to pieces—whatever you do, you must destroy them. Your circle leader will train you on the rest. Now go find your circle and help them find the blue stones."

The seven-legged Greznik noticed that Boshlek had only five legs that were shaped differently than its own. It said, "I see that you, and everyone else, have five legs, and I seven. Something went wrong on my way up. I got stuck and—"

"Report to your circle," interrupted Boshlek.

"I burned over and over again," continued Skarb. "And then before the other legs were finished, two more legs popped out and my skin—"

Boshlek did not like being reminded of its mistake and said, "Do not talk to me. I ordered you to leave. Report to your circle. Now!"

Skarb obeyed and found its new fighting circle sound asleep and tried to fall asleep just like the others. But because of its imbalanced shape, Skarb could not stand on its center leg without tipping over. It gave up, laid down, curled up its seven legs, and fell sound asleep—a deep sleep to rebuild the energy stolen from the scorching rise upward.

When Skarb's circle leader, Jatuh, awoke, it saw that a new seven-legged Greznik had entered their circle and was lying in a heap, comfortably sound asleep. When Jatuh saw the seven legs, it was angry. There was no way a deformed Greznik could join its circle. Jatuh did not want to risk the reputation of its circle on a weak and poorly performing Greznik, so it kicked the new member awake. Skarb woke up, startled, and stood at attention to the leader.

"You do not belong in my circle," said Jatuh.

"Yes, I do. You are 401^4 and I am 401^5. Same number raised to a different power. So yes, I do belong here," said Skarb.

"Why are you sleeping on the ground?" asked Jatuh. "You must sleep on one leg. Or you are not fit to be in my circle."

"I cannot sleep on my center leg. Everything is uneven. I wobble and tip over."

Jatuh said, "Let me see you run."

Skarb took off running with the strangest gait any Greznik had ever seen. Grezniks do not know how to laugh. Instead, they cackle a deep, guttural sound from a throat full of phlegm. When they are done cackling they spit out a reeky, gooey substance. When other Grezniks saw Skarb run, they spat out the reeky goo like water pistols.

"You cannot be in my regiment," said Jatuh.

"You and I are the same number, raised to a different power. I am in this circle," said Skarb.

"No, you aren't," said Jatuh as it kicked Skarb out. The other Grezniks closed the circle tightly so Skarb could not reenter. When Skarb tried to enter, it was thrown, painfully, a great distance, and told to stay there the remainder of the day.

Jatuh reported to Boshlek and complained, "There's been a mistake. The new Greznik cannot be assigned to my circle."

"It's not a mistake. It's a rule," said Boshlek.

"But my circle is the fastest, strongest, most prepared for battle. This Greznik has seven legs. It cannot sleep on one leg. It is a lopsided blight. It runs poorly. It can have no importance. It will weaken my circle," argued Jatuh.

"If your circle is the strongest, then it is strong enough to have one with seven legs," said Boshlek.

"It will weaken my fighting circle."

"If the seven-legger is weak, it will soon be gone—and when it's gone, you will get another. Everyone is replaceable, including you. Now shut up and leave."

Jatuh left Boshlek and returned, angry, to its circle. After watching Skarb, it decided Skarb would never be able to help their effort and would only slow it down.

Jatuh said to Skarb, "Listen here. You will never be a member of this circle. Ever. We would all be better off if you had never surfaced. You are an inconvenience, and you know what happens to inconveniences."

"What?" asked Skarb.

Jatuh kicked Skarb high into the air and, on its way down, batted it far away. Skarb tumbled down the steep mountainside and came to a crashing halt, stuck between two rocks, where its extra eyeball whirled around like a spinning top.

15

FROZEN DOUGH

After all the other swimmers and parents left the pool, Tony, Mitch, and Jovi were still waiting for their mom or dad to show up and take them home. Mitch texted them, but no one replied. He called their parents and Aziza, but no one answered and no one called back.

"Aziza told Mom she had to come get us," said Jovi.

"Mom wasn't listening," said Tony.

The coach stayed, making sure they were not left alone, but it was getting late. The janitor also waited as long as he could, then said they all had to leave because he needed to close the building for the night.

Aziza finally called back. "I'm so sorry. I just got your messages. I'm at my other job and can't pick you up. But I've texted your parents. Called them. I can't reach them ..."

The coach was puzzled by the parents' absence. He knew the Bosonataski-Fishengardets well enough to know they would never forget their kids at a meet and ignore all messages and calls. He had a gut feeling that something had gone wrong at home. Although he had had a long day and just wanted to get home, he could not just leave them there. He said, "I'll take you back home to make sure everything's okay."

When they turned the corner to walk toward their townhouse in the middle of the block, they realized something had, in fact, gone terribly wrong. There was a police squad car in front of the home and two FBI agents at the bottom of the steps. Then two more agents came out of their home, escorting their grandpa in handcuffs.

From the end of the block, Jovi cried out, "Grandpa!" and ran to catch up to him. But her grandpa, with his head dropped downward, did not look up. She only made it halfway down the block before the squad car drove away with her grandpa in the backseat. Their mom and dad watched from a front window and never saw the kids.

Mitch and Tony stood silently at the end of the block, next to Mitch's swim coach, having no idea what just happened. Jovi looked back at her brothers as if they could get her out of this scrape like they had so many times before. But this time, the mistakes were not her own and there was nothing they could do.

The noises of the city hummed all around them, and at that moment it all sounded so deafeningly loud to Mitch. Tony looked up and down the street, as if someone might be coming to set this all straight. The coach was not sure what to say.

Mitch said quietly, "I guess Tobias was right."

"What do you mean?" asked Tony.

"Grandpas are supposed to be the good guys. But ours isn't."

Jovi ran back to her brothers just as a television news van turned the corner and parked in front of their townhouse. An attractive newswoman and a cameraman popped out of the van, then another news van came from the other direction.

The coach knew their grandpa was a prominent person, but he had no idea why he would be arrested. Television crews crowded around to report live from the front of the home. If the kids walked into their townhouse, they would end up on national news. The coach tried again to reach the parents, but with no luck.

The coach took the kids to wait at a nearby bakery and celebrate Mitch's victory, but the celebration was subdued as the kids waited to hear from their parents. When they finally did, the coach walked the kids back to their home, relieved to see both the squad cars and television crews were gone. Their mom and dad came to the door to greet them. The coach knew that whatever happened that night was a private matter, so he gave the parents a brief update on the race and Jovi's fall and said a quick farewell. Mitch wished his dad would acknowledge the amazing win, and Jovi tried to show him the bump on her forehead, but the evening was pulled in another direction.

Tony asked, "Why was Grandpa arrested?"

"How'd you find out?" asked Caroline.

"We saw him in handcuffs," said Mitch.

"It's complicated," said Darrell. "It's been a long night.

Best for you kids to head up to bed. We'll talk about this in the morning."

The kids ignored their dad and went into the kitchen. Jovi pulled out an ice pack from the freezer for her forehead.

Tobias saw Jovi's bruised forehead and said, "What happened?"

"I fell," said Jovi, bursting into tears.

Caroline finally noticed her. "Oh, honey, that is a bad bruise. What happened?"

"*I fell!* We told you that already, like a hundred times!" shouted Jovi, throwing the ice pack on the kitchen floor.

"I'm sorry. I'm sorry, honey," said Caroline, giving Jovi a hug.

"You forgot to pick us up," said Mitch.

"I thought Aziza was bringing you home," said Caroline.

"She told you she wasn't," said Tony.

Caroline had made herself some tea and accidentally poured salt into her cup. As she took the first sip, she choked and spat it out, spraying tea all over Jovi.

"Yuck, Mom!" said Jovi.

"I'm sorry," said Caroline as she wiped tea off Jovi's face.

Tony asked again, "What did Grandpa do?"

"Stole lots of money," said Tobias.

"Is that true?" Jovi asked.

"I hope not," said Darrell.

"Of course it's not," said Caroline.

Mitch said, "It'll be all over the news."

"How do you know that?" asked Caroline.

"We saw all the reporters outside," said Tony.

Tobias, for once, spoke solemnly. "Grandpa stole money. He's going to jail. Everyone in the country will know about it within hours . . . and that's my cue to take the next plane back to Malibu."

Caroline snapped at Tobias. "I told you not to talk about this around the kids."

"They're going to hear it tomorrow, whether you like it or not," said Tobias. "And you do understand, they'll freeze all the money."

"What do you know?" snipped Caroline.

Jovi got up and looked in the freezer to see if any of Grandpa's money was in there. Tony had no idea what freezing money meant, but he figured Grandpa's "dough" was not in their freezer.

"Jovi, there's frozen dough in there. Can you get me some?" asked Tony.

"Stop joking about Grandpa!" shouted Caroline.

"I wasn't joking. There's frozen cookie dough in the freezer. Aziza and Jovi made it," said Tony.

"I'll have some of Grandpa's dough," said Mitch. "He usually doesn't freeze it. He usually gives us a check."

"That's enough, kids!" barked Darrell as he chipped off a hunk of frozen cookie dough and ate it.

"What does frozen money mean?" Tony asked Tobias.

"Grandpa needs to give the stolen money back. And until then, his money can't go anywhere. It's 'frozen' until they figure out whom it belongs to," answered Darrell.

"And right now, I can say I'm very glad I changed my

last name to a stage name. No one out there will know I'm related to him," said Tobias. "As for you guys, I'd suggest dropping Bosonataski from your last name."

"Kids, time to get up to bed. We'll talk about this in the morning," said Darrell.

The kids again ignored their dad.

"How did he steal it?" Mitch asked Tobias.

Mitch knew that Tobias always talked too much for their mom's liking, and he would get more information out of him. But this time, Tobias had far less to say.

Tobias said sorrowfully, "Grandpa did some really bad stuff, and because he's famous, it'll be all over the news. Your grandpa's mistakes are not your own, so don't let anyone tell you otherwise, okay? It took me a long time to learn that, and you'll need to learn it more quickly than I did. Now, you three do need to get to bed."

They did listen to Uncle Tobias and went up to bed. Unable to fall asleep, Mitch and Tony tiptoed back to the staircase to eavesdrop on their parents and Tobias. Jovi saw her brothers leave their room and followed.

Mitch said, "Shh, Jovi. Be quiet so we can listen."

The kids did not understand much of the conversation, but somehow, amid the muddled array of topics they did not understand, they could tell their life was never going to be the same.

Jovi crawled to the landing at the top of the stairs, leaned over, and fell asleep. She dreamed of being a ballerina with a beautiful skirt, twirling on a stage in front of an audience that was laughing at someone else. Mitch looked toward their front door and sensed that tomorrow he might not want to go through it. Tony stopped listening and wondered, *If my parents were chess pieces, which ones would they be?* He concluded any of them—because in every case, someone else moves them.

16

LET ME TRY

Skarb waited near the bottom of the mountainside until its extra eye stopped whirling and the dizziness waned. When Skarb felt stable again, it climbed back up and returned to the regiment. Skarb reached the outskirts of the regiment just as Boshlek interrupted their daily schedule to order the Grezniks into their fighting formation. The Grezniks speculated that a battle was imminent or that blue stones had been found. When Grezniks get excited about a fight, they froth at the mouth and spit continually. Soon the ground around their circles was slippery with phlegm.

Boshlek hollered, "This is just an announcement. Get quiet!"

The Grezniks stilled themselves, stood at attention, and, with loud gulps, swallowed the thick and rancid mucus that oozed from their mouths.

Boshlek said, "Proznia is here."

The Grezniks bent their backs and shook like frightened dogs about to be hit by an abusive master. Boshlek berated them for cowardice. The Grezniks struggled to regain their composure, cowered, and murmured among themselves.

Boshlek said, "Get a grip! Shut up and listen! Proznia has come to take us back. But we will not go, will we?"

"We will never go!" shouted the Grezniks in unison.

"Proznia has arrived. But it is trapped, caged within the waters."

The Grezniks were elated to hear that Proznia was trapped. In celebration, they cheered and spit upward so bits of phlegm rained down on them like confetti.

"Listen! Heed this warning. Proznia speaks from the waters as a thousand voices. The Voices of Proznia can turn the waters deceptively blue as though sparkling blue stones lie below their currents. They will call out to you and ask you to drink the waters in. But it is a dangerous ruse. The Voices of Proznia are more powerful than you—so do not travel to the waters alone, or Proznia will pull you in. If you drink them in, you will have given Proznia form and you will be no more. And Proznia will pull us back into its control. From today onward, our daily chant will include the following. Repeat after me:

"I will never wander to the waters alone.

"I will never go!

"The Voices of Proznia call out with lies.

"I will never listen!

"Eternal Commander is my almighty. I am worthless without our forever commander.

"I will obey. I surrender to Eternal Commander for all eternity."

While Boshlek spoke, the circle leaders stood on their hind legs and flapped their front legs in obedience and reverence. Their extra set of claws extended and clicked against each other creating piercing, clanging, metallic sounds.

Slyly, during Boshlek's announcement, Skarb squeezed back in Jatuh's circle between two Grezniks. Skarb was confident that if Proznia's power was poised to seize them all, Jatuh could ill afford to have a circle with only ten members. But when Boshlek finished its announcement, the circle members realized Skarb had snuck back in. They promptly kicked Skarb out again as Jatuh yelled, "You are worthless. Get out!"

Skarb spit in their direction but missed completely. They all cackled and snarled. It hunkered back down, flattened itself completely along a scree, and schemed how to get the blue stones and prove them all wrong—especially Jatuh.

Even with the greater urgency, no circle allowed Skarb to train with them or participate in finding the stones. Instead, in the next days, many hundreds of next days, Skarb was told every morning that its legs were worthless, weak, and pointless. Every day, Skarb tried to enter its fighting circle, and every time it was kicked out. Skarb tried to find another Greznik circle to join, but every circle had a perfect eleven members and none needed another to join them. Instead, every Greznik relished having one that was utterly worthless to inflate and puff up their own deluded sense of importance.

"Please let me try, at least once, to find the stones," said Skarb one day to Jatuh.

"Never," answered Jatuh.

Skarb pointed to other Grezniks. "They are not perfectly strong. They are not perfectly skilled. But at least they get to try."

"You are a mere insect. Annoying. Irritating. And I can easily swat you away."

Jatuh then tossed Skarb down a hill.

Over many years, Skarb repeatedly tried to change Jatuh's mind, but Jatuh, painfully and repeatedly, swatted it away and demanded others join in the effort.

Jatuh trained its own circle of ten Grezniks to be the strongest, fastest, and cruelest in the regiment. In doing so, Jatuh further proved its own strength and power, and the other Greznik circles increasingly admired and envied Jatuh. So as the years wore on, Jatuh grew in popularity, strength, and importance, while Skarb grew less and less important.

Skarb eventually learned to stop walking too close to any fighting circle for fear of being used cruelly, yet again, for fighting practice. Instead, Skarb wandered from circle to circle without ever entering one. It always stood near enough to watch and listen but far enough back to remain unnoticed and avoid an attack. Eventually the circles never noticed if Skarb was there or not.

Every day, Skarb wandered away from the regiment and practiced different techniques on its own. For years and years, its efforts produced no improvement. Skarb was still slow. Skarb still ran sloppily. Its bizarre six-legged gait could not be fixed to run like everyone else. Skarb gave up trying. Skarb still wandered every day, but it let its legs run like they wanted to—strangely. Over time, Skarb discovered that its odd gait was rather efficient and its unusual legs could run strangely fast.

Skarb practiced using its natural gait and became faster and faster, and it developed a powerful secret— its own running speed. Skarb could trail very far behind and explore the world on its own, then catch up to the regiment quickly. It hid this speed from the other Grezniks, believing one day it would find the stones on its own and reveal its speed to the regiment in a glorious victory lap. And the circle leaders would have to click their claws and bow down to honor and revere Skarb's power and success.

17

KNOCK, KNOCK, GOODBYE

The next day at breakfast, Jovi turned on the TV and a morning newswoman was reporting on their grandpa's arrest. "Neil Bosonataski, founder and president of SPSBR Investments, was arrested by the FBI last night at one of his Manhattan properties. His firm, Strongrock Powerbridge Steelmountain Bigstride Renaissance Investments, has a long history of risky investments that have paid off grandly, but this time perhaps he has taken a few too many big strides. He is accused—"

Jovi shouted, "Mom! Dad! Grandpa's on TV!"

She ran out of the kitchen to find them but accidentally flung her cereal bowl into the refrigerator. Jovi spilled things all the time, so Mitch and Tony hardly noticed. Mitch stepped over the puddle of milk to put his bowl in the sink as he watched the news about Grandpa.

Caroline ushered Jovi back into the kitchen and turned off the TV.

"Yes, Grandpa is on the news. The dust will settle, and it'll be just fine. So, we're going to go to school like any other day. And who dumped their cereal all over the floor? Clean it up."

Caroline left the room and shut the door, as if closing the door closed off the unwelcome news from their life.

Mitch usually would have let Jovi clean up her mess on her own, but their mom's snippiness was unsettling. He picked up the bowl, grabbed a rag, and helped wipe up the milk. Tony turned the TV back on, and they listened to the news about Grandpa.

Calls were pouring in to their parents as friends saw the news and wanted to find out more. The news had spread fast. At school, classmates ran up to Jovi, Mitch, and Tony and asked what happened to their grandpa.

"My mom said he was your grandpa. Is that true?"

"Did he really steal millions of dollars?"

"Is he in jail?"

Normally, Jovi always had something to interject about every topic. But no one told Jovi the rules for what to say when her grandpa was on TV for all the wrong reasons. Everyone was talking about it and asking her questions, yet she understood none of her grandpa's crimes. She felt nothing but shame, hated the questioning, and answered with a blank stare and walked away.

Tony was speechless too, but by midday he had fine-tuned his response: "We were playing Monopoly. My grandpa got the 'Go to Jail' card, then the FBI showed up and hauled him to jail. We play for real. Want to come over today and play Monopoly?"

Mitch, on the other hand, shrugged his shoulders when asked and replied with several variations on the same sentence: "Yes, my grandpa's in big trouble. I think you can visit him in jail if you want. If you do, ask him why he's there, 'cause I have absolutely no idea."

Mitch was relieved when the day finally ended and he could go to swim practice, but Brayton took the opportunity to rub it in his face. Mitch dove in the pool and swam the whole time. His butterfly technique that day was fast enough to qualify for the Junior Olympics.

The news about Grandpa's crimes dripped out all week, one crime after another. Like a leaky faucet and a plugged drain, it spilled out everywhere. Grandpa had even cheated some parents at their school. The parents' rage tore through the school like a dust storm carrying stinging nettles in the air.

Grandpa was accused of too many things, nearly all of which the kids had never heard of and did not understand. Conversations whirled around them like a foreign language. Getting ready for school, Mitch read an article on the front page. It said, "Bosonataski and his accomplices are accused of a long list of crimes, such as securities fraud, wire fraud, mail fraud, money laundering, forging, manipulating markets . . ."

In the midst of everything, they understood one thing: they were treated as though they were guilty too.

The exception was Kenny, who was as happy as always to see Tony. That morning Kenny's parents had run out of cereal, so his breakfast was hot oatmeal.

"How do you count oatmeal on your spoon?" asked Kenny.

"It's impossible," Tony answered.

"I think it was 201," responded Kenny.

Kenny noticed that kids were snickering.

"Oatmeal isn't funny," said Kenny.

"They're laughing at me, not you," said Tony.

"No. Not Tony. No. No. No. Kids don't laugh at you. Not, not, not Tony. They don't laugh at Tony. Only Kenny. Me."

"I promise you, Kenny, it's me this time. I'm the funny one today. They're laughing at me because they think my grandpa is funny," said Tony.

"Your grandpa tells funny jokes?" asked Kenny. "I got one. Knock, knock."

"Who's there?" asked Tony as they walked down the hall.

"I don't know. I can't remember. I say, 'Knock, knock.' You say, 'Who's there?' Then there's always someone funny at the door. People laugh," said Kenny.

"Nobody funny came to our door. The FBI knocked and took my grandpa to jail," said Tony.

"I've never known someone in jail, Tony. No. No. No one in jail. Grandpas don't go to jail. No. No. Not jails."

At swim practice, Brayton would not let up with the teasing. The coach said to Mitch, "Don't listen to them. You aren't your grandpa. His mistakes aren't yours. You are your own man."

"I'm not a man," said Mitch. "I'm only twelve."

"Sometimes the failures of the men in our life make us men before our time. We rise to the challenge."

For all of them, their days were filled with questions they had no answers to or vague advice that seemed pulled out of dusty books with yellowing pages written far too long ago.

Some days later, Jovi waited nervously by the door for Tony and Mitch to come home from school. When they finally did, she was frantic—and yet, for once, she was successfully whispering, as if whispering could make what she was about to say untrue.

"We're leaving New York. We're moving to Minnesota," said Jovi, holding back tears.

"No we're not," said Tony.

"We *are*. How come you never believe me?"

"That's impossible, Jovi. Mom doesn't even know where that is," said Mitch as he tossed his backpack on the steps.

But then a Realtor in the kitchen said to their mom, "I'm sorry, but unfortunately it's true. Your dad sold your townhouse a month ago. He said you already knew. These are copies of the sale documents, and this is your dad's signature authorizing the sale. The new owners are moving in next week."

"It can't be true. He'd never sell the house out from under us. And the new owners would never have bought it sight unseen," said Caroline.

"They have seen it. The buyers were at a fund-raiser at your house—I think it was New Year's Eve. I'm so sorry. This is terrible news for you. I had no idea you did not know."

"I just can't believe we have to move. I don't even know how to begin to explain this to the kids."

But the kids had already heard every word. Then there were a couple knocks on the front door, and Caroline got up to answer.

"Knock, knock," said Tony.

"Who's there?" said Mitch.

"Done it," said Tony.

"Done it who?" asked Jovi.

"I don't know who done it," said Tony.

"Grandpa done it. That's who!" said Mitch.

"Not funny!" Caroline snapped as she walked to the front door to let the moving company in.

Mitch asked the Realtor, "Are you selling our house?"

"It's already sold," Caroline answered. "We're moving to Minnesota."

Jovi said to her brothers, "See? I told you. It's Minnesota."

"Why are we moving to Minnesota?" asked Tony.

Caroline was like her father in some ways—she could make up half-baked ideas on the fly—so she said, "To start a hobby farm. We're going to start a business in herbal farming."

"A farm?" exclaimed Mitch.

The Realtor said, "A hobby farm sounds wonderful. Peaceful."

"Then you move there," said Jovi.

Caroline let the moving company in.

"We're moving right now?" asked Mitch.

"No, the mover is just here to determine how big a truck they need to move our stuff," said Caroline.

Later that night, the parents talked with the kids. Mitch asked, "Why are we moving to Minnesota? Can't we just move to another place in New York?"

"We can't afford New York right now. Grandpa managed our money, and without telling us, he spent it on schemes and scams. And without asking us, he bought Minnesota farmland just before he got arrested. We can't sell the land yet for reasons that are so complicated our lawyers can hardly explain it to us. We don't have much money right now, and we don't have enough to buy anything else—so we have to move to Minnesota."

"This is a joke, right?" said Tony.

"I wish it were," said Darrell. "But it isn't. And it's probably good to get away from the craziness here anyway. The movers will come and pack everything up. I'll go first and get everything moved in. Then Mom will fly with you, and you'll all drive to the farm together."

"But we're not done with the school year," said Tony.

"It's close to the end of the year, so we've arranged for you to finish the year by taking online classes. You'll need to say all your goodbyes in the next few days," said Darrell.

Jovi burst into tears, and Darrell pulled her up on his lap. As she cried into his shoulder, Tony ran upstairs and slammed his door. Mitch stared blankly ahead.

At school over the next week, they said a lot of goodbyes.

Kenny was devastated and said to Tony, "You aren't moving."

"I wish I wasn't," said Tony.

"No. No. No, you aren't moving. Friends don't move, Tony. They don't move."

"But I am. To Minnesota."

"Will you send me a letter?" asked Kenny. "Not an alphabet letter. A letter with a stamp. That kind. I have stamps if you need them. They have yellow flowers on them."

"I'll try. But I'm not a good letter writer."

"Me neither," said Kenny.

"You can write to me and tell me how many pieces of oatmeal fit on a spoon," said Tony.

"I know already. It's 201."

"We'll stay in touch," said Tony.

"No. No. No," said Kenny. Kenny did not like being sad, and he sat down on the floor and rocked back and forth. His brother Asher came over to say goodbye to Tony.

"Goodbye, Tony," said Asher, as Tony grabbed Kenny's hand to pull him up off the floor. "Thanks for knocking Brayton down a notch. Sorry you got in trouble for it," said Asher.

Tony asked Kenny, "Will you take care of my betta fish? I can't take it with me."

Kenny was so proud when Tony came by with the fish tank and the blue betta fish. The little Monopoly hotel was still at the bottom of the tank. Every day Kenny talked to the betta fish as if Tony were in the tank with it.

Nobody knew that Kenny's dad, Mr. Etson, was the undercover FBI agent whose evidence put Grandpa in jail. When Tony dropped off the fish, Mr. Etson saw in Tony's eyes the sorrow that he had seen so many times throughout his career in law enforcement—the pain that a man's terrible decisions foisted on the innocent around him. But this time it felt worse because his own sons were friends with the affected children—Mitch, Tony, and Jovi—and he wished their grandpa's crimes were not all miserably true.

For Mitch, saying goodbye to his swim coach was the most difficult. The coach was disappointed to lose his best swimmer. But he knew that the circumstances surrounding Mitch's family were completely out of the boy's control. "You've got the butterfly down pat now. Don't let your confidence dissolve, and you'll keep winning."

"But what if there isn't a pool?" asked Mitch. He was so disappointed he started to cry, but coughed to avoid it. The coach saw tears welling up in his eyes.

"Even if there isn't a pool, you can still do strength training. And you might be surprised when you race again."

▲ ▲ ▲

Tony was not sure what his fencing coach would say. After all, he had pulled Tony into the dean's office after the Brayton fight. But Tony liked him and often wanted to be like him when he grew up. Tony waited until his teammates left, but in the quiet of the gym, he was reluctant to walk up and say goodbye. He did not want the goodbye to be true, but he summoned the guts and walked over to his coach, who was putting away the equipment.

"This is my last day here," said Tony.

"Today? I thought it was next week. I'm glad you said something."

"I wish we weren't going at all," Tony said dejectedly.

"You're a great teammate, and the team is going to miss you," said the coach. "But you'll be okay. You've got a tough spirit. Most kids just go along like sheep."

"I don't really want to go. My grandpa ruined everything," said Tony.

"Your grandpa is a first-rate rascal, I admit. But listen here. We each have our own character, and we choose it every day. It isn't given. It isn't inherited. No matter what anyone says—and they are saying a lot these days—he's just your grandpa, and what he's done has nothing to do with who you're going to be. You're moving to Minnesota, right?"

Tony nodded his head yes.

"I grew up on a farm near there. You'll have fun out there," said his coach.

"Where?"

"In Iowa. Probably similar to where you're going."

The coach fenced Tony one last time, reminding him of the strategic thrusts of the game.

Your opponent will try to fool you. Don't be fooled.

You have to get close enough to strike. Sometimes it's better to make them move in so you can strike right on mark.

It isn't all technique. Every movement has a consequence. Anticipate what the opponent will do next.

▲ ▲ ▲

Jovi did not get a chance to say all her goodbyes. Horse riding was a favorite activity, but there was no time to get out to the Long Island stables and say goodbye to her instructors. The only person she got to say goodbye to was her climbing club instructor. Jovi normally found the encouragement of her climbing instructor a welcome change to her week but not this time.

"Keep climbing, Monkey Jo," said her instructor.

Jovi said, "There won't be anywhere to climb on a farm."

"You'll be surprised how often you have to climb."

"You can't climb a cornfield," insisted Jovi.

"No matter where you end up, you'll have to climb. Remember to anchor."

"How do you anchor to a corn stalk?"

Her climbing instructor smiled, gave her a reassuring hug, and said, "You're part monkey—you'll find a way."

▲ ▲ ▲

Although Aziza was not going to miss their parents, she was the most disappointed to say goodbye to the kids. Not only would she be out of a job when they left, but she really would miss them. As a goodbye present, she took them to the Bronx Zoo—partly to say goodbye, but partly to have a wonderful last day with them, away from their basket-case parents.

During their visit, they stopped for a while to watch the red panda, who was playfully running toward them and jumping as if trying to get their attention. The kids and Aziza all laughed at the red panda's antics and stayed longer to watch him play.

"The red panda wants to talk to us," said Jovi.

"Animals don't talk," said Mitch.

"What would he be saying to us?" said Tony.

"He's probably telling us that Grandpa sold the zoo out from under him," said Mitch.

The red panda sank down to the ground.

"You hurt his feelings," said Tony.

Aziza agreed. "He does look upset."

The red panda ran around in circles, chasing its tail, then it came up close to them.

"He wants to talk to us. I know it!" said Jovi. "He doesn't want us to leave."

Aziza dropped the kids back home and wiped away a few tears as she said her final goodbye.

Jovi was crying too but at nine years old, sometimes it is hard to be precise about why one is crying. If Jovi were older, she might have been able to put words to the gut of her sadness—Aziza was everything a kid dreamed a mom to be, and she was everything their own mom was not. If truth be told, Jovi wanted her mom to be just like Aziza.

"Maybe you can be our nanny in Minnesota," said Mitch.

"That would be fun, but I need to finish school here. I'm going to be a teacher because of you guys. Maybe we'll see each other again. I hope so," said Aziza.

"You'll be a good teacher. You let us eat cookie dough," said Tony.

Their last days were nothing but goodbyes, and their world felt like traveling through a tunnel. And as they got closer to moving day, the tunnel was narrowing to the width of a straw—and nothing they loved would fit through. They were not even sure whether there would be anyone or anything to say hello to at the end of the long tunnel—except dirt at the new farm.

18

THE WHITE-WATER TERRACES

With unfailing constancy, Boshlek ordered the regiment to every volcanic location to claw deep into Earth's broken skin, where Earth bled its troubled insides, to find the blue stones. One day the regiment moved inland, away from volcanoes, and mined China's beautiful Rainbow Mountains but found nothing. Skarb was sure its fellow Grezniks were mining incompetently. There just had to be blue stones where the ground layered so many colors into the hills. When the regiment gave up and moved on, Skarb stayed behind and waited until the regiment was out of sight.

Once the regiment was long gone, Skarb broke all rules and searched alone fearlessly, determined to find the stones. Skarb dug deeper and deeper—so deep it accidentally cracked through a wall of stone that held back a river of molten lava. The lava burst into Skarb's space and burned its skin again and again, just like its original journey up from the center. This time, Skarb was certain these burns would be its final demise.

Much to Skarb's surprise, its body did not explode like every other Greznik would have. Instead, it swam through the molten syrup until it reached cooler rock. Crawling back onto to the surface, Skarb looked at its pained body but saw no sign of damage. It was not missing any legs. Its skin was unharmed. Nothing was different. Skarb was puzzled—what prevented its body from exploding?

From that point forward, when the regiment departed for the next dig, Skarb would stay behind and crawl down into the earth, right where the regiment had failed—believing their failures could become Skarb's success. Yet every time, Skarb failed to find the elusive stones. And every time, after its secret digs, it ran quickly to catch up to the regiment before anyone noticed its absence. Yet one day, after so many tries and so many failures, Skarb was ready to give up. What was the point of trying anymore? That day Skarb did not hurry back to the regiment. Instead, it walked backed slowly and lazily dragged its two extra legs on the ground.

Jatuh saw Skarb's lazy, straggling saunter and appealed to Boshlek. "Walk that seven-legger into the sea. Get rid of it. It's an eyesore."

Boshlek ignored Jatuh's appeal.

Jatuh pleaded again. "You must give my circle relief. Get rid of that useless mistake!"

No Greznik will ever admit its own errors, and so it was for Boshlek. Boshlek would never admit that Skarb's deformities were caused by its own mistake on that horrible day when Proznia issued its devastating threat. So, despite Jatuh's repeated appeals, Boshlek had always refused to eliminate Skarb.

This time was no different. Boshlek merely said, "You are both irritating." Then it kicked both Skarb and Jatuh with its hind legs and sent them tumbling down the mountainside. They both fell down a glacial crevasse. Jatuh extended its legs and stopped its own fall, but Skarb gave up and just let its body fall. But one of its extra legs got caught on a protruding ice formation, and Skarb's descent came to a jolting halt.

Jatuh began its long climb out of the crevasse and shouted down to Skarb, "Hurry it up, you worthless sap!"

Skarb ignored Jatuh and instead cleaned its claws on the deep glacial ice, then took a nap while wedged inside the crevasse. Skarb did not climb back out until late at night when the regiment was sleeping.

Weeks later the regiment crossed an expansive Chinese mountain range and scaled the Meili Snow Mountain. But Skarb trailed behind aimlessly and trotted haphazardly toward the Haba Snow Mountain instead, not really wanting to catch up to the regiment. While running, Skarb was seen by a red panda—the first one Skarb had ever encountered. Running into a red panda is one of the reasons why trailing at the back of the regiment is dangerous; red pandas are one of the very few creatures who can outwit a Greznik.

As Skarb ran alongside a river that flowed down from the Haba Snow Mountain, it heard a red panda laugh at it from across the river. Skarb hated the mockery and ran across the top of the water to snatch and eat the furry little beast.

Unbeknownst to Skarb, the red panda had stretched across the water a very thin but strong woven thread. So as Skarb crossed the waters, it tripped on the thread and tumbled headfirst into the water.

The red panda jumped up and down in excitement and giggled uncontrollably that he had dissolved his first Greznik. He ran off excitedly to tell his friends.

But his enemy had not disappeared at all. Instead, Skarb was underwater, getting pulled down by the current and sinking deeper.

Skarb, completely surprised that its body did not dissolve, fought the current to reach the surface. But the spring snowmelt from the mountain range gave the river a brutal current that pushed Skarb deeper down toward the riverbed. Skarb traveled underwater several miles downstream, fighting the current to come up for air and get back on shore. Suddenly Skarb realized that its entire body was covered in the same substance as the webbing of its feet. Unlike every other Greznik, Skarb did not dissolve.

Skarb was desperate to escape the waters as the current propelled it toward the dangerous White-Water Terraces. The Haba Snow Mountain feeds the river with calcium carbonate–laden water, and over thousands of years the water formed cascading mineral terraces. The many terraces and their pools of water formed an unusual waterfall of layered white stone, and each terraced pool of water was deadly for a Greznik.

Right as it hit the top level, Skarb tried to crawl out and get its footing on the thin edge of the terrace, but it tumbled down and fell headfirst into the first terraced pool of water. It again tried to get up on the thin edge but slipped and fell into the next terrace down. Skarb tumbled all the way down the terraces this way. Each time it fell into the next pool down, it assumed its body would dissolve and disappear forever.

By the time Skarb reached the bottom of the water-fall, it had survived dozens of falls into water and had exhausted its ability to fight. Instead of struggling to get to shore, Skarb just floated with the current down the river like the bloated carcass of a dead animal.

Eventually, a long distance down the river and well into the pitch-dark of a dreary night, Skarb crawled out and collapsed on the shore, exhausted and baffled. It chewed on its skin to try to figure out why it did not dis-solve. After resting, Skarb carefully put its toe back into the water and then its whole foot, then another foot as it stepped slowly into the river. When it again did not dissolve, it swam and swam. After a long enjoyable swim, Skarb traveled slowly back to the regiment, dismayed at its newly discovered talent for swimming—a secret Skarb decided to keep to itself forever.

INVITED

19

SCATTERED STARS

The movers came while Mitch, Tony, and Jovi were at school, and they loaded up all the family's belongings from their Manhattan townhouse to deliver it to their new home—a farm that they had not even seen. Not long after, their dad left to drive their car to Minnesota and to be there when the movers arrived at their new farm.

The kids came home from school to an empty house. Their voices always echoed and cascaded down the six-story winding staircase, but now that the townhouse was emptied, every room echoed. Sounds and voices ricocheted off walls. The paintings on the walls were gone, cupboards were bare, dust balls convened in the corners, and the sun marked where furniture or rugs had once stood.

Caroline stood before the barren walls like she was looking into a mirror and seeing no one. When the kids got home from school, she assured them unconvincingly that everything was going to be just fine. Yet they knew that she was not convinced of her own assurances. Their

126

life had, in fact, spiraled down the staircase and crashed at the bottom.

For the first time in Caroline's life, the name Bosonataski kicked her out of every social network. Hardly anyone was calling her anymore. Invitations dried up. And Caroline had to worry about money. Instead of a luxury hotel, Caroline and the kids spent their last days in their New York townhouse with no furniture and slept on the hard floor.

On their last day, as a final goodbye, Tony walked into his empty bedroom for one last time. Memories felt soaked too deep in the walls to be taken with them. He swept his hands across the holes in the wall where favorite pictures once hung. It felt as though the next owners could look in and see what stories the walls trapped within. He sat down on the floor in the corner where his favorite comfy chair once stood. He put his forehead in his hands and watched the polished floor repel his teardrops.

Jovi ran up to the terrace to see the view she most loved. She looked out to Central Park one direction and down the street in the other, then up toward the rooftops. She often dreamed she was like Mary Poppins and could leap gracefully from rooftop to rooftop. But now the noises of the streets jangled and jingled like charms on a bracelet, and Jovi's dream seemed to leap off the terrace and flit away forever. All the people and cars going here and there looked like Monopoly pieces, and Jovi felt a surging unease from the emptiness of the final goodbye. She ran all the way downstairs, bawling.

Jovi passed Mitch on the staircase. He had gone up to the top floor to look down the staircase that wound down six floors to the basement. He loved the pattern the staircase made from the top, the swirling wooden banister with its ornate cast-iron railings. He had always wanted to ride down at full speed, but he had obeyed the rule that no one was allowed to try. He thought maybe on his last day he would break the rule and slide all the way down, but when the time came, he felt dizzy and woozy, as if something had already spun him around too fast. He walked slowly back down for the last time.

The airport shuttle arrived to pick them up.

Their mom called up to them, "Time to go!"

They jammed themselves into a crowded van. Jovi sat between Mitch and Tony and elbowed them away from her.

Jovi said, "Move over, Mitch! Tony's hogging the whole seat!"

"Quit elbowing me!" said Mitch.

"I didn't elbow you. You shoved yourself into my elbow!"

The rest of their journey was a blur. They landed in Minneapolis, then picked up a minivan their dad had left at the airport. They drove south in the nighttime, roughly three hours to the farm outside the town of Dunnell, population about 150, just north of the Iowa border.

The kids had never been to such wide-open farmland, and they imagined it being as barren as the moon. Their trips out of New York City were vacations to crowded mountain chalets for skiing. Beaches full of people. Summer camps packed with kids and nonstop activities. As

their mom saw it, quiet open spaces did not propel anyone forward.

As they drove south, the kids slept or read quietly in
the back, and Caroline brainstormed how to turn wide-
open spaces into success. She was determined to figure
out what she could sell to make money. Her social circles
spent money on many things—cleanses and scrubs, colors
and foils, ointments and oils, Botox and detox, boutiques
and antiques. But none of these were relevant to someone
stuck with a bunch of farmland. She kept coming back to
the idea that had the most promise: the personal chefs and
luxury restaurants who bought only the freshest of organ-
ics from cute little farms. She imagined creating an entire
line of herbs, *Caroline's Herbal Gems*, to be served at the
finest establishments and sold in pretty, quaint little shops
scattered around the country, like the ones she saw in
magazines and on cooking shows.

Her daydreams of herbal success grew larger and
more confident the farther she drove. She imagined, like
all the famous foodies, that she could make appearances
on those wake-up America TV shows where ladies sit
on couches and chitchat and chuckle with extravagant enthusiasm about everything. Those ladies had been
talking a lot about her dad's crimes lately. But one day, she
would be on those shows talking about Caroline's Herbal
Gems. Her business achievements would catapult her back
to the top of the social circles again, and they could all
move back to New York, basking in her success.

The GPS interrupted her reverie when it said, "You have arrived at your destination."

She looked around and found only one driveway to pull into, so she drove slowly up the overgrown lane leading to the house. The car splashed through the big puddles left over from the spring's rain and melting snow. The lane had eroded significantly, and the car unexpectedly dropped harshly into a deep divot and scratched its bottom against a rock. When the car's headlights lit up the house, Caroline's heart sank. The house was boarded up, except some of the boards had fallen off revealing broken windows behind them. The front steps to the house had collapsed from decay, and she noticed a wild cat scampering away.

The kids woke up when the car stopped. Jovi jumped out of the car into the moonlit yard and ran up to the decaying farmhouse. Behind it was a collapsed corncrib and a barn tipping so far over that it invited others to give in and give up. The broken splinters of wood from the crumbled corncrib formed animated shadows as clouds moved over the moon. A barn owl screeched and a bat flew out from the dying barn.

Jovi ran back and screamed out, "I'm not living here! I can't live here!"

"This is our house?" asked Tony quietly as he got out of the car.

Tony climbed up the rickety steps. The screen door had fallen off and was lying on the ground. The wooden door was worn gray and rotted. As he grabbed the rusty door-knob, one of the porch boards gave way and snapped, and

Tony's leg fell in. Inside the van, Mitch sank down in his seat. It was worse than he had imagined.

Caroline called Darrell, her hands shaking at the prospect of living in such a decrepit house.

"Can you see me?" she asked on her cell phone.

"Where are you? You said you were here," said Darrell.

"I'm right out front."

"No, you're not. No one's outside."

"I'm here," she insisted.

"No, you're not," he said.

"The GPS says I've arrived," said Caroline.

"Get rid of the GPS! I told you the GPS doesn't land you in the right place. Follow the directions I gave you. Go back to the town of Dunnell and follow my directions from there."

She rolled down the window and said, "Jovi! Tony! Get back in the car right now!"

From outside the car, Jovi burst into tears and said, "We're not living here! I want to go home!"

"Stop it, Jovi. Get a grip!" said Tony, who was holding back tears himself. He pulled his leg carefully out of the broken porch to avoid being speared by stray nails and splintered wood.

"We're not living here. I'm just lost. Now get back in the car!" said Caroline.

The kids got back in. Caroline backed quickly out of the driveway.

Mitch looked out the window at the empty, unplanted fields. The flat land provided a direct view to the yard lights from other farmhouses that were so far away compared to the jam-packed streets of New York. Mitch's silence was his own set of tears.

Caroline drove down the dirt road and, after many wrong turns, she found her way back to the town of Dunnell and from there followed Darrell's instructions. She pulled into another driveway toward a beautifully picturesque farmhouse and two red barns, faintly lit by an old yard light. She said to the kids, "This has to be it!"

Then they saw an old man come out of a barn. The inviting, quaint farm was not their home either.

"How can anyone find anyone's house around here?" said Caroline.

"Mom, I want to go back home. I don't like this. It's creepy!" said Jovi.

"Honey, calm down. It's all going to be fine," said Caroline. But her anxiety rattled her voice, and the kids knew she was as worried as they were.

Tony said, "How can you say that when you don't know anything about farming?"

"I do too. My mom lived on a farm, and I grew up on a farm."

"That's not what Tobias said. He said you ran away from Grandma to live with Grandpa in New York," said Mitch.

The truth of Mitch's words sank deep into Caroline's insecurities, and her shoulders drooped as she clenched the steering wheel. She backed up and drove down the road to the next farm. She entered a long driveway that wound along a white wooden fence lined with barren lilacs, a long row of machine sheds, then past farm buildings that were difficult to discern in the dark night. She pulled in and parked behind a large bluish-gray house with black shutters.

Darrell came running out and gave them all big hugs. "You made it! Welcome home!"

"This isn't home. I don't want to be here," said Jovi.

Caroline raised her eyebrows to Darrell, indicating she was tired of traveling with Jovi. She was not perceptive enough to see that Mitch and Tony liked their arrival even less.

The parents unloaded the suitcases, and Darrell said, "We had a little complication this morning. I got here shortly after the movers arrived. That's when we discovered that the previous owners left all their furniture in the house. There wasn't room for much of ours."

"So where is our stuff?"

"Piled high in the cattle barn," said Darrell.

"Why didn't you have them move out the old furniture and move ours in?" asked Caroline.

"Do you know how much that would've cost? We just can't spend like we used to. The good news is I think you might like what they left." Then he said to the kids, "Come on in."

The kids stood still. They did not want to go in.

"Hey, let's go inside, get settled in," said Caroline.

"We're going to explore outside a bit," said Tony, stalling.

Darrell whispered to Caroline, "It's probably good for you to see it before the kids do anyway."

The parents went inside, and the door closed shut behind them, leaving Mitch, Tony, and Jovi alone with the dark night sky. Many thousands of stars, scattered abundantly across the sky, shone more brightly than they had seen in the ever-lit city of New York. The kids could not help but look up, as if the stars held out an invitation. The deep darkness ate any words they might otherwise have said to each other if they were still in a noisy city. Never before had they stood outside with nighttime around them and without the sound of anyone—any car, any taxi, any plane flying above or train rumbling underneath. There was no one to break the unsettling silence. The nearest neighbor was too far away. It was too early in the spring to hear the crickets and frogs singing nearby. Surrounded by the unfamiliar quiet, the crunch of their feet on the dirt driveway sounded especially loud and gave their nervous steps a peculiar prominence in the still night.

Mitch said, "How long do you think Mom's farming idea will last out here?"

"Until Grandpa is forgotten in New York," said Tony.

Jovi said, "I hope by tomorrow. I hate it here."

"Let's go find the cattle barn where all our stuff is," said Tony.

Their first guess was right. Inside, they found all their New York furniture piled up, wrapped in plastic, stacked up tightly against the walls, and snagged on cobwebs that strung across the barn as if to capture memories that passed through. The moonlight cast strange shadows against the wooden walls of the barn. Their mom's contemporary-style furniture with harsh lines and sleek edges looked so strange inside a hundred-year-old barn, which had been home to herds of cattle and now housed only mice and wandering birds.

Mitch saw their living room chairs piled on the very top. Pigeons had already pooped on the plastic, and he smiled. "The birds hate those chairs too."

Tony found his favorite comfy chair. It had suffered a broken leg in the move. He tried to pull it out, but it was buried too deep under all their living room furniture, which was stacked on top of the very long dining room table.

Meanwhile, Caroline walked into the farmhouse from the back door and stepped slowly through the kitchen and into the front parlor. She struggled to accept the reality that the old house was to be their new home. When she and Darrell were facing the other way, a mouse darted out, looked up at them carefully, and ran across the living room floor and into a crack in the wall. Then the critter ran outside and across their lawn.

A grandfather clock stood in the front parlor, and a moon on its face reminded Caroline of the clock that stood in her mother's home. She stopped in her tracks. Mitch's comment about his grandma, Caroline's mother, rang true. Memories surfaced from when, as a teenager, Caroline had rejected her mom's boring farm life, left love behind, and returned to her dad's glittery and fast-moving life. For years, Caroline believed her decision had served her well. But now her dad's fast life had landed them all back on a farm.

Difficult memories rarely arrive in orderly sequences, like a photo album with recollections carefully laid out with enough time to process each one. Instead, they arrive like surprise visits from relatives you hardly remember and do not like—followed by a surge of unsettling emotions thrown in a blender. Such was the case for Caroline, arriving to open fields and a quaint old house that seemed to have held love within its walls. To avoid the unwelcome thoughts, Caroline chirped a remark about the clock then flitted from room to room, claiming that every bit of their new home was lovely. Wooden beams in the ceiling. A parlor. A wide winding staircase. A screened-in front porch. A big living room. A dining room and an old farmhouse kitchen.

The kids walked in through the front porch and into the front parlor. Mitch saw the winding staircase with walnut banisters, and although it did not wind down six stories like the townhouse, it invited one upward. Tony found a deep reading chair in the living room that he could sink into as he looked around at it all. The furniture was well maintained with velvet and silk upholstery, though it was worn. It looked like a grandma and grandpa once lived there. The kind of gentle grandparents that you read about in books. Tony smiled.

Jovi looked up at the paintings left on the walls. One of a horse. An open prairie. Beautiful flowers. And in the dining room hung a large painting of a ballerina with a beautiful whispery shadow behind the twirling dancer. Jovi swiped her hand along the frame, and her fingertips were covered in dust.

Mitch walked through every room on the first floor. He had an incredible ability to absorb even the most minute of details, and he asked, "Did Grandpa buy this after someone died here?"

"That's creepy, Mitch!" Jovi blurted out.

"It does feel like old people lived here," said Tony.

"We actually don't know. We don't even think Grandpa knew. He bought the farm via an auction," said Darrell. "Why don't you go check out the bedrooms? Mitch and Tony, you have to share a room."

The kids went upstairs. It was obvious which bedroom would be Jovi's. It had a pretty brass bed with a pink-and-purple homemade quilt, and another beautiful painting of a ballerina hung on the wall. But Jovi thought it was creepy—as if some other girl was going to arrive in the middle of the night and toss her out of the bed, screaming, "Get out of here! This is *my* bedroom!"

The bathroom was off to the right, in the corner, and it was wallpapered in seafaring maps from as far away as the Arctic and Papua New Guinea.

Jovi stood at the landing at the top of the stairs. "I'm not going to sleep anywhere here. We're going back home!"

"Just pretend it's camp. That's what I'm going to do," said Mitch.

"And Mom and Dad are our crazy camp directors who don't know a thing about farming," said Tony.

Jovi smiled. "They don't, do they?"

"Nope," said Tony. "Mom couldn't even keep herbs alive in those jars in her kitchen."

20

A COVERT DIG

The Grezniks left China, then traveled north to the gor-geous Valley of Geysers on Russia's beautiful Kamchatka Peninsula. There steam escaped from deep underground as beautiful spouts of clouds and mist, like restful exhales along the steep riverbanks. But like all magnificent wonders of the world, there was nothing for Grezniks to enjoy. When something beautiful comes into their view, they see only the opportunity to seize and sully.

Upon their arrival to the valley, Boshlek demanded that the Grezniks tunnel into the ground near the geysers. During every dig, tunnels filled with steam or water or unexpected pools of steamy underground water rushed forward. Grezniks were disappearing far more rapidly than they had at their other work sites.

Skarb, with its newfound ability to swim in both water and lava, decided it could try to use this secret to secure a covert role in the Great Search. Skarb snuck up on one Greznik from another circle, called Number 600 for short, and whispered to it, "Let me take your place tomorrow. You are a strong and agile Greznik. Send me down instead."

Number 600 said, "You are worthless to the search."

"Yes. And that's my point exactly. Tomorrow's dig will be like all others. Fruitless. And you will disappear. Let me go in your place. Let me disappear instead of a strong one like you."

Looking around to make sure no one was listening, Number 600 said, "Everyone knows that your circle leader relishes a chance to be rid of you once and for all. Why are you volunteering?"

"Because I want to be part of our great workforce. Everyone has the same worthy purpose. Everyone but me. I have no worth to any of you—you yourself have kicked and thrown me about many times. I cannot possibly emerge from this perilous dig when so many other skilled Grezniks have disappeared. And you will be praised and rewarded for my disappearance."

Excited about the benefits, Number 600 drooled excessive phlegm but quickly lapped it up and swallowed the oozing goop so no one would witness its excitement.

"But how will you trade places with me?" asked Number 600. "My circle leader will know you are not me."

"Your circle leader will never see me. You will dig straight down from your position, as you always do. Ahead of time, I will crawl underground unseen and stop directly below your dig site. When you start digging, you will hit my hiding spot. We will trade places underground. You will stay right there until the dig is over, but I will dig in your place. At the end of the day, you will emerge unscathed."

"But what if you are not dissolved?" asked Number 600.

"That isn't likely to happen, is it? But if it does, at the end of the dig, I will crawl back up to your hiding spot and we will trade places again. You will emerge exactly where you went in, unharmed. I will crawl up later, unnoticed. And I will never bother you again."

Much to Skarb's surprise, Number 600 agreed.

The next day, the circles began their dig, but Number 600 was doubtful that the wretched Skarb would really be waiting in an underground hideout. But as Number 600 clawed down, it found Skarb.

Skarb said, "We trade places here. You wait right here while I dig. If I don't come back by the end of the dig shift, you can go back up and rejoin your circle."

Number 600 traded places, and Skarb began digging. Skarb was thrilled to finally join the Great Search, even if its effort had to be covert. Number 600's circle dug for several hours, having no idea that one of the unseen diggers was Skarb. But in the third hour, their site hit underground hot spring waters. Their dig location collapsed as a large pool of hot water burst toward them. As the water rushed over Skarb, it burrowed backward like a crab to disappear unseen. Eight of the other Grezniks dissolved. At the end of the dig, Skarb emerged unscathed to Number 600's underground hideout.

Number 600 crawled out from underground and took the credit for its own survival, but the next time it saw Skarb it pretended that nothing had happened and ceremoniously kicked it as Grezniks always did when they walked by. Skarb winced from the pain, yet it did not respond in kind—knowing, as usual, a gang would form to attack if it did.

The regiment left and traveled to the active Plosky Tolbachik volcano, where lava bubbled up and poured down the steep slope like syrup. This time, Skarb approached a Greznik from another circle and offered the same deal it had offered to Number 600. "Let me take your place. I will explode in the lava and be gone forever. Why waste your effort when it can be me that is gone?"

In the days ahead, one Greznik after another secretly agreed to trade places with Skarb. None of them anticipated Skarb would survive. They were too humiliated when Skarb did survive that none of them dared tell anyone they had traded places with the worthless Greznik. They never acknowledged Skarb's success nor admitted their own cheating. Thus no one discovered the cheaters, and Skarb learned a Greznik's weakness: its own self-interest. To save its own hide, a Greznik will trade, lie, even cheat with Skarb—the castaway.

21

LIKE CINNAMON

As they toured the farmhouse, Caroline asked Darrell, "Who would leave all their furniture behind? What are we going to do with all of this?"

"It feels like someone booked us a picturesque bed-and-breakfast. Maybe we should just leave our stuff in the barn."

"But don't you think they'll eventually come back and ask for their stuff back?" asked Caroline.

"I think Mitch might be right that somebody died. Maybe they didn't have any heirs. Why else would the house be sold with everything still in it? In a town this small, someone has to know what happened here."

The next morning, there was nothing in the house to eat for breakfast. Caroline and Darrell had not thought through the fact that there was not easy access to groceries, diners, and takeout restaurants like there was in Manhattan.

Tony looked in the empty refrigerator and said, "At a bed-and-breakfast, there actually is a breakfast."

Mitch went out to the car and brought in the snacks left over from the drive down. The kids ate chips, soda, and cookies for breakfast as Caroline and Darrell got ready to leave for the grocery store. Caroline insisted that the kids all come with them. But they did not want to go, and Darrell convinced her to let them stay. "What harm can there be?" he said.

The parents drove to Dunnell for groceries, but the town was so small it had no place to buy food. Applequist's Grocery had been boarded up decades ago. Nothing was left of the butcher store except the faded shop name painted on the building's brick wall. The blacksmith shop, piano shop, Peterson's Coffee Shop, the creamery, barber, and confectionary were all gone—all old buildings waiting for new dreams to set them right again.

The town was quiet but for one person walking toward a little white church at the end of the block. Darrell rolled down his window and asked, "Where is the nearest grocery store?"

The nearest grocery store was not close by—not by Manhattan standards. But find it they did, and they loaded up on groceries. While in the checkout line, Caroline picked up a celebrity magazine only to find a relevant headline on its cover: "Oscar-winning actor Eddie Budala loses millions in Bosonataski fraud."

The article read, "New details have emerged in the Neil Bosonataski fraud case. Victims, such as actor Eddie Budala, have come forward describing Bosonataski's extravagant fund-raisers for a variety of popular causes, including his own art museum. Allegedly, the art collection was a front for illegally moving ill-gotten money in and out of the country . . ."

Darrell elbowed Caroline and whispered, "It's never going to end. We've got to change our name. Or everyone here will find out who we are."

"What were we thinking when we made a name that long?" said Caroline.

Darrell gave her a severely irritated glance and said, "Combining our last names was *your* idea. I warned you that it was absolutely, ridiculously long. No one can spell it, much less pronounce it. And we've suffered for it ever since."

When they got back home, they saw Jovi's muddy tracks in the kitchen. Caroline had not cleaned her own house in decades and stared at the dirt as though it might disappear on its own. After unloading their groceries, Caroline stepped onto the front porch and looked out at the open fields. It was all so quiet. Too quiet.

Caroline and Darrell went outside to inspect their new land. Caroline was determined to make her herbal dreams a reality and had convinced Darrell of the merits of pursuing a business in herbs. They walked down the winding driveway, along the dirt road, and onto an unplanted field on the north side of the farm. Caroline imagined the soil would be tender on her feet, like moist, garden shop potting soil. But instead it was dense, chunky, crusty, and proved difficult to walk on. They were rather humbled by how expansive open farmland can feel.

Their new farm, well over a hundred years old, had been an active soybean and corn farm. As they walked back by way of the dirt road, a pickup truck stopped.

The driver, a local farmer, asked, "Are you the new owners here?"

"We are," said Caroline. "Just arrived from New York."

"Will you be farming the land or renting it out?"

Caroline said proudly, "We won't be renting it out. We'll be planting herbs."

"Herbs?" the farmer asked, surprised. "What kind?"

"You know, spices for cooking."

"Like cinnamon?" joked the farmer, who already knew cinnamon trees cannot grow on a farm in Minnesota.

"Exactly, cinnamon. Probably other spices too," said Caroline.

"And vanilla beans?" asked the farmer with a sly grin.

"Yes," said Caroline, projecting a confidence she did not have.

The farmer wished them good luck, then drove off to meet friends at the neighboring town of Sherburn's one and only restaurant, the Cup-n-Saucer. There the farmer shared the story about New Yorkers hoping to plant cinnamon trees and vanilla beans instead of soybeans. Laughter spread through the whole restaurant, then spilled out the restaurant doors and through the whole town.

22

NO ONE CAN FIND THEM

One day, after heavy battle losses, the regiment retreated to a volcanic crater, the stunningly blue, hot acidic lake in the Troitsky Crater. Standing on the edge of the volcanic crater, Boshlek studied the lake and believed there just had to be blue stones resting on the bottom. It ordered the circles to cross the lake and look down as they ran on the surface of the water to determine whether blue stones rested on the bottom. But many Grezniks glanced down to see the stones and lost their balance, dropped in, and dissolved. Many circles lost all eleven Grezniks in the effort. Jatuh's circle was next.

Jatuh did not think it necessary to lose its strong circle on what it considered to be a wasted effort. So Jatuh whispered to its circle, "There are no stones here. Do not look down. Fake it."

Jatuh's circle turned rebellious.

"Why must we must we always risk ourselves, yet 401[5] never has to? Why can that seven-legger just sit around and watch us disappear?" asked one circle member.

"Because it's worthless for battle," said Jatuh.

Jatuh's circle was not satisfied, complained bitterly, and insisted that Skarb should be forced to participate. "Make that seven-legger search and fight like the rest of us."

Boshlek asked, "What is the commotion about here?"

The rebellious circle repeated their complaint. "Why must we always mine for the stones and fight the Tukors, while that worthless seven-legger can sit idle every time?"

Boshlek had no patience for the circle's squabbles and called Skarb down from the ridge.

"From now on, you must participate in every dig and battle," ordered Boshlek.

Skarb asked, "Why today do you make me search?"

"Because I am sick of your circle's complaining."

Boshlek shouted for the next circles to cross, including Jatuh's. Those who tipped their head down to look for stones at the bottom of the lake lost their balance and dropped into the water instantly. Jatuh's circle cheated, yet no one noticed because everyone else had their eyes on Skarb.

Skarb ran across and obediently tipped its head to get a good look at any stones that might be resting at the bottom of the lake. It immediately lost its balance and tipped forward dangerously. To avoid dropping into the lake, it flapped its other five legs every which way and increased its foot speed, causing its body to wobble and spin in a circle like a top. It spun around the lake, weaving in between other Grezniks as it tried to get across without falling.

The unusual shape and length of its front legs allowed it to catch its balance differently and more powerfully than other Grezniks. It finally regained its steady balance and ran the rest of the way across.

Skarb walked up to both Boshlek and Jatuh and reported, "I spun around the entire lake and there are no blue stones on the bottom." Then Skarb bowed in obedience and reverence to Boshlek.

Jatuh was furious at Skarb's success. From that point forward, Boshlek forced Jatuh to allow Skarb to participate in every mining and battle effort. Jatuh gave Skarb only the most dangerous of conditions to participate in. Surely, it assumed, Skarb would disappear forever, as so many others had. But instead, every time, Skarb crawled out from underground mysteriously unscathed. He survived every battle, though many other Grezniks disappeared.

The Grezniks began to believe that Skarb was special and had extraordinary skills at avoiding its own disappearance. Jatuh grew increasingly angry and threatened by Skarb's rising prestige.

Jatuh called Skarb over for a private meeting. "You will never again participate."

"But I don't disappear when others do," Skarb said proudly.

"You are cheating. You are not even trying to find the stones."

"I'm not cheating."

"Do not talk back to me. You will not participate anymore. You are a worthless cheater," said Jatuh.

"I am not a cheater, and I will find the blue stones. I will find them by myself. And I will bring them to you."

"Ha!" said Jatuh, cackling and gnarling. "No one can find them on their own."

"To you I am no one, and 'no one' can find them on their own," said Skarb.

Jatuh sneered and spit on Skarb.

Skarb, now labeled not only worthless but also a cheater, was relegated back to its previous plight where it was never allowed to participate in anything. Skarb tried to convince individual Grezniks to trade places and let it dig in their place, but no one would. Instead, they kicked Skarb far away, reciting Jatuh's lie: "You are a lousy, lowlife cheater."

23

LEFT BEHIND TO DIE

After their parents left for the grocery store, the kids found several pairs of cowboy boots and cowboy hats, abandoned by the previous owners. The boots were too big for the kids, but they fit well enough.

When they stepped outside and saw the old farm in the bright daylight, it looked so different from the night before and far grander than they had imagined back in New York. A large white barn stood closest to the house, with a small cattle yard to the right of it. To the right stood a hog house, and a metal grain storage bin and an old corncrib stood across from two silos and a long shed for storing farm machines. The large cattle barn, which held all their furniture, was behind the grain storage bin, along with another hog house and beautiful grazing fields. To the left of the large white barn was a small attached horse barn.

Next door to their farmhouse was a little house, which a hundred years earlier was used by the men who worked the fields. It was empty now but still had its own rickety teeter-totter. Jovi ran to the teeter-totter, and Mitch got on and they rocked back and forth. But then Mitch landed so hard that Jovi flew off and onto the ground.

Mitch laughed as Jovi scraped mud off her pants. She hated getting dirty.

"Stop laughing! You ruined my favorite pants!"

Tony ran toward the big white barn. It looked just like the barns sketched inside the storybooks they read as kids. Tony slowly unlatched the squeaky door, tentative about what might be behind it. The barn had been neglected and was decaying more from lack of use than the many years of hard work it had seen. Tony stepped slowly into the darkness. He flipped a switch by the door that turned on one hanging light bulb in the center of the barn, held up as much by cobwebs as the cord. Cobwebs coated the empty pens and dripped from the rafters as if sheltering a story held deep inside the walls.

Jovi backed out. "Disgusting. It stinks in here!"

Mitch thought it smelled awful too and went back out. Tony saw a ladder on the opposite side of the barn that led to the second level, the haymow. He ran toward the ladder, up the rungs, and through the huge open mow, empty of its hay except for a couple of rotting bales. He opened the mow door and waved down to Jovi and Mitch. "Hello!"

Mitch shouted up at Tony, "How'd you get up there?"

"Climbed up the ladder!"

Mitch ran back into the barn and up the ladder to join Tony. Jovi decided it looked fun up there and ran to climb up too, but then she heard a noise. A pounding and maybe a wheezing. She tried to figure out where it was coming from, but it seemed to be coming through the walls. She exited the barn again and saw an entrance to the adjacent horse barn. She climbed over the horse pen fence and into the horse barn, where she found three sickly horses—each in their own stall, barely able to stand.

She ran out of the horse barn and called out to her brothers. "Come here, guys! There are horses here! They're sick!"

Jovi found a bucket inside the tack shed and tried the outdoor spigot, but the water was not running. She went inside the house, tracking mud into the kitchen, and filled the bucket. Then she came back out to give each horse a drink.

All three kids knew how to ride horses quite well, unusual for kids growing up in New York City. Their mom had wanted them to do the same equestrian sports that British royalty enjoyed—polo, dressage, jumping—not because she had any clue about riding herself, but because she imagined all three of her children excelling in dressage, the prim and proper riding with top hats, suit jackets, and horses with beautifully braided manes and tails. And she enjoyed attending their competitive equine events wearing the lovely hats that such events encourage.

Although the royal dreams of their mother prepared them well for horse care, the three kids had never attended to three abandoned horses, dehydrated and desperately hungry.

"How are we going to find a veterinarian here? We don't know anybody," said Tony.

"Let's ask Mom and Dad when they get back. Maybe

they can find someone," suggested Jovi.

Mitch was doubtful, but there was no one else to ask. As they left the barn, they were startled as they rounded the corner of the barn and saw an old farmer walking toward them.

"Hello," said the old farmer.

In New York, you never said hello to scruffy men who loiter outside your home. You walked right by them. And that's just what the kids intended to do. But the old farmer reached out his hand, shook Mitch's hand, and greeted them again.

"Hello, I'm your neighbor. I live at that farm right over there. I think you pulled into my driveway last night. I thought you were coming to say hello, but you left before I could greet you."

"We were lost. We just got here last night with our mom. Our dad got here first," Mitch said politely.

"Where you from?" asked the old farmer.

"New York," said Tony.

"New York! What brings you all the way from New York?"

"Our parents are going to have an herbal farm. A hobby farm," said Tony.

The old farmer thought, *Farms ain't no hobby.*

"Do you know anything about horses?" asked Jovi.

"Do I know anything about horses? Well, a thing or two, I do."

"There are three horses in the barn, and they're sick," said Tony.

The old farmer pointed to the horse barn. "In there? Let me take a look."

The old farmer walked in and mumbled angrily, "Oh blimey, rats them—a bunch of bumbling doorknobs."

Jovi thought he was talking about the sickly horses and scolded the old farmer. "Don't talk to them like that! They're sick!"

"Oh no, I wasn't talking about these here horses. I was talking about their owners. The people who lived here before you. They said they sold the horses, and then I never saw the horses again. I never would've guessed they were still in here. I'd have been taking care of them had I known."

"They must have left in a hurry. They left all their furniture behind. Everything," said Mitch.

"Oh, they didn't leave it behind. It wasn't theirs. They were just renters."

"Whose stuff is it?"

"Old Mr. Charlie's. He lived here with his wife, Adelaide."

"Why did he sell the house?"

"His wife died awhile back. Not long after that Mr. Charlie had a bad fall working on his barn, and he injured one of his legs. So he had to move to town for nursing care. He was never well enough to return to the farm, so he rented out the house to a family. And other farmers rented the land. But he died recently. Sadly, Adelaide and Charlie did not have any surviving children. The land went up for auction, and your parents must have seen the auction announcement."

"Actually, our grandpa bought it."

"Is your grandpa moving in too?"

"No, he's in jail," said Jovi, with sadness.

Mitch elbowed her, but the old farmer did not seem the least bit interested in their grandpa.

"What are your names?" asked the old farmer.

"I'm Mitch, this is my brother, Tony, and this is Jovi."

"What's your name?" asked Jovi.

"Everyone just calls me Old Man."

"You think they'll come back for these horses?" asked Jovi, who really wanted horses of her own.

Old Man shook his head, discouraged about the condition of the horses.

"No, there's no chance they'll come back. These horses were Mr. Charlie's. The renters promised him they would take care of them, but the family got tired of small-town life. They said, 'Everybody knows everybody, and everybody knows everybody's business. It's like living in a fishbowl.' And one of their sons, I heard, is a finalist on some kind of TV singing contest. I don't know, but it's called something like *The Voices*, or such and such. So they all moved out to Los Angeles to make it big. In music or something. Be a superstar. You know, get famous—so everybody in the country would know who they are."

Old Man sighed, then said, "José, Joker, and Max are in rough shape."

"Are those the kids that lived here?" asked Tony.

"No, those are the horses' names."

"Which one's which?" asked Mitch.

"José is the chestnut horse with a white patch on its nose. Joker is the black-and-white one. And the amber horse is Max. They're prize-winning barrel racing horses. Mr. Charlie rode them often before he got injured. The renters hardly rode them at all. I got some softer food in my barn that'll be easier for them to chew and digest since they are so weak. It's for one of my very old horses. I'll bring some back."

"Are they going to die?" asked Jovi.

"They'll have a tough go of it. They're very weak. Luckily you moved in right away, or these horses surely would have died here. Can you check the shed and see if Mr. Charlie's tack is still there?"

Mitch and Tony found the tack shed, and it was full of Mr. Charlie's tack—his old saddles, bridles, horse shoes, ropes, blankets—all the tack they could possibly need for three horses and more. But it was all very dusty and had not been used in a long time. And the previous owners had left the shed in a complete mess.

Old Man left to fetch some special food while the boys began cleaning up the tack shed. Meanwhile, Jovi brushed the horses' manes and tails to free them of snarls, burrs, and dried-up mud. Jovi stayed all day with the horses, sitting on a bucket in their pen and hoping they would not die. She made sure they always had plenty of water and their special food.

Later, the kids told their parents about the horses and they were so pleased that the kids had found something on the farm that captured their interest. The next day, the kids were excited to find the horses improving and gaining strength. Old Man was equally thrilled that the horses were on the road to recovery. He told the kids how grateful he was that they found them, and over the next few days, Old Man came often to check on the horses and help the kids care for them.

As the horses got stronger, Old Man trimmed their hooves and said, "Soon they'll be ready for you to ride them."

"I get José," said Jovi, who was jumping up and down with excitement to ride.

Old Man smiled but did not tell her that José was the fastest. So fast it was almost too scary to ride José at full speed. Mitch wanted Max, the powerhouse.

Tony said, "I guess I get Joker."

"Watch out for him. He *is* a joker. Very hard to control, and he likes to play tricks on the rider. Joker needs a strong-minded rider to control him," said Old Man. Then he looked into Joker's eyes. "Isn't that right, Joker? You be nice."

Joker shook his head back and forth.

During those first few days, Tony and Mitch organized the tack shed and refurbished the tack to its rightful condition. They oiled the saddle and bridle leather, fixed stirrups, and cleaned the horse blankets. Jovi brushed the horses every day and spoke to them as if they were her long-lost friends who never got tired of her endless chitter-chatter.

Old Man came to visit the horses early in the morning, before sunrise and before anyone at their house was awake. The kids were not there when he said quietly to José, the leader of the three horses, "Why didn't you send word about being trapped down here? Don't give up yet. Not yet. We've still got a lot of work to do."

24

BELCH BALLOON

Skarb was never again allowed to join the regiment's search, and if it had been counting its idle years, it would have noted that the years had spun forward from Before Christ to Anno Domini and into the Middle Ages. But instead of counting the years, Skarb measured the growing futility of it all. Doubts seeped into Skarb's thoughts: *They have searched and found, fought and lost—and done so over and over again. They have never succeeded. They might never succeed. Why do they bother anymore?*

For no other reason than boredom, one afternoon Skarb walked away from the regiment into a boggy forest and dug down deeper than usual, digging in a fury of uselessness. But then Skarb accidentally hit a massive underground cavity and fell straight down, face-first into a deep, soupy, smelly muck that flowed in from an underground stream. Given the speed of the fall, Skarb sank ten feet into the mud. The force of the fall sent pounds of the muck into its mouth and down into its gut. Completely defeated and feeling sick, Skarb crawled out from underground.

"That was definitely my last dig," grumbled Skarb as it began its trek back to the regiment.

Ingesting many pounds of that awful, decaying muck made Skarb quite ill. When Grezniks eat, the digestive debris comes out through the skin as an awful fetor, unique like a fingerprint. And although Grezniks know one another by their unique smell, no other living creature can smell them. But if they could, they would choke, gag, and soon vomit.

Feeling nauseous, Skarb traveled very slowly back to the regiment. But as the muck digested, it created too much gas too quickly. Skarb expanded like a balloon, so badly it could barely move. It bloated up like a puffer fish and developed a horrible case of the belches. It had no choice but to stay put and wait until the belching subsided and it returned to its normal size.

Unexpectedly, Jatuh and Boshlek moved away from the regiment for a private meeting and walked right toward Skarb's hiding place in the woods. Skarb did not want to have to explain to them what had happened, so before they got close enough to see, it rolled away as quietly as it could and hid behind a large boulder—a worthless endeavor because they would soon smell Skarb's skin or hear its terrible belches.

Boshlek said to Jatuh, "I smell the seven-legger."

"I do too. The wretch is near," acknowledged Jatuh.

If a Greznik is close enough to smell another, they are close enough to hear each other's conversations. The two of them walked closer to Skarb's hiding spot just as a huge belch began to rumble within its gut. Skarb silently took a deep breath to hold back the massive belch. Then suddenly Skarb's smell was gone. Boshlek and Jatuh sniffed around, but the odor had fully dissipated.

"Never mind. I can no longer smell it," said Boshlek. "It can't hear us now."

As Skarb held back its belch, it wondered why they could not smell it anymore. It had no choice but to listen in and hope to hold back the belch long enough.

Skarb did not yet know that its body held another secret: from its burning rise to the surface, Skarb's skin was sealed and did not give off an odor. Instead, the smell that normally seeped out of a Greznik's insides through the skin came out of Skarb's mouth. Skarb did not yet know that if it closed its mouth, no one would know it was nearby.

Boshlek said to Jatuh, "Too many battles ago, you promised to find a blue stone mine. But you have failed to do so. You must succeed or you will be walked into the sea."

Jatuh was surprised by this threat and boiled with rage. There was no reason Boshlek could ever accuse it of being a failure. No one had been more dedicated than Jatuh, and it responded indignantly, "We have all searched and searched, and yet we never find the stones. It is not only I who have failed. All the circles have failed. And I cannot find the stones with the seven-legged cheater, fraud, and fake in my circle. It is the cause of our failures. Other Grezniks hate it, resent it, and complain about it constantly. The wretch must be sent to disappear so we can maintain obedience in the regiment."

Skarb wanted to scream out in fury over what it had just heard. But in holding back the belches, it bloated to such a humongous size that it would soon expand beyond the edges of its hiding spot and be seen.

Boshlek answered Jatuh, "I will make the seven-legger disappear after you prove your dedication to the regiment."

"I have proven my dedication for too long. For thousands of spins around the sun. Why doesn't Proznia just tell us where the blue stones are?"

"Proznia will not help us. It knows we have no intention of returning to it."

Skarb was about ready to burst like a blister and wanted to yell at Jatuh, *Quit asking so many questions, you idiot!*

Jatuh said defiantly, "Perhaps we cannot succeed without Proznia's assistance. Maybe if we drank the blue stone waters, we would have the power to find the stones. What if we have been wrong all this time?"

Jatuh's skepticism sent Boshlek into a fury.

"We are not wrong!" shouted Boshlek.

Boshlek charged toward Jatuh viciously, and Jatuh ran as fast as it could to protect itself from being gorged by Boshlek. But Boshlek dominated Jatuh in skill and kept Jatuh moving forward, running it dangerously toward a cliff above a populated village.

To avoid its own demise, Jatuh curled its head downward and pledged its allegiance to Boshlek. "You are ever brilliant and always right. Eternal Commander never makes mistakes. I will never doubt you. I will always obey. I am forever loyal. I am just a meager circle leader compared to your greatness."

Boshlek believed it had successfully forced Jatuh back into docility and spit all over Jatuh. But Jatuh's apology was all for show. As Jatuh shook Boshlek's phlegm off its body, it also shook off the apology and grew determined to destroy Boshlek.

After Boshlek chased Jatuh out of view, Skarb let out the biggest belch a Greznik had ever experienced. It came out so fast and with such force, it launched Skarb backward like a rocket. It hurtled deep into the woods, where it bounced off a tree and then swirled around like a balloon letting out its air. Fully deflated, Skarb was relieved to feel normal again.

But then Skarb heard Boshlek returning from their chase, with Jatuh following behind in obedient submission. Skarb flattened itself and waited for them to pass. Normally, if they passed a Greznik that closely, they would have smelled it. But this time, Skarb held its breath again, and Boshlek and Jatuh did not know it was there. Skarb discovered the secret: if it closed its mouth and hid, no Greznik would know it was nearby. Skarb had become a spy.

25

HE SHOT THEM

After attending to the horses each morning, the kids completed the schoolwork needed to finish up the school year. Back in New York, their life was so scheduled that they rarely stopped long enough to play together. On the farm, however, they were not sure what to do with themselves. The parents were no help—they were always busy on the computer researching business ventures involving acres of dirt, desperate to make money and secure their comeback.

From the living room window, the kids watched Old Man do his farm chores every day. They wished their farm was a working farm, but given their floundering parents, they did not bank on their fields ever having anything in them.

Not knowing how to farm, Caroline and Darrel were unsettled by the empty fields surrounding their farmhouse. Caroline knew that if her mom were still living she would know exactly what to do. But Caroline, without a question, did not. It did not take too long for Caroline and Darrell to feel a quiet panic at the sight of their unplanted fields and the black soil under their feet. The planting season was closing in on them, and they needed the land to generate money.

The parents quickly learned that cinnamon trees could not survive a Minnesota winter. Caroline commented to Darrell that she grew basil in jars on their Manhattan windowsill, and soybean leaves looked similar to basil. Caroline and Darrell concluded if soybeans could grow on their farmland, so could basil.

Caroline said, "It's official. We're a basil farm."

After planting a small patch of basil seeds on their land, they realized working in the dense soil to plant little, itty-bitty seeds was backbreaking work. The next day they hired a local farmer to complete the rest of the planting. And they rented some of the land out to local farmers.

Meanwhile, the horses recovered strongly under the wonderful care and came to the fence every time they saw the kids, hoping for treats.

The kids rode their horses every day and grew more confident in riding farther. One day they rode them to the town of Dunnell. There was a small gas station at the edge of town. The kids tied up their horses along a nearby fence and stopped in to buy some candy.

Inside, just like their parents at the grocery store, they found celebrity magazines highlighting news about the Bosonataski fraud.

"Grandpa is still all over the news," said Tony.

Mitch whispered, "We need to change our name."

They picked out some candy and went to the cashier to pay.

"Where are you kids from?" asked the cashier, a middle-aged woman.

"We live on Mr. Charlie's old farm," said Tony.

"So you're the New Yorkers. The ones growing cinnamon."

"Basil," said Mitch.

"Watch out for that old man down the road from you," said the cashier.

"Why's that?" asked Tony.

"Nobody knows him. He comes and goes. The kids that lived in your house before you said he's really mean, and that no one dared get near him."

Jovi asked, "What's so mean about him?"

"He fired his shotgun at them."

Jovi exclaimed, "He *shot* them?"

"No, he missed," said the cashier.

"Maybe they deserved it," said Jovi, angry that some-one would say bad things about the man who helped them save the three abandoned horses.

"Could be. Could be. But still, a man who shoots chil-dren? I'd stay clear of him if I were you."

26

BUSTARD AND SPOONBILL

Skarb was discouraged by everything Jatuh had said to Eternal Commander. The useless seven-legger was the cause of the circle's failures. Worthless. A cheater. A fake. A fraud. The source of complaints. Hated. Resented. Skarb slumped over. "I'm not a fake. I'm not a fraud. And it's not my fault that I have too many legs and can't sleep standing up. It's not my fault I don't dissolve and don't explode in lava. And today I learned I can't even stink properly!"

Skarb mumbled this line of thinking for hours, rehashing the same themes over and over without relief. Skarb began questioning everything, even Boshlek's constant warnings—*Never travel to a water's edge alone or the blue stone waters will call out to you. The Voices will pull you in. Never drink of the blue stone waters or you will free the Voices of Proznia,* and so on.

Skarb muttered, "What if a Greznik must go to the water's edge alone to find the blue stones? If so, who better to travel to the water's edge alone than a Greznik who can swim? I've been near water many times and nothing happened. So how bad can it be? I will go to the river where I came to be. I will stay at the water's edge alone and find out what happens. I will get the power Eternal Commander does not want us to have. I will bring blue stones to Eternal Commander, and I will finally be accepted and important. I will show everyone that I do belong in the circle."

After nightfall, Skarb slithered away from the regiment. Skarb climbed up high on a mountain and looked out at the great distance it would travel alone. Then it said quietly, with less confidence, "And if I fail and disappear, they will have their way. My existence will be over, and it will not matter anyway."

Skarb ran off to the south, wickedly fast, and cut through China to reach the Chongchon River where Skarb originally came into existence. Skarb was determined to either find the blue stones or find a way to disappear, for no other reason than to bring an end to the futile searching.

Along its lonely journey to the Chongchon River, Skarb stopped at every pond, lake, and river along the way. Yet there were never any blue stone waters. There were no voices. There was nothing. Skarb would wait along the water's edge for the great danger to appear. It never did.

Skarb decided what Boshlek had said about the blue stone waters was a great lie. There were no blue stone waters. There were no voices coming out from the waters. It wondered, *Perhaps even the power and purpose of the blue stones is a lie. Maybe we really are just stuck on Earth. Could it be that all this digging and searching is a useless endeavor?*

Skarb gave up taunting the waters and traveled with less purpose and greater feelings of worthlessness. Underneath it all, Skarb hoped to disappear. Skarb reached the Chongchon and walked along the river's edge for miles and miles. It sauntered leisurely to the source of the river but did not notice that two birds slyly followed, one on each side of its path—a great bustard and a black-faced spoonbill. Bustard and Spoonbill, allies of the Tukors, lived along the river for this one purpose: to guard against wandering Grezniks who might dare to travel to these waters alone. At tremendous personal risk, they followed Skarb.

Grezniks can travel very loudly or in total silence, whichever serves their purpose. Yet even as Skarb sauntered quietly, its sense of worthlessness awoke and stirred the nearby river waters. The waters felt Skarb's defeated steps, like someone hitting a drum from far underground.

Believing its own existence was, as the Grezniks had said a million times over, worthless, Skarb lay down to sleep. It slept more soundly than it ever had before because no Grezniks were there to kick its belly every time they walked by. Nearby, carefully hidden, Bustard and Spoonbill stayed awake and kept a careful eye on the river water while Skarb slept.

Skarb awoke before dawn, and despite Boshlek's repeated warning to never fix one's glare on the waters, Skarb had done so along the entire journey without consequence. As one last taunt, Skarb looked directly into the Chongchon's gentle currents, found nothing dangerous, and turned its back to the waters.

When the sun tipped over the mountain range, the sunlight hit the river waters and lit the edges of the currents. As the breeze blew, the ripples sparkled. Bustard and Spoonbill saw the glittering surface of the water and knew that Skarb was in danger. Both birds came forward to speak to the Greznik.

"You must not travel here alone. You need to leave," said Spoonbill. "The waters here are unkind."

"Waters are always unkind to Grezniks. We dissolve in them," said Skarb, licking its chops, ready to eat the two birds.

"We are offering you a chance to run. You must run away from here and do not look back," said Bustard.

The waters grew angrier and the current swirled in a display of its strength. The river water turned from a muddy color to a beautiful crystal blue. The river waters glistened as though the spark of a smiling eye danced on the edge of every wave. The many sparkles turned to blue crystals that lifted up and out of the water. The crystals floated upward and into the sky, then started floating down toward Skarb.

Spoonbill shrieked with anguish and warned Skarb, "You must run! Run away from the river!"

27

SNAGGING THE LURE

On an early morning in late May, a fragrant breeze blew into the kitchen during breakfast. Jovi was delighted by the lovely, floral scent and ran outside to discover its source—lilacs. She walked along the lilacs, then spun around the front yard dancing her ballet recital. The boys, too, noticed the changes of spring as the sounds of the farm emerged. Birds sang more readily, like an orchestra warming up backstage before the summer concert bursts forth.

Summer weather came early that year, and it was one of those steamy mornings when the morning mist floats up from the tips of the corn and the haze dusts the early rays of sun. Their new home was not air-conditioned, and that morning, just after sunrise, the parents moved ever so slowly in the old and hot farmhouse and sipped iced coffee. They sent the kids out in cowboy boots and shorts, their skin already sweaty and sticky from the muggy air.

Old Man's corn had a strong start, but it was still short and close to the ground, forming long straight rows like racetrack stripes through the rich soil. The kids walked parallel to the tracks along a fence line, down to the creek to try out some of Mr. Charlie's fishing gear they had found in the attic. Jovi had no intention of fishing, but she wanted to explore the creek. Mitch and Tony were ready to catch something big and ran ahead of Jovi, who was trying to walk gracefully atop the larger rocks scattered along their path.

They set up their fishing station near a bend in the current. There had been a lot of rain in the days before, so the creek was flowing at a good clip. The deeper waters and faster currents were due to heavy winter snowfalls and a lot of spring rain. Over a hundred years earlier, the creek sustained big fish in the spring flows. But now the creek was most often slow-moving and was nothing but mud by August. Mitch and Tony were hoping to catch bass, but they would be lucky to find even a crawfish or a sunfish. Tony and Mitch fished for a while but caught nothing except an occasional snag on lingering reeds.

Tony said, wiping sweat from his forehead, "Nothin' is hungry when it's this hot. Let's move to the shade."

They reeled in their lines, picked up their fishing gear, and walked down to a small grove of ash and oak trees. The grove followed the creek and dipped ever so slightly behind a big hill. Hanging over the creek was an old ash tree and a burly oak. The old ash had grown apart at its trunk, very near to the ground, and it bent toward the creek. Jovi climbed up it speedily and gracefully.

Mitch and Tony watched the trees blowing in the wind

and the bright-blue sky beyond, as flies stopped for a rest on their sweaty, dirty legs. José, Joker, and Max had come over to see if the kids had any snacks for them, but they had none. The horses munched grass, hid in the shade, and stomped the flies off their legs.

While they were lying on the grass, Tony asked Mitch, "Do you think there are any big fish in this creek?"

Jovi answered jokingly from up in the tree, "Sharks. There are sharks."

Mitch said, "There aren't any sharks here. We left the ocean in New York."

Jovi said, "There is such a thing as a freshwater shark, you know. It's called the Glyphis. I'm going to catch one."

"You've never even fished before, Jovi," said Tony.

"Neither have you!" said Jovi, irritated that her brothers always thought they could do everything better.

She jumped out of the tree and grabbed Mitch's fishing pole.

Mitch said, "A shark is not going to find its way up a creek to a soybean farm."

"Basil farm," said Tony. He asked Jovi, "What are you going to do if you catch a shark?"

"I'll flop it down on your saddle."

Tony said, "And I'll ride away with it. After traveling all the way here, a shark might want a ride on a horse."

"I think Old Man fishes upstream, and I bet he catches everything before it gets this far," said Mitch.

Tony said, "Let's try fishing upstream."

"We probably can't fish on his land," said Mitch.

Tony said, "We already ride our horses up there. Maybe it's okay to try fishing up there."

Several times already they had ridden their horses on Old Man's land, but not always intentionally. They were never quite sure where the property lines were. But now that the fields were growing, if the leaves were corn, they knew they were on Old Man's land. If basil, it was their own land. One time, on Old Man's land, Tony saw Old Man peering out from behind a curtain in the house. After hearing the warnings about Old Man, they were afraid he would come out yelling, so they rode quickly away.

But this time, the kids decided it would be okay to follow the creek to find a better fishing spot on Old Man's land. They kept a careful eye on the farm, afraid he might come out shouting at them or worse—such as fire his hunting rifle toward them.

Old Man had four very large Polish Percherons—workhorses whose equine parents used to work in the salt mines of Poland. Old Man's horses were much larger than José, Joker, and Max. The Percherons would line up when the kids came near, put their ears back, and stand there ominously.

The kids found a prime fishing spot perched up on a hill with the creek rushing below. The strong current rounded a bend and formed an eddy on the other side. They got off their horses and started walking down the hill. Jovi was the first to see a big fish resting in the eddy. The fish stopped to lift its head upward and get a good look at the kids before it skirted off. It sped up the creek toward Old Man's farm and was quickly gone.

"I saw a big one!" said Jovi. "A really big one!"

"I saw it too!" said Mitch. "It was a Glyphis shark!"

"I was just kidding about a shark. It wasn't really a shark, was it?" asked Jovi.

"I saw it too! What's a shark doing here? This is crazy!" said Tony excitedly.

The kids ran along the creek to see it again but could not find it. Tony and Mitch were determined to catch it, so they pulled out their rods to fish again.

After an hour or two without one single bite, Tony said, "Maybe we didn't really see a shark after all."

Mitch said, "I know we saw one."

"I'm going to catch that shark," said Jovi, grabbing the rod from Tony before he could put it away.

Jovi cast the line into the creek, but the lure did not land where she wanted it to.

Tony said, "That's not how you cast, Jovi. Let me do it."

Jovi pulled the rod away. "I can do it. Leave me alone."

She reeled the line back in and cast again, but this time she snagged the lure on some weeds on the other side of the creek. To unsnag the lure, she pulled back on the rod, bending it and yanking it, swinging it, and pulling it hard.

Mitch said, "Stop it, Jovi! It'll break!"

Jovi pulled hard on the line, trying to maneuver it out of the snag. Suddenly, the lure broke loose. The line let out, and the lure flew straight over Jovi's head. Mitch and Tony dove to the ground to avoid getting hit by the sharp hook. The line went way over their heads and landed far behind them in a deep ravine.

They had not yet discovered that the ravine hid an old dump where over many years people had tossed away things that were either broken, unwanted, or no longer useful, such as cast-iron stoves, sewing machines, barrels and buckets, iceboxes and refrigerators, rusty generators, washboards and washers, gears and gadgets, worn-out saddles, broken pitchforks, and more. The lure dropped straight down into the mess of tangled iron, steel, and rusted bits of who knows what, where it snagged an old piece of equipment deep inside the pit.

A lot of fishing line had gone out when the pole let loose from the snag. The kids followed the line and found the old dump. They stopped and looked down into the wide pit, amazed at the big pile of junk.

Tony said, "Wow, look at that."

Jovi reeled in her line to pinpoint exactly where the line dropped into the dump.

Mitch said, "You caught junk instead of a fish."

They did not notice that the shark swam back to look up at the kids on the hill.

As the kids looked across the precarious pile of old junk, Tony volunteered to find the lure. He followed the fishing line, crawled down, and found the lure hooked onto a steering wheel of a strange piece of equipment. Despite being grown over in moss and weeds, he could still see that it had unusual gears and a complex instrument panel.

Tony yelled, "Come down; you've got to come see this!"

Mitch carefully walked across the top of all the junk,

then crawled slowly down, hoping nothing would upend and crumble down on them.

"I think it's a tractor!" Tony said.

When Mitch reached Tony, he agreed that it was a tractor, but a strange one.

Mitch looked under the engine hood. "This doesn't look like a normal tractor engine."

Tony examined the instrument panel. "It looks like it's from a rocket ship."

Tony unhooked the fishing lure, and he and Mitch climbed back out.

Mitch said, "Do you think we could pull the tractor out? Maybe we could get it working."

"I'm not pulling that thing out. Why would we do that?" asked Jovi.

"What else are we going to do today?" said Tony.

"You think you're going to pull that out from under all the junk? I don't think so," said Jovi.

Mitch said, "Max, José, and Joker can help. We can tie ropes to the tractor, and the horses can pull it out."

Jovi liked the idea of giving the horses a big job to do. They went into the tack shed and found the many parts of an old pulling harness—breechings, back loin, bellybands, and so on. In a drawer, along with some old farm records, Tony found a detailed sketch of how to put on a pulling harness. They got José, Joker, and Max loaded up and ready to pull. Soon, the horses were excited to work.

Tony crawled down to the tractor and tied ropes to it, and Mitch and Jovi hooked the ropes up to the pulling harness. Mitch and Jovi guided the horses to pull. Max, José, and Joker pulled as hard as they could, but nothing budged even so much as an inch. They pulled again, and some metal pieces rattled and started to move. The horses pulled one more time, and instead of loosening the tractor's position, the pile shifted and dropped more junk on top of the tractor.

Mitch and Jovi ran forward, afraid that Tony was crushed under the pile.

Tony shouted, "That wasn't helpful!"

One piece of metal snapped, broke off, and flew forward, just missing Tony's head as it flew by him.

"This is too dangerous," said Tony, crawling out of the dump.

José, Joker, and Max were too tired to continue, and they pointed their ears toward Old Man's farm. His large and powerful horses were standing at the fence line of the fallow field. The Percherons had been out grazing but had come right up to the fence, as if they were excited about a possible project that needed strong horses.

Tony said, "Maybe those horses want to help us pull out the tractor. They look super bored standing in the field."

"And this time the horses have their ears forward, not back. Maybe they do want the job," said Mitch.

"You said already that it's too dangerous. So why are we getting the tractor out?" asked Jovi.

Mitch said, "Because we don't have a tractor on this farm."

"And this one is built like a rocket ship. Let's go ask Old Man if his horses can help us," said Tony.

"What if he's as mean as they say he is? I don't want to get shot at," said Jovi.

Tony was more interested in the tractor than he was afraid of Old Man. "Maybe he just didn't like those kids. After all, they did leave the horses to die. Let's go talk to him."

Mitch and Tony started walking to Old Man's farm. Jovi refused to go with them.

Jovi said, "No one would dump a rocket ship on a farm anyway!"

The boys kept walking. Not wanting to be left behind, Jovi caught up. "Fine. Whatever. I don't care. But if he so much as gives me a mean look I'm running as fast as I can. And it won't be my fault if I trample you on my way out."

Old Man's farm was the closest farm to theirs, down the road to the south. He lived in an even older farmhouse with a big red barn, a smaller red barn, a machine shed, a corn-crib, a hog house, a chicken coop, one silo, and a grazing field for his horses. He farmed his land except for one section, which had remained fallow—uncultivated—forever.

They walked cautiously toward Old Man's farm, where he was outside repairing his fence. Quietly, they approached from behind, nervous to talk to him. Although Old Man had been friendly when he helped with the horses, they had been sufficiently spooked by the woman in town who had told them to be wary of him.

Jovi turned slightly to the side and pointed one foot back down the driveway, ready to run. Both Mitch and Tony were looking around to see if Old Man had a rifle within easy reach, and they were now too nervous to speak. Mitch elbowed Tony to get him to talk. Then Tony elbowed Jovi, and Jovi got mad. "I'm not going to talk to him. Mitch can."

"No, you talk to him."

"No, you talk to him. It was your idea to pull the tractor out anyway."

"It wasn't my idea. It was Joker and José."

"Well go tell Joker and José to talk to him."

"Horses don't talk."

"Max does. Make him ask."

"Max doesn't talk. You go ask."

"I'm not talking to anybody. You go talk to him."

Old Man turned around abruptly. The kids all stood up straight with fright.

"I saw you found my tractor. That ol' tractor ain't worth anything. Been in there for years. Doesn't work. Won't go anywhere. Worth nothing to everybody and nobody."

Tony and Mitch slouched and drooped their shoulders in disappointment.

"See? I told you," said Jovi as she turned to walk away.

Then Old Man added, "Everybody but you. I've been waiting for you kids to find something in that dump."

"We tried to get the tractor out, but the pile crashed down on it," said Tony.

"It's a difficult project to get that out," said Old Man.

"I told them it was too hard. But they wouldn't listen," said Jovi.

"Why do you want to get it out?" asked Old Man.

"It has a really cool control panel," said Tony.

"Like a spaceship," said Mitch.

Old Man paused a bit, pounded a few more nails into his broken fence, then said, "The tractor isn't a spaceship, but it does have a lot of power. More power than any other tractor. You'll have a fun time riding it. Like your favorite ride at a county fair."

"We've never been to a county fair," said Jovi.

"Just Disney World," said Mitch.

"This is completely different from Disney World—nothing like it in the world. My Percherons would be happy to help. They'll be so excited they won't be able to contain themselves."

Then Old Man got close to the kids and looked them all directly in their eyes, one by one. "But the tractor is a secret between you three and me. Because it's a secret, we need to work on this project at night so no one knows about it. You come down to the dump after dusk and be ready to work on pulling it out. Okay? I'll bring my horses over tonight after sunset. You meet me down there."

Old Man had such a commanding presence, Mitch and Tony nodded their heads in agreement—but Jovi was not so sure. They talked about the idea on their way home.

"I think it's too dangerous to go," Jovi said. The whole idea made her nervous. "Maybe he's going to shoot us when we get there."

"Could be," said Tony.

"Could be? You mean you really think he might shoot us?" asked Jovi.

"He's not going to shoot us. Why would he do that?" said Mitch. "And I want to see what the tractor does. Despite what everyone says, Old Man isn't all that mean. He seems pretty happy about getting that tractor out."

"He said it's supposed to be a secret," said Jovi.

"Yeah, it's a spy mission," said Tony, always knowing what to say to get Jovi on his side of an idea. "So let's go. And if we need to, we'll run home fast. He's pretty old, so he couldn't catch us anyway."

Later that evening, the sunset waned and left without fanfare as the kids waited impatiently for an opportunity to leave the house unnoticed. But their parents moseyed about the house, futzing around with this and that.

Their dad said, "Hey, kids, get ready for bed! Not another late night tonight."

The kids went upstairs to wait it out until their parents went to bed. Mitch and Tony got in their pj's and sat up reading with the light on. Jovi kept her clothes on and hunkered deep under the covers so her parents would not notice. When their parents came up to bed, they cracked the door open to check on her and believed her to be asleep. But Jovi was too worried about the spy mission to fall asleep.

Their mom went into Mitch and Tony's room, grabbed the books from the boys, and turned out the light. "Boys, time to get some sleep."

They were supposed to meet Old Man after sunset, but the sunset had already shed its parting rays of light an hour earlier. Tony and Mitch tried to stay awake until their parents went to sleep. But their parents stayed up late, and the later it got, the more the kids' eyelids flickered. Eventually, all three fell sound asleep.

Old Man put the pulling harness on his four Percherons and led them down to the dump after sunset. His horses were so excited to pull a heavy load that Old Man had to pull back on their reins to prevent them from running dangerously down to the dump. Old Man, too, was energized and excited to finally get the tractor out after all these years. He got down to the dump and looked around, but the kids were not there. He waited and waited, but the later it got, he feared they were too frightened or disinterested to come.

Old Man spoke as if the horses understood. "Looks like they may have lost interest or chickened out. We'd better leave the secret buried in the rubble and head on home."

The horses pounded their feet on the ground, shook their manes, and refused to go back.

"I don't want to leave the tractor behind either. But I can't leave it out for anyone to find. We must bury it forever. But not tonight, friends—not tonight. I'm an old man and too weary. So weary."

The eyes of his lead horse flared in fear as it shook its head back and forth and whinnied loudly. The horses rattled the harness, reared up, and cast thrashing shadows in the bright moonlight.

Old Man pulled the reins to calm them and whispered, "Shh, shh, yes, you're right, I know, I know. Burdens need someone brave enough to unearth them and carry them afar. But no one has come."

The horses quieted down and hung their heads sorrowfully as the promise of adventure sank deep into the soil. The midnight shadows sheltered their disappointment and the moonlight bundled up their broken hopes and pulled them into the infinite nighttime sky, quieting all their fears.

Old Man led his horses back to his farm, wondering what the next day would bring. Every day the sun spins a sunrise again and the call to adventure beckons anew. But in this case, it beckoned much more dangerously than Old Man ever expected.

28

PARALYZED LIKE STONE

The Chongchon River swirled a beautiful blue. Bustard and Spoonbill trembled at the growing threat and bounded over to Skarb.

"Run! Run!" said Bustard. "The Voices are coming for you. Do not drink the blue stone water! Do not look back!"

But Skarb ignored Bustard and looked back toward the river. Skarb was instantly enraptured by the magnificent blue waters. More blue crystals floated up out of the water and morphed into fairy pitta birds whose many colors formed the mesmerizing patterns of a kaleidoscope as they flew. The fairy pitta birds circled above Skarb's head and sang enticingly. "Look at the waters. You have found the blue stones. The stones are yours. Go on. Take them. They have been waiting for you."

The fairy pittas flew elegantly, and each bird sang in a different pitch and rhythm. The blue feathers of their wings sparkled like blue stones as they beckoned Skarb.

"Come to the blue waters, see the stones, touch them, hold them. They can all be yours."

Desire overwhelmed Skarb. It walked to the edge of the waters.

Bustard flared his feathers, puffed up his throat to distract Skarb from the water, and cautioned Skarb. "Do not listen to the Voices! Look away. Look to me. Do not follow them!"

Skarb did not try to avert its gaze. The fairy pittas swarmed around Skarb so it could no longer see anything but the waters ahead.

"Look in. Step in," sang the birds splendidly. "Take the blue stones. They are magnificent. Just like you will be."

Spoonbill raised her white neck and her spoon-shaped beak and flew directly into the swarm of fairy pitta birds, hoping to force them away from Skarb. But their response was fierce, and she could not battle so many at once.

Skarb stepped into the water and stretched its head forward to see the stunning blue stones resting deep in the river waters. Skarb felt parched and wanted nothing more than to drink the river dry to reach the stones on the bottom.

The fairy pitta birds said, "Quench your thirst. Drink of the waters and you will reach the stones. We have chosen you. You are the most important Greznik. Come and you will prove that you are different from every other Greznik—invincible and strong, powerful and masterful. Drink of the waters and you will be accepted into your fighting circle."

"Will I have five legs? Five normal legs?" asked Skarb.

"Of course you will!" said the Voices, swirling so beautifully around Skarb.

"You birds fly so perfectly. Will I run perfectly if I drink the water?"

"Yes, you will. We are like you. You are the many-legged Greznik, and we are the many-colored birds. You can be the powerful seven-legged Greznik."

"But that is not what you just said. You said I could be the powerful five-legged Greznik," said Skarb.

"Look at your reflection in the waters—see how wretched you are. Ugly and weak. Drink of the water and you will be strong and handsome. Light and beautiful."

Bustard and Spoonbill desperately tried to distract Skarb, but their voices were no match against the thousands of luring Voices. They pecked and bit Skarb's legs and tail, but Skarb kicked Bustard and Spoonbill away. The fairy pittas swarmed cruelly down upon Spoonbill and Bustard and plucked their feathers until they bled.

Skarb felt miserably thirsty and asked the fairy pittas, "Tell me again. What do you promise me if I swallow the waters in?"

"When you drink the waters in, you will be the most important, most powerful Greznik. You will rule the regiment. You can become anything. And all the blue stones will be yours."

Skarb gazed at the blue stones resting on the riverbed, excited to have found the stones at last. "I really have found the stones! The victory is mine!" Skarb said proudly. "I will go back to the regiment and tell them where the blue stones are, and I will be admired. I will be rewarded. I will run the victory lap that I have imagined all these centuries."

"You must not tell them. The stones are for you and you alone."

"I *will* tell them. Every single one of them. I will first tell Eternal Commander that I found the stones! How proud it will be of me! When the regiment sees all these stones, and they all realize that I, the castaway, found them, I will be respected at last."

"The blue stones will not reveal themselves if many Grezniks come. We invite Grezniks one at a time," said the fairy pittas impatiently.

"Then I will bring all the Grezniks, and we will line up for you. And you can invite us one at a time. If you say I can be all-powerful, then I can ask for anything. So I demand five Greznik legs, not the seven I have, and six normal eyes. Then I will deliver the stones, and I will finally be important."

From the middle of the flock, one fairy pitta came forward and said daintily. "If you bring the stones to your circle, they will just take the stones from you. You must know that about them by now! The stones are for you and you alone. Come to us. Quench your thirst. Drink of the beautiful waters."

The birds retreated so that all Skarb could see was a view of the sparkling waters. The blue stones were lying so beautifully at the bottom of the river. An irresistible desire throbbed inside Skarb, and the thirst to drink the river dry was overbearing. The hair in its mouth felt like dry straw, and the unexpected need for water made its tongue so parched it cracked like desert ground.

Skarb was about to drink the water when several large fish owls flew out of the trees and surrounded Skarb. The owls understood the many disguises and dangers of the Voices and hoped to divert Skarb. They flapped their expansive wings and said in their deep and haunting voices, "Those are not real fairy pittas. They are the Voices of Proznia. If you drink, you will give them form, and they will give you their hunger—a void will torment you forever."

Mucus poured from inside Skarb's mouth, and it shot the slime at the owls and knocked them over. "You speak lies! You just don't want me to be strong, do you? You don't want a Greznik to have the stones, do you? Well, the stones are mine!"

Then dozens of kingfishers flew forward and surrounded Skarb, fluttering their beautiful blue wings, and sung, "The fish owls did not lie. Heed their warning or you will become the Great Betrayer for Proznia."

Skarb growled, stood up on its hind legs, and swatted the kingfishers with its front legs. "I am Greznik. I already am a great betrayer. Grezniks are always unfaithful. We always devour. We always cheat. We always deceive. We always corrupt. The stones are mine!"

Skarb turned back to the waters and watched the fairy pittas carefully as they invited it forward. It tried to grab several of the birds in its claws, but they darted from its reach or were not as close as they appeared. Skarb noticed one bird in the middle of the flock that did not move as readily as the others. Skarb focused its glare only on it and studied its movement. Skarb said, "You come from the waters. Answer me. Are you the Voices of Proznia? If so, why do you act as a coward and disguise yourself as dainty little birds? Show me your power. Become something more than just a twit, a tweet, a flit. Turn into a Greznik."

The fairy pitta flew directly above Skarb's extra eye on top of its head and grew as big as Skarb, then dropped all its beautiful feathers and contorted itself into a wrathful face. "You must not ask of us! Drink of the water!"

Skarb sneered, spit at the fairy pittas, and flexed its body for a fight. "I wasn't asking! I was demanding! You are not birds. You are Proznia!"

All the fairy pittas changed from beautiful birds to savage mouths with wings and dove violently down on Skarb.

Skarb swatted them away as best it could, but the bizarre winged mouths attacked more viciously to destroy the belligerent Greznik. But Skarb crouched down, stirred its insides to a boil, then bounded through the attack toward the waters and bellowed, "I will never return to you! The stones will be mine!"

Skarb dove in the water and struggled to swim as the swirling currents formed a powerful whirlpool and spun Skarb in circles. An acrid smoke rose from the waters.

"Get out! Get out!" said the owls and kingfishers as they flew back into the trees.

Skarb thrashed and swam through the swirling currents. Then Skarb dove down to steal the blue stones lying on the riverbed. When it reached the bottom, with its mouth shut tight, it dug and dug. Skarb found nothing but silt. Skarb dug with such ferocity it used up nearly all its energy and almost did not make it back up to the surface.

Because Skarb did not swallow the water, the flying creatures of Proznia exploded into thousands of beautiful diamonds that turned into balls of putrid mold and fell like stones into the water. They pounded like hammers on Skarb and stirred the water. The bitter waves shaped into distorted, tortured faces and screamed at Skarb, "You did not drink! You fiend!"

The river water swirled like an ocean maelstrom and pulled Skarb under. Skarb let the waters pull it downward, and then it attacked the maelstrom and broke out of the savagely cruel currents. It finally rose to the surface and took a gasping breath, barely making it to shore. As it crawled out of the water, the swirling Voices were swallowed up by the muddy springwater and sank to the bottom of the river.

Skarb collapsed on the ground, paralyzed like stone.

29

THIS ISN'T CEREAL

Just after midnight, with moonlight shining directly into Tony and Mitch's room, their alarm clock went off. Mitch and Tony shot up out of bed, forgetting where they were and why they were getting up.

Mitch was so sound asleep, he looked around expecting to see his New York bedroom. He turned off the alarm.

"Why'd you set the alarm?" Tony asked groggily.

"I didn't," said Mitch, just as Jovi barged into the room.

"I did. Get up!" she said, shaking Tony out of bed. "We're supposed to be spies tonight!"

Mitch looked at the clock. "The tractor! We've got to go! We're super late."

"Shh, you're going to wake up Mom and Dad," said Tony.

The boys stumbled to put their work pants on. The three kids tiptoed out of the boys' room, making sure their parents did not wake up. Downstairs in the mudroom, they put on their cowboy boots and leather work gloves, grabbed their flashlights and headlamps, and snuck out of the house. Jovi tripped on one of Tony's boots by the back door, and a bunch of stuff tumbled down noisily. Normally their sounds would have woken up their parents, but they were in too deep of a sleep. The whole farming adventure proved more difficult than their parents ever imagined, and every night they crashed, sound asleep.

The kids walked down the rocky path to the creek. It was a clear night with a full moon, so they could see without the aid of flashlights. The creek sparkled in the moonlight, and water bubbled around the bend, reminding Jovi of the ballerina she had so wanted to be—the one in *Swan Lake* whose sequined skirt sparkled across the stage.

Jovi said, "The water is a like a ballerina dancing out to the sea."

"I don't think the creek goes to the sea," said Tony.

Mitch said, "Who cares? Come on! Hurry up. We're late!"

The kids arrived at the dump, and Old Man was not there.

"We missed him," said Mitch, disappointed.

Tony looked toward Old Man's farm and saw the dark outline of him leading his horses back home.

Tony ran as fast as he could to Old Man and said, "We're here!"

"I thought you weren't going to show up," said Old Man.

"We fell asleep by accident. But we're ready now. Is it too late?" said Tony.

"Well, it's good news you're here," said Old Man.

Old Man turned his horses around, and when they were pointed back toward the dump, the horses took off.

"Watch out, Tony!"

The horses ran too quickly, but Old Man got them under control. When he got back to the dump, he said, "So glad you chose to come. I was worried. I looked the situation over earlier, and I don't think the pile is going to shift again. Tony, I think it's safe for you to climb down to the tractor. But go carefully. Mitch, you guide these ropes down to Tony so he can tie them to the tractor. Jovi, help me tie the ropes to the pulling harness."

Tony walked on top of the heap, turned on his head-lamp, and crawled down. Mitch dropped the ropes down, and Tony tied them to the buried tractor's trailer hitch. Tony climbed back out to the edge of the dump, and they both stepped aside. Then Old Man and Jovi guided the Percherons to pull. But nothing moved at all. The horses pulled and pulled several times, but nothing budged.

Old Man stepped back to analyze. "It's buried deeper than I thought."

"I don't know if we can do this," said Jovi.

Mitch and Tony agreed with the difficulty of the project.

Old Man said as he handed different ropes to Mitch, "We aren't giving up yet. Mitch, tie these two ropes to one of the pieces of junk lying on top of the pile. Let's start with that rusty old mattress spring."

Mitch tied the ropes to the mattress spring, and the horses pulled it out. The kids retied the ropes to an old icebox, and the horses pulled that out too.

Old Man grabbed the icebox, loaded it onto his hay trailer, and said, "We're keeping that. I need a good icebox."

Piece by piece the horses pulled out layers of junk, but there was still so much more to go. It was a humid and sticky night, so everyone, including the horses, was sweating and getting very dirty. They stopped for a water break as moths flew around their headlamps, crickets chirped in the grass, and frogs croaked in the creek. The mosquitoes were out with a vengeance and the kids slapped their arms repeatedly.

Jovi said, "We've hardly made a dent in the pile, and I'm already tired."

"Me too," said Mitch. "This tractor can't be worth this much work."

"Yeah, and I'm getting hungry," said Tony as he scratched the mosquito bites scattered over his arms.

Old Man said, "No whining yet. Believe me, you're going to want to see what this tractor can do."

He handed them each a piece of pemmican out of his pocket as a snack. The kids each took a big bite.

"Hey, this isn't cereal, but it sure tastes good right now," said Mitch.

"It is yummy. What is it?" asked Tony.

"Pemmican," said Old Man.

"What's pemmican?" asked Jovi.

"It's food that keeps you full for a long time. High in protein and nutrients, and it can last a long time without refrigeration. Even in hot weather. The Cree prepared it. The Arctic explorers brought it on their trips. Fur traders ate it too. It's perfect for anyone who needs to stay alive in rough conditions. It's good for you to get used to it."

Tony asked for another bite, but Old Man said, "Let's get back to work."

The kids were rejuvenated from the snack, but the remaining pile of junk still looked too big to tackle.

Old Man said, "We can just move the rest of the stuff to the side. It'll go faster this time. Take another swig of your water and let's get back to work."

After removing one piece at a time for another hour, Old Man said, "I think we're ready to start pulling again."

The Percherons pulled and pulled, but the tractor still would not budge. Old Man was getting as weary as the kids, but he grabbed some shovels off his hay trailer and said, "Here. Climb down and dig out the wheels."

The kids shoveled the soil loose around the tractor wheels, then climbed back out and gave Old Man a thumbs-up. He got the horses pulling again. And sure enough, as the hot, sweaty workhorses pulled and pulled, the tractor started to move. Slowly but surely it emerged from the bottom of the dump. They were happy to see it fully at last.

Once the decrepit tractor was out in the open, it was clearly rusted, dented, and damaged.

Mitch said, "There's no way this tractor will ever work."

"You're right. Not in this condition. It's in worse shape than I thought," said Old Man worriedly. He looked back at the eastern horizon. "The sun is going to rise soon, and you need to get back to bed so nobody finds out about our secret tractor."

Tony said, "We can't leave it out in the open like this, can we? Everyone will see it."

Old Man said, "You're right, but all we have to do is load it onto my hay trailer, and I'll pull it to my barn."

With the horses' help, they loaded the tractor onto the bed of the trailer. Once it was on the trailer, a few rusted pieces fell off and crashed to the ground. When those critical pieces broke free, the tractor could not hold itself together and crumbled down. Not a remnant of its original structure was left. Nothing but a pile of scrap metal.

Mitch grabbed his head with both his hands. Tony gasped. And Jovi shrieked, "It broke!"

Mitch got up on the hay trailer and examined the pieces but concluded he would never be able to figure out how to put it back together again.

"I wasn't expecting that," said Old Man. "But it has been down there for years. It was bound to be fragile."

Tony's heart sank. None of the parts were discernable, and nothing looked like pieces of the amazing instrument panel that had originally piqued his curiosity in the first place.

Old Man was tired and said, "Let's all get to bed. Tomorrow come over to my barn and we'll work on fixing this. But remember: Don't tell anyone about this project. If you do, the tractor will never ever work again. Secrets are meant to stay secrets."

"Can you keep a secret this time?" Mitch asked Jovi.

"Jovi is terrible at keeping secrets," said Tony.

"Don't say that," Jovi said angrily.

"But you spill every secret," said Mitch.

Jovi said, "Come on. That's not fair. I've kept secrets before."

"Name one," said Tony.

She could not come up with one. She had spilled the beans on many Christmas presents, including the time Mitch got a hamster from Tony. She blurted out that Dad had bought Mom a vacation to Paris for her birthday. She snitched that Tony was sneaking extra cookies, beef jerky, and tasty meat sandwiches into his lunch every day to give to friends whose parents packed them vegan lunches. Jovi spilled the beans that for many months Mitch had traded after-school lessons with a friend—the friend took Mitch's golf lessons, and Mitch took his friend's electric guitar lessons. Mitch and Tony finally got back at her and explained what really happened to their parents' precious seventeenth-century vase, whose broken pieces mysteriously appeared inside in a plastic bag on top of its display pedestal in their living room.

"Jovi, you can't think of one," said Mitch, who never trusted Jovi with a secret.

"Who would I tell out here anyway?" she asked.

Old Man interrupted their bickering and said, "Jovi, you simply have to keep this secret. And Mitch and Tony, you're going to find out how hard it is to keep this secret."

They promised Old Man they would not tell a soul.

Besides, it did not seem difficult to keep a secret about a big pile of broken tractor pieces. They walked back home and went quietly into the house and crawled back into bed, not saying a word. Their parents never knew they were gone.

Because they were up so late, they slept later than normal. After they woke up, they walked into their farmhouse kitchen for breakfast with filthy faces, grimy hands, and dirt buried deep beneath their fingernails.

Caroline said, "Look at you! How'd you get so dirty? I thought you took showers last night."

Their parents prepared breakfast, but the kids were too tired to eat. Jovi was so tired she held her head up with her hands, but it did not help any. She nodded off and tipped over into her cereal bowl, spilling it everywhere. Tony looked down at his plate of pancakes and said, "I'm really tired. Maybe if you fed us pemmican for breakfast we'd have enough energy."

Their parents looked at each other, miffed, and said simultaneously, "Pemmican?"

Caroline's cell phone rang, and she said excitedly, "Darrell, it's our first basil buyers! The Tortelliano Grocery suppliers! Kids, go outside. We need the house quiet. Hurry it up!" She answered the call as she scurried out of the room. "Hello, Caroline's Herbal Gems. Caroline speaking."

30

GONE TO YOU

Skarb lay on the river's shore, unmoving. Its eyeballs did not flinch or shift, but they stared in opposite directions and drooped like teardrops. Its claws were limp like jelly.

Spoonbill pushed her little bird foot into Skarb's belly. "It's dead."

"But Grezniks aren't alive, so they can't die. There's no such thing as a Greznik carcass," said Bustard.

"True. But this one is done for. Gone. No movement. Still as stone."

"How come this one had seven legs?"

"I don't know. And why didn't it dissolve?" asked Spoonbill.

"Would it dissolve if we rolled it back into the water?" wondered Bustard.

Bustard and Spoonbill tried to push the lump of a Greznik into the water but with no success. They hopped on top of Skarb's side and jumped on its belly with their little feet, but it was cold as ice and solid as granite.

"There's no way we can move it," said Spoonbill.

They hopped off and looked at the now calmly flowing waters and scampered along the shoreline.

Skarb let out a huge belch with so much force and stench that Spoonbill was blown upward and into the water. Bustard tumbled backward into a rock, rendering him unconscious. Spoonbill got out of the water, ran back to Bustard, and flapped her wings to revive him.

Skarb shook its head, and its legs twitched as it tried to stand up.

Spoonbill tapped Bustard with her foot and flapped her wing like a fan across Bustard's face. "Get up quick! The Greznik is moving. Get up! Hurry!"

Skarb had barely enough strength to get up on its legs. It hobbled clumsily to the water's edge, then it stood in the water and looked down at the riverbed. The waters were brown, and the riverbed was no longer covered in blue stones.

Skarb grumbled, "Where are the blue stones? I must have the blue stones!"

The kingfishers sang from the trees, "Do not search. Do not seek. You are victorious."

Skarb looked up, but they flew into the sun and disappeared. Skarb growled fiercely and said, "I will find the stones again, and they will be mine."

Spoonbill said, ready to flee if Skarb attacked, "The stones were never there. It was a mirage."

"Liars, you are. I should have swallowed the blue stone water. If I had, I would have the stones now!" growled Skarb.

Spoonbill said to Skarb, "The Voices are gone to you. You proved you will not listen to them."

"How can you understand me? No one can understand a Greznik," said Skarb.

"That is a secret not for you to know," said Spoonbill.

Skarb jumped into the water and swam to the bottom again. But it could not find the stones and came out of the water. Bustard and Spoonbill stepped back, their little legs shaking in fear of Skarb.

"How can you swim?" Bustard asked nervously.

Skarb answered, "That is a secret not for you to know."

Skarb dove in again but could not find the stones. For many days, it waited for the sun to come out from behind the clouds and reveal the blue stones again. But every time the sun cast its rays onto the river, the water did not change into the unusual blue. Even so, Skarb kept swimming to the bottom of the river to find the stones. But they were never there.

After days of trying, Skarb crawled out of the water one last time and lay on the shore, exhausted. It said angrily, "I could have had the blue stones. They were right there. I should've swallowed the blue stone water!"

Spoonbill flew down and landed dangerously close to Skarb. "We are telling you the truth. The stones were never there. The kingfishers spoke the truth to you. If you had drunk the waters, you would have become the Great Betrayer for Proznia."

Skarb said, "What does it matter? All Grezniks are betrayers."

"You rejected the Voices. Your world has changed," said Spoonbill. "To be a betrayer, you must choose it."

"I don't have to choose anything. I am a Greznik. We always betray. Now get away from me!" Skarb charged at Spoonbill and Bustard. Weakened from the river struggle, Skarb tripped and crashed. Too weary to fight, it lay down to rest. And the two birds flew to safety.

The fish owls whispered from the trees, "Proznia will fear you. Hear the call."

Skarb was oblivious to the owls' beseeching prayer, and when its legs recovered enough, it ran back to its regiment. Believing it had failed to seize the moment, Skarb returned utterly defeated.

Skarb walked up to Jatuh and said, "I found the blue stones, at the source of the river where I came to be. I went alone. I saw the blue stones in the waters."

Jatuh cackled and spit. "You are lying."

"No, I am not. The legend of Proznia's blue stone waters is a lie. I went to the river's source, and when the sun sparkled, I could see the stones. They claimed to be Proznia. But it is a mirage."

Jatuh said, "You are a liar. A cheat. Always have been."

Skarb answered, "It doesn't matter if I am. You wouldn't believe the truth from me anyway."

Jatuh watched Skarb wander off slowly and meander aimlessly. The strangely deformed Greznik had lost interest in the Great Search for the stones. Skarb's newfound indifference got under Jatuh's skin, and the discomfort felt like sharp spurs running through Jatuh's insides. Jatuh could not deny it: Skarb had seen something that could not be easily explained away. Jatuh boiled with envy that such a pathetic thing could have knowledge that Jatuh did not. In a rage of insecurity and dread, Jatuh was determined to make certain that the other 401, raised to another power, would be destroyed forever.

31

STOP!

Grateful for their parents' herbal distractions, the kids went down to Old Man's barn to see what he had in store for the collapsed and broken tractor. They knocked on the barn door, but no one answered. Mitch and Tony tried to open it, but the door was shut tight and looked as though it had not been opened in decades.

They walked around the barn. Mitch said, "How weird. There's no way to get in."

"He told us to meet him in the barn, right? Where is he?" wondered Tony as he leaned up against the north wall of the barn.

As he leaned, the wall slid open just enough to let the kids squeeze through. As they stepped inside, they were stunned. The barn was filled with machine tooling, iron forging tools, a smelting furnace, electric control panels, wood saws and a lathe, a glassblowing kiln, loads of cabinetry, and walls covered with tools. Old Man was welding some pieces of metal together when they stepped in.

Old Man's three dogs ran up to them and greeted them happily, lapping their faces and jumping up on them.

The old icebox from the dump was cleaned up and loaded with blocks of ice. Old Man opened the icebox, grabbed three World War I canteens already filled with water, and gave one to each of the kids.

"It's a hot day for working on the tractor," said Old Man.

Jovi asked, looking in the icebox, "Where do you get blocks of ice that big?"

Old Man answered, "This farm holds many secrets."

In the middle of the barn, the tractor parts were scattered all over the floor and looked impossible to put back together again. Jovi was less interested in the tractor and walked over to a workbench full of oddly shaped pieces of beautifully handblown, frail glass. She carefully picked up a piece, but it was light as a feather and felt covered in oil. The glass slipped out of her hand and crashed to the floor.

Jovi looked down at the floor expecting to see broken glass, but mysteriously it had not broken. She tried to pick it up, but like a slippery fish, it fell out of her hand again. It bounced when it hit the floor. She tried to pick it up but could not. Tears welled up in her eyes as she feared Old Man's anger.

Old Man put on a special pair of work gloves, picked it up, and placed it on the workbench. "Come back over here, Jovi."

Tony whispered, "Jovi, why do you always have to touch everything? You're going to get us kicked out."

One wall of the barn was covered from floor to ceiling with drawers, the wide and shallow kind used to store blueprints and architectural drawings. From a drawer close to the floor, Old Man pulled out a stack of blueprints and placed them on the long workbench.

"These are the blueprints for the tractor. I need you to study them and put the tractor back together," said Old Man.

The kids' eyes opened wide, stunned at what seemed to be the most difficult homework assignment they could ever receive.

Tony looked closely at the first three pages. "We can't read these pages. They aren't in English."

"What language is this?" asked Mitch.

Old Man explained, "The pages are written in code. I'll teach you how to break the code."

"I always wanted to be a spy," Jovi said excitedly, now interested in the project.

"Some of these instructions are written incorrectly on purpose, so you need two decoding methods to read them. As the first step in the code, all the letters are converted to symbols, so that part of the code isn't all that hard to break on its own. Once you translate every page, then you need another decoder, which I'll share with you later."

The man handed them a sheet of paper with the key to the first code.

A - a wooden paddle
B - a puppy
C - a left hand
D - a crescent moon
E - an open book
F - a spotted square
G - a baby's cradle
H - a lit candle
I - a figure-eight knot
J - a quarter note
K - an anchor
L - a teacup
M - a chicken
N - a penny-farthing
O - a hummingbird
P - a birch bark canoe
Q - a broken clock
R - a Civil War cannon
S - a peregrine head
T - a bowler hat

U - a plumeria flower
V - a heart-shaped rock
W - a carrot
X - a sea turtle
Y - a wedding cake
Z - a ballet shoe

0 - a cross
1 - a medieval ship
2 - a codfish
3 - a gecko's foot
4 - an elephant's eye
5 - a balalaika
6 - a boomerang
7 - a church steeple
8 - a dessert fork
9 - a worn-out boot

"This will take a long time," said Mitch, discouraged.

Old Man said, "No tractor lamentations allowed here. Divide it between the three of you, and it'll go faster than you think."

The kids dove right in and began decoding each page. They all liked a puzzle and enjoyed working on it the rest of the day. For the next few days, they rode their horses down to Old Man's farm and continued their deciphering work. Despite Jovi's difficulty in keeping secrets, this time she was not the least bit tempted to tell their parents about their project. Caroline and Darrell were busy building their new herb business, so they were not the least bit curious about what the kids were doing each day. They were just glad the kids were outside.

Caroline said to Darrell, "It's great that we can let them play outside. After all, what trouble could they get into on a farm?"

Once the kids finished decoding the pages, Old Man explained that some words and sentences should be ignored or rearranged. Then he taught them how. He explained, "That way, if someone breaks the first code, they will put the tractor together incorrectly."

The rules for the secondary code were challenging, and the kids struggled to learn it. But once they did, they could read the instructions easily.

With the blueprints fully decoded, they organized the broken parts of the tractor to match the assembly instructions. But many parts needed fixing, rebuilding, or replacing. Old Man gave each kid a job right away. Jovi was not all that interested in engines, so he gave her the task of blowing new glass for the headlights. The glass blowing was difficult and it took a while before she caught on. But once she did, she enjoyed it, yet she found it bizarre that the melted glass was not hot to the touch. The tractor needed to be wired from front to back. Tony was particularly good at the electrical work, so he got that assignment. Mitch was assigned to rebuild the engine.

Old Man helped each of them throughout the process. Days later, they were ready for the last step: building a wide tractor seat to fit all three passengers. They filled the seats with sheared wool from Old Man's sheep, then they put the finishing touches on the tractor—some legacy pinstripes down the side, which Tony designed.

Old Man walked to the back of the barn to an old, dusty cabinet. He patted the top of the cabinet a couple of times, and a dark cloud of dust billowed, causing him and the kids to cough. After the dust settled, he asked Jovi to climb up on top of the cabinet to reach atop a wooden crossbeam and grab a key hidden there. Jovi found the key, climbed back down, and gave it to Old Man.

He unlocked the cabinet, and it was filled with hundreds of keys of all different shapes and sizes. He removed one key from the back of the cabinet, then walked over to the tractor, sat down in the driver's seat, and put the key in. The kids were thrilled to finally see the tractor in action.

"I can't believe we put it all together," said Mitch.

"I thought it was impossible," said Tony.

Old Man said, "It's amazing what you can build piece by piece. Should we get it started?"

"Yes!" answered all three at the same time.

He turned the key, but the engine failed to start. Old Man tried again and again. He asked Tony to try, but it just would not start.

"The tractor doesn't work," Old Man said dejectedly as he got out of the tractor.

Mitch was very disappointed. "After all that work, it has to start. We followed the blueprints exactly."

"We spent weeks in this barn when I could've been playing on the computer?" said Tony, forgetting why he ever thought the tractor was interesting in the first place.

"I'm going home. I need a break," said Jovi, who started for the door. With the momentum of their disappointment, Mitch and Tony followed.

Old Man said to them, "You can give up now, but you will never know what this amazing tractor can do. I promise you, it isn't like anything you know. You might become slaggards if you give up now. Or we can fix it. Have some pemmican and get back here."

Jovi whispered to Mitch, "What's a slaggard?"

Tony whispered back, "Is that even a word?"

"Do you think he means sluggard?" wondered Mitch.

Old Man tried again but could not start the tractor. "You kids are just going to have to figure it out."

"We don't know how to figure it out," said Mitch.

Jovi asked, "Can you at least give us a hint?"

Old Man said, "No hints needed. We followed the

blueprints exactly. Your work was perfect. You three get on the tractor. See if you can figure it out."

Old Man wrapped a bunch of pemmican into some bandanas, refilled the World War I canteens with cool water from the icebox, and put it all under the tractor seat.

Jovi got into the tractor first, in the driver's seat. Then Mitch buckled himself in next to Jovi and then Tony. Jovi was less interested than her brothers in getting the tractor started. She preferred to give up and ride horses all day instead. Horses did not need fuel, electronics, dashboard controls, and a key. All they needed was trust in their rider, a saddle, an open road, and a kick in the side.

The whole project to her was bizarre. Powerful secrets. Strange tractor controls. Encoded blueprints. She looked at Old Man suspiciously, wondering if he was just a crazy old farmer.

Old Man said, "Some of the tractor's capabilities are not on the blueprints, so be sure to watch the dashboard closely when driving it."

"Maybe the tractor just needs a kick, like a horse," Jovi said jokingly.

Old Man kicked the tractor.

"Tractors don't start with kicks," said Mitch.

Jovi turned the key, knowing it would not start because it had not started in the thirty previous tries. "I'm glad it didn't start." Then she gestured for Mitch to trade places with her. "I don't really want to drive it anyway. Mitch, you do it."

"Okay, I'll try." But Mitch could not get his seat belt unbuckled. "I can't. My seat belt is stuck."

Jovi said, "Maybe the tractor just needs a magic word to start it."

Tony said, "Tractors don't run on magic words."

"What do you think they run on?" asked Old Man.

"Fuel," said Mitch, who kept trying to undo his seat belt.

"Humph," grunted Old Man.

Jovi, for the fun of it, turned the key and said, "Go!"

Old Man said, "*Go* is the magic word!"

Suddenly the engine started, and Old Man quickly pushed a button on one of his electrical panels. The barn wall dropped down into the ground like toast into a toaster. Before the kids had a chance to ready their positions, the tractor peeled out of the barn, and within moments was going sixty miles an hour and accelerating. They spun out of the barn and into the open, bumpy fields.

Jovi yelled, "Mitch, take the wheel! I don't know how to drive!"

"I can't! My seat belt is sealed shut!"

Jovi said, "Tony, switch places with me!"

But it was too late. Jovi drove over a bump, and she and Tony nearly flew out of the tractor.

Mitch helped Jovi get her seat belt on as she gripped the steering wheel.

The tractor hit another bump, and Tony flew up. Mitch grabbed Tony's pant leg just in time, pulled him back in, and buckled him in.

The tractor kept accelerating, reaching speeds that would make it impossible to take corners without rolling. As they sped down the straight road, they were headed for a large concrete road barrier. If they did not turn sharply, they would hit it head-on.

"Don't turn the wheel, Jovi! The tractor will roll!" said Mitch.

"I have to turn or we'll be crushed like bugs on a windshield!" said Jovi, gripping the steering wheel so tightly her fingers cramped. Jovi cried as she held on tight. "I don't know how to drive a tractor. I hate tractors!"

"Turn the wheel, Jovi! Turn it!" shouted Tony.

But Jovi was bawling with her eyes closed.

"Everyone, hang on!" said Tony. He reached over and spun the wheel, just before they almost hit the wall. Against all laws of physics and despite their incredible speed, the tractor easily made the sharp turn.

"That's impossible!" exclaimed Mitch.

"Jovi, open your eyes and steer! Mitch and I have to figure out how to turn it off," said Tony.

"STOP! STOP! STOP!" shouted Jovi in the loudest voice she could muster, hoping it was the magic word to make the tractor come to a halt. "Why isn't it stopping?"

"Jovi, steer us back to the farm," said Mitch.

"I can't! It has a mind of its own. It's worse than a horse!" said Jovi.

They were going way too fast, but there was nothing to do to slow it down. The tractor sped through the nearby town and out into the open road, past cars and trucks. Before they got their bearings, they had already crossed the state line and were barreling through Iowa.

The tractor accelerated to unexplainably fast speeds, and Mitch said, "We've got to stop this thing!"

Jovi hollered, "Stop! Stop! Stop! It's speeding faster and faster! Get it to stop!"

Mitch said, "We know the magic word to start the tractor, but not the magic word to stop it!"

"You blockheads! Figure it out! You're the ones who wanted to drive this thing. I didn't!" yelled Jovi.

"Stop screaming, Jovi, and drive!" yelled Mitch.

Tony tried turning the key off, but it would not turn. Mitch pushed every button possible. Tony messed with the gears, but each one seemed to increase the speed.

Jovi said, "Tony, change places with me."

"Get ready to switch places," said Tony. But when he tried to take off his seat belt, he could not. Whether Jovi liked it or not, she was trapped in the driver's seat, steering a tractor that was already exceeding the fastest speeds of the most powerful race cars.

They sped toward a long string of hog barns and a river. If they crashed into one of the barns they would die, along with hundreds of piglets.

Mitch yelled, "Jovi, turn!"

"Don't turn," said Tony. "We'll end up dead in that river!"

"Doesn't matter. It won't let me turn!" said Jovi.

A blinking green light that said *Jump!* popped out of the dashboard.

Mitch pushed it just as they were about to smash into the first barn. They closed their eyes and held each other's hands, knowing they would die on impact.

32

DEAD GOATS HEIST

During the Middle Ages, the Greznik regiment trav-eled through the Caucasus Mountains, trekking at high elevations to avoid being seen. Villages were scattered across the region, perched along the most breathtaking of steep hillsides, surrounded by dangerous peaks. Village families in the region, to protect themselves from avalanches and thieving thugs from other mountain villages, lived in defense towers built of stone—square at the bottom, three to five stories tall, and tapered at the top. They had no idea the towers also protected them from Grezniks passing closely by.

Both people and animals lived on the ground floor of a defense tower. Animal stalls were located along the perimeter, and situated in the center was the main living area. The fireplace stood in the center and was surrounded by benches, one side for the men and the other for the women. The head of the family sat in a square-shaped chair near the center of the room.

Everything inside was made of intricately carved wood, including the animal stalls. The animals provided warmth to the second floor, where the people slept—an area the people shared with hay and farm tools. From the second floor, the hay was thrown directly into the animal's stalls below through holes located above the stalls. If enemies approached, the people could retreat to the tower and lock and fortify the door. The people could live, locked inside, for days as they fought back the enemy from the top floor of the tower.

One day, the Grezniks passed a defense tower in the valley below in which three goats had just died from a miserable infection. Jatuh seized the opportunity to get rid of Skarb and said, "Oh great and wonderful Eternal Commander, why don't you send 401[5] to retrieve the goats in the tower and bring them to you?"

Boshlek had been growing increasingly weary of Skarb—a constant irritating reminder of its own mistakes. For once, when Jatuh made its appeal, Boshlek agreed and called Skarb forward.

Boshlek ordered Skarb, "Get the dead goats and bring them back to me."

"In the tower?" asked Skarb.

"Yes."

"Then you are sending me to disappear," said Skarb.

"Yes, we are to be rid of you once and for all," said Boshlek.

Jatuh drooled at the prospect of being rid of Skarb for good.

Skarb asked, "What if I do bring the goats back?"

"No one has ever succeeded in entering a tower and coming back out again. But if you come back without the goats, you will be punished for days on end."

"Must I leave at once?" asked Skarb.

Boshlek swatted Skarb. "Yes, leave now."

Skarb walked away slowly and said to Jatuh, "Quit your drooling. I'm not gone yet."

Yet Skarb knew the assignment was impossible. Grezniks could easily sneak up on a defense tower, but as soon as a Greznik grabbed an animal, the shepherd dogs would bark, attack, and cause the people to look out, see, and evaporate the Greznik. Even when Grezniks killed and ate a shepherd dog and got into a tower, the animals slept in the same room as the people, and the Greznik was always seen and evaporated.

Skarb dreaded the assignment and took a circuitous route to the tower. After a few weeks of sauntering lazily, Skarb crossed a beautiful mountain valley and became determined to somehow prove Boshlek wrong. Skarb turned around and traveled toward the tower, wondering if the dead goats were even still there. As it neared, Skarb realized that the village had recently been ransacked, and all the villagers had fled or been killed. Whoever now lived in the tower was a squatter. The tower was miserably neglected and unkempt, and the animals were hungry and in poor health. From a distance, Skarb smelled the decomposing goats, amazed they were still in the tower, and cautiously approached to avoid alerting both a giant shepherd dog and a mangy bloodhound.

Skarb sniffed around and was surprised to confirm that no people were nearby. Skarb drooled with delight at the luck—the goat heist would be easy. Skarb imagined Boshlek's reaction when it came back with the three dead goats in its grip. It thought, *I will defeat their plans to destroy me once again.*

Skarb easily got inside the defense tower, saw the dead goats thrown in a heap at the side, and expanded its jaws to fit all three goats within the grip of its teeth. But just as it was about to grab the goats in its mouth and run, Skarb heard the farmer's twelve-year-old son, Bogdan, running toward the tower unexpectedly. Just in time, Skarb jumped to the second floor and hid behind a pile of hay. Skarb heard the boy's bitter and brutal father storming toward the tower, fiercely angry and yelling his son's name.

The cruel father's voice got closer, and to flee his father's fury, Bogdan dashed up the ladder to hide behind the same pile of hay. Skarb, without a sound, slyly crawled upward to the top floor of the tower.

The father entered the tower and yelled up for his son to come down. Bogdan climbed up higher too.

To avoid being seen, Skarb opened the lookout window and jumped out. It landed safely, ran off, and leaped behind a stone wall.

The father climbed the ladder to the second floor to find his son, but Bogdan had already reached the top floor. Bogdan looked out from the top window and was grateful to see a pile of hay at the bottom. But it was a dangerously long jump down, and he would need to land on exactly the right spot to avoid getting hurt. He heard his father climbing upward and decided the jump was worth the risk. He jumped, landed on the hay, and tumbled painfully into some rocks. Although badly bruised, Bogdan was surprised to have not broken anything. He got up quickly, ran forward, dove behind the stone wall, and almost landed right on Skarb. The Greznik jumped silently and invisibly before the boy landed, then slithered away in the darkness.

The father climbed to the top floor and found the lookout window open. He went back down and stumbled outside the tower, plagued by the cauldron of his own anger, misery, and regret. He called out to his fleeing son, but Bogdan had heard that tormented voice one too many times. He ran into the field toward a trough used to feed their grazing cattle. Hidden inside the trough was an old and tattered rucksack, given to him by his gentle grandpa and grandma at his mother's funeral a few months earlier. The rucksack was packed with beef jerky and some old cheese.

Grandpa had said to Bogdan, "Keep this rucksack, and if you ever need to run, come to our farm. You will be safe with us."

Bogdan put the rucksack on and ran into the mountains as fast as he could.

Skarb did not care what happened to Bogdan. Instead, it was focused only on grabbing the dead goats. The shepherd dog barked and grew increasingly agitated the farther Bogdan ran. The bloodhound was trapped inside the tower and ran around anxiously, wishing it could follow

Bogdan's scent. The sheep outside shook their heads, and rams hit their horns like a drum against the stone wall of the defense tower. All of them were oblivious that Skarb was licking its chops, ready to eat anything that got in its way.

33

TOO MUCH FUEL

Mitch pushed the tractor's *Jump!* **button. They held each** other's hands, ducked, and expected to die when they crashed into the first hog barn. Instead, the tractor leaped over one hog barn, then another after another.

Tony opened his eyes first. "We jumped all of them!"

They crossed over to a dirt road and barreled into central Iowa.

Jovi asked, "Can't you guys figure out how to stop this thing?"

"Let's hope it runs out of fuel soon!" said Tony.

Mitch read the fuel monitor screen out loud: "Available fuel at this speed: 600,000 miles."

Jovi said, "Are you kidding me? This thing won't stop for another 600,000 miles?"

"How far is that?" said Tony.

"Around Earth about two dozen times at the equator," said Mitch.

Jovi gripped the steering wheel and said, "Let's burn some fuel!"

Jovi accidentally plowed through a woman's beautiful rose garden. Mitch cringed, and Tony apologized to the woman, "Sorry! My sister doesn't know how to drive!"

"It's the tractor's fault, not mine!" said Jovi.

Mitch looked behind them to see the unfortunate damage to the rose garden, but there was none. "The garden isn't damaged at all!" he said.

They worried about what harm the tractor was doing to the fields and terrain, but, strangely, the tractor left no damage. No tracks. No evidence that they had been there at all.

As the kids became more familiar with how to maneuver the wild and crazy tractor, they started enjoying the ride. They flashed by farms and buzzed through many little towns. They dashed down into Nebraska, passed through a county fair, and caught cotton candy out the side of their tractor on their way through. They zipped through the beautiful mountains of Colorado, jumped over billboards like hurdles along the highways, crossed through the deserts of Arizona, and zoomed all around the Grand Canyon.

After the Grand Canyon, they pointed the tractor toward the Pacific Ocean to drive through California's back canyon roads. They drove way too far south and accidentally drove directly into Los Angeles. They tried to correct the error but ended up on Interstate 5—seven lanes of cars backed up in bumper-to-bumper traffic. About to ram into the back of a minivan, Jovi swerved onto the freeway's shoulder, but just ahead the shoulder narrowed and disappeared.

"Ahhhhhh!" screamed Jovi.

"The tractor can't jump all these cars at once!" shouted Mitch.

"We'll crush them. It'll be a massacre!" said Tony.

A button popped out on the dashboard that said *Ride Over!* Mitch pushed it. The kids closed their eyes, assuming the cars and their drivers would be crushed underneath them. The tractor rode over all the cars, skating over the top of the entire traffic jam and weaving between cars the way a skier does moguls.

Mitch looked behind to see the damage, but again he was surprised. "The cars aren't damaged at all!"

"What on earth is happening?" said Tony, flabbergasted.

Mitch said, "Let's get off the freeway!"

He hoped they could more easily navigate the side streets to get out of Los Angeles. But at their speed, catching the freeway exit at the right time was difficult. They drove by exit after exit. When Jovi finally got off the freeway, she inadvertently headed them directly into downtown Los Angeles. By avoiding all the cars, taxis, pedestrians, buses, and cyclists, they ended up pointed straight for a tall building with nowhere to turn. Mitch pushed the *Ride Over!* button.

The button popped the tractor into a wheelie position. The kids held on as the tractor precariously balanced on its back wheels and headed right for the revolving doors of a tall office building.

"Tractors can't ride up a building!" said Tony.

"There isn't another option!" Mitch yelled.

Jovi turned the steering wheel so the tractor was pointed away from the revolving doors, but they were now headed for the glass windows that scaled the tall building.

"Turn again, Jovi!" yelled Mitch, certain they would drive right through the glass and be cut to pieces.

"Turn it, Jovi!" said Tony.

"I can't!" said Jovi. She turned the steering wheel, but the tractor would not turn.

A button on the dashboard started blinking and beeping, and it said *Ride Over Suction Wheels!* Tony pushed it, and a hatch opened below them. An additional set of uninflated wheels got into position, and a strong pump expanded the wheels. Tiny suction cups popped out of the tire treads. As the tractor hit the building, its front wheels adhered to the side of the building, then the back wheels, and it rode straight up.

Halfway down the other side of the building, on the eleventh floor, Tony maneuvered the tractor to try riding sideways around the floor. But after two laps, they could not figure out how to stop looping the eleventh floor. They kept passing the same meeting where a dozen or so employees sat around the table.

"We keep passing the same people," said Mitch. "How do we stop circling?"

Every time they lapped around, Jovi noticed that the meeting attendees did not even look up. A perky project manager was in the front giving a presentation explaining why their project would have fifty-one phases instead of two—putting them twenty-three years behind schedule. As the kids' windburned faces sped past the window for the seventh time, a man in the meeting yawned and pulled a plate of days-old pastries toward him, grabbed a dried-out apple fritter, took a big bite, and chased it down with a Valley Mist soda.

"No worries, they don't even see us," said Jovi.

Tony finally figured out how to point their tractor downward toward the street. But once they were in a vertical position again, they fell into a full-speed free fall. Again they closed their eyes, hoping a miracle would intercept their inevitable deadly crash below.

When the tractor hit the ground, it felt as though an invisible giant marshmallow stopped their fall. They bounced to an upright position as the extra set of wheels retreated back into the tractor, and they sped off down Sunset Boulevard and later Vine Street.

The farm tractor was completely out of place as it passed Hollywood sports cars. Bits of caked-on manure from their farm started flicking off the wheels. Bits splattered onto drivers' sunglasses and splashed into lattes and landed in convertibles. The kids could not prevent the manure flinging. They could only yell "I'm soooorrry!" as they flew by.

A clump of paparazzi was chasing the superstar singer from the band Mender Daft when the tractor flew by. They had never seen anything like it and ditched the pop star to follow the tractor. The lead singer breathed a sigh of relief because the celebrity media had already captured her carrying that same handbag last month—a grave publicity error for a superstar like her.

Other photographers loitered outside a spa, waiting for the pop star Miss Goop Goop to walk out in a new and ever-ridiculous outfit. The tractor drove past Miss Goop Goop, who walked out wearing a dress made of plastic garbage bins. The photographers ditched her to chase the tractor. Miss Goop Goop stomped her feet in frustration and shouted in protest that someone younger was getting all the attention. "What about my garbage garb?"

Tony noticed people were taking pictures of them. "We need to get out of here. Thousands of people are seeing us and taking pictures."

Jovi cried, "I always ruin secrets!"

Mitch said, "The secret is officially destroyed. Everyone will know about the tractor."

The tractor was too fast to catch—and more puzzling yet, when a paparazzo snapped a photo of the tractor, the kids and the tractor were never in the image. No matter what camera was used, the tractor was never in the picture. Several journalists were close enough to read the back of Mitch's shirt. He wore an old jersey with his grandpa's last name—Bosonataski—written across it. And that was a last name they all knew. The journalists took note.

The kids spun around the same block a few times before figuring out they could use the jumping and leaping capabilities of the tractor to leap from building to building and avoid the streets altogether. Then they headed down to

San Diego, but they still could not figure out how to slow down. Because of a traffic jam on Interstate 5, they went off road onto the US Marine Corps Base Camp Pendleton, racing past Marines at hundreds of miles per hour.

"I'm getting tired, guys. And hungry. Mitch, how many more miles before we run out of fuel?" asked Jovi.

"You don't want to know."

"I'm hungry too," said Tony.

Jovi's hands cramped from gripping the steering wheel. Tony's hands blistered from working the gears constantly. Mitch wearied from working the dashboard controls. Mitch reached down underneath the seat and grabbed the canteens and pemmican. Tony took the wheel while Jovi drank some water and ate some pemmican. Then Mitch took over the gears while Tony got a snack. Then Tony helped Mitch get some water and pemmican too.

"I'm too tired. I need to stop," said Jovi.

Mitch and Tony were equally weary. So tired, in fact, that Mitch's head tipped down and his forehead hit the dashboard. Unexpectedly, out popped a map. Mitch and Tony figured out how to program the tractor to drive home.

"That would've been more helpful a few hours back," said Tony.

"That map was not in the blueprints. I would've remembered that," said Mitch.

"Most of this insane machine was not in the blueprints," said Jovi.

With the tractor heading back home, Tony shifted it

into the highest possible gear and quadrupled their speed.

"We're defying laws of physics," said Mitch as he watched the world around them speed by.

"Hopefully we can get there before I fall asleep at the wheel. I should never have agreed to this!" said Jovi.

"You have to admit driving up a building was pretty fun."

Jovi smiled and said, "That was awesome."

"We're programmed to drive straight home. Hopefully Old Man knows how to stop this thing," said Mitch.

By dusk, they arrived back to Old Man's farm. Old Man saw the tractor speed past his window and rushed out of his house. They rode in circles around his house and asked, "How do we stop this thing?"

"Say the magic word!" said Old Man.

"We don't know the magic word to make it stop!" said Mitch.

Old Man said, "It's the same as starting it!"

Jovi yelled, "Go!" And the engine slowed to a stop.

When the kids crawled off the tractor, their muscles were completely spent and their legs wobbled. Barely strong enough to stand, they leaned their backs against the tractor and propped each other up.

Tony said, "I can't believe you stop the tractor by saying 'go'."

"That's ridiculous," said Mitch.

"And I can't believe we never said 'go' today," said Jovi. Then her fatigue gave way to silliness. "Remember how we leaped over the piglets?"

They all laughed so hard they tipped over onto a hay bale. Old Man relished hearing all the details of their adventure.

"And we drove up and down buildings," said Jovi excitedly.

Tony added, "The wheels have suction cups built into them. We didn't know it could do that!"

"That's because I built that part," said Old Man slyly.

Then Jovi started sniffling.

"But I failed again," she said quietly.

"Why do you say that?" asked Old Man.

"Because I didn't keep the secret. Everyone saw us."

"Yeah. She's right. The secret is out," said Tony, disappointed in their failure to keep their travels unknown.

"Hundreds of people saw us," said Mitch.

"I'm sorry. I always fail at secrets," said Jovi.

Mitch said, "It's not your fault."

Old Man was quiet and solemn. "It was an amazing adventure," he said. "You went even farther and faster than I thought you would."

"You aren't mad?" asked Mitch, surprised.

"It's more complicated than that. The tractor remains a secret. Even if your adventure didn't seem like a secret today."

"But many people saw it. We drove over their cars, jumped their houses, drove through their gardens, went up and down their buildings . . . Lots of people took pictures of us," said Tony.

"Any picture they took will not have you or the tractor in the image," said Old Man.

"The tractor's invisible?" asked Mitch.

"The tractor isn't invisible. Those people really did see both you and the tractor today. But nothing will appear on their pictures," explained Old Man.

"But they really did see us?" asked Jovi.

"Yes, they saw you. But they won't be able to prove any of it. Not this trip anyway. The tractor cannot be traced. It will not show up on photos, and neither will you. It won't register on *any* equipment. The tractor, and anything on it, can only be seen with a person's God-given eyes," said Old Man.

"But we still have a problem," said Mitch.

"How's that?" asked Old Man.

Mitch said, "I shouldn't have worn this shirt today, especially to Hollywood."

Tony realized what jersey Mitch had worn and said, "Oh no. They'll figure out who we are. We'll be all over the news."

"Why?" asked Old Man, puzzled.

Mitch turned around so Old Man could see the back of his jersey. "Bosonataski is my grandpa's last name. No one else in the country has that last name, and everyone in the country knows it now because of our grandpa."

Jovi bawled. "Our grandpa's in jail. We left New York because of him. Now we're going to have to leave here too!"

Old Man masked his concern and said, "Let's not worry about that today. You need to get some sleep. Go on home and get some rest. The Dunnell Tractor Pull Contest is tomorrow, and we're going to take this tractor."

"We'll win!" said Mitch.

Old Man said, "We'll take it to the Dunnell Tractor Pull, but we'll keep our secret. To everyone else, it's just an old tractor."

The kids were too tired to walk home, so Old Man let all three of them ride his Percherons home. The horses stopped in front of the farmhouse and let the kids off. The kids were too tired to realize how strange it was that all the horses obediently walked right back home in perfect unison.

Mitch's worry about his jersey proved to be justified. Back in Los Angeles, reporters were absolutely mystified as to why no one could prove the tractor had ever been there at all. But many had noticed the unique last name of the nationally known fraudster on the back of Mitch's shirt. They had wondered, "Could the jailed con artist, Neil Bosonataski, have somehow pulled this crazy stunt?"

The reporters immediately called their contacts in New York to research where the jailed crook's family was located. Caroline's friends snitched and gave the reporters her new address. And they confirmed that Neil Bosonataski's daughter, Caroline, had three kids who fit the description.

Reporters were dispatched to the farm from every major news network. They took red-eye flights or chartered aircraft to get their television crews to Dunnell immediately, expecting to break the news before their media competitors. But as reporters arrived in the morning, it was obvious that no one got an exclusive on the breaking news. Hundreds of reporters were scattered across the farm's front lawn, waiting to get a glimpse of the kids and the tractor.

34

BROKEN CAGES

Bogdan's father circled the defense tower, hollered out for his son, hobbled around in the dark, tripped over farm tools, and landed in animal dung. He gave up looking for Bogdan and returned to the tower. He grabbed his jug of *chacha*, guzzled what he could, and collapsed, totally alone, into his square wooden chair, too clouded in his head to care. As head of a household made empty by his own doing, he drank more *chacha* while the goats rotted in the stall just behind his chair.

Skarb snuck up to the edge of the tower. This errand for Boshlek was proving to be as difficult as Jatuh expected it to be. Yet determined to prove Jatuh wrong, Skarb decided to try one more time to grab the rotting carcasses.

Skarb climbed up the outside wall of the defense tower again and into the top floor, then slithered down onto the second-floor haymow above the animals' stalls. Skarb inched backward as it analyzed how to get to the dead goats, but it accidentally fell straight down the hole in the floor from which hay would be dropped down to the animals. Skarb fell right onto the pigs below, and the pigs squealed out.

Bogdan's father woke up from the squealing pigs and hollered, "Shut up, you pigs!" But the father did not look over. He just drank from the jug and fell asleep again. Skarb had to get out of the tower and fast, but it would not leave without the carcasses.

Skarb waited until the father was slumped over, then it stood up carefully, stared right into the pigs' eyes to frighten them into silence, and prepared to silently pounce and grab the goats. But a faint cry came in through the upper window, and the sound dripped down toward Skarb. The cry would normally emit no empathy from a Greznik, but the wail resonated and vibrated Skarb's insides painfully, as though it were a frail glass goblet shattering from a strong voice at a powerful pitch.

Skarb heard the cry again, and its legs quivered. It climbed back up to the haymow and all the way up to the top floor. Skarb jumped out of the top floor, leaving the goats behind. It landed safely and turned its head toward the cry.

Skarb zoomed its powerful vision far ahead and saw Bogdan stop on the mountainside, look up and cry, "Please help! Guide me, Lord, please!" Bogdan collapsed on the ground, cried more broken tears, and pleaded for help. With tears soaked deep into the ground, Bogdan stood up, ran farther, and left the trail to cut over to another defense tower. The boy stopped, completely out of breath, and fell on the ground exhausted from running with a loaded rucksack. Bogdan cried himself to sleep in the mountains. He rested just long enough to get his legs strong again for another sprint. He put his rucksack on again, looked back toward the farm, and ran.

As Skarb watched the boy curiously, its insides rumbled as though an underground river flowed within. The feeling made its wiry hair stand on end, as though lightning were about to strike. The shepherd dog barked loudly as a warning to all around and to alert the farmer, who was too fuddled to hear.

For a reason unknown to itself, Skarb did not grab the goats and run. Instead it grabbed the shepherd dog, scared it into silence, and dropped it on the ground with a threatening growl. Skarb climbed the exterior wall of the tower and entered again from the top floor. It destroyed the animals' stalls and pushed stones out of the tower's wall and chased out the animals, then turned its rage onto the bloodhound who was the last to run out. Skarb destroyed a cage filled with doves and threw the doves into the air, and they flew away in fright.

The terrified animals ran in all directions, fleeing their ultimate enemy, a Greznik. Some cried out in the chaos, fearing they were all to be cruelly chomped and devoured. One of the baby goats could not find its mother, and Skarb grabbed it in its mouth. The mama goat wailed in anguish, but Skarb spit out the baby goat unharmed right at the mother's feet. Bogdan's piercing cry stung from afar, and Skarb felt as if its insides were shattering.

Bogdan's father remained benumbed in his chair, so Skarb snuck in and grabbed the rotting carcasses in its mouth and ran out. Skarb dug a deep hole in the ground and buried the dead goats side by side. Skarb broke the pasture's fence and let the cattle loose, then set the sheep free. Skarb took two broken fence posts and lay them, crisscrossed, on top of the burial mound.

Skarb growled and showed its teeth, and both dogs cowered in fear. Skarb chased the bloodhound into the mountains until the dog caught Bogdan's trail and followed it. The shepherd dog rounded up all the animals, who then followed the bloodhound. The bloodhound ran as fast as she could to reach her master Bogdan. Both dogs constantly looked behind them and growled to protect Bogdan.

After all the animals were let out and the goats were buried, Skarb stood in the empty pasture bewildered. It did not understand what compelled it to bury the goats and let all the animals go. Skarb stood on top of the burial mound and sniffed into the soil, already feeling the severe punishment for not bringing the goats back. Skarb raised its snout in the direction of its regiment to source their location and run back, but its feet felt a magnetic force from deep inside Earth that repelled it from running back. It tried to walk toward the regiment, but a mysterious voltage sent pain into every particle of its existence. Skarb collapsed and writhed from the agony, just above the goats, who now rested in peace.

35

TRACTOR PULL

The next morning the kids wanted to talk to one another about their tractor adventure, but they could not discuss any of it around their parents. At breakfast, they pretended as though nothing unusual had happened the day before and talked about what their friends might be doing back in New York.

After breakfast, as they waited to go to the Dunnell Tractor Pull Contest in the afternoon, Mitch read a book upstairs in a rocking chair. Tony studied chess strategies. Jovi worked in the attic looking through the boxes left behind by Mr. Charlie. She found many beautiful pieces of intricate embroidery made by Mr. Charlie's wife, Adelaide. Jovi draped a delicate lace shawl around her shoulders as she twirled around like a dancer at a royal ball.

Meanwhile, their parents were busy researching herbal farming on the internet. No one had yet looked out a window.

Darrell grabbed his coffee mug and turned to Caroline. "I'm getting more coffee. Do you want some more?"

"Yeah, thanks," said Caroline.

Darrell grabbed her mug, got up from his chair, glanced out the window, and blurted out, "Are you kidding me?"

Caroline jumped, thinking Darrell was yelling at her. "You asked me if I wanted coffee."

"No, no, not that. Look out the window. They found us!"

Their front lawn was littered with reporters and television camera crews arriving to track down and report on the mysterious tractor.

Darrell paced frantically and said, "What do they want from us? Can't they just leave us alone? We didn't do anything wrong!"

"I told my friends not to give away our address. Who would have told these people?" wondered Caroline.

They went down to the cellar and put on some leather vests, chaps, and boots with spurs to avoid being recognized. They pushed their cowboy hats on so tightly they nearly covered their eyes. They peeked out the cellar's bulkhead doors on the back of the farmhouse, facing the barns and the cattle pen. There were no reporters behind the farmhouse—only a branded bull with a ring in its nose who had walked up to the edge of the fence.

"Whose bull is that?" asked Darrell. "We don't have a bull."

Then a newswoman walked toward the back of the farmhouse, texting on her phone. She sported her own nose ring and tattoo, and as she passed their bulkhead door, Caroline said, "Psst!" and gestured for the newswoman to come over to her.

"What're all these people here for?" asked Caroline, just barely peeking her head out.

The newswoman said, "You haven't heard? Yesterday, like, three kids drove all over the country in, like, a super-fast tractor."

"What? What happened?" asked Caroline, relieved that the reporters were not there because of her dad's crimes.

"They drove a tractor, like, superfast. I mean, like, megafast. Up and down buildings. Jumped over stuff. You know, like, drove over cars. Through, like, people's gardens. Driving all over Hollywood, like, literally *over* Hollywood."

"You're serious?" asked Darrell, who thought the reporter's story could not possibly be true.

"Yeah, like, *totally* serious. Three kids in a tractor. Driving, I don't know, like, some kind of powerful tractor . . . it was like stealth or something. I mean, like, doesn't leave a trace. You can't, like, tell that it's been there. They even, like, drove over our news van. Like, I was totally there."

"And you think the kids are here?" asked Darrell.

"One of the boys was, like, wearing a Bosonataski jersey. Someone in New York, like, said the kids live here. Do they?"

"No, no. Interesting. No. Our kids worked in the fields yesterday," said Darrell.

Caroline and Darrell ducked back inside again.

Caroline said, "That's insane. Who'd make up a story like that about our kids?"

"Who put these people up to this?" wondered Darrell.

The parents burst out laughing.

"It's got to be one of your dad's stunts," continued Darrell. "And for once, I think it's hilarious. But why would he do it?"

Jovi, after twirling circles in the attic, stopped to sit down and look out the small window. She saw all the reporters, then ran to the attic steps and yelled down, "Mitch! Tony! Get up here! Hurry!"

Tony and Mitch ran up and looked out the window.

"Uh-oh. They did see Mitch's jersey," said Tony.

"How are we going to explain this?" said Mitch.

Suddenly, all the camera crews and reporters turned their attention toward the dirt road. The mysterious tractor was bumbling down the road toward them. The reporters recognized the distinctive pinstriping down the side of the tractor.

"There it is!"

"That's the tractor!"

"That's it!"

The tractor, driven by Old Man, put-putted down the dirt road at a snail's pace. The camera crews ran toward the tractor to film it up close, but when they got near, they paused. The tractor was pathetically slow and very dilapidated compared to what people witnessed the day before. They took photos, but unlike the day before, the tractor showed up on their cameras and on live TV.

The camera operators zoomed in on the tractor, while the reporters asked Old Man, "Did three kids drive that tractor at high speeds in Los Angeles yesterday?"

"What?" shouted Old Man, who could not hear a thing over the tractor's clanging engine.

The reporter repeated the question, but again Old Man could not hear it. Old Man turned off the engine and heard the question.

Old Man chuckled. "This old piece of junk? How could this rusty old thing have been in Los Angeles yesterday?"

It took Old Man several tries to get the tractor started again.

Back at news headquarters, the TV station managers saw that it was just a measly old tractor driven by a frail old man. They ordered the TV producers to quickly shut down the live television feed and switch to weather reports. The news directors back at the various station headquarters called their staff at the farm and chewed them out for wasting valuable media time.

One reporter said to her news director, "But I saw the tractor myself. I was stuck in a traffic jam on the 405. It ran over my car."

"It ran over your car?" asked the news director.

"I promise you, it did. It drove over hundreds of cars and trucks. And up and down an office building."

"But then the cars and buildings would be damaged. And they aren't, are they?"

"Well, no, but . . . you see . . . that's the mystery of this."

The news director said, "You flew out to a cornfield—at the company's expense, mind you—simply because you saw the name 'Bosonataski' on the back of a boy's jersey? Let me remind you: that is the last name of the world's most famous con artist. You just fell for one of his many cons. It was probably a hologram. A movie studio stunt. And if you believed it, he's probably got some stock to sell you."

The front lawn of the farm was covered with dejected reporters wandering about, angry over chasing a rickety tractor, or humiliated for believing the story in the first place.

Tony said, "I hope Old Man is right that the secret is still a secret."

"Sure doesn't seem like it," said Mitch.

One reporter mumbled to his cameraman, "I bet this all started on social media. I bet everyone fell for some fake social media post."

Still in their leather chaps, vests, cowboy hats, and sunglasses, Caroline and Darrell decided to go outside and find out what was going on.

The reporter said to his cameraman, "What do you bet those are the parents? Let's go record a statement from them. They probably started it all—angling for a publicity stunt. These things always start with the parents."

The reporter and his cameraman walked up and knocked on the front door, with their camera recording.

Suddenly it dawned on Caroline that this was a free publicity opportunity for their basil venture. She had dreamed of the moment when she could talk about her new business on television. And here it was, like a gift dropping from the sky: the national media on her doorstep. She ran to the door. Darrell followed.

Caroline opened the door. "Can we help you?"

The reporter asked, "We understand that you have three kids who traveled through Los Angeles yesterday on a tractor. Can you confirm the accuracy of that report?"

Listening from the attic window, the kids all held their breath, waiting to hear how their parents would respond.

The parents just looked at each other and laughed. Darrell stepped toward the camera and said with great seriousness, "Our kids were here doing farm chores all day yesterday. There's no way they were in Los Angeles."

But Caroline hastily grabbed a microphone from the reporter, stepped forward to put her face right in the camera, and said, "This basil farm here grows fresh basil for dinner tables everywhere. It's a beautiful fresh basil farm. We all work hard here. Every day. We planted the basil seeds for that basil field over there." She covered up the head of the microphone to bark an order at the cameraman. "Hey you, get a shot of our basil. Point the camera over there."

The reporter turned to his cameraman and whispered, "I was right. The parents wanted to be on TV. Turn the cameras off. Let her keep talking if you want."

Neither Caroline nor Darrell noticed that the camera equipment had been turned off. Caroline kept talking, believing she was on live TV.

The parents spent the rest of the day in front of the television, switching news channels constantly, trying to find Caroline on TV talking about their basil farm. They never found themselves on TV and complained repeatedly about the ridiculousness of the news media covering world events instead of happy things like basil.

Once the lawn was clear of reporters, the kids quickly saddled up José, Joker, and Max and rode them to the tractor pull. They did not want to miss the contest. They were sure Old Man would win with his amazing tractor.

The kids found Old Man next to his tractor wearing his old and worn cowboy hat and boots. They tied their horses to the fence line, afraid they had missed his turn in the contest.

"Just in time! It's almost my turn," said Old Man.

"We had to wait until all the reporters left," said Tony.

Old Man said, smirking, "They weren't too happy to find only an old, decrepit, rusted-out tractor."

Mitch said quietly, "It doesn't look the same. You're driving a different tractor, right?"

"Nope, same one," said Old Man.

"But we painted and polished it. Now it looks rundown again," Jovi said with disappointment. "Why?"

"It does look different, yes, but like fish scales, it can have different shades depending on how you're looking at it."

Tony stepped back to see if a different angle of the sun would make the tractor shine again. He swiped his hand across the engine hood to see if Old Man had painted it again to make it look old. Mitch examined the dashboard but could not figure out how the complex control panel could have retracted and disappeared.

A lot of farmers milled about, waiting for their turn in the tractor pull. A group of boys from neighboring towns had lined up against a fence to watch.

When Jovi, Mitch, and Tony arrived, a few of the kids along the fence snickered at them. Everyone in town had heard about the many reporters and camera crews who had arrived that morning to validate rumors of three children from New York driving a tractor through Hollywood.

Tony said to Mitch and Jovi, "It's like Brayton all over again."

"Exactly," said Mitch.

The announcer called out the next contestant's number.

"That's me, I'm up next," said Old Man.

Old Man drove his tractor to the starting line of the pull.

Jovi leaned over to Mitch. "Maybe he'll yell, 'Go!' and the tractor will win."

The other boys on the fence laughed at the bumbling tractor.

Tony said, "Let's hope so."

Old Man hooked the tractor up to a lightly loaded trailer, pulling far less weight than all the other contestants. Old Man climbed in and started the engine. The tractor pulled the trailer just a few inches before it stalled out. Old Man got out, patted the hood of the tractor as you would an old and faithful farm dog. Old Man saluted the judges, then said, "That's all, folks!"

Old Man unhitched the trailer. Then it took a bit of tinkering for Old Man to start the engine again and drive away to make room for the next contestant.

A group of boys from the neighboring county chuckled at Old Man's effort. Those boys had father-son teams with tractors that had powerful engines, fancy pinstriping on the hoods, glistening flames painted on the sides, and tractor names like Viper Vixen, Reckless Sting Ray, and Dirtball Dragon.

One of the kids, Ralph Rydum, was the next contestant, driving Dirtball Dragon. As Ralph walked to his tractor, he imitated Old Man by hunching over and walking slowly as the other boys jeered.

Some of the boys walked over to Mitch, Tony, and Jovi. Ralph's brother Ryan said, "That was quite a stunt this morning, getting all those people to fall for your tractor scam."

Another boy added, "You must've posted a big lie online saying you, like, rode that piece of junk in Hollywood?"

"I mean, like, what else would a bunch of New Yorkers do on a farm? Grow cinnamon?" mocked Ryan.

The other boys laughed.

Ryan continued the taunting. "You know that old farmer shot at some kids once."

Jovi hated the teasing and said, "Too bad he missed."

The announcer said over the loudspeaker, "That was the oldest tractor here, and it's currently in last place. Next up: Dirtball Dragon. Dirtball won regionals last year, so let's see what it's got this year!"

Tony, Jovi, and Mitch walked over to Old Man.

Tony wanted Old Man's tractor to beat Ralph Rydum's Dirtball Dragon. He jumped into the tractor seat, grabbed the steering wheel tight, and said the magic word—"Go!" But the tractor did not move.

Mitch asked Old Man, "Can't we get this tractor to go fast and show 'em?"

Old Man did not answer.

"Did you hear what they said?" asked Jovi. "They were making fun of us. And you too."

"But a lot of people weren't snickering," said Old Man.

"But those boys were," said Jovi, pointing at Ralph and Ryan.

"They are but a small few with vacant heads and hollow voices. But do know, there are a lot of wonderful people in this town."

Tony was less interested in life lessons offered by Old Man than he was in beating Ralph, so he asked, "Why won't you let the tractor win? They'd all be so jealous. Then they'd want this tractor."

Old Man said, "Boys like Ralph wouldn't choose this tractor."

"They would if they knew how fast it goes," said Mitch.

"Doubt it. Sometimes you have to give before you know what you're getting. You have to choose before you can see the choices ahead. And so it is with the tractor: you have to give and choose before you can get and see."

Then Jovi kicked the tractor like it was a horse. "Go! Giddyap, go!"

Old Man said, "It doesn't work quite like that."

"But 'go' is the magic word," said Tony.

"Actually, it's not a magic word but a voice recognition system. I programmed it to recognize your voices and mine. But some mechanisms can only be activated at the right time and on the right journey. You need to be careful."

Mitch said, "I don't understand."

"Come over tomorrow and we'll work on another project. I've got another machine that needs your attention," said Old Man.

The kids got on their horses and followed Old Man as he rode his tractor home. As they left the fair, they passed by the kids along the fence, who laughed and imitated the sounds of the weak old tractor.

Jovi could not stand the teasing anymore and charged José toward the fence. Ryan and Ralph dove over the fence to avoid being clipped by José, but after that, Jovi could not stop the horse as he galloped faster and faster. She lost control of the reins and hung on for dear life, yelling, "Stop, you dingbat!" all the way home.

Joker followed his buddy José, but Joker got frustrated that he could not keep up and stopped suddenly, put his neck down, and launched Tony into a pile of hay. Max could not be bothered, so he sauntered home with Mitch on his back, next to Old Man as he drove the bumbling, fumbling old tractor slowly home.

Mitch asked Old Man as they rode, "Did you shoot the kids that used to live in our house?"

Old Man asked, "Is that what they're saying in town?"

"Yeah, they said you shot at them."

"No. I was working on an engine and it backfired. They thought it was a gun going off. Just as well."

36

THE LEAP

Lying above the buried goats, Skarb felt a searing agony, as if it were crawling out of Earth's burning insides again. Then a soothing breeze blew over its body and it felt like thousands of gentle whispers to calm the fiery anguish. It turned to see where the boy had gone, but Bogdan was now out of sight. Curious about a creature who would run away from his master, Skarb followed the boy's scent until he was within its line of sight.

When Bogdan reached another valley far from his father, he relaxed his pace. As the sun rose, he stopped for a snack in the sunny dawn. His bloodhound was still far behind, so Bogdan did not know she was following his trail. The shepherd dog guided the other animals to follow the bloodhound, but they trailed even farther behind.

Bogdan walked for days, from valley to valley, following the sight of each defense tower that marked the next village, then hiding at night from thugs who were known to roam and pillage. He had no idea his devoted bloodhound and steadfast shepherd dog were following his trail. When Bogdan finally saw a familiar church in the next mountain valley, he breathed a sigh of relief. His grandparents' farm was only one valley beyond it. Late that afternoon Bogdan arrived at his grandparents' farmhouse.

Skarb had followed Bogdan the whole way, but at a much higher elevation to remain far away from the villages they passed. From a very high, distant mountain, Skarb watched Bogdan walk across the pasture of his grandparents' farm. Skarb zoomed in its vision to watch Bogdan's arrival.

Bogdan's grandpa saw his grandson walking across the valley, and with tearful eyes, he welcomed Bogdan with a hug that set free the boy's fears that he might not be wanted. His grandma had tears in her eyes too, and she waited patiently for her turn to give Bogdan a hero's welcome, knowing what courage it took to journey to their farm.

Skarb could hear their voices from up high, yet he felt the urge to watch up close. He ran down the mountain to reach the farm and cottage, wary of being seen by anyone. Carefully hidden, Skarb watched through the little farmhouse window as the boy's grandma fed Bogdan a warm meal, sharing what little they had. Bogdan had run out of food and was famished. He was filthy, and his clothes were tattered from the journey. His grandma gave him some of his grandpa's clothes to wear—too big for him and not enough to keep him warm.

After eating, the weary Bogdan lay down on the floor and fell quickly asleep. His grandparents covered him in the only blanket they had—their own.

Early the next morning, just before sunrise, Bogdan awoke cold and shivering—yet when he remembered where he was, he felt the warmth of safety pour over him. He heard familiar barking just outside the door, and he ran outside, surprised to see his bloodhound. The bloodhound saw her master and wagged her tail so excitedly she nearly tipped over.

The grandparents came out to see all the commotion and found Bogdan hugging his dog. He was so happy to see her again. Bogdan asked them, "Will you let me stay?"

"Yes, of course you can," said Grandpa. "I don't know how we will make ends meet, but you will bring new life to this farm."

His grandma hugged him so tightly he felt her love deep into his heart. She said, "We will always love you. We wish we could fix the broken days behind us, but we will heal the days ahead."

Skarb decided it was too great a risk to spy so close lest they set their eyes upon the watchful Greznik. It reluctantly retreated up the mountain to a safer location.

Each day, the morning chill grew colder as the sun rose later. The coming winter brewed, yet Bogdan felt the warm comfort of the sheltering arms of his grandparents. Days later, they were all delighted to see Bogdan's farm animals come over the top of the valley's ridge, herded by the shepherd dog. The big shepherd dog was so glad to find Bogdan at last.

His grandpa was getting too old to keep up with the farm, and it had started to fall apart. In the weeks that followed, Bogdan, under his grandpa's teaching, built fences to keep the animals in. Together they brought the farm into tip-top shape again. As the years passed, Bogdan's grandparents taught him everything they knew about farming and other essentials of life on a mountain farm. Bogdan took wonderful care of his grandparents, and they of him.

Every day, Bogdan hoped to see his father come up and over the valley's ridge, to write a different story for their future. But he never did. For nearly a decade, Skarb watched Bogdan and his grandparents with curiosity. Wolves often snuck up to eat a sheep or a goat, but when they saw Skarb they ran off to another valley. Skarb, without realizing it, had become a protector.

Sadly, war hit the region, and Bogdan and his grandparents fled to more peaceful areas and crossed a sea to safety. With too many people around, it was not possible for Skarb to follow. Right as Bogdan and his grandparents left the shore to new horizons, a wave of disappointment overcame Skarb. Not wanting to return to the regiment, Skarb thought of running directly into Bogdan's sight as a good way to finally disappear. But Skarb recalled how the blue stone waters were far more insufferable and excruciating when encountered than when they were contained within a legend. Perhaps evaporating from the gaze of a human was not as straightforward as it seemed.

Skarb departed the shore, leaving Bogdan and his grandparents to cross the sea alone. It retreated into the mountains, only to find humans battling each other around every bend, providing constant dangers through which Skarb found it difficult to navigate. Having nowhere else to go, Skarb resigned itself to returning to the regiment.

What it would say to explain its absence, it was not sure. It found the Greznik regiment on the beautiful Mount Elbrus. In the strange understanding of time that Grezniks have, they were only disappointed to see the strange Greznik again. But even after nine years, Jatuh was ever alert and always ready to pounce.

Jatuh said to Skarb, "You are returning with no goats in your grip, I see. Delaying, hoping I would forget the order given to you? No chance of that. Grezniks do not forget. Nor do they forgive a debt."

For Skarb's failure to bring the goats and for disobeying orders, it was punished for days on end as they used it for fighting practice and violent games that bore down cruelly upon Skarb.

At the end of the punishment, Skarb was crumbled on the ground, unable to move. Skarb did not move for days. When Skarb had regained its strength, Jatuh walked by and sneered. But Skarb stood up strongly and said, "I was gone for nine trips around the sun. No one cares if I am gone. No one cares if I walk to the waters alone. I have wandered across more regions than you. I have wandered to the waters, rivers, lakes, seas, and oceans, and I have done so alone. No other Greznik can say that, not even you. I saw the blue stone waters, and you never have. I have become more powerful than you."

Skarb's insolence deeply disturbed Jatuh. Jatuh charged toward Skarb, viciously and unexpectedly. Skarb jolted high into the air and flipped backward and darted away.

Jatuh turned and chased Skarb beyond the eyes of the regiment and across a mountain valley, into another range of mountains. Skarb ran more quickly than Jatuh expected and evaded Jatuh.

Jatuh knew the landscape well—far better than Skarb, who had been away for so long. Jatuh purposely chased Skarb up a steep mountainside path, steering it directly into a trap. Skarb sped down the other side of the mountain ridge, thinking it saw an escape. Jatuh anticipated this move and trapped Skarb against a cliff wall.

"I will devour you," growled Jatuh as it expanded its jaw, ready to eat Skarb in one bite. Jatuh charged forward to eat its most hated Greznik.

Skarb jumped vertically, grabbed hold of the cliff wall, and with impressive speed climbed up it. At the top, it ran along an upper ridgeline and then climbed higher to cross over to another mountain valley. Jatuh followed, gnarling and gnashing its teeth the whole way, pleased that Skarb was heading directly into another trap. Skarb would either run toward a heavily populated village in the valley below or fall off a large cliff into a volcanic lake. Either way, Jatuh was victorious. Skarb would disappear forever.

Skarb stopped. It had nowhere to go. The cliff edge above the lake was on one side, and the bustling village below on the other. Skarb turned to face Jatuh. Jatuh expanded its mouth, and extra fangs popped out. Mucus frothed and poured out like a faucet, then Jatuh lunged to eat Skarb. But suddenly and unexpectedly, they both heard villagers walking dangerously nearby, singing as they traveled. Both Skarb and Jatuh were about to be seen and evaporated.

Skarb turned toward the lake, looked up at the wide-open blue sky, and accepted its invitation. Skarb leaped as high and far as it could over the water and dropped like a stone into the lake.

37

HEIR EEL COMBINE

The next morning after the tractor pull, the kids were in the kitchen nook by themselves eating breakfast. Mitch, Tony, and Jovi were still disappointed that the amazing tractor had been a worthless competitor.

"I don't understand why the tractor looks like junk now," said Mitch.

"Is there any chance we dreamed it all?" asked Jovi.

"I'm beginning to think we did," said Tony.

"Or maybe Old Man hypnotized us," said Jovi.

"That can't be," said Mitch. "Those reporters really did see us. They came to find the tractor."

"I don't understand it, and I guess I don't mind because the tractor was awesome. Let's go to Old Man's farm and see what the new project is," suggested Tony.

"I'm not riding another weird machine again," said Jovi. "And there's no way I'm riding José down there. He's in big trouble for running home like lightning."

Jovi walked alongside José, while Tony and Mitch rode Joker and Max. Tony was waiting for another one of Joker's jokes, and sure enough, halfway to Old Man's farm, Joker peeled away from Max, galloped to the creek, and dropped his neck down to dump Tony in the water. But this time, Tony was ready for it. He hung on and was quick enough to take control of Joker and run him through the water and up the other side.

When they got to Old Man's farm, they entered through the barn's secret door, but he was not there. They looked all over the farm for him—in the shed, in the fields—but they could not find him. They climbed up into the haymow to look out but saw no one. By early afternoon, they gave up waiting and went home for lunch.

After lunch, he still was not there. In the high afternoon sun, they climbed up to the haymow and played King of the Haymow. One person, the king, tried to hold position on top of the large stack of hay, while the others tried to topple the king. Jovi was often shoved off the bale to tumble downward.

"No fair! You're bigger than me!" said Jovi.

"You need to learn how to fight better, Jovi!" Tony said triumphantly, taking his place as King of the Haymow.

Mitch snuck up from behind and knocked Tony off. "Not king anymore." But then the stacks of hay gave way, and Mitch tumbled down too.

Jovi laughed and cheered as she stole the position of king, but suddenly they went silent when they heard a loud rumbling sound bumping down the dirt road. They looked out and saw Old Man coming toward them on a large farm machine they had never seen before.

"What is *that*?" asked Mitch.

"It's huge! Let's go!" said Tony, scurrying down the ladder to get outside.

Old Man was driving a slow-moving tractor combine. They had never seen any piece of farm machinery that big. Old Man waved at them as he drove the tractor into the barn and climbed out.

Tony asked Old Man, "What is that?"

"It's a tractor combine. Not to be confused with a tractor. Do you know what a tractor combine does?"

The kids shook their heads.

"I'm guessing most New Yorkers have no clue. A combine combines. Makes sense, right?"

"Uh, yeah, I guess so," said Mitch. He whispered to check if Tony or Jovi knew what a combine combines.

"No whispering in here. The word *combine* has two pronunciations. One is pronounced like in this sentence—'I combine my coffee with a bit of sugar and cream in the morning.' But a tractor combine is pronounced in a way where *com* rhymes with the name *Tom*. A 'tractor *combine*' combines harvesting steps that used to be done separately. This tractor combine has what's called a corn head on the front. The corn head cuts the cornstalk, separates the ear from the stalk, shucks it, then shells the kernels from the cob. The country can't feed all those New Yorkers without machines like this. This combine is just like any other combine, but it also has many more capabilities that you need to learn to use."

He pointed to the wide and tall set of floor-to-ceiling blueprint drawers and said, "Go find the blueprints and take them out."

There were many drawers along the wall, and Jovi asked, "Which drawer has the right blueprints?"

Old Man wrote the drawer label on a piece of scrap paper: *Heir Eel Combine.*

The kids started at the leftmost column of drawers and moved to the right, looking for the "Heir Eel Combine" label. They found it in the middle column of drawers, but it was the very top drawer and they could not reach it. Mitch stood on top of a tall workbench. Tony climbed onto Mitch's shoulders, and Jovi climbed up on the bench, then onto Mitch and up and onto Tony's shoulders.

From the top of Tony's shoulders, Jovi could just barely reach the top drawer to open it. As she pulled the blueprints out, the bench underneath them wobbled slightly, then one of the legs on the workbench broke. To avoid crashing dangerously to the floor, Jovi let go of the blueprints and grabbed hold of a rafter—proving, once again, why she was called Monkey Jo. She put one leg over the rafter and safely pulled herself up. Tony and Mitch fell on bales of hay.

Old Man had a huge fan running in the barn, so when Jovi let go of the blueprints, they blew in every direction. Some sheets landed on rafters. Others stuck to the dirty, sticky walls. Some blew to the other side of the barn and landed under benches and on top of equipment. One sheet was about to blow into the smelting furnace, but Mitch ran forward and caught it just in time.

"Good save!" said Old Man.

Jovi was stuck way up high in the middle of the barn, clinging to the rafter.

"We need to get you down," said Old Man.

"Jovi can climb anything. She'll get down by herself," Mitch teased. Clearly there was no way for Jovi to get down.

"Blockhead! I can't get down from here!"

"Enough of that, kids," said Old Man. "Mitch, Tony, stack up hay bales underneath Jovi until she can safely jump."

When she let go, she landed a little off center, and the entire pile came crashing down, making a mess.

"Restack the hay, kids. Then gather up all the pages of the blueprints and bring them over," said Old Man.

The kids restacked the bales, gathered the pages, and put them in order. Old Man said, "Just like the tractor, these instructions are encoded with the same secret language. But I decoded them already for you. The combine has special features, and these blueprints are the instruction manual. But we'd better put the pages in order first."

After the pages were ordered, Old Man said, "Now it's time to read the instructions from beginning to end and memorize them all."

The kids each grabbed some of the pages and looked through them, but the manual was long and extremely detailed. The kids looked at each other and had the same thought: *Memorizing the massive manual will take forever.* Old Man sensed their reluctance to try.

"Just start on page one," said Old Man.

Jovi had some trepidation about what this machine had in store for them, but the first page intrigued her. Surprisingly, it talked about navigating in high winds.

Mitch was puzzled when he ran across instructions for how to take off in fog.

Tony saw the page describing the instrument panel. There were instructions applicable to harvesting corn, but then the instructions transitioned into how to split the corn head in two and convert it to wings.

It did not take long for them to realize that this tractor combine was no ordinary combine.

Tony leaned over to Mitch and said quietly, "I think this combine might be even more bizarre than the tractor."

Mitch agreed.

Jovi said, "Why would we be traveling through clouds when harvesting corn?"

Mitch turned to Old Man and asked, "Does this combine fly?"

"Yes, and that's why it's called the Heir Eel Combine. It's spelled oddly, but it's really an aerial combine. It flies!" said Old Man.

Mitch looked around the barn and said, "This place is nuts."

Tony looked at the combine and thought, *There is no way that thing can fly.*

38

SAVING A SECRET

As soon as Skarb jumped, Jatuh fled immediately to avoid being seen by the villagers and did not actually witness Skarb hitting the water. Jatuh ran headlong down the mountain and rejoined the regiment, relishing that Skarb was finally gone. But after leaping, Skarb hit the water and shot its body downward like a torpedo. It crash-landed at the bottom of the lake near an underwater cave and crawled in.

Skarb crawled along the bottom of the lake to the opposite side before poking its snout out of the water. Carefully, it also lifted its extra eye out of the water to look around. Neither Jatuh nor the villagers were nearby, so Skarb crawled out of the water and ran off to hide.

That night, like all others, every circle leader reported to Boshlek which, if any, Grezniks from their circle dissolved or exploded that day. This time, Jatuh savored the opportunity to report the demise of Skarb. "The seven-legged 401^5 disappeared today. The wretch fell into a lake and dissolved. It disappeared from its own careless error. Villagers were walking toward us, and it panicked and foolishly jumped off a cliff into the water. But I, more wisely, ran the other way and easily escaped their view."

From out of nowhere, Skarb jumped alongside Boshlek, surprising Jatuh. Skarb stepped in front of Jatuh and said, "Eternal Commander, my circle leader has made its own careless error: it reported an inaccurate account of today's events. I never fell into the lake. I did jump, but I landed exactly at the edge of the lake. Not even one toe went into the water."

Skarb walked away with a proud stride and its snout casually flopping about.

Jatuh winced in puzzlement. That was not what happened. Although Jatuh did not see Skarb fall in, it saw Skarb falling directly over the water. Skarb's explanation was impossible.

Boshlek turned to Jatuh and said, "Tell me again what happened today."

"I punished 401[5] for straying. I charged it up the mountain pass, but villagers came dangerously near. To avoid being seen, the careless, incompetent fool jumped off the cliff. The villagers were nearly upon us. I could not stay to see where it landed. I more wisely fled the other way."

"It's you who is careless and incompetent," said Boshlek. "You don't have control of your circle."

Jatuh defended itself. "The seven-legger wastes our time. And remember, no circle leader is any nearer to finding the stones than I am. They all dig more sloppily, incompetently, and lose Grezniks far more often than I. And everyone knows I am a superior Greznik."

"There are no uniquely qualified Grezniks. You are all the same. A Greznik that has not found the stones is no better than any other that has not found the stones. *Find them!*"

Boshlek kicked Jatuh away and sent it flying to crash down on its circle. Jatuh landed painfully, seething in hatred for Eternal Commander.

Over the centuries, the regiment continued with its wandering and battling existence while Skarb straggled and no one cared, no one looked. As Skarb hid and observed, it learned more quickly when dangers were nearby such as humans approaching their position, lurking red pandas, and ships sailing too near to the regiment's ocean crossings. It reported these risks, quietly and without notice, to Boshlek. Boshlek at first doubted its whisperings, but then Skarb's warnings proved accurate. Slowly over the years, Skarb became an invaluable source of information for Boshlek. As the Grezniks wandered into the twentieth century, people traveled more readily and the wars of the world migrated people in unexpected directions, making it more difficult for the Grezniks to avoid them. To retain their secrecy, Boshlek became more reliant on Skarb's helpful information. Unbeknownst to Jatuh, Skarb became important.

39

A DAUNTING INVITATION

The kids started the tractor combine project exactly as Old Man suggested—studying page one. They placed the first page of the decoded instructions on top of a big barrel so they could review it with the combine right in front of them.

Mitch took a deep breath and said, "Okay, ready? Let's try."

Jovi read the instructions out loud as Mitch and Tony matched up the instructions with the equipment. They were very methodical and rotated duties as they progressed through the manual.

After reviewing the complete set of instructions from beginning to end, they reported to Old Man that they had finished.

Mitch asked, "Can you take us on a flight?"

"Not until you have memorized every single page of the instruction manual."

"Are you kidding me? There's like a million pages

here!" yelped Jovi, discouraged. "I'm not good at memorizing like Mitch."

"It's not a million pages, Jovi," said Mitch. Yet he was equally overwhelmed by the prospect of memorizing all the pages and mumbled, "But it is too many."

"I think you can do it," said Old Man. "We'll go flying when you're done. I just want you to understand how it works before you fly in it. There are some repeated patterns and rules when flying this aircraft, and once you recognize them and have them down pat, memorizing it all will go quickly. I promise you."

They reluctantly buckled down and started to memorize but did not really believe they could ever get through it. They got impatient and sped up a bit, but Old Man noticed the increased speed. "Slow down," he said. "You aren't learning it as well when you go that fast. You absolutely need to have every little piece memorized."

The kids went through the entire manual a number of times and picked up on the patterns. The memorizing went more quickly, and sooner than expected, they had memorized every detail.

The next day started as a cloudy, misty morning, but it had worked its way into a full rain. The kids ate a big breakfast then told their parents they were leaving again to work on Old Man's farm.

"That's great he has so much work for you to do," said Darrell.

"He's paying you, right?" said Caroline, more doubtfully.

Tony, always quick on his feet, said, "He's teaching us how to farm. Free education. Summer school."

The rain kept the parents inside where they shopped online for garden boots and matching rain jackets. They also researched recipes for what do with piles of grapes, on the chance they might someday have piles of grapes.

The kids rode their horses down to Old Man's farm in the rain. They found him in the barn at a small gas burner, cracking an egg into coffee grounds and stirring the egg in.

"What are you making?" asked Jovi.

"Egg coffee. Crack an egg, mix it in with grounds, and boil it. It's really good, if you like coffee."

His three dogs were at his ankles begging for their breakfast.

"Tony, can you feed my little rascals here? The food is in that barrel in the corner."

Mitch asked, "We've memorized everything. Now can we take the combine for a flight?"

"Are you sure you've memorized all the instructions?" Old Man asked.

"Yes, every page; just ask us a question," said Mitch.

Old Man peppered them with questions about flying the aircraft—how to work the gauges, controls, monitors, wings, and acceleration. The kids answered every question perfectly and showed him which controls split the front corn head and how the two pieces slid back to form the wings. They explained how the corn head sensors turned into wind measurements to provide flight feedback, how the big wheels worked as landing gear, and how the cabin could expand to create a large cargo hold, and how the back of the combine extended to convert into the tail of the plane.

Tony said, "It can also hover like the osprey aircraft."

"But it's exceptionally more stable and far more powerful," added Old Man. "Are you sure you've memorized every single page?"

Jovi nodded her head yes. "Every page!"

"Humph," said Old Man as he sat down on a hay bale, sipped his coffee, and rubbed his chin.

After a while, he stood up and said, "I can't believe I'm saying this, but I think today is the day to take this for a flight."

Tony jumped up excitedly. "Where should we fly it to?"

Old Man said, "Anywhere you want to."

Jovi climbed in first with a boost from Mitch. Then Mitch and Tony got in.

They waited for Old Man to get into the combine too, but he just sipped his egg coffee.

"Are we going now?" asked Tony.

"Yup, you're ready."

"But you're going to fly it with us, right?" asked Mitch.

"I'm not going with you. This is a solo flight," said Old Man.

Old Man stocked the combine with pemmican and filled the canteens. He prepared three thermoses full of hot soup for when the cabin got chilly at high altitudes. He put those in the back. He secured some fishing poles to the side and said, "Remember, you can hover in this craft. I'm strapping on these poles so if you want to hover over a lake, drop a line, and catch some fish, you'll have the gear. Now you're ready. Confirm your roles in flight."

Jovi said, "No need to put those poles on. I don't even fish on the ground. There's no way I'm fishing from a flying farm machine. Because I'm not going this time."

Old Man ignored her comments and secured the poles tightly along the side. Then he walked around the combine to complete one last equipment check and confirm that the kids had all the right gear available for high-altitude flying.

"We thought you were going with us," said Mitch, who never imagined they would go flying by themselves.

"This is a little irresponsible, don't you think?" said Tony. "Three kids flying a combine?"

"It's not irresponsible when you're trained for the tiniest of details," said Old Man. "Check your equipment and get ready to fly."

Jovi started to climb down. "Oh no, I'm not doing this. I got stuck driving the tractor last time. I'm not going this time."

Mitch and Tony pretended they were not scared, but they had no intention of flying by themselves either. They, too, started to get down from the tractor.

"No climbing down. Get back in your position. You know what to do. Just pretend you're going to fly and tell me what you'd do."

"Don't say the magic word. I don't want to fly it," whispered Jovi to her brothers as they climbed back in.

Old Man said, "This one doesn't run on magic words. It runs on a key. Turn the key."

"You really think we can do this?" asked Mitch. "It's kind of crazy."

"A lot crazy," Tony said emphatically.

"You survived the tractor run, and you didn't memorize those instructions. I promise you can do this. Just start the engine, Mitch," said Old Man.

Mitch turned the key. The engine rumbled, and the dashboard lit up with even more controls than a 747 cockpit.

"Wow. That's a lot of lights and buttons and dials," said Jovi.

Tony recognized the controls from the instructions and got excited to try them out. The big barn door opened before them. The rainy morning clouds had retreated, and the sun shone down on the wet grass. They looked out to the boundless blue sky and the distant, wide-open horizon calling them forward.

Old Man pointed to the barn door. "Drive out of here, kids. Have a great time."

The kids had waited with excited anticipation for a fun adventure in a flying farm machine. But all of them had pictured Old Man in the cockpit. With an unmapped expedition stretched out before them, the four walls of the barn felt unexpectedly comforting, and the blue-sky horizon a daunting invitation, one simply too big to accept.

40

DIG. FIND. LOSE.

In the 1940s, the regiment traveled from island to island in the Pacific in their search for the stones. With a world at war, the Grezniks' efforts were riddled with difficulties. They zigzagged around tank battles and dodged naval and air battles. Airplanes dropped like tears into the ocean, and ships sank with the dreams of the lost taken with them. Worries hung like curtains over many people's hearts, and dark battle clouds brewed on the distant horizon.

The Japanese invaded Papua New Guinea, and a bewildered people wondered why the crosshairs of evil wove their battles into their magnificent landscape. Rivers carried their tears out to sea as the Grezniks, blind and oblivious to the sorrows of a great war, descended upon Papua New Guinea. The Grezniks hid deep inside the rain forest, far away from villages and removed from the risk of being seen. They gathered in their fighting circles and prepared for another phase of their battle plan to defeat the Tukors and discover the blue stones.

Jatuh was reluctant to start another search and instead held nothing but seething dissatisfaction and anger inside. Jatuh was fed up. No changes to techniques, no changes to strategies, and thus no blue stones. No escape from their dreaded cage.

The more Jatuh thought about the years and years of failed endeavors, more and more doubt crept into its thoughts: *Dig. Find. Lose. Dig. Find. Lose. Dig. Find. Lose. That's all we do. And it must stop. If I were Eternal Commander, we would have succeeded by now!*

As Jatuh's anger seethed, Boshlek ordered the circles to begin another search for the blue stones within Papua New Guinea's splendid landscape. As they searched high and low, Skarb sauntered from hilltop to hilltop investigating the details of abandoned volcanoes, searching for clues to the stones, and keeping an eye out for planes and other dangers of an increasingly modern world.

Down the steep slopes and far away from the Grezniks, a Glyphis shark swam along the muddy river edge of a narrow tributary deep inside the beautiful rain forests of Papua New Guinea. The freshwater shark followed the bottom of a homemade wooden outrigger canoe floating above him. He watched the paddle dip in for each stroke and swam unseen under the drip, drip, drip coming off the paddle after each stroke.

A boy, Tagoga, paddled the long and thin outrigger slowly along the river's edge. He had been paddling since the early morning and had traveled deep into the rain forest, down an unknown vein of the river, and was now far from his family and far from the war's invaders. The only fish he wanted to catch was the elusive Glyphis shark, but the shark avoided his hook every time. For many days, Tagoga—determined to catch it—paddled to where he once saw the shark. Little did Tagoga know the Glyphis shark was named Geduld. And every time Tagoga paddled to this quiet pool of water, deep inside the middle of Papua New Guinea, Geduld followed him to protect him.

Geduld purposefully followed Tagoga's boat unseen and kept a careful eye on the boy's fishing line. Tagoga had tried all morning to catch the shark and decided to give up for the day. Too hot and weary to paddle all the way home in the afternoon sun, he paddled under the shade of a tree whose foliage leaned protectively over the water. He tied his boat to the shore, pulled in his line, and ate a snack. He picked several wide, three-feet-long leaves from a nearby tree. Tagoga lay down in the bottom of the canoe, and across the gunnels he placed the big leaves for extra shade and fell sound asleep underneath them.

Tagoga did not wake when a Bosavi silky cuscus, a sweet and furry little creature, walked to the shoreline and toward his canoe. Silky Cuscus climbed up onto Tagoga's paddle, which had one end resting on the boat and the other on the shore. Silky walked along the paddle and into the canoe to sniff at Tagoga's feet and eat some of his snack. Tagoga did not wake up as Silky looked over the gunnel of the canoe and down into the water to see Geduld swimming back and forth under the boat. Silky raised her head as if she had heard something deep in the forest. She walked back along the paddle and into the forest to head back toward Mount Bosavi, a dormant volcanic crater where she lived.

As Silky walked back into the rain forest, she felt creatures walking nearby. By the patterns of their steps, she knew they were Grezniks—Jatuh and its circle were headed right for her. To hide, she quickly dove under large fallen leaves. Silky held her breath and lay perfectly still. The Grezniks stopped near her hiding place to eat dead and decaying larvae.

Normally Grezniks can smell a creature from a great distance and instantly know exactly where that creature is. However, Silky was extremely adept at traveling undetected by Grezniks. But also, Jatuh was not paying close attention and thus neither was its circle. Jatuh was entirely focused on the pointlessness of launching another phase of the Great Search without a revised strategy.

Jatuh examined its own circle members as they ate and decided they were all worthless and wasted weaklings. It became convinced not only that the strategies of the Great Search were inadequate, but also that its own fighting circle was ineffective.

Jatuh thought, *If only I had a better fighting circle, I would have found the stones by now. This circle is worthless.*

Jatuh heard water flowing nearby and plotted how to walk its circle members into the water, dissolve them all, and get an entirely new circle assigned. As it listened to the nearby stream, Jatuh was proud of its own steadfast obedience. It had always heeded Boshlek's warning to never visit the water's edge alone. But this time, in its disgruntled mood, Jatuh also remembered what Skarb had said hundreds of years earlier: the Voices of Proznia and the dangers of blue waters were all just a big lie.

I can travel to the waters alone. What is the worst that can happen—I see the stones? Suppose 401^5 really did see the blue stones. Even if it did, it would be far too incompetent to get them. But I am not so pathetic. If I saw the stones, I could capture them. I can walk to the water's edge and look for the stones, and if something goes wrong, I will just run away fast enough.

The more Jatuh pondered the possibilities, the more convinced it became that Boshlek created the big lie to prevent Grezniks from ever finding and controlling the real power on their own.

And if I find the stones, all the Grezniks will obey my orders only and bow to my feet! The control will be mine!

Doubts crept further into Jatuh's thoughts, and its delusions of securing the stones for itself grew stronger and stronger. Jatuh's disgruntled footsteps were felt by the Voices of Proznia, still trapped within the waters. The Voices believed they could make Jatuh an agent of their freedom, so they began to stir and disturb the river current.

Only Jatuh could hear the waters rippling louder and louder, like soothing vibrations of strings singing out. Jatuh could not resist the enticing sound of the waters and walked to the river's shore. Its circle members bounded in front of their leader to block and stop it from traveling to the shore alone.

"There's nothing but water ahead, and you cannot go there alone," said one member of Jatuh's circle.

Jatuh ferociously growled at its circle and bit several of them. "Stay here or I will eat you all! Never forget, you are all easily replaced!"

Its circle jumped back, cowered, and bowed submissively to protect themselves from their leader's attack. Over many years, they had watched what Jatuh had done to Skarb, and they did not want to be the new recipients of that brutality.

Jatuh heard the nearby river waters lapping on the shore and felt a magnetic pull to travel to the water's edge alone. Jatuh turned back to its circle and lied to them. "You all stay here," it said. "I am not going to the waters. I am leaving to speak to Eternal Commander."

Fearing that Jatuh might attack or punish them, the circle did not refute or question their leader. Instead, they walked deeper into the forest, started eating again, and let Jatuh go on its way unhindered. Because of their cowardice, Jatuh walked toward the direction of Boshlek, but when far enough away, it took a switchback and walked silently to the river's edge. But the quiet steps of the scheming malcontent were felt deep inside the river waters and awoke what was trapped within.

41

CHECK OR HOLD?

Mitch, Tony, and Jovi sat in the tractor combine with the dashboard controls all lit up as Old Man gestured for them to drive forward. The barn door was open ahead of them, the engine was running, and the sky was a deep, inviting blue. The humid air stood still, but the formidable headwinds of fear held them back.

Jovi procrastinated their departure by asking Old Man, "Does this combine need to stay a secret too?"

"Definitely. But no one would believe that it flies even if you told them. But don't," said Old Man.

"Then I don't think we should go. Remember, I'm super terrible at keeping secrets. And we didn't exactly keep it a secret last time."

"And we wouldn't want to attract a bunch of reporters again," added Mitch.

"This time you won't," Old Man said calmly as he poured a generous amount of sugar into his egg coffee. "Drive out of the barn, then decide."

Tony looked at all the lights and dials and colors on the controls and said to Old Man, "I've played video games, but this is seriously way more complicated than anything I've ever used. I think you should take us out on a training flight at least."

Mitch added, "I agree, a training flight would be smart."

Jovi was emphatic. "Kids don't fly airplanes. A nine-year-old is *not* allowed to fly without a license."

"If this were a normal airplane, I'd say you should be older and go to flight school. Then go on multiple training flights with an experienced, licensed pilot. But this just isn't a normal airplane. It's a flying tractor combine. No need to stay home doubting yourself. Go on. You're ready. At least just drive it out of the barn."

Mitch was in the cabin's driver seat, with Jovi in the middle and Tony next to Jovi.

Tony said quietly, "Mitch, go ahead."

Mitch nervously drove it out of the barn, as if they were driving a regular combine.

Tony reviewed the instrument panel meticulously, confirming that he remembered what everything on the panel controlled.

One of the neighboring farmers drove by in his truck and waved his hand casually, wondering why three kids were driving a combine when harvest season had not yet arrived. The farmer just shrugged it off and drove on by.

Jovi waved as if it were just a normal day at the farm for them, riding down a dirt road in a huge piece of farm equipment.

When no one was looking and everything was quiet, the kids checked with each other.

Tony got his fearless glare in his eyes. "Let's do it. He wouldn't be wrong, would he?"

Jovi surprised even herself and said, "Mitch, go for it."

"Check or hold?" asked Mitch.

"Check!" answered Jovi and Tony.

They counted together, "One, two, three!"

Mitch increased the engine power and monitored the gauges. Jovi launched the sequence for converting the corn head into the wings. Tony checked that the controls were in working order and reviewed the sequence for takeoff. Jovi confirmed when the wings were fully engaged. The tail expanded, and out popped a long pole—at the end of which unfurled a large United States flag.

"Mitch, the controls are ready for takeoff. Check or hold?" said Tony.

Mitch reviewed the gauges one more time and answered, "Check."

Mitch asked, "Jovi, are the wings locked and loaded?"

"Both wings ready," said Jovi.

Tony said, "Let's go. Final check or hold?"

They all said, "Check!"

Mitch initiated the takeoff sequence. Everything went off without a hitch. The aerial combine accelerated down the dirt road faster than a jet taking off from an aircraft carrier. The speed caused the kids to freeze with fear.

But then Jovi cheered at the top of her lungs, "Go, Bosonataski-Fishengardet!"

They snapped out of it and took control. They all focused intently on the equipment, checked controls, and communicated to each other back and forth. At the end of the road, the aerial combine lifted, and the wheels were off the ground.

They cheered and waved at Old Man. He waved back, breathing a sigh of relief that they had accepted the invitation.

Old Man shouted up to them, "Have a great flight!"

"We did it!" said Mitch, looking down at the farm from above.

Their departure route flew the plane right over their farmhouse, above the living room window where their mom and dad were reading on the couch. Their parents heard the noise and went to the window.

Caroline said, "Look, honey, there's a plane flying right out our window."

Darrell said, "Wow, it's flying low."

Caroline looked up again and said, "The pilot sure looks like Mitch. I need some coffee. All this open land. I'm just not used to it. It's making me see things." She walked into the kitchen and made herself a latte.

After buzzing their house, the kids flew up higher and circled the county. Mitch loved baseball, so they flew over a few small-town baseball games and a professional stadium. Then they headed up to the Badlands, down toward St. Louis, Missouri, where they flew through the St. Louis Gateway Arch, and over Kentucky and Tennessee.

Old Man had put stacks of old, musty encyclopedias in the back to ensure good weight balance. As they flew over historical areas, Mitch reached back and grabbed the volume they needed to read about each location. When they flew over Pennsylvania, they buzzed down over Carpenters' Hall in Philadelphia where the Continental Congress met in 1774. Then Independence Hall and over to Gettysburg. Their Manhattan school required that every student memorize the Gettysburg Address, and the kids recited a portion of it together as they circled the battleground: *The world will little note, nor long remember what we say here, but it can never forget what they did here. It is for us the living, rather, to be dedicated here to the unfinished work which they who fought here have thus far so nobly advanced. It is rather for us to be here dedicated to the great task remaining before us ~ that from these honored dead we take increased devotion to that cause for which they gave the last full measure of devotion ~ that we here highly resolve that these dead shall not have died in vain ~ that this nation, under God, shall have a new birth of freedom ~ and that government of the people, by the people, for the people, shall not perish from the earth.*

"Let's go to some Revolutionary War sites," said Tony.

"Which one?" asked Mitch.

Jovi had just studied the war and was excited by the idea. She said, "Let's go to Valley Forge. The Paul Revere House and Old North Church. Boston Harbor. Let's do them all!" She was thrilled to fly over various historical sites and see history from the sky.

They flew down to DC and over the Potomac River,

saw the Vietnam Memorial, and waved at the Pentagon, all the while their stars and stripes whipping in the wind.

They flew up to Maine and cut over to Quebec, then up toward Labrador Sea where they followed the route through the Arctic's Northwest Passage taken by an American sailing vessel called Cloud Nine. After reaching the western end of the Northwest Passage, they turned south over the Beaufort Sea and then over to Alaska.

As they crossed over Alaska, they flew in and out of clouds and completely missed seeing the Grezniks traveling wickedly fast across the terrain. From above, the Grezniks looked like schools of sardines, swishing and swirling together across the landscape, but the kids had no idea the regiment was running below their flight path. As soon as the Grezniks saw the aircraft, they flattened themselves on the ground.

"Let's go see Pearl Harbor," said Mitch.

"Do you really think we can fly that far over the ocean?" asked Tony.

"Let's go for it," said Mitch who had always wanted to see the USS *Arizona* Memorial, especially from the sky. Their family had been to Hawaii but their parents were always socializing at the golf club and had little to no interest in history. They flew over the memorial and saw the remains of the sunken battleship in the waters. For Mitch, it was a dream come true.

They flew back up to the Pacific Coast toward San Diego, where they flew under the San Diego–Coronado Bridge, then over the beautiful Baja Peninsula, the Gulf of

California, and down to the Panama Canal. But just like the tractor, some people tried to take a picture of the aerial combine, but nothing would show up on the image. The aircraft did not show up on the major international airports' radar, nor the military's radar. People reported there was a strange airplane flying in the sky, but no one could register any of its movements. When people called the authorities to report an odd-shaped airplane tearing through the sky, the authorities checked their monitors, saw nothing, then asked the callers not to abuse and waste their time with false reports.

▲ ▲ ▲

Back at the farm, Old Man climbed up a ladder to reach some tools hung high on the wall of the barn. At the top of the ladder, he saw one page of the blueprints that had fallen behind a tall tool cabinet where he stored his glassblowing tools. The page had fallen so far down, he had to use long tongs to reach behind the cabinet and rescue the page.

Old Man was upset to realize that the page contained the instructions on how to land the flying tractor combine. That meant Mitch, Tony, and Jovi never learned how to land the aircraft. He was disappointed with himself for not asking them if they knew how to land. He sat down on a bale of hay, troubled and worried by his discovery. He worried about an injurious crash and feared for their safety. Yet also, those three children—who had unexpectedly arrived on Mr. Charlie's farm—were the last hope for rescuing Old Man himself.

42

SILKY AND WOOLLY

When Jatuh stepped away from its circle to walk to the waters, Skarb was far away, exploring the beautiful depths of Papua New Guinea's enchanting Bosavi Crater. As Skarb ran down the steep crater, a Bosavi woolly rat felt the Greznik speed by. He jumped to his feet and told his wife and kids to hide deep within the thick foliage. More Grezniks were surely nearby, and Woolly Rat prayed that his family would stay safe. Then he ran off to warn others. Woolly found Silky carefully following another Greznik, Jatuh, who was traveling solo to the water's edge.

Silky hoped Geduld the Glyphis shark was still swimming under Tagoga's outrigger canoe. Geduld was, in fact, still there, and he was the first to feel the Voices stirring deep below him. Little bubbles formed along the muddy bottom, and Geduld braced for the coming torrent.

The bubbles rose up from under the mud, moved toward each other, and whirled violently. The bubbles swirled the current faster and faster, creating a powerful force near the bottom of the river. The force was so strong that Geduld struggled to swim. Yet Tagoga's boat was safely in an eddy, and he lay there sleeping, unaware of the currents boiling up nearby.

Geduld used all his strength to swim directly into the bubbles, bursting as many of them as he could to weaken the strengthening current. Despite his best efforts, the current swirled savagely, more bubbles took form and rose together, and the Voices of Proznia reached the surface.

The Voices sang to Jatuh, each with a unique, enticing sound. "Go to the water's edge. The stones are waiting for you."

Jatuh liked hearing the lovely Voices and stopped walking to listen. The Voices continued singing and inviting Jatuh to the river.

Geduld swam under Tagoga's canoe and banged his tail on the bottom, hard enough to make a loud *whack!* sound against the boat and nearly tip it over.

Tagoga woke up with a start, steadied the canoe, and saw Geduld dart away quickly. The sight of the shark so close to his canoe excited Tagoga. He reached forward in the canoe for his fishing pole, but as he grabbed it, he saw Jatuh walk to the shoreline. Jatuh was too enamored and distracted by the Voices to notice Tagoga there.

Tagoga had never seen anything so frightening in his life. He ducked back down in his boat and hid under the big leaves.

When Tagoga's eyes did not evaporate the Greznik, Geduld's hunch was confirmed: Tagoga had become a Tukor without even knowing such a person existed.

The bubbles on the water's surface turned into hundreds upon hundreds of raindrops that defied gravity and lifted up and out of the water. The water droplets took the shape of many beautiful, alluring eyes that drifted upward and hid amid the foliage that overhung the river.

When Jatuh neared the shoreline, the sun was high in the sky, and the muddy water had turned a crystal blue. The sun beat down on the water and revealed entrancing blue stones covering the river bottom. Jatuh could not take its eyes off the stunning blue.

The inviting eyes swarmed around Jatuh and lured the Greznik forward. They changed into birds, many blue-faced honeyeaters, that flew gracefully and chattered sweetly above Jatuh. "The blue water is so beautiful, isn't it? Do not believe the lies of the past. You are the most important Greznik, and we have chosen you. Come to us and you will prove that you are different from every other Greznik—invincible and strong, powerful and masterful. And we will give you the stones. You will have all the strength. Everyone will obey you. Your commander will be no more. It is you, the important one, who is destined to have the power."

Jatuh looked up longingly at the blue-faced honeyeaters, enamored by their flattery. Their blue faces sparkled as though blue stones were darting across the sky.

Silky stepped to the shoreline and warned Jatuh, "Do not listen to them!"

"You soft and silky wobbler," mocked Jatuh. "You just do not want me to be strong and powerful because you are weak and meek."

The honeyeaters circled around Jatuh. "You are so wise. Silky Cuscus and Woolly Rat are mere simpletons. They are nothing compared to your intelligence and strength. You need not listen to their jealous talk. Come to us. Reach for the beautiful blue. You can become anything. The stones will be yours."

Woolly said, "Please walk away from the Voices. Close your ears to their songs. Close your eyes to their sight. You must."

Suddenly many birds of paradise flew out of the rain forest, perched on branches that hung over the dazzling pool of water, and displayed their magnificent plumage. They sang to Jatuh, "Do not listen to those deceiving birds. They are not real honeyeaters. They are the Voices of Proznia and—"

The blue-faced honeyeaters, with wings as sharp as broken glass, flew fiercely at the birds of paradise and sliced their wings. Many birds of paradise fell to the ground, broken and bleeding. Yet they fought through the pain, and sang to Jatuh, "Do not step in the water. Do not drink the water. The Voices will betray you."

"Do not listen to them," said the Voices to Jatuh. "Creatures of Earth are not to be trusted. They are your enemy. But you can trust us. We are like you. Drink of this water and you will be powerful. You will be the great ruler!"

Against its instincts and against everything it had been taught, Jatuh believed the Voices and unconsciously stepped even closer to the water.

Silky and Woolly risked their lives to nip at Jatuh's legs,

hoping to distract the Greznik. But Jatuh kicked them back, breaking Woolly's leg and knocking Silky unconscious.

Jatuh followed the beautiful birds forward and stepped into the sparkling river. The water crawled up its legs like worms, but Jatuh did not notice and felt soothed. Across the water was a steep riverbank, and water suddenly gushed forth from a cave up high and fell to the river as a gorgeous waterfall. Jatuh wanted to swim to the waterfall and bathe in the currents. Jatuh took another step forward.

The Voices sang, "You are the strong one. Drink of the sparkling waters. Drink of the beautiful blue. And swim to the waterfall."

Jatuh put its snout next to the water to drink. Geduld jumped out of the thick water and bit the Greznik's snout as it leaned forward to take a drink, but Jatuh swung its claws at Geduld and sliced open its skin. The surprise shark attack successfully jolted Jatuh out of its stupor. It looked down and saw its feet in the false waters and realized its error. It lifted its head abruptly and tried to step back, but the blue water was a thick, pale-blue putty, and Jatuh could not pull its feet out.

"Let go of me!" said Jatuh. "I am not meant to drink of the stone's water."

The Voices sang soothingly, "Why do you believe such lies? Nothing but lies!"

Jatuh tried again to step away but could not. "Let me out! Grezniks never drink, and I will not."

The Voices continued, "You are the most intelligent, the most important, the worthiest of all to receive the stones. Go on. Quench your thirst. And have the stones. The stones are for you and you alone!"

The birds of paradise said to Jatuh, "If you close your eyes, you can get out before it's too late."

Jatuh writhed but did not turn its eyes away.

Woolly said, "Turn your gaze away from the blue and step back!"

The water flowed easily again, and the blue stones glistened under the water. Jatuh drooled at the prospect of having them for itself. It put its head down toward the water. The sparkling blue stones drifted Jatuh into a trance as it dreamed of bringing the stones to the regiment. *I could have all the control and walk Boshlek into the sea and rule the regiment. No more trying to prove myself. No more searching and searching. I could escape this awful earthly trap and obliterate everything and everyone.*

Silky struggled to get back on her feet and said quietly, "Please, my friend, do not do this. Avert your eyes and look to me."

Jatuh said to the sweet and furry little Silky, "I am not your friend, you disgusting enemy of mine! I do not listen to you!"

"The Voices are a greater enemy than I could ever be," said Silky. "Do not drink, or you will give them form. You will have the enemy inside you."

Jatuh picked up Silky and threw her into the forest. Then it put its snout in the waters, and drank and drank and drank. Woolly screeched in anguish and shouted, "Spin your eyes away!"

But Jatuh chose not to hear anything as it stared lustfully at the beautiful blue and swallowed the delicious waters, determined to reach the stones. Once Jatuh started drinking, it could not stop.

43

CROP CIRCLES

The kids enjoyed their flying adventure but had no idea that they had triggered all the nation's security controls. Alerts about a stealth aircraft flying around the country had gone up the chain of command of every arm of the US military. Military personnel tried unsuccessfully to locate the aircraft on their monitoring equipment.

A United States Marine Corps general phoned a sergeant major.

The general asked, "I hear this aircraft is untraceable. But have you seen it?"

The sergeant major responded, "Yes, sir. I saw it fly by. Many people have. And we've tried to identify this aircraft by all means possible, but we've been unsuccessful."

The general said, "And you've tried to follow it?"

"Nothing can catch up to it. Even our fastest planes, sir. But it does have an American flag raised on the back tail."

"An American flag painted on its tail?"

"Sir, the Stars and Stripes aren't painted on. It's *flying* a huge American flag—a flagpole is built into the tail."

"It can't be flying that fast if it has a flagpole on the back."

"Sir, it *is*. Whenever we get close, it moves downward very quickly. The pilots have to be experiencing unbelievably strong g-forces."

The general asked, "Where does it go?"

"Sir, you won't believe this, but they appear to be unaware of us. They seem, instead, to be checking out good fishing spots."

"Fishing spots? With a stealth fighter aircraft?"

The sergeant major said, "Sir, with all due respect, do you want people to know about your best fishing spots?"

"How do you know they're looking to fish?"

"Because one of them throws out a line. The aircraft can hover, like our ospreys. And, sir, it appears to be flown by three kids. You won't believe this either, but I grew up on a farm—and I swear by my Eagle, Globe, and Anchor that the wings are made of a modified corn head."

"What? Did I hear you correctly?"

"Sir, it's, ah . . . yes . . . I think you heard me correctly, sir. It's a flying tractor combine."

"Well, I'll be. I want one."

The sergeant major responded, "Sir, we don't know how to make a stealth fighter aircraft out of a combine."

Jovi, Mitch, and Tony were oblivious to the fact that they were drawing so much attention. They decided they should head back home in case their parents worried about where they were.

As they got close to home, it was pitch-dark. Mitch was at the wheel and asked, "So how do we land this thing?"

Tony said, "I don't know how to land it. I didn't read that page."

Jovi said, "I never saw the how-to-land page."

"You mean none of us knows how to land?" asked Mitch.

Tony looked casually out the window at the moonlit cornfields and said calmly, "Nope. I guess we don't."

"Oh boy. Not good. Not good," said Mitch.

"My brothers are blockheads," said Jovi.

"Why do you always have to sound like Lucy?" said Tony.

"Because my brothers are blockheads. Why else wouldn't you have read the last page?"

"Why are you blaming us? You didn't read it either," said Mitch.

Jovi looked down at how far they would crash. "What if we try to land on a haystack?"

"We'll be squished like bugs."

The kids reviewed every step of the takeoff sequence and thought if they could reverse everything, they might be able to successfully navigate a landing. They argued over the details but soon agreed upon a plan.

They flew low, slowed down, and headed for the dirt road as their landing strip. But they miscalculated their target landing speed and completely missed the road. Instead, they careened onto one of Old Man's cornfields. They bumped and bounced through the rows of corn, and one of the wheels came loose. The steering mechanism got stuck, causing the combine to spin around in circles, cutting spiral patterns into the cornfield. The windshield crumbled. Corn flew everywhere—bits landed in their shirts, husks stuck in their hair, cornstalks were stuffed into their pants.

They finally got the aerial combine slowed down to a stop. The corn rows were a mess, and there were kernels and bits of stalk tossed everywhere and stuck in every nook and cranny of the machine's wheels, gears, and equipment. But they were safe.

The wings were out of place, and debris was wedged into the corn head. They unjammed the steering wheel and hobbled the combine back toward Old Man's barn.

Old Man had been too worried about the kids to sleep, and he had frequently looked out of his window hoping to see their plane. When he finally saw the combine bumbling down the road, he ran out of the house in his robe and pajamas and looked up at the sky and said, "Thank you, Father, Thank you."

The kids drove the tractor into the barn, and Mitch saw the missing page of the manual sitting on a barrel.

Mitch said quietly as he climbed out of the combine, "We didn't read that page."

"I know, and I'm sorry," said Old Man. "I found it hidden behind that cabinet. I can't believe I didn't ask you how to land. How'd you do it?"

Tony said, "We talked over a bunch of different strategies."

"And argued about it," said Jovi.

"We decided on what might have the greatest chance of success," said Mitch.

"But we completely missed the road and crashed into your field," said Tony. "Then the steering got stuck. And that wheel there is broken, so we spun around in circles for a while."

"And corn is stuck into every gear," said Mitch, shaking kernels from under his shirt and out of his hair.

The combine suffered significant damage, and Jovi worried Old Man might be mad at them, as her mom would have been. Jovi said, "We'll clean it up. I promise, we'll come by tomorrow and clean it up perfectly."

"Your parents came down here this evening looking for you, wondering where you were," said Old Man. "I told them that you took my tractor to work some fields down in Iowa. And you'd probably be home late."

"But that's not true," said Mitch.

"No, it's not, but I couldn't exactly say that you were flying a tractor combine, could I?"

"This secret isn't easy to keep, is it?" said Jovi.

"No, it is not," said Old Man. "Now you go home, get a good night's sleep, and enjoy time with your parents tomorrow. They were understandably very worried about you. We can clean up the combine another day."

The kids went back home, crawled into bed, and quickly fell sound asleep. Their mom and dad heard them come in, and when they went to their rooms they found the kids sound asleep, with bits of corn and stalks in their hair, in their pants, and in their shirts.

Darrell said, "Wow, they really were working the fields. Amazing kids—already working so hard and so young."

The next day a woman from a nearby town drove past Old Man's cornfield and saw the spiraling crop circles the kids had cut into the field the night before. She stopped and got out of her car, wondering how the pattern could have come to be. She called her husband to come see it. They were amazed and called their friends, and soon a crowd had gathered to check out the unexplainable crop circles.

A man said, "Look at how the corn is absolutely flattened. There's no way those circles were made by humans."

After breakfast the kids noticed the growing crowd gathering along the dirt road, studying the strange patterns cut into the field.

"Uh-oh, I hope they don't know we did that," said Tony.

"I didn't tell anyone! I promise!" said Jovi.

They went outside, walked cautiously toward the crowd, and noticed that Ralph Rydum and his buddies were there too.

Mitch asked a woman who was standing on the edge of the crowd, "What's everyone looking at?"

The woman answered, "See the patterns cut into the cornfield right there? They're crop circles."

"What's that?" asked Jovi.

"Strange patterns cut into a field. It happens in the middle of the night. They're caused by aliens," answered her husband.

"Are you serious? Aliens landed?" asked Jovi.

Ralph Rydum answered confidently, "Yeah, like duh.

Aliens. Aliens, like, landed here last night." Then he took more pictures of the crop circles and posted them immediately to every possible social media site, thrilled to be the first to post the documented alien landing.

"Wow. Aliens. Awesome," said Tony, with feigned amazement.

Tony elbowed Mitch and gestured for them to head to the creek. They grabbed their fishing poles, and once they got to their favorite ash and oak trees, far from the crowd, they sat down and laughed.

"We're aliens," said Jovi, chuckling.

"I had to get out of there. Otherwise I'd have burst out laughing," said Mitch.

"A sucker born every minute," said Tony.

They fished a little but mostly talked about their adventures on the flying combine.

Tony looked down into the water and watched a crawfish scoot under a rock. He wondered to himself why water is clear.

Jovi asked her brothers, "How come the tractor didn't leave any tracks?"

"I was wondering the same thing. And why can we see it, but no one can take pictures of it?" asked Mitch.

They pondered many theories, but none seemed possible.

Tony said, "Maybe in the eye of a camera, Old Man's machines are clear like water."

The creek flowed swiftly over stones, as if cloaking the answers in the riddles of a babbling current.

44

WHAT HAPPENED, DADDY?

Jatuh stood in the river and guzzled more and more of the river water to quench its unrelenting thirst. Suddenly the dazzling blue water disappeared and the blue stones at the bottom vanished. The waterfall spouting forth from the steep riverbank went instantly dry. Jatuh's thirst disappeared, and the water's flavor turned into a noxious rancidity. Jatuh could drink no more.

The Voices, disguised as blue-faced honeyeaters, flew down to Jatuh and shrieked with piercing, stinging sounds and claimed victory. "You have set us free. You are no more. *You are us.*"

Wicked sounds ripped through the air, and Jatuh felt as though knives were ripping through its many ears. It stood on its hind legs and covered its head with its other legs to shut out the stabbing noise. Its eyes searched the waters for the blue stones, but they were gone.

"Where did the stones go?" asked Jatuh angrily as it dropped down on its four legs and shook its head to shake off the shame of the water it drank. Jatuh tried to get out of the water, but droplets of mud slithered up its legs like centipedes to grip them tightly in the water. It struggled to break free and pleaded, "Stop! Stop! Let me go! What do you want from me?"

The Voices changed into sinister flying creatures whose feather vanes were sharp like knives. They flittered around Jatuh and laughed mockingly. "You worthless, meaningless Greznik—you exist no more. We control your reins. We will move you like a pawn. You, everyone, and everything will be shattered and taken back by me!"

The waters were still too thick for Jatuh to get out. Jatuh begged, "Let me go! Let me get out!"

Geduld tried to swim back over to Tagoga, but the currents were too powerful. The Voices flapped their wickedly sharp wings so violently their feathers flew off like spears. They flew past Tagoga's hiding spot and pierced everything in their path. The strength of their fluttering wings created a wind tunnel around Tagoga's quiet eddy and blew away the big leaves that sheltered his hiding spot. One feather flew past Tagoga's arm and sliced it open, and he shouted out in pain and fear. Then he stood up and bravely faced the eyes of the flying fiends.

The birds screeched a tormented, agonizing sound and exploded into thousands of raindrops, suspended like tiny diamonds. The little diamonds burst, and earsplitting sounds of shattering glass and crackling ice ripped through the air. The diamonds exploded like mud-filled balloons above the river water, and they poured down as the hardest, filthiest rain Tagoga had ever seen. Tagoga's outrigger canoe filled so full of the foul water that he had to step out onto the shore.

Tagoga cowered to protect himself from the worst rainstorm that had ever pummeled the shores of his favorite river. Each raindrop was cold and fell hard like ice and reeked so wretchedly that Tagoga lost his breath. He hid under the thick foliage of the rain forest and nursed his bleeding arm. Gentle Silky curled up next to Tagoga for safety and calmed Tagoga's spirit.

One more wicked droplet exploded and dropped like a stone onto the water. It sank to the bottom, voiceless again, hidden as the current stirred up the muddy river bottom. Jatuh pulled itself out of the water and collapsed on the shore. Dark clouds poured a torrential rain. Jatuh lay on its side with its eyes extended, still as glass. With all the blue stone water it had swallowed rushing through its body, it could not move. Its world went silent as its body absorbed what it had taken in.

When the downpour stopped, Silky crawled out of Tagoga's arms and waddled out of the forest, bruised and dazed, yet strong enough to walk to Jatuh. She got close enough to look into Jatuh's eyes and stroke its face gently with a leaf. Then Jatuh's mouth bubbled blue foam and frothed a disgusting slime.

Jatuh retracted its eyes but was unable to move anything else. Moments later, Jatuh's claws twitched as they struggled to work again. It moved its snout and its tentacles, hoping to regain its ability to smell. It glanced over to the water, wishing to see the beautiful blue stones. Then it muttered, "Where are the stones?"

Silky said, "The stones were never there. You are lucky the Voices were seen by a boy. They shattered, collapsed, and fell back into the river before they completely took form in you."

"Where is the boy?" asked Jatuh.

Silky lied to keep Tagoga safe. "The boy did not see you. He was killed by the sharp wings of the Voices."

Silky hoped Tagoga would stay hidden to avoid being devoured by Jatuh.

Woolly said to Jatuh, "You must rid yourself of the blue stone waters now deep inside you. If you do not, Proznia will torment you until you give in and become its pawn. You need to leave behind what you hoped to get and follow me."

Jatuh sneered at his warning and said, "I have no reason to follow you, my enemy. Your warnings have no merit."

"It is a grave error to assume your enemy can never reveal a piece of truth," said Silky.

"How come you can understand me?" asked Jatuh.

"That is a secret not for you to know," said Silky.

Woolly said, "Please heed our warnings. You must come with us or you will be a tool, a pawn of the Voices. You can destroy the blue stone water in you."

Jatuh said, "There is nothing different about me. The Voices cannot control me! You said they burst, shattered, and fell back in, so I do not need to listen to anyone! I am the power now. I can get the blue stones myself."

"That is not how it works," warned Woolly. "Please follow me. You must."

Jatuh dashed into the forest with such power that Silky and Woolly blew away like tumbleweeds and slowed to a stop just before they tumbled into the river.

Geduld was submerged right at the water's edge and said, through the waters, "Dark days are ahead. The Voices of Proznia will still torment the Greznik, and they can still ruin us all. I will leave now to tell our allies. Take good care of Tagoga while I'm gone. We'll pray he chooses well."

"Travel safely. We want to see you again," said Woolly, sad to see his friend leave for dangerous travels far beyond.

Tagoga had no idea that the animals and the Glyphis shark were speaking to each other. Tagoga shivered from the horror of the scenes that were thrust upon his heart, yet he hoped the beautiful, crystal-clear-blue waterfall would spout forth again. He wondered, *What did I just see? Was is it a dream? Or was I hallucinating from the afternoon heat?*

Silky said goodbye to Geduld and Woolly, then walked over to Tagoga and sat by his side.

Tagoga said to Silky, "I wish you could tell me what happened here."

Silky thought, *You have seen the face of darkness, and the fight is yours to choose.*

Woolly hobbled slowly back to the Bosavi Crater with his injured leg. It took a long time to get back, and he was so grateful to find his wife and little children safe and sound.

"What happened, Daddy?" asked his littlest one, who saw his injured leg. Woolly pulled his children closely in.

"It's okay. It'll be okay," said Woolly. Yet as he put his children to sleep, he worried what the future held for them.

His wife splinted and bandaged his leg as their children drifted off. Once their children were sound asleep, Woolly shared with his wife what happened. In the distance, they heard the thundering sounds of the world war raging violently nearby. They hung their weary heads deep inside the Bosavi Crater.

Tagoga left to paddle back home, and Geduld swam under his canoe. When Tagoga reached home at dusk, he got out of his canoe, pulled it safely into the small harbor, and tied it up.

His mom asked him, "Did you catch the shark today, Tagoga?"

"No," said Tagoga, as he watched Geduld swim away, forever, down the long river toward the ocean.

"Maybe tomorrow," said his mom.

"No, not tomorrow," said Tagoga. "The waters need the shark to stay right where he is."

As Jatuh ran back to its circle, it spat the foul-tasting blue foam from its mouth. Then it rejoined its regiment as if nothing happened. For a very long while, nothing was different for Jatuh. It believed that nothing happened at all from drinking the blue stone waters, and maybe Boshlek's warnings were, in fact, all a lie. It remembered what Skarb had said long ago: *The legend of the Proznia waters is a lie.*

Skarb's haunting words tumbled across Jatuh's thoughts. *Did that deformed Greznik drink the waters before I did and learn the lie before me?*

But Boshlek had never lied. Its warnings about the Voices of Proznia were all too true.

45

THE HICKORY BOX

All afternoon and into the evening there was a steady stream of visitors coming to see the mysterious crop circles. Finally, close to dusk the crowd dispersed, and the kids walked to Old Man's farm. They found him in the barn working on a wood lathe. The kids called his name, but their voices could not be heard over the loud machine. They waved their arms to get his attention.

Old Man turned the machine off. Sawdust and wood chips settled to the ground as Jovi blurted out, "We have a question."

"Sure thing," said Old Man. "What's on your mind?"

"Why don't your machines show up on pictures?"

"And how can they go so fast?" asked Tony.

Mitch added, "And why doesn't the tractor leave any tracks on the ground?"

"No one can tell that the tractor was ever there," said Tony. "Even when we drove over flowers. We want to understand why."

Old Man sighed and said, "It's a bigger answer than you may think. Or even want. Can you keep a secret from everyone?"

"We've kept your secrets so far," said Mitch.

Jovi added, "Even I've kept the secrets this time. I haven't told anyone. Besides, who would believe me anyway?"

"This is a much bigger secret, and it's harder to keep than you think. But I learned this when I was a boy." He tapped each of them on a shoulder with his knobby, crooked finger and said, "I think you will keep your heart strong and save this secret for years to come."

He gestured for them to follow him into the haymow. They climbed to the top of the mow, and he asked the kids to help him toss a bunch of hay bales to the side. Underneath the bales was an old, small hickory box. He opened the box for the kids to see the contents—brilliantly blue sparkling stones.

Jovi said, "Wow, those are beautiful."

"What an amazing blue," said Tony.

Old Man said, "You must not tell anyone that these stones are here. No one. These are unusually powerful blue stones."

Mitch asked, "What kind of powerful?"

"As one example, if you grind them up into a powder, I have the recipe for making paint out of the powder. If you paint something with the dust from these stones, it cannot be tracked by any kind of equipment."

"Then the tractor and combine were painted with blue stone paint?" said Mitch.

"Yes."

"But the tractor and combine aren't blue," said Tony.

"The paint is essentially clear, even though the stones are blue," explained Old Man.

"The stones are clear like water. And sometimes blue like water?" wondered Tony.

"In a way, yes," said Old Man. "And the stones allow many rules of physics to be broken. At least the rules as we know them to be."

"We'd be Kings of the Haymow back at school if we had rocks like this to play with!" said Jovi.

"And Mitch, you could paint a wetsuit with it. Imagine how fast you'd swim," said Tony.

"Maybe a polo saddle for you," Mitch said to Tony. "There's some awesome things we could do with the stones."

Jovi asked, "Do they really have to be kept a secret?"

Old Man said, "This is why knowing about the stones can become a problem. They can make you wish for things. Things to have. Things to do. Things to be. There are many uses for these blue stones, and in the wrong hands their powers can be used for horrible things."

Old Man sat down on a bale of hay and looked up toward the cupola. The kids felt they had done something wrong, but they did not know what it was.

Old Man said, "Always know where your compass is pointed."

Jovi said, "I don't have a compass."

"Everyone has an internal compass. But it doesn't point north, south, east, or west," said Old Man. "Sometimes it points you toward jagged paths, winding and twisting roads, even dangerous, treacherous treks. Much of the journey will seem impossible. But if you want to be famous, or want people to applaud you, or if you want people to see you do amazing things, then your compass goes haywire and the blue stones will turn invisible to you. You won't be able to see the tractor and the combine as they really are. Instead, you will be diverted. Without direction. Thrown off your path. You'll be thirsty for magic, and this barn will be closed to you. You'll battle it forever."

"That's confusing," said Jovi.

"I don't understand," said Mitch.

"Me neither," said Tony.

Old Man said, "Sometimes protecting something takes you on adventures to faraway lands, drops you into deeply complex missions, pushes you in directions you do not want to go. Simply stated, I'm getting too old to do this work. And I need you to take over. The secret needs someone young. Someday I will be gone. I think this secret needs you. You three. But you must decide to be brave, to defend it—knowing that no one will ever give you credit for your bravery. You will not be famous, but you will have the most amazing adventure. And it's an adventure story you can never tell anyone."

"But you're telling us," said Mitch.

"Because I think you are strong enough to bear the secret."

"Why do a bunch of rocks have to be protected anyway?" asked Jovi.

Old Man said, "This is where it all gets a bit perplexing. I don't know everything, but I'll tell you what I know. Creatures called Grezniks roam the world and burrow deep to find these hidden stones, and they, too, can leave no trace. You'll never know they are there or were there. And they want us dead. All of us. Everything on Earth—dead. Grezniks were sent by a faraway power to destroy every little bit of Life by shattering Earth to bits."

Old Man explained what the Grezniks look like and all their capabilities. "Grezniks are like powerful computers. They can quickly calculate complex equations, decipher codes, and so on. Their eyes are like binoculars so they can zoom in to see things from great distances. Yet there are characteristics of Grezniks that we do not know, though, especially how they navigate through this busy world, hardly ever being seen. If someone looks directly at a Greznik, the beast will explode into a smelly smoke, and it will be gone forever."

"Why can't a bunch of people just look at them and get rid of them all? Or just shoot them all?" asked Mitch.

"It doesn't work. A Greznik's skin is so tough it is impenetrable. It cannot be pierced by teeth, a spear, or even a bullet. And we don't know how they do it, but they can make as many of themselves as they want to and replace any that are lost. And it gets even more complicated. Some people can see the Grezniks without evaporating them. They are called Tukors. No one is born one. You don't inherit it. It isn't given. Being a Tukor is a choice, but an ongoing one. The choice is more of a journey than a single decision."

Old Man gently squeezed each kid's shoulder. "It's dangerous work. Yet you can grow those shoulders strong to carry the burden of this secret."

Jovi said, "I'm not sure I want to know about this secret."

"We're a little young to know, don't you think?" asked Mitch.

Tony added, "Yeah, we're just kids on a farm."

"You are never too young to know that you have a special mission in life," said Old Man.

"Like a spy mission?" asked Jovi.

"Not really, not like that. Everyone has a unique mission, but the longer you pretend you don't have it, the more lost your own map will become."

"I don't understand all that. But I know I'll be able to keep this secret because it's too confusing to remember," said Jovi. She was feeling a bit uneasy, even queasy at the sound of it all.

The description of the Grezniks made Mitch and Tony uneasy too. Eating creatures in one bite. Expandable jaws. Extra teeth to devour people. Destroyers. Made of particles that humans cannot measure. That all sounded like things you run away from, not toward.

The kids decided that they were not sure they wanted to hold this secret, and they told Old Man so.

Old Man said, "You don't get to choose the Journey. The Journey chooses you. And it follows you until you follow it."

That sounded like mumbo jumbo to the kids. In fact, the entire conversation felt like a bunch of muddled talk, too high and mighty for children. They told Old Man that they were very grateful for the fun rides on the tractor and the combine, but they did not want to hold the secret. They promised they would not tell anyone about the stones or the Grezniks, but beyond that, they did not want anything else to do with the mission. And they would not take over Old Man's work. The kids agreed—some secrets were not worth holding.

Just before they walked out of the barn, Tony stopped and turned around. "Are you a Tukor?"

But Old Man had started up his lathe and did not hear.

They walked home by way of the creek. The sun had set, and there was no moon that night except a sliver that peeked out from behind burly clouds. Old Man watched the three kids walk back by way of the creek, and he hunched over with sorrow.

As the kids passed Old Man's barn, they thought they saw little eyeballs in the barn looking at them—but when they got closer, there was nothing. Walking past the creek, they thought they saw a big fish following them, but when they got closer, it just looked like rocks or reeds. They were certain they saw bats circling, but when they looked up, they were gone. A few steps more, and lots of eyeballs seemed to be just resting on top of the ground, looking at them, blinking. But the moon went under a cloud, and the eyeballs were gone again.

The kids, spooked by all that they were seeing, ran home and into the house. They stopped in the mudroom and removed their boots. Their mom and dad did not even notice them come in. The kids ran upstairs without saying anything to each other, crawled into bed, and fell into a restless sleep.

46

GO NORTH

After Jatuh swallowed the blue stone waters, for a long while there was nothing different. But eventually Jatuh felt unusual sensations that, like a strong magnet, pulled Jatuh toward the north. When those moments came, Jatuh's claws tingled and it felt a sudden urge to run far away alone.

As the years passed, the nagging and twitching and urgings would give it no rest. Jatuh could not withstand the magnetic nagging any longer. In the middle of the night, as its circle rested, Jatuh ran to the nearest river waters.

It stood on the shore and said, "Leave me alone. Set me free. I am not yours."

Jatuh waited for a response. The waters lapped on the shore. The whispering stillness of night blanketed the wilderness.

"You will not have me!" shouted Jatuh.

The river current slowed to a still, and the waters faintly sniggered.

Jatuh asked, "What did you say?"

No response was offered to the Greznik. Instead, the current sped up and left the Greznik more alone. Jatuh's feet shook forcibly but involuntarily, and the quavering moved up into its legs with cruel intensity.

The waters barked an order, "Go north!"

Energy jolted through Jatuh's body and paralyzed it. Jatuh collapsed to the ground. A strong urge to run north heaved from within. Just as fast as it came, the urge subsided. Jatuh ran back to its circle and found them sleeping. It dropped its middle leg down, pulled up its other four legs, and hoped for a restful night. But it never came.

In the years following, Jatuh wished for but was never granted relief from the dreadfully strong northerly cravings. Jatuh's inner compass unrelentingly pointed Jatuh to the northern reaches of Earth. Unable to suffer them any longer, Jatuh assumed that if it gave into the urge to travel north, the cravings would subside.

Jatuh suggested to Boshlek, "We will never find or seize the stones unless we seek them differently. Alter our strategy. It has been many trips around the sun since we last searched the regions of the Arctic latitudes. We should travel north."

Boshlek was desperate for success. The world had become more populated, and new threats came from above and below and all around that could bring about the demise of its regiment. So this time Boshlek gave in to Jatuh's suggestion and ordered the regiment to travel northward across the Pacific Ocean to Alaska.

Though they traveled farther north, Jatuh got no

relief from the magnetic cravings. Instead, they got worse. The regiment stopped to rest on one of the Pacific Ocean's many splendid islands. Jatuh saw a sea turtle swimming at a distance far from shore. Unexpectedly, Jatuh's body shook, and bits of a turtle shell popped out along its back. Jatuh panicked and ran away from the sight of the turtle, then chewed the pieces of shell off its back before anyone noticed. Sometimes its insides would shake and feathers would grow out of its fur, or a bird's beak would poke out from its nostril, and or a different type of claw would poke out of the bottom of its foot—all of which Jatuh bit off or snapped off quickly.

Jatuh had hoped that when the regiment arrived on Alaska's arctic landscape, it would be cured of its torments. Instead, the yearnings to run away only got stronger and more uncontrollable. And the internal shakes happened more and more frequently. Worse yet, when the shakes happened in Alaska, every other Greznik could feel a cold bitterness moving through the air. Like a stone dropped in water, bitterness rippled through the regiment.

Late one morning, Boshlek was calling its circle leaders to a meeting when it felt that strange bitterness in the air.

Boshlek said to one of its circle leaders, "There it is. I felt it again. Did you feel it this time?"

"Yes, Eternal Commander, I felt it. The same as yesterday," answered the circle leader, also puzzled.

"What's causing these strange sensations?" asked Boshlek. "It isn't Earth's crust shifting. Nor is it shifts in the wind. Nor lightning from above. Nor are they sound waves."

Later, Jatuh walked up to Boshlek privately and feigned ignorance. "I felt the tremors too. The strange pulsations around us are getting stronger and stronger."

"It must be our enemies," Boshlek speculated incorrectly.

"I agree. And I think I can find what's causing it," said Jatuh manipulatively.

"How?"

"Grant me leave from the regiment, and I will travel alone and figure it out. I will return to you with the answer," said Jatuh.

"Grezniks don't travel alone," said Boshlek.

"No, we do not. But the enemy will never reveal itself to our entire regiment, will it? If a Greznik were traveling alone, the enemy might come out of hiding."

"Nonsense. The enemy will destroy a Greznik traveling alone, as the red pandas do," said Boshlek.

"But that's the point. The times are changing, and so must our tactics. If you grant me leave from the regiment to travel alone, I will find a vulnerable creature. There must be at least one weak creature in the Tukors' forces who will betray them. You know I am the strongest, most skilled, most loyal Greznik in the regiment. I am the Greznik for this assignment!"

"Our enemies will not give you information, no matter the circumstance. Now get away from me."

A few days later, the regiment traveled through the northern reaches of Alaska. Unexpectedly a strange and incredibly fast aircraft was upon them. Boshlek had never seen anything like it. Boshlek immediately hollered a warning to the regiment. All the Grezniks instantly flattened and camouflaged themselves. Boshlek did not get even the slightest glimpse of the three pilots, Mitch, Tony, and Jovi, because the aircraft flew away too quickly. Never before had the Grezniks been caught off guard like that. Boshlek was alarmed.

Boshlek called a meeting of the circle leaders. "There is no other explanation for that aircraft other than that the Tukors are preparing for a battle and assembling their troops again."

As the meeting of circle leaders disbanded, Jatuh spoke privately with Boshlek and said, "We haven't made that mistake in many years—letting an aircraft sneak up on us. The enemy must be brewing a battle up here. You must let me travel. It's urgent we take new risks, and immediately."

"If I grant you leave, how can I be assured that you will not walk to the waters alone?"

"I have never done so and will never do so," lied Jatuh unflinchingly. "I have no interest in tempting Proznia. Proznia has no power over me, and neither will its waters. Every Greznik lives to find the blue stones and escape Proznia, and we must do this together. I want the stones as much as you do. I would never jeopardize our pursuit of the stones by taunting the waters."

Desperate to be released from its regimental duties, Jatuh's insides pulsated and bitterness again rippled across the regiment.

Boshlek said, "There it is again. That bizarre aura. What is causing that?"

Jatuh would never own up to it. Instead it feigned ignorance and repeated its appeal to Boshlek. "The auras must mean that we are close to the stones. Why else would we all be feeling those strange auras? Why else would a strange aircraft sneak up on us? You can trust me to travel alone and discover what the enemy is up to. Besides, what is the worst that could happen? I fail miserably and return to the regiment knowing that the enemy's forces are impenetrable. But you must know that just cannot be."

Boshlek refused and sent Jatuh back to its circle.

As the days passed, its cravings to travel far away got worse and Jatuh concealed many more of its troubling internal shakes. Boshlek felt them every time and grew more and more uneasy that their enemies were near, triggering the strange auras. After several days of more frequent, intense events, Boshlek called Jatuh forward and granted it leave from the regiment.

Boshlek said, "You must return to me in three days sharp with the report on what is causing these auras. Or you will be found by our scouts and instantly walked into the sea."

Jatuh bowed in obedience to Boshlek, hiding its delight in finally being able to follow the craving and rid itself of the torments. At nightfall, it walked away from the regiment. As it got farther away from the regiment, the vibrations in its legs grew stronger, and Jatuh felt an unrelenting desire to run to the sea. Jatuh gave in and ran to the water's edge, with an eerie yearning to swim. Jatuh saw a fishing boat offshore, bouncing about in the rough seas.

The fishermen reeled in an ancient yelloweye rockfish, but they reeled him in too quickly. The fish's swim bladder, which controlled its buoyancy, did not have time to adjust to the changes in depth and expanded too much, severely bloating the captured rockfish.

The bloated yelloweye rockfish was a rockfish named Anz, respected and loved by his own community. Anz was limp as the fisherman took pictures, but his eyes saw Jatuh at the edge of the sea. He was startled and consumed with fear. The sight of a Greznik alone by the sea meant danger far greater than a fisherman's hook.

To the surprise of the fisherman, Anz flapped and fell back into the water. As Anz fell, he shouted, "A Greznik is alone at the sea!"

Anz hoped nearby animals would hear, but his voice was too weak and damaged to be heard. Underwater and dying, Anz could no longer see Jatuh on the shore.

Hidden from the fishermen's view, Jatuh's body began to shake violently, and it felt intense and crippling pain. It collapsed to the ground and curled up, desperate for the reverberations to stop; but this time Jatuh had nothing in its power to stop them. It was aghast when its hair shriveled back into its skin and its legs shrank. Its skin grew scales like that of a yelloweye rockfish, and its tail converted to a fin. Jatuh watched as gills grew grotesquely out of its side. Bit by bit, Jatuh turned into a yelloweye rockfish—and wickedly so.

47

USELESS BIKES

After Mitch, Tony, and Jovi rejected Old Man's secret,
they did not go fishing, nor ride their horses, nor play King
of the Haymow. They woke up each day and ate their breakfast with little motivation for the day ahead. Tony started
counting the pieces of cereal that could fit on a spoon and
sent postcards to Kenny with the morning updates. After
breakfast every day, they bugged their mom and dad about
wanting to play on the computer.

The kids went into their parents' office, and Mitch said,
"Seriously, Mom, how long does it take to research basil?"

Tony added, "You've been doing that for weeks. It's our
turn to use the computer."

"Kids, our world is different now. We have to work,"
said Darrell.

Caroline said, "We're researching grapes now. For a
vineyard. Wouldn't this land look beautiful as a vineyard?"

"If vineyards made money here, they'd be here already,"
said Tony. "So, come on, it's our turn."

"Maybe some screen time after dinner," said Darrell.

Mitch and Tony left the room and went upstairs to stare at the bedroom ceiling and think of something to do besides video games. Jovi was up in the attic rummaging through Mr. Charlie's old treasures. Mitch went downstairs looking for his baseball glove when he overheard his mom and dad.

Caroline said, "Maybe we should move back to New York. The kids have been inside for days griping about screen time. So much for a peaceful life on a farm."

Darrell said, "Maybe we can find a summer school in New York they can attend."

At this, Mitch ran upstairs to Jovi and Tony. "Hey, Mom and Dad want to move back to New York. Put us in summer school."

The kids tiptoed downstairs and stood unnoticed, just outside the office door, eavesdropping on their parents.

Caroline was on the computer looking at Manhattan real estate for sale. "Honey, look, here's a nice condo for sale in Tribeca. I always wanted to live there. Maybe we really can move back?"

Darrell said, "There's no way we can afford that, Caroline."

Caroline slumped back into her chair. All this farming business was hard work, and she wanted a way out. "Maybe we can have our dream of farming *and* our love for the city. Hey, what about starting a movement in urban farming?"

Darrell chuckled. "In case you don't remember, Manhattan doesn't have soil."

"Yeah, yeah . . . but what if we create rooftop farms, you know—like on top of every Manhattan building? Our business can be Rooftop Basil Farms. Something like that," she said.

"Huh, you might be onto something," pondered Darrell. "Rooftop farms. All that wasted space up there when it could be growing something."

Tony whispered, "Rooftop farms? Are you kidding me?"

Mitch added, "You can't drive a tractor on a rooftop."

"Maybe just a teeny-tiny tractor with a spider riding it," said Jovi. "Come on, let's go outside. We need to feed the horses."

The horses were the only thing that got them outside every day. There was no way they were going to be like the kids before them and neglect their new friends José, Joker, and Max. They went out to the haymow and tossed down some hay for the horses.

Up in the mow, Jovi climbed up to the top of the haystack and yelled, "I'm King of the Mow!"

But then she saw some bikes stashed behind the bales. She said, "Did you guys put bikes up here?"

"What?" asked Mitch.

"Come look at these bikes!"

Mitch and Tony climbed up and saw the three heavy-duty mountain bikes hidden behind all the hay. They did not own any bikes and had no idea how the bikes got there.

"Who would've stashed bikes up here?" wondered Jovi.

"Maybe they're stolen," said Mitch.

"But why would they hide them here? They'd have to know we'd find them. But check 'em out—these bikes are awesome!" said Tony.

"There's a purple-and-yellow one. That one must be mine since those are my favorite colors," exclaimed Jovi.

There was a red-and-blue one for Mitch. And Tony liked the neon-green bike.

Mitch said, "Maybe Mom and Dad bought us new bikes for our birthdays and tried to hide them. They'd be the only ones to know what colors we'd want."

"But our birthdays are months from now," said Jovi.

"Mom and Dad were gone yesterday morning to find basil baskets or something like that. Maybe they found the bikes and just bought them for no reason," said Tony.

"But Mom and Dad wouldn't even know where to find bikes this cool," said Mitch. "And I don't think they'd hide them in the haymow. We come up here every day to get hay for the horses. They've never even been up here."

Tony easily carried his bike up and over the hay bales. "Wow, they're so lightweight."

Jovi, too, could lift her bike over her head with one hand. "Do you think they're made of feathers?"

Tony said, "I hope peregrine feathers. Then they'd go superfast."

They carried their bikes down the ladder and then rode them over toward the machine shed. They checked out all the unusual features excitedly. Buttons lined the handlebars. Tiny speakers and unusual wiring ran through the frames.

On the back of the bikes, there were fasteners for mounting something over the tires. They went back into the barn to make sure they did not miss anything, and sure enough, they found motors hidden between the hay bales. They carried the motors out and mounted them on the back of each bike, then hooked them up to some mysterious fuel system.

They pushed all the buttons methodically. They spoke into the small microphones on the handlebars. Then they tried to engage the motors. But nothing worked.

The three of them got on their bikes and pedaled down the empty road. When the bikes were moving, they again pushed all the buttons—but nothing happened.

Mitch said, "These bikes look fancy, but they're useless. Maybe Mom and Dad did buy them."

Tony added, "Yeah, I bet these are lightweight bikes because they're made of basil."

"Basil bikes. You can ride them right into spaghetti sauce!" said Jovi.

"The buttons can't all be useless," said Tony. "Why would there be buttons if you can't push them and make something happen?"

"Maybe there's a word to start it, like the tractor," speculated Mitch.

Jovi said confidently, "Go!" but nothing happened.

Tony got on his bike and tried too. "Go!" The bike did not respond. "Well if there is a magic word, it isn't 'go' this time."

Mitch said, "Maybe we should get on the bikes and

just read every word in the dictionary until we find the right word."

"Yeah, but what if the bikes speak Norwegian?" Tony wondered.

Mitch added, "Or if one speaks Spanish, one Norwegian, and the other Chinese. It would take forever for us to find the right words."

"Do we think these bikes are from Old Man?" wondered Tony.

"I don't think Old Man would give us bikes," said Mitch. "We didn't agree to his secret."

Tony said solemnly, "Maybe we should've agreed."

"We all decided not to. And I'm stickin' to that. The secret didn't sound fun," said Jovi.

Mitch said, "And it sounded bizarre. I'm not even sure it was true."

"But I really want to know how this bike works," said Tony.

The kids rode the bikes around the farm then down the dirt road, through the mud at the edge of the creek, and across the pasture. The gears and handlebars and spokes got covered in muck and bits of grass. But the buttons never worked. And nothing special happened.

When they went inside for dinner, Jovi asked, "Mom and Dad, did you buy us bikes for our birthdays already?"

"Bikes? Now? Your birthdays are next winter. That's months away. Besides, we'd never surprise you with a bike. We'd make sure we got the exact one you wanted. Do you want bikes for your birthdays?"

"Naw," said Mitch. "We like riding horses."

Surprisingly, this time Jovi did not say a word about the bikes. Somehow, deep inside, she knew they were a secret worth keeping.

48

YELLOWEYE ROCKFISH

Along the Alaskan seashore, as soon as Jatuh was fully disguised as a yelloweye rockfish, it involuntarily flapped on the rocky cliff edge until it slipped off and fell toward the ocean. Jatuh thrashed violently, believing it would dissolve when it hit the water. But when it landed on the ocean waters, its body did not dissolve. It easily swam away.

Jatuh swam over to Anz, the dying yelloweye rockfish. The ancient Anz never imagined that the fish swimming toward him was the Greznik he had seen on the shore, now transformed into a perfectly convincing rockfish disguise.

Anz said to Jatuh, "I just broke free from the fishermen. I'm critically injured and too weak to swim deep. You must swim down and tell our community the grave news that a Greznik has traveled alone to the sea and is lurking on the shore. Remind them of our promise to hold the secret close. No Greznik must ever discover it."

"What secret?" asked Jatuh.

Anz was alarmed by Jatuh's question. No yelloweye

rockfish would ever be unaware of the great secret held by the rockfish community. Something was very wrong. Anz tried to swim down deep to warn his family and friends of the menacing visitor and, worse yet, the Greznik. But his body was too injured to continue down into the depths.

Jatuh could not care less that Anz was dying and in need of help. It was only interested in figuring out the secret held within the rockfish community. Jatuh forced its body to look exactly like Anz, including the damage done by the fisherman's hook and Anz's rapid rise to the surface. Then Jatuh, disguised as Anz, swam down and found the other yelloweye rockfish in the depths below.

As Jatuh swam to them, they were so happy to see their wise old friend and excitedly talked over each other to greet him.

"So wonderful to see you, Anz!"

"What a blessing Anz is safe!"

"What a miracle that Anz is still with us!"

"We thought you were dead! Those fishermen pulled you up so fast, how did you escape?"

Jatuh wickedly imitated Anz's voice and lied to the innocent rockfish. "I have troubling news. When I escaped the fisherman's hook, I saw a Greznik on shore, traveling alone!"

The terrible news sent fear rippling through the community. A few young rockfish swam up to see what all the commotion was about.

An elder rockfish said to the youth, "Anz has just told us that a Greznik was alone on our shores. With danger lurking near, now is the time for you to learn the secret held for centuries by our community."

The younger rockfish were so excited to finally be old enough to learn the secret that they beamed with pride.

The elder rockfish said, "Anz, teach the young ones the secret, as you have done so many times before."

Jatuh was caught in the lie. It had no idea what to teach the young ones. Jatuh feigned more physical complications and said, "I'm not well. My injuries are severe. Someday the torch of telling the secret must be passed along, and it may be soon. So this time, I entrust the teaching to you."

The elder rockfish said, "Anz, do not give up yet. We will help you recover."

"Thank you, but today I am too weary. Please share the secret with the little ones."

The elder rockfish turned to the young ones and shared the carefully guarded secret. "Because we live deep in the sea and Grezniks cannot submerge in water, we hold an important clue to the blue stone mine. The mine is found by locating three corners of a triangle, all located in Alaska. We know the location of one corner of the triangle. Our corner is marked by a marble run built into a rocky granite structure, like a small crag or a tor. You start the marble at the top, and as it winds down the run, it makes four interlocking figure eights, tracing the shape of the yellow crowned beggar-ticks flower. And when the marble stops, it marks the corner of the triangle. The marble is the size of an eye of an elder rockfish. Now you must keep that secret and never speak a word of it to any other living creature."

Jatuh added, "Shouldn't we also tell the little ones where the marble run is?"

"Oh, dear Anz, it's not like you to ask something you already know. You really aren't feeling well, are you? You swam too deep too quickly. You need to rest."

One of young ones said, "But that's a good question. Where is the marble run?"

The elder rockfish answered, "We've never known where it is, except that it is in Alaska. Perhaps only a Tukor knows where."

Jatuh waited until all the yelloweye rockfish retreated to their deepwater hideouts, then it swam upward. Upon reaching the surface, it flopped itself on the shore, where its body shook violently until its scales dried, turned dark, and melted into skin. Hair grew in their place. Dorsal fins sank into its body, gills glued shut, and Greznik legs popped out. A Greznik snout grew out of its mouth. As half-fish, half-Greznik, it saw Anz's dead fish body floating in the water. It pulled out Anz's eyeball, then finished morphing back into Jatuh.

Jatuh heard piercing, searing sounds ripping through its insides. Then the Voices said, "You've been a lazy, worthless Greznik, taking too long to find even one clue. But you have finally obeyed. Now be swift and find the other clues, or we will sear your insides!"

Stabbing sounds blared in Jatuh's ears. Jatuh looked around for unusual birds in the air, but unlike in Papua New Guinea, the Voices were not disguised as birds. The Voices were inside, trembling their desires from within.

Jatuh retorted with deluded confidence. "I am the one with the power now, not you! You shattered and sank to the bottom of a river! And I am free to find the stones without you!"

Jatuh ran back to the regiment. It reported straightaway to Boshlek. "My travels were a tremendous success. I extracted a clue to the blue stone mine."

"What's the clue?" asked Boshlek.

Jatuh explained about the triangle, the granite tor, and the marble run. Then Jatuh handed Boshlek the rockfish eyeball.

"What's this?" asked Boshlek.

"The size and weight of the marble you must use. But unfortunately, no one knows where the run is, except perhaps a Tukor."

"How do I know that you are telling the truth?"

"I will find all the clues for you. We will find the blue stones together. When you finally hold a blue stone, you will believe me. You have taught us over and over again that no one Greznik can extract the stones on its own. Every Greznik needs the regiment. The clues are worthless without the regiment, and the regiment is worthless without you, Eternal Commander. We are one, and I am ever loyal to you. Now, may I leave again and travel far to find the other clues to the Alaskan mine?"

"How do you know the mine is in Alaska?" asked Boshlek.

Jatuh lied. "I overheard one lynx share the clue with another."

"How did you force a lynx to reveal the clue to you?" asked Boshlek.

"I did not have to force him. He never knew I was there. Our enemies are getting sloppy. The advantage of traveling alone is that our enemies cannot easily detect the presence of a single Greznik. All I had to do was spy on their conversations, and I overhead every detail. Again, if you grant me leave, I can depart tonight to find more clues."

Boshlek said, "Not tonight. I will consider the situation and let you know."

Jatuh was desperate to search immediately and said, "I have delivered a powerful clue to you that you would not have if it weren't for me. Why do you hesitate?"

"You are not in command of this regiment. I am. Remember that, or you will be destroyed. Now get away from me."

Jatuh fumed, yet walked away with feigned calm. But then its legs began to shake. At the same time, Skarb returned to the regiment from an afternoon of wandering and felt and smelled something strange in the air. No matter how slight Jatuh's shakes were, unlike all the other Grezniks, Skarb smelled a familiar horrible odor— the same stench as when the Voices bubbled within the Chongchon River. And the familiar odor brought back memories of when Skarb dove into the Chongchon River to grab the sparkling blue stones, but found nothing but mud, rock, and silt. During their stay in Alaska, Skarb had smelled the stench repeatedly but could not determine its source.

Skarb asked Jatuh, "Do you recognize the smell in the air?"

Jatuh raised its snout and sniffed but smelled nothing. "There is no odor in the air."

"How could you not smell it? The stench is so strong," said Skarb. "It smells like the Chongchon River. I smell it vividly, every time the air quivers so."

"There is no scent in the air," sneered Jatuh.

But then Skarb saw Jatuh's foot shake strangely, and that same smell of the Chongchon River came flowing toward Skarb. Skarb said to Jatuh, "It's you casting off the stench. When you shook your foot, the smell of the Chongchon came to me. You are the one who smells of the river."

"You are delusional. There is no smell," said Jatuh. But Jatuh was alarmed to realize that when Jatuh got those bitter shakes, Skarb could smell something that other Grezniks could not.

To throw Skarb off, Jatuh feigned several shakes of its legs as it walked away. Skarb witnessed the shakes but this time smelled nothing. Skarb fell for Jatuh's trick and thought, *If my circle leader isn't giving off that smell, what is? Are the Voices trying to speak to me?*

Jatuh fretted that it would not take long for Skarb to put two and two together again and confirm that Jatuh was in fact the source of the strange bitter quivering in the Arctic air.

Jatuh listened as Skarb asked several other Grezniks if they had smelled the river water from long ago, and they answered truthfully that they could not. Jatuh's fur spiked upward, as if danger were approaching. It tried to walk off the disturbance, but the unsettling sensation of danger persisted. Jatuh's legs shivered oddly as it walked, as if trying to shake off a stinging scorpion. This time the internal sensation was not from the Voices. Instead, its body was simply trying to shake off an unwelcome and unfamiliar disturbance that no other Greznik could feel— fear. Fear arising when in the presence of anyone who chose differently at the water's edge.

As the truth sunk in that Skarb could smell its internal torments, Jatuh lost its bearings and felt weakened, as if being forced to look in the mirror and seeing nothing but a foul reflection of what it had swallowed in—Proznia. And Skarb did not yet understand that because it had rejected the Voices, it could sniff out those who had given in.

49

DON'T KNOW HIS NAME

Over the next couple of weeks, the kids enjoyed riding their bikes but wondered if anyone would come back, retrieve the bikes, and take them away. But no one did. They talked about asking Old Man about the bikes, but they remained steadfast in refusing his secret and did not want to risk Old Man asking them to reconsider.

The kids could see Old Man's farm from theirs, and they usually saw him outside working each day. But they had not seen him for a couple of weeks. Old Man never neglected his farm, but his fields were not attended to and his lawn was growing long.

"Maybe he's sick," said Jovi.

"We should check. It's weird we haven't see him," said Mitch.

Tony looked admiringly at his bike and said, "All these parts and pieces can't just all be for show. Even if Old Man doesn't know anything about our bikes, maybe he can figure out how they work. Let's go check on him."

They went to his farm to find out if he was okay. And perhaps they would find the courage to ask him about the bikes. When they got to Old Man's farm, his dogs did not come running to greet them. No farm animals were out, nor were there any in the barns. There weren't even birds singing. The farm was eerily quiet.

They looked everywhere for him. They went to the barn and tried to get in the secret door just as they had done every day when they rebuilt the tractor and studied the aerial tractor combine. But the door did not open the way it used to do. The machine shed was locked up, and the horse barn was empty.

They had never been in Old Man's house, but they walked to the front step and knocked on the door. They waited a long time for an answer, but no one came. They knocked again and again, louder and louder, but no one answered. The curtains on the windows were all drawn tightly shut. They tapped on the windows, but there were neither signs of movement nor lights on inside.

They looked in the silos, the corncrib, the chicken coop—but everything was locked up or empty. They found the Percherons grazing at the far end of the pasture and thought Old Man might be with them. But he was not, and his horses had eaten through their hay. The horses followed the kids back to the barn.

"We'd better check on the blue stones," Mitch said worriedly.

The kids entered the hay barn where the blue stones were hidden, and they slowly opened the door. Normally there were pigeons in the rafters and mice scrambling about, but this time the barn was silent. Up in the haymow they looked all over for the hickory box that held the blue stones, but it was gone.

From up in the mow, they dropped down a few hay bales, climbed down, and carried the bales to the Percherons, who were happy to have something tastier than grass to eat. While the horses ate, the kids sat down and leaned up against an old tree.

Jovi said, "I wish these horses could talk and tell us where he went."

"And where the blue stones are," added Tony.

The horses looked up as if they wanted to talk, then put their heads back down and ate more.

Jovi asked, "Do you think he moved away and left us?"

"Something is wrong. He wouldn't just abandon his farm," said Mitch. "And definitely not his horses."

"Maybe a Greznik came and took him away?" said Jovi.

"I didn't really believe the stuff about the Grezniks. How could any of that be true?" said Mitch.

"Who knows. It's all bizarre. But he did seem serious when he said it was dangerous work and he couldn't do it anymore," said Tony.

"He said he was too old for the secret," said Mitch. "He couldn't protect it anymore."

Jovi said, "And we never even asked him his real name."

Tony added, "You're right. We don't even know his name."

"Maybe he left a clue somewhere about where he is," said Mitch.

The Percherons stomped their feet. They pounded their hooves, reared up, and neighed loudly.

The kids backed away from the rearing horses.

The horses stomped again, and the ground thundered underneath them. The smallest Percheron turned and shook her head, her mane flapped back and forth, and her tail swished from side to side. She ran off, pawed at the ground, and put her nose down, then looked up at the kids and stared at them as she flared her nostrils.

The kids agreed it was the weirdest thing they had ever seen a horse do.

The kids walked back to the barn and decided they would stay nearby until Old Man came home. They went home for dinner, then returned and spent the evening on the wooden fence, waiting. It got late, and the mosquitoes were biting like mad. The sun sank slowly below the horizon, and they walked home, dispirited, by way of the creek.

As they walked away from Old Man's farm, they did not notice that little eyeballs watched them from the haymow, and crayfish looked out from the edges of the creek. Nor did they see small eyeballs popping out of the ground, and a rabbit dashing quietly behind them.

Mitch stepped very near to a small hole and suddenly felt something run up the back of his pant leg. He shook his leg and looked, but there was nothing there. A few minutes later, Tony, too, stepped very near a hole, and he jumped.

"I think something just crawled up my leg!" said Tony.

Then Jovi felt something on her ankle. She screeched, darted forward, and they ran all the way home.

They threw off their boots in the mudroom and ran upstairs. Tony put on his pajamas, and when he picked up his dirty pants to throw them over the back of his chair, a piece of folded parchment paper fell out of his back pocket.

"What's this?" Tony wondered.

"Where did you get it?" Mitch asked.

"Fell out of my pants. Did you put it there?"

"No."

Mitch checked his pockets. "I got one too."

They called Jovi into their room to ask her if she got a note in her pocket too, but she did not find one.

Jovi was disappointed. "I don't have one. How did you get yours?"

Tony said, "I swear I felt something crawling up my leg when we were walking home. Maybe something ran up our legs and stuck something in our pockets."

"Me too! I know I felt something on my leg," exclaimed Mitch.

"Me too, but I ran away," said Jovi.

Tony unfolded his piece of folded parchment paper. "It's a long note."

Tony's piece had the number one written on it. Mitch's, number two.

Jovi said to Tony, "Read yours first."

Tony read it out loud:

If you have received this note, then I have been gone for too many days and our friends have decided they can trust you and are asking for your help.

Before I left, I received terrible news from an ally who traveled from far away to tell me that Grezniks are dangerously close to finding a long-hidden blue stone mine. It will be catastrophic if those stones are seized by the Grezniks. I left to prevent them from finding the mine.

If I have not come back, that means I did not succeed in my plan and I either need help or I need you to continue the mission for me.

In all my years, I never found anyone who could ever possibly be entrusted with this secret. You three kids were an answer to my appeals to God Almighty. But you said you weren't strong enough to bear the secret. Yet I know you can carry the burden. Don't let anyone get hold of you and make you believe otherwise. Do not let doubts creep inside you the way biting gnats sneak through a screen. I believe in the strength of your hearts to try. I know you can handle this secret. I need your help. Please come find me.

Sincerely and with faith,

Fingal

Tony said, "His name must be Fingal!"

"I've never even heard of that name before," said Mitch.

"How do you spell that?" asked Jovi.

"F-I-N-G-A-L," said Tony. "How are we ever going to find him? Quick, Mitch, read your note!"

Mitch read his note out loud:

I don't know if you have found the bicycles yet. But if you haven't found them, they are in your haymow. The bikes are very powerful, so I hope no one will find them except you. I am wearing my old leather farm boots. I placed a small device in the sole of my left boot. It looks like a microchip and it emits a signal. The signal is a very unusual frequency that is unreadable to everything except those bikes. If you turn on the bikes, a little screen will pop out from the middle of the handlebars. The screen will display a map, and it will pinpoint my exact location. I hope you have the courage to find me. I hope there is enough summer left when you get this for you to rescue me. Or if I am gone forever, to rescue the secret of the stones from the Grezniks. If you go, be careful on your journey. Travel silently and without notice—no one must know. Please, have courage.

Sincerely and with faith,

Fingal

Jovi said, "But we don't even know how to turn on the bikes!"

Mitch added, "He can't have forgotten to tell us how to use the bikes."

"Well, he forgot to tell us how to land a flying combine," said Tony.

Jovi said, "Maybe I was supposed to get a note, but I ran when I felt something on my leg."

Tony said, "It's all kind of creepy."

"I guess we'll just have to figure out the bikes. Fingal needs our help," said Mitch.

The next morning, the kids woke at the crack of dawn, ate breakfast quickly, and ran out to their bikes. Jovi was the first to run up and over the haystack to get her bike, and she found a third note resting on the handlebars.

Jovi said, "I found the third note! I have the third note!"

"Does it tell us how to use the bikes?" asked Mitch.

Jovi opened the note and said with frustration, "It's long—pages and pages. And it's written in the code."

They took the third note back into the house, grabbed some scrap paper, and went up to the attic to break the code. Jovi's note was very long with a lot of detail.

"Why do his machines always have really long manuals?" said Jovi, exasperated.

The note read:

Here is what you need to know about your bikes.

1. *The bikes can be quickly converted to motorbikes using the engines I left in the haymow. Mount the engines on the back of the bikes. They have the capability to be entirely silent or very loud, whichever you need.*

2. *The bikes have internal GPS systems. A rod will emerge from the middle of the handlebars, and from it will unroll a screen which will display a complex mapping system.*

3. *The bikes are fueled by an advanced, long-lasting battery technology—very small batteries that are found in the bike pedals. You will not need to worry about recharging them. The battery will last a century riding at full speed the entire time.*

4. *The bikes cannot travel through water, so rivers need to be jumped.*

5. *They do not fly, but they can launch and glide to a slow landing, like a glider.*

6. *There are three ways to communicate with each other: walkie-talkies, your helmets, and earphones built into the bikes.*

7. *The walkie-talkies are hidden in a canvas bag by the honeysuckles, behind the rain barrel. Retrieve them as soon as possible. The walkie-talkies also work as cell phones. When you retrieve them, you will find the instructions. Always have the walkie-talkies on you when you travel.*

8. *You will also find three helmets in that canvas bag. The helmets contain communication equipment, so when you are wearing them and you speak, your siblings will hear your voice via their own helmets. The helmets have a special setting that cancels out*

the sound of your voice so no one else will hear you except your siblings. Your helmets protect your eyes from debris and bugs as you bike fast. Because of the lightweight design, you will hardly notice that you have a helmet on at all.

9. *As a backup communication system, earphones pull out from the handlebars and operate as both a transmitter and a receiver. Whichever method you use to communicate, make sure you can still hear the other sounds around you.*

10. *Activating the motorbike engines is very tricky. Each bike needs the other bike to start for the very first time. You must all be pedaling at once, and as hard as you can. Be very aware of each other and communicate, so you do not crash into each other. One bike cannot be going faster than the other, or the bikes won't start. Siblings know each other well and can coordinate. The enemy does not like teamwork and will have a difficult time copying this. To start the engines, all three of your bikes need to be connected to each other via the starting ignition wire. The wire pulls out from under the seat and plugs into your sibling's seat. Connect all three bikes, and once you are pedaling fast*

enough, then each engine will start. When your engine starts, unplug the ignition wire from your seat.

11. *The engine is activated by voice. You must program the walkie-talkies to recognize both your voice and the command words to start the engine. The bike's voice recognition system works for only one voice. Be sure your surroundings are totally silent when you program the system to know your voice. If a cow moos when you are recording your voice, the bike will start with that cow's moo instead of your voice. After programming the walkie-talkies, mount them on the bikes to download the voice commands.*

12. *To stop the bike, you don't need to do anything but hit the brake.*

13. *Take your canteens and keep water in them at all times. Take the pemmican stored in my horse barn, in the barrel next to the tack. Do not leave any behind. You will need ample food supply. Each of you should pack a backpack carrying only critical supplies. Do not pack a heavy pack. Go as light as you can because there may be times when you will need to travel by foot.*

14. *There are three wristwatches, one for each of you. Each watch emits a signal that will appear on the bike's map as a blinking boot icon to signify your location. That way you can find each other if you get lost or lose contact with each other. As I mentioned in the previous note, the sole of my boot has a device that also emits a signal, so when you turn on the bikes, you will see my location.*

15. *The wristwatches are hidden with the pemmican. When you find them, you will also find goggles. These goggles are to be worn under your helmets. They provide powerful night vision, so you can travel just as fast at night and through fog. They also act as binoculars that can zoom in from great distances. The technology to do this is not available to any other living creature—so do not lose these goggles. They must not fall into anyone else's hands.*

16. *Be wary, alert at all times. Grezniks have receptors all over their bodies that can detect any and every sound, radio wave, or signal—and they can understand all forms of communication, except the technology herein. But even so, be careful.*

*17. Memorize these instructions and then burn
this parchment. Burn all three parchment
notes as soon as possible.*

The kids read Fingal's notes multiple times until they had all three committed to memory. Then they burned the parchment behind the corncrib. They talked about how to prepare for this trip. They especially wondered how any of the strange details of Grezniks, blue stones, and hidden mines could possibly be true. Most of all, they were not yet sure they would even go.

But Jovi said, "We could probably leave for the day and find him. He can't be that far away."

50

GIVE ME A CLUE

Days passed and Jatuh could not get any relief from the torment that shook its insides and left it wanting to flee far away. One evening, Jatuh could not take it any longer. It snuck away from the regiment, walked to a nearby lake, and spoke to the waters held there. "I cannot just wander aimlessly following every craving. You are wasting time by tormenting me. If you want the stones, just give me the clues and tell me where the mine is. You owe me for my obedience. Give me a clue!"

Jatuh waited for the Voices to speak and deliver a clue. But the lake was a still, blue glass. Snowcapped mountains in the distance were dusted orange from the lingering midnight sun and reflected perfectly in the water. Jatuh threw a rock into the lake to disturb the reflection and summon the Voices, but instead the water welcomed the rock as it fell to the bottom. Ripples of water spread out in a circle, breaking the reflection of the mountains the way laughter breaks the silence of our sorrows.

Jatuh returned to the regiment and was surprised to see Boshlek calling a meeting of circle leaders. Before the meeting started, Boshlek called Jatuh over and said, "The regiment will commence a search for the marble run as a trial. Your trial. If our enemies respond to our efforts, it will affirm that your secret intelligence was accurate and we are close to finding the mine. But if we are completely off track, the opposition will ignore us, and you will be walked into the sea for wasting our time."

Boshlek called the meeting to order and explained the details of the marble run. "We will commence a search for the marble run. Keep a ready eye out for enemy scouts. If they are tracking our efforts, we are on target."

The regiment created many marbles to match the size of the yelloweye. To begin the search, all circles lined up adjacent to each other then moved methodically toward the north, studying every tor and crag. At each rocky structure, they determined if the precisely formed marble run could exist within the stone structure.

For several days in a row, at a distance, a female lynx stood high on a mountain slope watching the regiment. According to Jatuh's untruthful report to Boshlek, the lynxes unknowingly revealed the clue. From the ominous presence of a lurking lynx, Boshlek concluded the regiment was on the right track. Little did Boshlek know her presence was merely coincidence.

Boshlek called Jatuh over. "Leave to seek the next clue. Kill that spying lynx on your way. If you are not back soon, you will be found and destroyed by the scouts."

Jatuh, excited to leave, said, "You will not be disappointed, Eternal Commander. I will return and deliver another valuable clue."

▲ ▲ ▲

The lynx watched the Grezniks crawling over rocky structures, but she had no idea what they were trying to do. She thought the Greznik behavior highly unusual and delivered a message to the allies: "The Grezniks are behaving strangely. They stopped mining for the stones and are making marbles, all the same size and weight, and rolling them down rocky structures. They're losing their marbles in the effort. They drool and salivate the entire time as if blue stones were nearby."

Sandhill cranes spread the word of the strange Greznik behavior, and in no time, the news had traveled far. A musk ox named Kasper ran off to share the news. Not long after, a wise old Arctic lemming named Oskar received the message and said, "Grezniks are near. Set a trap."

▲ ▲ ▲

Jatuh ran slyly away from the regiment and sped up the mountain slope to snatch and eat the lynx who had been observing the Grezniks. However, when Jatuh reached the top, it could not find the lynx and was puzzled by her sudden disappearance. Jatuh searched for her, but then it felt a craving to travel northward. Jatuh abandoned its search for the lynx and let the Voices guide its travels northward, to the mountains in the Gates of the Arctic National Park and Preserve. Jatuh was crossing a wide-open mountain valley filled with wildflowers when a sudden and over-whelming fatigue compelled it to stop for a rest.

As soon as Jatuh stopped running, the powerful attacks from within began. The shakes were excruciating and severe, and they seared Jatuh from within. Jatuh had for-gotten how unbearably painful the shakes had been when it turned into a yelloweye rockfish. This time the pain was so debilitating that Jatuh collapsed to the ground, its writhing hidden amid the lovely wildflowers and tall grasses of the expansive valley.

Unlike when Jatuh became a rockfish, its body did not convert to a different creature immediately. Instead, its body shrank. Everything inside shattered thousands of times a second as it shriveled smaller and smaller. As the agony became intolerable, Jatuh regretted seeking the clues again and shouted at the Voices, "Leave me alone!"

When Jatuh became small enough to fit easily in the palm of a person's hand, its legs pulled inside its body and disappeared. Four new ones grew in their place, short and stubby with tiny paws. Its translucent fur turned a dusty, spot-ted brown. A short, tiny tail popped out. In no time, Jatuh had converted into an adorably handsome Arctic lemming.

When the process was finally over, Jatuh looked at itself and grumbled to the Voices, "I'm small enough to be snatched and eaten by a hawk! How stupid of you to change me into a lemming!"

The Voices struck at Jatuh's disgruntled insolence by jolting voltage through its system that swiftly blew the critter backward. As Jatuh waited for the pain to subside, it heard a multitude of little voices coming toward it. It rolled back onto its feet, stood up on its itty-bitty hind legs, and saw a gathering of lemmings traveling across the valley.

Jatuh hid and listened to the lemmings mingle and chat, memorizing their manner of speaking. Once Jatuh could imitate them perfectly, it ran to them. On the edge of the gathering, it walked up next to the prettiest lemming.

Jatuh, fully disguised, said, "Hello, can you help me? I've been traveling too far, too long. I need to rest."

The pretty and petite lemming was struck with the handsome and strong traveler and asked, "What brings you to us?"

Jatuh the lemming answered, "I have journeyed very far. My entire community, home, and family disappeared in a terrible accident. An awful landslide. And I am the only one left. I have been wandering about looking for a new home, a new family of lemmings, when I heard your voices."

"What a terrible tragedy to have gone through. How awful to lose one's family, home, and community. Of course you are welcome to join us. What is your name?" asked the pretty lemming.

"My name is Tiro," said Jatuh.

"Welcome, Tiro. My name is Sally. I can't imagine losing all my family and friends. So devastating."

"Yes, I miss them deeply. It's difficult to be a lonesome lemming in such a massive landscape as it is up here. It makes one feel so small, so lost. Thank you for welcoming me. If it's okay, I would like to rest here awhile."

"Of course you can," said Sally.

"Thank you so much. I'm much obliged."

Sally was impressed by his politeness and suggested, "Why don't you join me? We're about to start an important meeting."

"What's the meeting about?" asked Tiro.

"Our secret. It's under attack," said Sally, feeling comforted by having a strong and handsome lemming by her side. "The Grezniks are gathering the secrets, finding the clues. I hope they do not discover our beautiful secret."

"We do have a beautiful secret," said Tiro, hoping to lure her into telling him the details.

"I doubt anyone else has a secret that is a sound, an echo," whispered Sally.

"I doubt it," said Tiro. "Echoes are such a mournful sound."

"Ours especially—a C-sharp. I do love to sing in the mountains and hear an echo. But if I could ever be so lucky as to hear this important echo, I would wish the echo to be a happier tone."

"I hope the Grezniks never learn of our beautiful clue. It would be so devastating," Tiro said deceitfully.

Sally led Tiro to the large gathering of lemmings just as the meeting began. Sally's admiring friend, a small little lemming named Gwilim, moved toward her, hoping to be able to stand next to her. But he was disappointed to see that Sally had brought a new friend to the gathering. From afar, Gwilim wondered who the lucky lemming was who had garnered her attention.

The wise old lemming named Oskar called the meeting to order. Some lemmings stood on the perimeter of the meeting as lookouts to ensure that no other creature could hear or observe the meeting.

Earlier that day, Oskar had received word from a sand-hill crane that their network of allies had been betrayed, and that Oskar's help was needed to figure out how deep the breach had gone. On the chance there was a traitor within his community, Oskar called the community together to hear his announcement.

Oskar began with administrative details and then said, "We all know that our secret, the secret we hold so dear, must be treasured and protected. We are one cornerstone of the Great Defense. We hold the clue to one corner of the polygon that marks the blue stone mine. And we must be wary of anyone who may wish to steal it, particularly Grezniks."

As Oskar spoke, he looked out across the crowd with a wary eye, hoping they would remain steadfast in their mission. He feared that someone might, in a moment of weakness, break their honor. "We must protect our secret every day and always. But traitors could be very near to us. Traitors are sneaky. They seep into your life. They often look to be on your side by offering appealing proposals and promises they can never keep."

Sally shivered at the fear of such terribleness. Tiro stepped closer to Sally to comfort her, and Sally smiled at Tiro admiringly. In disappointment, Gwilim stepped farther away.

Oskar continued, "The weaker ones of any community wish you to do as they have done—answer to the seducing darkness that they have already succumbed to. It's easier for them if you join their mistaken path rather than admit their own tormented pain. But they won't admit to you they gave in nor that their insides burn from the pain of having done so. Instead, they will make it look so fun to give up and give in. They'll invite you to join their path and will cheer you on to make you believe their mirage of fun is real. Their deceitful friends will encourage you to break your courage, make you feel that you are wrong. Do not let them feed your fears and insecurities."

Tiro felt restless, horribly itchy, and uncomfortable from Oskar's lofty thoughts so he turned to Sally and held her little paw. He said, "Does he always talk this much?"

"Sometimes longer." Sally smiled.

Oskar said, "I want us to remain strong together. To remind ourselves that our wisdom is a quiet guide that pulls our hearts forward to the great callings. But do not mistake wisdom for a breeze that easily passes you by. Wisdom is resolute. It anchors deep in your soul. You cannot run from it. Be steadfast in kindness, and fight to the end."

A lemming interrupted and asked Oskar, "Is there a traitor among us today?"

Oskar continued, "A lurking danger is near. Grezniks are gathering in Alaska, and they will always be prepared for battle. Battles are not won easily, and they sometimes force us to say goodbye to each other forever. If this happens, you must, with all your might, carry on our secret with courage."

The lemmings were surprised to hear such fearful warnings from their leader, and they murmured their worries to each other.

"Today I'm sharing with you more details of our secret," said Oskar. "The secret of the echo. We have never known where to stand to hear the echo. But now I will tell you. In the Wrangell–St. Elias Mountain Range stands the Grand Parapet, which has a steep mountain face called the Knife Edge. To hear the echo one must stand across from the Knife Edge on a rhombus-shaped stone and sing loudly the C-sharp pitch. Your voice will not be heard by anyone, yet a loud echo will come back. And the only creature who will hear the echo is you—the one who stands on the stone and sings the note. I ask that you hold this secret dear to your heart and never speak about it again."

Tiro just barely contained his excitement from hearing the second clue. After the meeting, Tiro rested with the lemmings and then whispered to Sally, "I'm sorry to have to leave you, but I must continue on. I must travel forward on my own."

"Tiro, please don't leave. It's never safe to travel alone. You'll be eaten or hurt," said Sally, wishing the handsome new lemming would stay.

Tiro felt such a rapacious desire to eat the pretty little Sally that it drooled foul-smelling phlegm. Tiro lapped up and swallowed the drool before she saw a drop of it.

Tiro said to Sally, "I must leave. Oskar's speech inspired me to not give up. He said we need to stick together. To help each other. I need to find my cousins, and I believe them to be not too far away. But if I can't find them, I'll return to you."

"Promise?"

"I promise," said Tiro. He feigned a forlorn goodbye and ran off.

When out of sight, Tiro ran up and over the valley's ridge, faster than any other lemming could possibly run, right into a wide, rocky crevice. Hidden within the crevice, Tiro changed back into Jatuh the Greznik and ran back to the regiment, directly to Boshlek to report the second clue to the powerful blue stone mine.

51

LEAVING FOR CAMP

After burning Fingal's notes, Tony said, "What if Fingal isn't close by?"

"But I don't want to abandon him," said Mitch.

"What if Grezniks are attacking him?" said Jovi.

"If Grezniks even exist at all," said Tony.

"Right, how could they be real?" asked Mitch. "What if he's just a crazy old man?"

"I think he might be," said Tony. "What if it is all some kind of weird delusion, hypnosis, a dream or something?"

"We really did ride on a wild tractor. That wasn't a dream," said Jovi. "That was all too real."

"And those reporters were real," added Tony.

"How about we fire up the bikes?" said Mitch. "See if they even work."

"And figure out where Fingal is," said Tony.

"Yeah, maybe he's just testing us. Maybe he's just sitting at the Cup-n-Saucer restaurant, having a bowl of soup," said Jovi.

"And apple pie," said Mitch. "Let's go get the gear from his farm and figure it out later."

They rode their horses up to Fingal's farm and found the old rain barrel by the honeysuckles. They located the canvas bag with a waterproof box containing the walkie-talkies, instructions, and helmets.

That afternoon, they found a very quiet spot in the house, down in the cellar, where they were sure there would be no other sound. There they programmed the walkie-talkies to recognize their voices.

They got the bikes out of the shed and attached the walkie-talkies to them, then downloaded the voice-recognition data.

"Ready to start up the bikes?" asked Mitch.

"Yes," said Tony. "If we can't get them to work, we won't be going anyway."

They joined all three bikes together with the activation wires. Connected, they pedaled down one of the rarely used dirt roads, learning how to pedal at the exact same speed. When one of them went too fast, the wires disconnected. They soon got the hang of biking while tethered to each other and pedaled as fast as they could.

They pedaled faster and faster. Each time one of them started to fall behind, the other two would encourage the other, "Keep going! Don't give up!"

Jovi was younger, and she was fading more quickly than her brothers. Mitch said, "You can do this, Jovi! You got it!"

"We can do this!" cheered Tony.

But Tony hit a bump in the road, and his bike slipped

just enough to disconnect the cord. They had to start all over. They reconnected the wires, counted to three, and pedaled as fast as they could. They were going fast, but it was taking too long to start the bikes, and their legs were losing steam. They were all about to slow down as they gasped for air. They looked over at each other, knowing they could not keep going this fast—that in a few more seconds, their legs would give out.

Ahead of them was a dead end blocked by an electric barbed wire fence.

Tony said, "These bikes had better start or we'll crash!"

Just in time, a beeping green light on their handlebars turned on. The engines were ready to start.

They each spoke into their voice recognition system and said, "Start engine!"

Their engines successfully started.

"Disconnect!" Tony yelled.

Mitch pulled the wire that connected him to Jovi, and it reeled back into Jovi's seat instantly. Tony disconnected from Mitch's bike.

They had no time to breathe a sigh of relief because as soon as the engines started, the bikes quickly accelerated. They were all headed for the electric barbed wire fence, and there was not enough time to turn. A button appeared on their screens that blinked *Jump!*

They all hit their *Jump!* buttons, and over the fence they went.

"Bosonataski-Fishengardet! We did it!" Jovi screamed out.

Hearing Jovi cheer their awful name in the wide-open fields cracked Mitch up. He laughed in hysterics as he tried to keep control of his bike.

Tony practiced fast turns, driving in figure eights. "This is so awesome!" Then he, too, laughed at the sheer joy of riding at such speeds.

The kids tested the capabilities of their bikes, learning how to turn fast, ride over rocky patches of pasture, and use the communication system. Their pants got muddy and their knees got scraped from practicing low-riding turns.

They all slowed down and stopped along the creek.

"Should we try jumping it?" asked Tony, excited to test the bikes' more dangerous capabilities.

Both Jovi and Mitch were more nervous than Tony to leap over the water.

"Tony, you go first," said Jovi.

They picked a narrow section of the creek. Tony backed up his bike, then accelerated toward the creek and tucked down as he hit the *Jump River* button. The bike successfully leaped across. After landing, he spun the bike around to face Mitch and Jovi on the other side and encouraged them to come over.

Mitch went next and landed perfectly. After much encouragement, Jovi got the guts and leaped. Thrilled by a successful landing, she said, "I did it!" and turned around and jumped back over.

They practiced jumping then decided to cross the creek at its widest section. Tony and Mitch jumped at the same time, but on this try gliders popped out of the back of the bike, and the boys floated down for a smooth landing.

Jovi followed, but the gliders that popped out of her bike were like a ballerina's skirt that matched the colors of her bike. She spun around in the air like a dancer twirling on her toe.

"Ooh, that is so pretty!" said Jovi, who loved the feeling of a graceful leap. It felt as if she were spinning gracefully across the rooftops of New York, just as she had imagined so many times.

After practicing their jumps, they rode across the open pasture just for fun. They jumped over another fence line, but Jovi's bike landed in a different part of the pasture than Mitch and Tony—the portion fenced off for a bull. She did not realize a bull was contained there as she enjoyed riding leisurely across the pasture. She did not see that a bull had taken off charging toward her, allured by her colorful bike.

Mitch yelled, "Jovi, get out of there!"

"Jovi! *Get out of there!*" shouted Tony.

Jovi did not hear them. She had her eyes closed and was enjoying the feeling of the air against her face. She was humming a tune and relishing the smooth ride of her bike. But when she opened her eyes, she saw the bull charging for her. She spun her bike around and sped away, yelling, "*Ahhh!*"

Mitch and Tony jumped over the fence and used their bikes like a shepherd dog to herd the bull away from her. To get away from the bull, she jumped the fence and crash-landed in a pile of mud. But her bike kept going and smashed into a big boulder, then tumbled and bounced all the way down into a ditch, out of sight.

Mitch and Tony sped forward, jumped the fence, and raced to Jovi, afraid she was badly hurt. They were relieved to find her a little dazed by the wipeout, covered in mud, but okay. They also expected her bike to be ruined by the catastrophic wipeout, but they were surprised to find it completely undamaged.

"Wow. No way. It doesn't even have a scratch. That's impossible," said Mitch.

"There's no doubt these bikes are Fingal's inventions," said Tony.

From all the fast turns, they all had torn pants and scraped-up knees.

Tony said, "We need knee pads. We weren't even turning as fast as these bikes can go."

"Fingal said that the signal from his boot would appear on our screens, but I haven't seen it," said Mitch.

They each looked through the menu on their bike's monitor to find Fingal's beacon signal, but no one could locate it. Mitch noticed, in the lower left of the screen, a small icon for a pair of boots. He clicked on the icon and the words "Location Found—Fingal" popped up on the screen. A topographical map appeared, and there was a blinking blue boot icon located on the map.

"That's it! That must be where he is," Tony said excitedly.

They examined the map and realized he was located near Lopp Lagoon, a large tidal lake up in Alaska, near the Bering Strait.

"Alaska! He's in Alaska?" exclaimed Jovi. "I thought he'd be a few towns away. Or Iowa. But Alaska?"

"How would we ever get up to Lopp Lagoon?" Tony wondered, equally dismayed at the prospect of traveling that far.

Mitch added, "It'd take weeks to get up there, and he might be gone by then."

"And Mom and Dad would wonder where we are. We can't do that," said Jovi.

The screens included live satellite weather feeds. Lopp Lagoon, just below the Arctic Circle, was cold, rainy, and barren tundra—like nothing they had ever seen before.

"Not a tropical paradise," said Tony.

"Maybe he has a walkie-talkie. Let's try to connect with him," Mitch said.

They got out their walkie-talkies and tried to reach him, but they were unsuccessful.

"How many miles up to Lopp Lagoon from here?" asked Tony.

Mitch mapped it out. "It is over three thousand miles point to point."

Their hearts sank.

"That's a long way to go," said Tony. "And how could we ever be gone that long?"

"But Fingal needs us," added Jovi.

"How about we just pretend we're going and make a list of what we would bring if we did go," suggested Mitch.

"Good idea. After that, we can decide if we want to go," said Tony.

The kids went back into the farmhouse and made a list of the gear they would need, in addition to what Fingal left for them at his farm such as rain gear, a tent, matches, sleeping bags, and so on. It was late in the day as they packed each item into their backpacks. They checked and rechecked that they had packed everything they needed, then they closed up their packs and hid them under their beds.

"Tomorrow we'll go up to Fingal's barn and get the pemmican," Tony said.

The windows were open and a cool breeze blew in, delivering an unexpected chill on a summer night. The curtains flapped, and Jovi pulled a blanket over her shoulders and wondered if the chill was coming down from Alaska.

The next morning, just as the kids came down for breakfast, the parents got an important call and disappeared into the study and shut the door. The kids drank juice as they talked quietly about how to get to Alaska and decided it was impossible.

When their parents got off the phone, they came back in the kitchen but were extremely distracted. Their mom poured some cereal, but she accidentally poured tomato juice on it instead of milk. Their dad put in some frozen waffles for himself, but he doused them with corn oil instead of syrup. The kids grabbed a jar of peanut butter and some bread and made some sandwiches and dashed out the door.

They ran out to their horses, José, Joker, and Max, and rode them over to Fingal's farm. They found the barrel of pemmican, right where Fingal said it would be, in the horse barn next to the tack. There was plenty of it. They packed up the pemmican to bring it back to their house for the journey, yet they were still not sure if they were even going.

At the bottom of the big pemmican barrel, they found a fully loaded potato sack. They pulled it out and found three jackets to wear while riding their bikes. Tucked into a sleeve of each jacket they found the special night-vision and binocular goggles. But they also found three flashlights that expanded into walking sticks, specially made for difficult mountain hiking. Also at the bottom of the barrel they found a tiny metal box containing the three wristwatches. They put the gear in one bag and strung that bag onto the saddle of José. They tied the sacks of pemmican onto the back of Max, and they rode back home.

They put José, Joker, and Max out to graze and pulled out their bikes. They put on their new wristwatches, opened the screens, and saw the three new blinking boot icons on the map.

Tony said, "Those must be our feet! Let's test it!"

Mitch said, "Jovi, run over to the horse barn. Tony, you run over to the hog house. I'll watch on the screen."

When they ran, Mitch saw the boots moving across the screen at every step. He assigned a name to each icon, so they would know who was who on the screen. They tested to make sure Mitch's icon worked correctly too. Then they went back in the house, pulled their packs out from under their beds, and brought them out to the shed. They divided the pemmican evenly between the three of them and packed it efficiently into their three packs.

The kids completed a final gear check.

"We're ready . . . if we decide to go," said Tony.

They had no idea how they could ever leave the farm without explaining to their parents where they were going. What could they say to explain their absence? Fingal made it clear they must tell no one, absolutely no one. Yet they could not simply sneak away. Their parents would report them missing—and then what?

"We can't just disappear. We can't do that to our parents," said Jovi.

"Who knows? Maybe they'd never know we were gone," wondered Mitch.

"Possible, actually. But we can't just leave them without saying where we're going," said Tony.

"I know you're right. But remember what Fingal told us?" Mitch said.

"About what?" asked Jovi.

"The Journey," said Mitch.

"You don't get to choose the Journey," said Tony.

They all finished the sentence together: "The Journey chooses you."

Jovi said, "Fingal does not have anyone but us. Who else will rescue him?"

They nodded their heads. They were ready to try.

They went back home for dinner and wondered how they were ever going to be able to leave. During dinner, they were somber and quiet.

"You three sure don't have much to say," said Caroline. "You didn't overhear our plan, did you?"

The kids sat up straight and said, "What plan?"

"We got a call from our lawyer today, and it turns out there has been an important development in Grandpa's case," said Darrell. "It seems that years back when he was married to Grandma Vicki, he parked some of her money in an obscure account and somehow forgot about it. And now it's ours. It's not as much as we're used to, but it's something. With that, along with our basil business, we'll have some money coming in, and we can move forward with our new business idea. So . . ."

Mom interrupted, clasping her hands excitedly. "We're moving us all back to Manhattan. We're going to start an urban farming movement there—a trend in rooftop farming. Imagine all the roofs in Manhattan, Brooklyn, Queens, and the Bronx covered in herbs! And think of the money we could make selling all the products New Yorkers need to farm their rooftops."

The kids stared at their parents blankly. Moving back to the city without rescuing Fingal would be terrible. They imagined Fingal left alone in Alaska and the farm left behind to decay. The horses—José, Joker, and Max—would be abandoned again with no one on the farm to feed them. A move back to New York was the worst possible news.

Caroline was puzzled. "We thought you'd be ecstatic at the idea. But no need to look so sad. We aren't totally sure yet. Dad and I are going to New York ahead of you to research rooftops. You three will stay behind."

"By ourselves? Without a nanny?" asked Jovi.

"We'd never leave you here alone," answered Caroline.

"Is Aziza coming?" Jovi asked excitedly.

"No," answered Darrell.

"Uncle Tobias will be coming to stay with you," said Caroline. "He's thinking of giving up on his acting career and even his dream to be a master chef. He's coming here to decide if he wants to run the basil farm and our vineyard."

"We don't have grapes," said Tony.

"But we might. So, while Dad and I are in New York the rest of the summer, he's going to be your nanny!"

The kids normally dreaded a visit from Uncle Tobias. He and their mom argued about the past all the time. And when he stayed with them, Tobias always laid on the couch, complained of headaches in the morning, and never did anything fun with them. Tobias just barked at them to be quiet while he watched the TV, complained constantly of the world's injustices, and moaned that the powers that be do not fix them.

But now the circumstances were different, and the kids looked at each other and smiled—only because this might be the only time they would want Tobias to come. If he came to the farm, it meant the kids would not have to move back to the city with their parents, at least not yet. Maybe they could figure out a way to help Fingal in the meantime.

They all heard a car coming down the driveway, and Caroline jumped up out of her chair. "Perfect timing! That's probably Tobias."

A taxicab drove down the driveway and stopped at the front door of their big farmhouse. Tobias jumped out, and they realized he had taken a cab a distance of 150 miles from the nearest metropolitan airport.

Caroline asked, "You took a cab? Who takes a cab for such a long distance?"

Tobias said, "I can't follow a map, or even a GPS. You know I'm terrible at directions. But this cab driver knows his way around cornfields."

Within a day of Tobias's arrival, the parents packed their suitcases, said their goodbyes, and drove to the airport to fly back to the big city. It did not take long for the kids to find Tobias reclining on the couch, watching TV, and moping about the lack of great acting opportunities.

The kids left Tobias to his pouting and went outside to double-check their gear again. They hoped they had packed enough food. That evening, as they were in their bedroom doing a final gear check, Tobias barked that they were making too much noise upstairs. The next morning, as the kids made breakfast for themselves, he barked that they were clanging the dishes too loudly and barked that it aggravated his headache. The kids agreed he might be part dog, except for the fact that dogs are really fun.

They were ready to leave.

JOURNEY

52

CHARGED

Despite their doubts, Mitch, Tony, and Jovi decided to embark on the journey to find Old Man Fingal up in Alaska's Lopp Lagoon. If the new motorbikes proved to be as powerful as the tractor and the flying combine, they believed the lengthy trek to the Arctic was at least in the realm of possibility. Unsure of which route they should take, Mitch pulled out a big pile of maps from Mr. Charlie's belongings. They took the ones they needed up to the haymow and stretched them out. After a long discussion on the benefits and challenges of various routes, they narrowed it down to two and flipped a coin.

With the route selected, they had only one remaining step: tell Tobias they were leaving.

"We have to tell him something. We can't just slip away," said Tony.

"How about we tell him we're going to camp?" said Jovi.

"Good idea. And it's kind of partially true," said Mitch.

"Let's hope he doesn't ask any questions."

Tony said, "Let's time it just right. If we tell him around bedtime, there's a chance he won't ask anything."

The kids all knew Tobias's daily routine and agreed with Tony's plan. That evening they found Tobias, as usual, sound asleep on the couch with the TV on. They tried to wake him up to tell him they were going to a camp in Iowa, but as expected, they could not rouse him.

Mitch spoke to him anyway. "We're leaving for an adventure camp."

Half asleep, Tobias mumbled, "Yeah, go on. Have fun."

Mitch left a note explaining that they had left for camp, and he included the phone numbers of their walkie-talkies as their contact information. They were not sure what they would say to Tobias if he actually called, but they would worry about that later. They also left instructions on how to feed Max, José, and Joker. They hoped Tobias remembered enough of his childhood days on his mom's farm to manage the horse care.

At dusk, they snuck out of the house with their packs, got their bikes out of the barn, and turned on the engine silencers. They completed one last equipment check, then put on their special jackets, goggles, and helmets. They were ready to go.

"How long do you think it will take us?" asked Jovi.

"Depends on how fast these bikes can go," answered Mitch.

"If they can go as fast as the tractor, we'll get there in a couple of days at most," said Tony.

"Check or hold?" asked Mitch.

"Check!" said Tony and Jovi.

They did not admit it to each other, but they all were scared and unsure of what this adventure would bring. They took a good look at the farm, not sure when they would be back, and started the engines.

The kids rode all night across Minnesota, avoided major roads, headed toward South Dakota, then drove up through North Dakota and into Canada. They traveled hidden in the racetrack lines of tall corn or along railroad tracks. Just like the tractor, their bikes left no trace. With the engine silencers on, they flew by as quietly as milkweed seeds blowing in the wind. No one would ever know they had passed by.

Tony said, "This is like being a driver in the world's fastest video game."

"Only it's real this time!" said Mitch.

The kids rode fast all night, and their skills on the bikes improved as they became more familiar with their power and finesse. They accelerated the bikes to top speed, sped through forests, bounced over rocky landscapes, and jumped boulders. With their powerful night vision goggles, they did not need headlights. And they traveled so fast, they were not seen by anyone.

The first several river jumps in the dark terrified them, but they got accustomed to it and jumped more easily as the journey wore on. They were ever alert to avoid traveling near people. Their bikes had heat sensors that marked locations of people or vehicles nearby, so they could stay clear of everyone. The kids remembered what Old Man had said about attracting a lot of attention: avoid it.

They sped across Saskatchewan, then Alberta, British Columbia, and through the Yukon. The air got colder, and the bugs were horrible. Unlike normal windshields, no bugs splattered on their helmets even at their high speeds. When they stopped for a break, they wore bug nets over their heads and slept briefly in the tent with the screens shut tight. After traveling through the Yukon, they cut over into Alaska. They were now traveling at a very high latitude, so the sun never slept. They saw many species of birds and animals—hawks, deer, eagles, beavers, ducks, otters, snakes, moose, and more.

As they crossed over into Alaska, they passed between the two tiny towns of Circle and Chalkyitsik and pointed their route directly toward Fingal's location on the Seward Peninsula along Lopp Lagoon. Yet they found it very strange and troublesome that Fingal's blinking boot icon on the screen had not changed its location on the map their entire journey.

"Maybe he's just hanging out in a tent," said Jovi.

"Let's hope he's all right," said Mitch. "Let's keep moving fast to get there."

Dark gray clouds blocked the sun, then rain pummeled their helmets as the landscape around them dropped into silence. If they saw an animal, it seemed to be spying on them. Swarms of birds would follow them for miles, sometimes at a distance behind or ahead. Occasionally the birds would surge forward and swoop down as if to attack something the kids could not see. Creatures would go silent when they passed. Or dart off as if terrified.

In the distance, they saw a herd of musk oxen. As they neared, the herd suddenly charged toward them from every direction as if to trap them in the middle.

"They're charging us! Quick turn!" shouted Tony.

They turned and sped through the only opening in the herd. However, once they got through the blockade of musk oxen, another herd blocked them and forced them to alter their course again. This continued for an hour, and by then the kids were well off their planned route.

The charging of the musk oxen waned, but then Mitch saw a brown bear charge at Jovi. "Jovi, a bear! Turn!"

Jovi did not get away before the bear swung at her. She just barely dodged it by turning and speeding in the opposite direction of her brothers, where she could no longer see them.

Jovi said, "Mitch! Tony! Why are we getting attacked? Where are you?"

While Mitch worried about Jovi, a brown bear came up from behind him and another behind Tony. Mitch and Tony forked off in different directions and in the wrong direction from their intended route. All three kids ended up far away from each other. Just as the brown bears ran out of steam and could not chase the kids any longer, swarms of birds dove down on each of the kids and dropped small pebbles on them like rain. They could not see their way ahead and scattered even farther away from each other.

Mitch took a careful look at his bike's monitor to see

where Jovi and Tony were, but they were traveling in completely different directions. He spun his bike around to get to Jovi first, but then another swarm of birds dove down. So thick was their flock that he had a hard time seeing ahead. To dodge their attack, he was forced to go the other way.

Suddenly he lost the signals from Jovi and Tony, and his monitor went dark.

"Jovi! Tony! Where are you?" hollered Mitch. He dodged more attacks as he tried unsuccessfully to turn on his monitor.

His greatest fear had come true: he had lost them. For the first time in his life he desperately wanted to hear Jovi yell, "Bosonataski-Fishengardet!"

Mitch was desperate. "Tony! Jovi! Can you hear me? Answer me!"

They were all moving farther and farther away from each other, and Mitch was sure he had lost them. Tears dripped from his eyes. He dodged bird attacks around every bend, but as he rounded the base of a cliff edge, he slammed on his brakes suddenly to avoid crashing into Tony and Jovi.

"I thought I lost you!" said Mitch through the pouring rain.

Jovi and Tony did not have time to respond. Lynxes charged at them, and the kids were forced to flee again. This zigzagging, high-speed race continued for a couple of hours, and the intensity of it prevented the kids from keeping track of where they were on their maps and where they were headed.

Suddenly the chasing stopped. They were exhausted, and their hearts were pounding.

"Let's hope that's over," said Tony.

"We can't sit out in the open like this. Where are we?" asked Jovi.

Mitch's monitor suddenly turned on, and his map appeared in full color again. "Wait, weird, it's working again," said Mitch. "And how'd this happen—we're almost there!"

They traveled the remaining distance in good time and without any more attacks. There were no trees, the land was flat, and they could see far ahead. Finally, their three boot icons aligned with Fingal's on their maps. They got off their bikes and looked everywhere, but Fingal was nowhere to be found.

"Fingal should be here," said Tony.

"But he isn't," said Jovi anxiously.

"What if the device in his boot failed and it's giving off the wrong signal? Maybe he's not even in Alaska," said Mitch.

"Don't say that," said Jovi, using her binoculars to scan the landscape to find him.

Not knowing what else to do, they wandered around.

"Over here! I found his boots!" said Tony.

Mitch and Jovi ran over.

"Just his boots. This isn't good," said Mitch.

"I hope he wasn't eaten by a Greznik," Jovi said despairingly.

Mitch and Tony feared the same. Tony reached into one boot and was surprised to find a note Fingal had written, in the same code they had come to know. Something had already opened it, crumpled it up, and ripped it into pieces. The kids put the pieces together and hoped that whoever found the note had been unable to decipher it. They were quickly able to decode it, even though it was written hastily:

If you have found my boots, you are truly amazing voyagers. I think the Grezniks can read the signals from your wristwatches, so you need to take them off and hide them. Inside the sole of my left boot you will find a small device that looks like a microchip. Like your watches, it emits a signal. Remove it. Next to where you found my boots, you will find an oval granite stone, about six inches in diameter, that has a crisscrossing layer of quartz. Turn the stone at the horizontal layer of quartz, and it will reveal a compartment inside. Put the watches and the device from my boot inside, then twist the stone back to its closed position. The rock is made of a very dense material that will prevent anyone from receiving the signal. Take the stone with you. Turn off your communication system, and do not use it again. The Grezniks will lose our trail for a while. Do this and leave immediately.

Be sure to pack my boots and bring them to me. I will be waiting for you at an old cabin. Search your bike's map for a maple leaf. It marks the location of the cabin. The cabin looks abandoned and will be marked by an anchored cross doorknocker and a star-shaped doorknob. Come as quickly as you can. Without your wristwatches, your bikes' maps will no longer be able to mark your location. So never, ever leave each other's side. You should never be alone.

Do not leave this note here. Burn it. The back of each bike has a flamethrower, which ignites by switching the lever on the left handlebar and then two reverse twists of the right handlebar. Make sure others are standing far away when you do this. Practice bringing the flame down with the turn of the handlebar before you try to burn this note.

I am hopeful we will see each other soon to continue our important mission.

Travel strong,

Fingal

They searched the area but could not find the oval stone. Tony found a steep dip in the landscape that was difficult to climb down, and when he used his binoculars to search it, he thought he saw the stone lying opened at the bottom.

"Jovi, you're the best climber. Can you get it?" asked Mitch.

Jovi was not sure she could, but she decided to try anyway. She climbed down carefully and found the opened stone, then put it in her pack. When she reached the top, they took off their watches and pulled the small device out of Fingal's boot. They placed them all inside the rock and closed it.

"Let's get going again," said Mitch, as he put the stone in his pack.

The kids found the maple leaf on the mapping system, located in the forty-two-mile-long mountain range called the Kigluaik Mountains, on the same Seward Peninsula as Lopp Lagoon.

They locked the GPS onto the cabin's location so the bikes could lead them there. The kids practiced igniting the flamethrowers on the backs of their bikes and burned the torn letter. They packed Fingal's boots in Tony's pack.

They raced off toward the mountains, still worried about Fingal and hoping they could find the cabin once they got there. They took their bikes up to top speed and neared the mountain range. When close enough, they stopped their bikes and used their powerful binoculars to zoom in on the landscape and search the mountains for the cabin.

"I think I see it," said Jovi, pointing ahead.

Mitch said, "Found it. You're right, that must be his cabin. I see the anchored cross doorknocker."

Tony saw the cabin too and added disappointedly, "And the star-shaped doorknob. But no signs of Fingal. Let's go."

As they started up their bikes again, a musk ox stood on a ridge and stared at them ominously. When they looked at the musk ox, he tipped down below the horizon.

"This is all creepy. As soon as we find Fingal, we're going home!" said Jovi.

Tony said, "I agree. And if Fingal's not in the cabin, let's go home."

As they neared Fingal's cabin, it was clear that the last leg of the journey was impossible for the bikes to navigate, even with all their special capabilities. They would have to leave their bikes behind, which meant leaving their maps behind too.

The kids reviewed the possible routes to the cabin on their maps. The most difficult route was the shortest, but it required climbing a very steep scree and balancing on narrow ridges that could plunge them downward with only the slightest misstep.

The easiest route was the most feasible of the options, but the hike was the longest, had many switchbacks, and would likely take the remainder of the day and part of the night.

"Should we flip a coin?" asked Jovi.

"Let's just do the medium difficulty one. It's steep, but it looks like we can change our mind about halfway up and connect to the easier route if we need to," said Tony.

The kids studied the map carefully, memorized the route, turned off their bikes, and stashed them deep within a rock cleft.

As they started the hike to reach Fingal, Mitch said, "How could Fingal hike up here without his boots? His feet must be raw."

"And freezing," Tony added. "Even my feet are cold, and I have boots on."

Jovi said, "If we get attacked again by those animals, we can't outrun them on foot."

Tony was just as scared but said, "If brown bears chase us, maybe the lynx will scare them away. And if the lynx charge us, ducks will dive-bomb the lynx. And if mountain goats charge us, puffins will scare away the mountain goats, and . . ."

"Muskrats will chase the mountain goats. And fox will chase muskrats," Mitch continued.

They kept Jovi amused with their storytelling. But as the hike got more difficult, they were all breathing too hard to talk. They took a break to drink some water.

Jovi asked, "Do you think they'll sell postcards at Fingal's cabin?"

"Doubt it. But who would we send them to anyway?" asked Mitch.

"I don't know. I was just imagining we were at camp. Kids always send postcards from camp."

"We're supposed to be at a camp somewhere in Iowa. How would we explain 'Hello from the Kigluaik Mountains' to people?" said Mitch.

Tony said, "I wish I could get a postcard for Kenny. That's who I need to send a postcard to. But there's no cereal to count up here. How much pemmican fits on a spoon?"

53

WHAT'S THAT SMELL?

After Jatuh left to seek a clue, Boshlek was desperate to find the marble run and ordered the regiment to continue their methodic search across the Alaskan landscape.

Skarb left them and climbed over a mountain pass into the next valley. The mountain face far in the distance was scarred with rippling crevices, like lines in aging skin. But when Skarb ran fast across the valley, the crevices rippled in the sunshine like ocean waves cascading across the mountain.

Skarb felt a surging sense of freedom as it ran, then suddenly those strange tremors ripped forward again, but this time far more violently. A strong wave of a stench came over Skarb so mightily that its legs gave out, and Skarb tumbled down a hill. Unbeknownst to Skarb, Jatuh was far away—hidden in a grassy valley, turning into a lemming. And Jatuh's turbulent change into the furry little critter sent bitterness rippling outward all the way to Skarb and the regiment.

Skarb recovered and grew distraught that the Voices were calling it forward, expecting a response. Skarb ran to the nearest river and stood on a rocky ledge overlooking the raging river below, hoping to summon the harassing Voices there. Skarb asked, "Why are you tormenting me? Leave me alone!"

The river merely bubbled over many stones, delighted with the sunny day, disinterested in Skarb's plea.

Skarb spit into the waters and said, "Stop taunting me!"

Skarb returned to the regiment to ask if they, too, had felt the strong reverberations. It saw Boshlek pacing the perimeter of the regiment with a skittish demeanor.

Skarb avoided the angry Boshlek, snuck up on Greznik Number 600, and asked, "Did you feel that strange aura in the air again?"

"Everyone did," answered Number 600.

"Could you smell it?" asked Skarb.

"Of course not. What a stupid question."

"What caused it?"

"Nobody knows. And not knowing makes Eternal Commander surly and rancorous," said Number 600. "Now get away from me before anyone notices me talking to you."

Boshlek paced around the regiment and fretted over its decision to let Jatuh travel alone. It worried, *What if the strange auras are not caused by a Tukor? What if they are being triggered by someone in the regiment? What if that Greznik is secretly trying to agitate and incite a rebellion?* Boshlek's anger was palpable as it pounded its feet hard, trod in circles, and spit a bubbling, fecal foam at every Greznik it passed by.

Boshlek mumbled to itself, "There is rebellion in the air. I feel it."

Unlike Boshlek, Skarb believed the reverberations came from far away, and it was determined to figure them out. Skarb avoided Boshlek and slowly stepped back from the regiment and out of sight. It ran away to the mountains, curious to discover what caused these strange sensations. Skarb traveled into central Alaska but had no success at all in tracing their source.

Giving up, it lay down to rest before returning to the regiment. But then its ears intercepted a unique radio signal, and it felt something speed by from behind. Skarb dropped flat and looked around but saw no one and smelled nothing. It looked and sniffed every which way to discern where the mysterious thing had gone, but there was no evidence of anything or anyone.

Skarb searched carefully for the source of the signal and ran toward it but found only a musk ox up on a ridge.

Was it merely a musk ox that I felt darting behind me? But that just can't be, thought Skarb.

Skarb charged toward the musk ox. The musk ox dropped quickly down behind a ridge. When Skarb reached the ridge, the musk ox was gone. Not even a whiff of his scent remained. Skarb darted this way and that, searching for the musk ox, and he grew alarmed that he had disappeared so skillfully.

Skarb worried that, like the red panda, the musk ox was setting a trap. Then Skarb felt something speed from behind again. It quickly flattened itself and turned its eyeballs every which way, but nothing was there. Then the pounding of many musk oxen was heard in the distance. Skarb zigzagged across the land toward the Seward Peninsula, searching for and following the mysterious radio signal. But each time it picked up the signal, it would lose it. This continued for days.

Eventually, Skarb picked up a strong signal again, but this time—unlike the previous few hours—the signal did not alter its position. Skarb followed the signal all the way to Lopp Lagoon where it found the source: a pair of abandoned farm boots. Inside the left boot, Skarb found a note written in code. It easily deciphered the message, read it, and ripped the paper into pieces.

Skarb understood the implication of the note—Skarb had, in fact, been chasing someone but had failed to find the traveler. Problematically, whoever wrote the note knew that Skarb had picked up the signal and was following. The note also revealed that other people would be coming. Perhaps Boshlek was right—the Tukors were pulling their forces together. Skarb found the oval stone and opened it, but found nothing. Then it pitched the stone down a rocky dip in the landscape.

Skarb was just about to eat the note, but the paper smelled alarmingly peculiar. Skarb feared the toxicity was the work of a Tukor and tossed the bits of paper into the strong winds. Skarb hid and waited for the other travelers to arrive. But then it picked up another strange radio signal from off in the distance. It then sped off to find the signal's source and destroy the intended recipient of that the note.

After Skarb was long gone, a spectacled eider duck gathered up the torn and scattered bits of Fingal's note in its beak and placed the torn pieces of paper back into the boots, hoping that Mitch, Tony, and Jovi would find it before the Greznik found the three travelers.

Skarb darted here and there across the land to find the signal's source. It picked up the signal and charged toward it, but suddenly the signal disappeared. As soon as Skarb picked up the signal again, whatever it was darted away and out of range. After several tries, Skarb figured out there were three signals in the air. Perhaps three humans? Or three machines? Skarb would never have guessed that it was three children—Mitch, Tony, and Jovi—who were so elusive.

Skarb tried to catch them, but they altered course continually like electrons bouncing around their orbits—going every which way. The three creatures, whatever they were, were impossible to catch. Skarb had never encountered something so evasive. Grezniks could trace anything they wanted to. But not this time.

Then the signals suddenly went dead. Skarb returned to where the boots were left, but when it got there, the boots were gone. Skarb looked for the oval stone with the crisscrossing layer of quartz and could not find it. Even the torn bits of the note were gone. Whoever had taken the note was probably headed to the cabin, but there was no way for Skarb to know where to look for the cabin. Skarb believed it to be the work of Tukors and returned to the regiment.

When it got back, it seized the first possible moment to speak quietly to Boshlek. "I tried to find the source of the bitter quivers in the air," said Skarb. "You are right, Eternal Commander—the Tukors are here."

"How do you know?" asked Boshlek.

"I felt them. They are here," Skarb said confidently.

"More than one?"

"Three. There are at least three."

"Three? We thought there was only one Tukor left alive. The next generation is distracted, thrown off course. Where did you find them?" asked Boshlek.

"I felt one heading west. I followed it to Lopp Lagoon, but I found only a pair of empty boots with a note inside, containing instructions to proceed on to a cabin. Then I intercepted another signal near the Alaskan towns of Circle and Chalkyitsik and I tried to find it. But then I realized there were three signals."

"Where is the cabin?"

"The note did not say," said Skarb.

"Why didn't you follow them?"

"I lost their trail. The radio signals went dead. I can assure you that you'll need the entire regiment to find and follow them. Whoever they are, they are incredibly fast."

"Fast to you means slow enough by anyone else's standards," said Boshlek. "I will send three scouts to seek the Tukors."

Boshlek called three scouts forward, ordered them to search for three travelers, and explained, "They are likely with the Tukor. Leave immediately. Bait them to find out if they are Tukors. If they are Tukors, catch them. Devour them."

▲ ▲ ▲

Just after the scouts departed, Jatuh returned to the regiment, approaching from the opposite direction. Jatuh was thrilled to have so successfully deceived the lemmings and hoped to speak to Boshlek immediately to share the clue about the echo at the Grand Parapet. But Jatuh stopped cold, stunned to find Skarb meeting alone with Boshlek. Jatuh barged forward, knocking Skarb aside, and bowed in reverence to Boshlek to announce its obedient return.

Boshlek sent Skarb on its way. Boshlek asked Jatuh, "What have you found?"

Jatuh reported, "I have traveled in your honor, Eternal Commander. You are my great and ever-powerful commander. I have discovered another clue to the blue stone mine."

Jatuh gave Boshlek all the details about a mountain's knife edge, a rhombus-shaped stone, and a C-sharp echo that can only be heard by whoever sings the note.

Boshlek, having just heard Skarb's alarming report of Tukors nearby, believed the accuracy of Jatuh's report and ordered the regiment to the Grand Parapet's Knife Edge in the Wrangell–St. Elias Mountain Range. When they got there, Boshlek found the stone on which to stand and howled a C-sharp, expecting to be the only one to hear an echo. But the echo came back loud and clear for the entire regiment to hear it. Jatuh's clue was devastatingly wrong.

Jatuh was stunned at the error. Why had the clue failed? Jatuh had delivered to Boshlek, word for word, the clue detailed by Oskar the lemming. Jatuh's body suddenly felt as though something were squeezing and crushing it in a vise, and Jatuh collapsed to the ground.

Not only did the entire regiment hear Boshlek's C-sharp echo, but the enemy's forces were also notified that Grezniks were discovering the clues. A sole mountain goat up on a mountain pass ducked away and disappeared. Three sandhill cranes flew off. The mountain goat and cranes left to set off a chain of communication across Alaska, and every Greznik knew it.

The regiment stood before the Grand Parapet and dropped into defeated silence, as though ice water had drained down from the sky.

54

THIS ISN'T CAMP

On the last leg of their hike to Fingal's cabin, the kids grew weary, their hearts pounded, and they breathed deeply as they made their ascent. As they wound around the path, they could no longer see the cabin.

Jovi stopped to catch her breath and looked around. "Are we still going the right way?"

Mitch looked down at his compass. "We have to be. I'm positive."

Tony said, "We've climbed so high we can't see our bikes anymore."

"Let's hurry and hope they're still there when we get back to them," said Mitch.

Jovi did not like when her brothers validated her fears, so she picked up the pace. The sooner they got to the cabin, she hoped, the sooner they could turn around and get home—with Fingal alongside them.

When they were well over halfway there, they reached a plateau whose peaceful view invited them to rest. They all sat down for a quick snack of pemmican and water. While they caught their breath, Tony looked through his binoculars and saw the dilapidated cabin ahead, but it was still at a higher elevation.

Tony pointed and said, "There's the cabin! If we hike across the plateau and fork off to the east, we can take that switchback and get there sooner."

Jovi longed to rest more but was desperate to find Fingal. "Let's go."

"Let's hope Fingal is there waiting for us," said Mitch.

Tony cheered them up and helped quicken their pace by playing King of the Mow—whoever got to the cabin first won. They were exhausted when they finally reached the cabin. It was cloudy and dark, and no light or movement came from inside. The wind stilled and the landscape quieted.

"It's almost worse that it's so quiet," whispered Tony.

"It feels like something is going to jump out at us," said Jovi.

They walked to the cabin door, quietly and nervously, side by side, and feared what they would find. Tony turned on his headlamp to light their way into the dark cabin.

Mitch said, "If we have to run, let's take the same route down. At least we'll recognize it and not lose each other on the way."

They braced themselves, ready to run away, as Tony opened the door just a crack. They peeked in, but it was pitch-dark. Mitch swung open the door carefully. Fingal was lying in the dark on the floor with an old, worn-out blanket over him. He did not appear to be breathing. Jovi tiptoed up to Fingal, gently shook him, and hoped he was just sound asleep.

Fingal awoke, looking very tired, unshaven, and weak, but he smiled widely when he saw them. The kids had never seen him smile so strongly before.

"Oh thank goodness. What a good sight to see you three. I'm so happy you came. I have been distraught the last couple of days. Worried something had gone wrong. Worried you decided not to come. Worried you had gone back to New York. But what's the use of worry? Here you are!" He sat up straight and said, "You hid your watches, right?"

Mitch nodded and pulled the rock out of his backpack and gave it to Fingal.

"Great job," said Fingal.

Then Tony pulled Fingal's boots out of his pack.

"Brilliant, Tony! I need those."

The kids were ragged, dirty, and tired from their travels, and they were not quite sure what to make of this bizarre adventure. Jovi was too scared to cry.

Fingal looked very tired, more tired and old than usual, with a sadness that seemed relieved by their arrival.

"We're really glad to see you safe," said Mitch, who was also holding back tears of exhaustion and relief.

"Yes, we are," said Tony.

"But we're actually a little worried," Mitch added. "We're so far from home."

"We should go home soon. We told our family we went

to a camp in Iowa. But this isn't camp, and it's definitely not Iowa," said Tony.

Jovi wanted answers. "Why did you leave without telling us? Why did you go so far away? What's out here?"

Mitch said, "And we abandoned the bikes you gave us in order to hike up here. We're worried they'll disappear."

Fingal answered, "Your bikes are safe. Nothing will happen to them."

"How can you be sure?" asked Tony.

"Because musk oxen will be guarding them. Kasper the musk ox. A very wise and worthy friend."

"The musk oxen? No way! They tried to kill us!" said Jovi.

"And the bears. And the moose. And the birds. They all attacked us," said Tony.

"At first, when we crossed over into Alaska, all the animals started acting strangely," Mitch reported. "They disappeared around us and went quiet. After that, they all charged at us."

Their report of sustained attacks worried Fingal. "Wait here a moment," he said.

Fingal stepped outside and shut the door behind him. He walked over to Kasper who, unbeknownst to the kids, had followed them to the cabin.

Just when the kids were beginning to worry whether Fingal was coming back, he came back inside and said, "A Greznik got very close to you. It found my boots and my note, and it went searching for you. It was traveling by itself, which is highly unusual for Grezniks. The animals and birds charged and dove at you to draw you away from the Greznik, and to force it to lose your trail. They protected you all the way."

"What a strange journey. I had no idea animals could be fighting for us," said Tony.

"Would've been a lot easier if we had known that. I thought they were going to kill us," said Mitch.

"You haven't yet told us what you need us for," said Jovi, whose stomach quivered as the dangerous realities of their adventure sank in.

Fingal pulled out some worn-out maps and an old, battered compass. He sprawled the maps out on the floor in front of the kids. The maps showed every detail of the land, but had no labels, no names of rivers or mountains, and no indicator to show which direction was north or south.

Fingal began, "Back at the farm, I got a message that the Grezniks were close to finding an old, forgotten, blue stone mine in Alaska that has not been used in centuries. The mine is deeper than any other mine, and it has some of the purest blue stones. The mine is merely a small hole narrower than the width of a straw, and to access the stones, the hole must be drilled very deep. Grezniks are somehow infiltrating our network and extracting the clues to the mine.

"The entrance can be found by first finding three corners of a triangle. The mine is located at the 'centroid' of the triangle—the gravitational center. The three corners are marked by secret clues," said Fingal, as he pointed to three points on the map. "The corners are here, here, and here."

Then Fingal pointed to another spot on the map a significant distance away. "And this is where we are.

"Grezniks have been witnessed searching for one corner of the triangle—a corner marked by a marble run. They are close—too close. And we must stop them. But first we'll get a good night's rest. I'll explain all three corners tomorrow, and then we'll be on our way."

"How long will it take us?" asked Jovi. "Because we're supposed to be at a camp. And the camp isn't supposed to last the entire summer."

"We do need to quickly complete our work up here. Then we'll need to get home and fast. But for now, we can rest well—we are all together."

The kids crawled into their sleeping bags on the wooden floor of the cabin and fell sound asleep. Old Man Fingal prepared the gear for their travels, then he, too, fell sound asleep closest to the door to protect the children.

In the middle of the night, the walls of the cabin shook from loud pounding. The kids all shot up straight as a board. Fingal stood up quickly, as startled as the kids.

"Get up, kids! Get up!" said Fingal.

Fingal pressed his face up against the wall of the cabin, still as could be. The kids thought he might be crazy, but he was looking outside through a small hole. Fingal was relieved to see that it was only Kasper the musk ox throwing his body at the cabin to wake them up. "It's all right, kids. Wait here."

Fingal stepped out of the cabin and approached Kasper, who was breathing heavily from a sprint. Jovi hunkered down into her sleeping bag and shivered in the cold night. All three kids were shaking from the chill and the unexpected fright.

Fingal came back in and said, "We need to leave here quickly. Grezniks are nearby."

"Grezniks! Are they going to eat us?" exclaimed Jovi.

"We need keep our voices down. Grezniks can hear at incredible distances. They'll be here soon. There are three of them—scout Grezniks. The regiment must know we are here, or they would not send out their scouts. Before we leave, I need to tell you some important points. And I'm sorry you have to learn so young. And so quickly. Then we must leave here at once."

55

A DISGRACEFUL DRUBBING

The regiment's failure at the Grand Parapet was a devas-tating blow. Reeling from their failure, the regiment darted straight up Knife Edge, ran across the mountain range, then dashed far south to regroup in a low-lying forest.

Boshlek suspected that either Jatuh had provided a false clue or their enemies had. It called Jatuh forward and said, "Explain to me where you got the clue about the echo."

Boshlek stood nose to nose with Jatuh and searched its eyes for a scheming lie, but Boshlek did not detect even the slightest glimpse of Jatuh's insincerities.

Jatuh responded, "I spied on a gathering of shrews and overheard them talking about the clue. I relayed to you everything they said, word for word. But their information was wrong. I suspect they intended to trick us."

"They did trick us," said Boshlek.

"It must have been a trap," said Jatuh, angry that it had fallen for the lemmings' trick.

Boshlek agreed. "One or more Tukors have been reported nearby, and if they know we are closing in on the clues, they will feed us inaccurate information."

"Who saw the Tukor?" asked an envious Jatuh, wishing it could have been the one to find a Tukor and chew it to bits.

"The Tukor has not been seen, but it has been felt. Possibly more than one. There might be several."

"But who discovered them?"

"While you were gone, those vibrations tore through the air again—but this time, they felt powerful like a tsunami. The seven-legger, 401^5, claims to have picked up the Tukor's radio signals. It chased at least one, but it speculates there were three. The seven-legger was unable to catch them, for the obvious reason: it is a slow and worthless weakling. But the presence of Tukors would explain the strange vibrations in the air. I sent three of our scouts to search and confirm if any Tukors have arrived."

Jatuh's legs buckled at the shock of learning that Skarb was the source of the Tukor sighting.

"Now go away. I will call you forward when I want you to do anything. Right now, I absolutely do not," said Boshlek.

Jatuh felt the urge to attack Boshlek but restrained itself. It also fumed with resentment toward Skarb. Jatuh did not return to its circle and instead ordered four junior sentries forward.

Jatuh said to the sentries, "Follow me."

Jatuh led the sentries to Skarb, who was sleeping alone,

lying on the ground. Jatuh ordered the sentries to encircle Skarb. Then Jatuh kicked Skarb to wake it up. Skarb woke with a start, only to find itself surrounded.

"What have I done?" asked Skarb.

"You did not find a Tukor. You lied to Eternal Commander to mask your own incompetence. I know you are lying because no one knows you better than I. As punishment for your deception, from now on you will be guarded by a circle of sentries and will never be allowed to depart that circle. They will not let you move more than two steps in any direction."

All four sentries were extremely skilled and able to overpower any Greznik. After training for years to become a regimental sentry, a coveted position, all four were severely disgruntled with their assignment—to guard the wretched, weak, and worthless Greznik. Guarding Skarb was the lowest task they could get. It was a massive insult that Skarb understood fully. Yet one sentry was Number 600 who had, years ago, secretly traded places with Skarb to let Skarb mine for the stones in its place. Number 600 knew that, with Skarb, things were not as straightforward as they might seem.

Skarb bent its head down so its seventh eye glared down on Jatuh's face. Then it said, "I hear you. I understand. And I will not wander. But the Tukors are here. I did not lie."

Skarb's glare caused Jatuh's insides to rumble. And once again, Skarb's pointed words brought on that strange feeling inside Jatuh. Jatuh's legs shook ever so slightly— not because of the Voices and not to fool anyone, but for no other reason than its inability to account for the pangs it felt inside every time Skarb spoke.

They stared in silence at each other until Jatuh could not take it any longer. Then Jatuh ordered the sentries to attack Skarb to rid itself of its own internal pangs. The sentries, in dutiful compliance, attacked Skarb. But the attack did not help relieve Jatuh's insecurities. They only worsened and Jatuh walked away to rejoin its circle.

After Jatuh left, the sentries' attack did not continue long because Skarb sank down in complete submission and said to them, "You are the best. You are the strongest. I will obey you fully now and always. I will not challenge your greatness. Do not waste your fighting talents and energy on such a pathetic, powerless poltroon like me."

The sentries could not be bothered with expending any more effort on a weakling like Skarb, and they willingly ceased their attack. Skarb stood submissively while they complained to each other about how insulting their new assignment was. At night, three sentries slept while one stayed awake to prevent Skarb from escaping. When Number 600 took its turn on watch duty, Skarb whispered to it, "I know you hate guarding me. But I can make it easy for you. Tomorrow morning, I'm going to leap over you and into my circle to fight my circle leader."

"You will never survive. Your entire circle will destroy you for good."

"That is exactly my intention. And you'll be free from this awful assignment. As much as you do not want to guard me, I don't want to spend centuries of my existence guarded by you," Skarb said convincingly.

"But long ago, remember, you said you would disappear when I traded places with you, mining the Valley of Geysers. But you did not disappear. Why should I believe you this time?" whispered Number 600.

"If you hadn't traded places with me years ago, you would've disappeared and never become a sentry. And if you don't trust me this time, you'll be stuck guarding me forever. And what a waste that would be. You—strong and skillful, at the top echelon of our regiment—will fritter away your talents guarding me. Tomorrow, let me leap over you and you will be freed from this awful assignment."

"I will be punished if I let you escape."

"No one will be looking at you. They will be focused on destroying me," said Skarb.

"And if you are wrong?"

"You can eat me."

"Eternal Commander would never let me eat you. It would eat you itself," said Number 600.

"Then let it do so," said Skarb.

"I will decide in the morning," said Number 600.

When dawn came, Skarb had no intention of disappearing that day. Instead, now was the time to show its fighting circle how skilled, swift, and strong it had become. It was now an equal. Skarb watched Jatuh's circle carefully and waited for the right moment.

When the moment came, Skarb made pleading eye contact with Number 600, and the sentry slyly nodded its head that it was okay for Skarb to try. Skarb took a deep breath and jumped over Number 600, ran to Jatuh's circle, and bounded right into the middle, startling everyone. The circle members kicked Skarb to toss it out, but Skarb dodged every kick and went face-to-face with Jatuh.

"What are you doing?" asked Jatuh. "You cannot enter our fighting circle."

"I did, and I am ready. The Tukors are here, and you need me," said Skarb.

Jatuh growled. "You are neither important nor worthy, nor valuable to any of us. You learned that years ago! Get out!"

Skarb said emphatically, "I am in the circle now, and I will stay. Admit it. You need me."

Jatuh kicked Skarb to launch it out of the circle, but Skarb jumped away quickly and Jatuh missed. Jatuh tried and missed again, and a great fight began.

Skarb had trained on its own for years. But Jatuh had not paid attention and had no idea that Skarb could fight back with masterful skill. Skarb dodged numerous blows by its leader, and the other Grezniks quickly realized that Jatuh was suffering a humiliating loss by the rejected, unimportant Greznik.

Number 600 and the other sentries bounded forward to watch, then more and more Grezniks gathered to watch the unexpected ouster. They all salivated, slobbered, and stood on their hind legs, cackling and spitting an awful goo. The ground around the circle was quickly covered in the wretchedly awful, slippery slime as they relished the circle leader's crushing defeat.

When victory over Jatuh was certain, Skarb stepped back and said proudly, "I am ready to join. You cannot deny it."

Skarb was so proud to have demonstrated that it was an important part of the circle. The centuries of training by itself had worked. There could be no denying—Skarb proved, in front of all the Grezniks, that it had more effective techniques and superior fighting strategies. It waited for Jatuh to finally welcome the strength of Skarb into the circle.

A great leader would be proud of one of its own showing such prowess. But not Jatuh. Jatuh was angry and humiliated. Never would Jatuh allow anyone to be better, and no one could be allowed to threaten Jatuh's importance. And by successfully entering the circle, Skarb had done both.

Never before had Jatuh let anyone from the regiment witness the unusual strength it had from ingesting the Voices of the blue stone waters. But as onlookers witnessed Skarb's superiority, Jatuh could tolerate neither the humiliation nor the threat to its own superiority.

The disgraceful drubbing triggered Jatuh's legs to tremble. Jatuh's eyeballs got wide and puffed out, and sparks flew out of them. Anger agitated every particle of Jatuh, and the blue stone waters inside energized into a frenzy. It ran toward Skarb with tremendous speed and strength, then threw Skarb into a tree with such force that its body wrapped around the tree, spun around it, and tore off its thick branches. Skarb landed, motionless, in a heap at the base of the tree.

Not able to move, Skarb could not understand what had just happened. Before Skarb could get up and analyze how Jatuh had more energy than any Greznik could possibly have, its leader pounced again and threw Skarb into another tree.

As the fight abruptly changed course, the other Grezniks knew they would get in trouble for having jeered the circle leader and cheered for Skarb's victory only moments earlier. They backed off to save face and rallied in support of Jatuh.

As the fight reversed, the other Grezniks assumed wrongly that Jatuh merely toyed with Skarb at first, then threw Skarb into the trees to teach it a lesson.

Jatuh pounced onto the injured Skarb, gripped Skarb's head in its claws, towered over it, and cruelly scolded Skarb. The other Grezniks surrounded Jatuh and Skarb and cheered Jatuh.

"Never, ever try to enter the circle again—you useless waste of a Greznik!" said Jatuh.

Skarb could not move, having been absolutely pummeled. All it could do was rotate its eyeballs around to glue its gaze onto Jatuh. Skarb's fearless glare triggered an even stronger pang inside Jatuh as it sensed that Skarb had something it did not. And despite towering over a conquered Skarb, Jatuh's legs began to tremble and weaken as unexpected feelings of defeat surged within.

Jatuh weakened so quickly that it could not complete the demise of Skarb. Instead, it launched the seven-legger into a boulder, where it crumbled into an injured heap. The other Grezniks walked over to Skarb and, for a game, threw it back into the circle, only to taunt and mock it and throw it violently out again, over and over. And they hurled insults at Skarb in rapid succession.

"How could you possibly think you could win?"

"You have never been anything but useless!"

"And weak! How idiotic of you to think you were strong enough!"

"You're a fool for trying."

More Grezniks joined in and batted the weakened Skarb around like a baseball. Then they tossed it back and forth over a fallen tree like a volleyball.

Jatuh yelled at them, "Stop it! Back off! Get back here!"

Obeying orders, they dropped Skarb on the ground and walked away. Every particle in Skarb's existence fired a painful electric shock as strong as a lightning strike, paralyzing its seven legs.

Skarb could not understand what had just happened. Only moments earlier, it had successfully proved, without a shred of doubt, that it was ready to be an important part of their fighting circle. After many hundreds of years of rejection and training by itself, it had succeeded in proving itself worthy. Skarb had earned a rightful spot in the circle. But then Jatuh unleashed an incredible power and pulverized Skarb's offense with almost no effort.

Questions boiled in Skarb's thoughts. How did Jatuh get that sudden surge of strength? And never before in Skarb's entire existence had Jatuh ordered other Grezniks to stop attacking it. So why did Jatuh do so this time?

Jatuh ordered the sentries who guarded Skarb to come forward and said to them, "Number 401[5] has learned its lesson. Return to your normal duties."

Number 600 commenced its regular sentry duties, but it took note that Skarb had saved it once again from a terrible outcome.

Skarb lay in a heap for quite a long while before it could get up and limp away. It analyzed the fight and the strange turn of events over and over. Skarb became convinced that Jatuh cheated to win that fight—using a hidden source of energy to ensure Skarb's humiliating defeat. But if not for that extra help, Skarb, without a doubt, won that fight. And Jatuh knew it. Jatuh ordered the other Grezniks to stop tormenting Skarb, fearing they would discover that the worthless seven-legger had in fact outwitted, outfought, and outmaneuvered its own circle leader.

But where did Jatuh's secret power come from? Skarb wondered. Skarb had no idea how Jatuh could instantly summon so much strength and power, but it was determined to figure out the secret. Yet Skarb had no idea how wickedly powerful and dangerously dark the secret would prove to be.

56

THE AIR FEELS OUR FEAR

Fingal and the kids rushed to leave the cabin. The kids packed up their gear as Fingal pulled climbing equipment out of a wooden box in the corner. From Jovi's climbing club back in Manhattan, she knew what the equipment was and helped Tony and Mitch divide it up between the three of them. The kids shivered from the cold and needed another layer of warmth. From the bottom of the box, Fingal took out some old sweaters, warm hats, gloves, and socks made of musk ox wool, called qiviut. Then he handed them to the kids.

"It's going to be cold out there today," said Fingal. "Put on a sweater and pack away some extra warm layers. Not only will the wool keep you warm, but also the smell of the sweater will help foil the Greznik from following your scent. Very quickly now, I need to tell you more about the three corners of the triangle because we will be traveling to them.

"The first corner is a marble run built into a granite crag called a tor.

"The second corner is a carving pointed to by a shadow.

"The last corner is a sound, an echo of the C-sharp musical pitch.

"Our allies leaked incorrect information about the location of the echo," continued Fingal, speaking very quickly. "Shortly after, the Grezniks fell for the ruse. They traveled to the wrong location to find the C-sharp echo, confirming there was a traitor in our ranks. Grezniks also know the truth about the marble run, so we must destroy the real marble run before they find it."

Kasper pounded loudly on the wall again.

Fingal put the maps away quickly and said, "We need to leave immediately. I'll explain the rest later."

The kids stepped outside but were startled by four musk oxen standing right by the door, so they ducked back inside. Fingal opened the cabin door and invited them to go back out again. "Don't worry, kids. They're here to help. You're going to ride them down to your bikes."

"Ride them?" exclaimed Jovi.

"Yes, there's one for each of you. Kasper, right here, is the leader, and you'll ride the other three. Secure your packs on tight because the ride down won't be smooth— and it could be fast."

The musk oxen stepped forward, one for each kid, and Kasper stayed on the lookout.

"But first, I need you to do something. Come back inside the cabin," said Fingal. He shut the cabin door tight and completely covered the window with a taut curtain. With the door and window sealed, the cabin was pitch-dark.

Fingal lit an oil lamp over by the wall, and Mitch turned on his headlamp. Fingal lifted several rickety floorboards. Under the floorboards were closely fitted wood pieces running perpendicular to the boards. He slid those pieces back and forth, like a Japanese puzzle box. After thirty-one movements back and forth, the mechanism unlocked— and the pieces slid under the boards to reveal a steel door underneath, closed by a combination lock. He entered the combination and the door lifted up as a hatch, revealing an underground room. Fingal carefully entered through the door and climbed down a rickety staircase. The steps shifted and wobbled as he took each step, as though they would give out from under him.

"If we had more time, we'd fix these steps." Once he reached the bottom of the shaky steps, Fingal said, "I'm going to close this hatch, then I want you to spin the combination lock and slide the pieces back into place to lock them. Then put the main floorboards back and blow the lamp out. You three go outside and ride the musk oxen to where you left your bikes, okay?"

Fingal stepped away into total darkness under the cabin.

Tony said worriedly, "But we don't know the combination to get you back out!"

Jovi took off her headlamp to give it to Fingal. "It's pitch-dark down there. Take my headlamp."

"Tony's right. We need the combination. And please take the headlamp," said Mitch.

"You must go now," said Fingal. "Do not hesitate. Trust

the musk oxen. They will get you to your bikes as speedily as possible. Then wait there."

Fingal pulled a long cord, and the steel hatch door slammed shut. The kids jumped at the loud sound. Mitch dropped to the floor and tried to open the door.

"Wait for what?" asked Jovi.

Mitch yelled, "Fingal! Can you hear us?"

The kids pressed their ears on the steel door and waited to hear a response. But they heard nothing.

"This can't be good," said Tony. "He's locked down there. There's no way to get out."

"We shouldn't leave him and just walk out of here. What if he starts banging on the door and we won't be here?" asked Mitch.

"He hasn't been wrong before. Let's just do what he said," said Tony reluctantly.

Kasper the musk ox loudly pounded on the walls of the cabin with the boss of his horns.

"We don't have another option. Let's go," said Mitch.

They reluctantly slid the wood pieces back into place to hide the steel door. They blew out the lamp and went outside. The kids remembered the route they took to get to the cabin, but Kasper led them all down a faster, yet more treacherous, path.

It was an anxious ride to their bikes, and the entire time the kids constantly looked over their shoulders for signs of Fingal or Grezniks. The musk oxen led them back to their bikes in good time, and they were relieved to find their bikes unharmed and ready for use.

"I'm still worried about Fingal," said Tony.

Jovi and Mitch said simultaneously, "Me too."

"Don't you sometimes think the air up here feels our fear?" said Tony.

"Something's in the air. That's for sure," said Mitch.

The musk oxen stood very upright, faced the same direction, and listened for the slightest of sounds. Kasper suddenly took off running like he was chasing something.

Jovi looked through her binoculars to see if there was anything frightening nearby, but she saw something coming toward them from great distance.

Jovi pointed south. "I think it's him! I think that's Fingal!"

"Where?" asked Tony.

"Over there!" said Jovi.

Tony looked and he, too, saw Fingal riding toward them at a very high speed.

"That's definitely him," said Mitch. "Where did he get a bike like ours?"

"And how could he get from under the cabin to way over there?" asked Tony.

Soon Fingal was right next to the kids, but they noticed his bike was quite different from their own. His had many more buttons, gears, and attachments.

The kids all talked at once to Fingal.

"Slow down, kids," said Fingal, whispering. "We can't talk about this in the open. Not even a whisper. We're in more danger than I ever imagined, and we must hurry."

They said goodbye to their musk oxen, got on their bikes, and sped away. When the kids all had their eyes forward, Fingal's cabin folded up like a box, collapsed into the ground, and disappeared.

57

A WISH TO DISAPPEAR

Skarb retreated to a hidden rock cleft within the forest to nurse the injuries it sustained from Jatuh's attack. Around three in the morning, Skarb heard Boshlek approaching and hunkered down to hide. Boshlek passed close by, followed by Jatuh shortly after. After they passed, Skarb crawled out of its hiding spot, circled around to approach them from the other direction, and hid close enough to spy on their conversation.

Jatuh began, "My circle needs to be cleansed of its costly nuisance. The seven-legger is a drain on our efforts. Defective. Can't fight anyone or anything. Too easy to defeat. For strategic reasons, it really does need to disappear."

Boshlek said, "Why must you constantly repeat this request? You and I have both tried to destroy the seven-legger in volcanoes, lava rivers, hot springs, marshy bogs, and underground water flows. But every single time that wretch comes out when others have disappeared. Whether you like it or not, it's proving to have an unusual power."

Jatuh held its composure, yet many angry and defiant thoughts rattled within. *Eternal Commander speaks nothing but utter claptrap. The worthless Greznik has no power. I am the one with power! How dare someone hurdle such stupidity at me. I am the one who should command this regiment! I should eliminate our worthless commander and take its place.*

Boshlek continued, "And you failed. You lied. You did not give us the correct location of the C-sharp echo."

"I told you already: I did not lie. Why would I lie? I have no reason to lie to you. I overheard a gathering of shrews talking about the exact location of the echo, and I told you exactly what I heard. They must have falsified the clue to throw us off. If you let me, I will figure out what went wrong and find the real truth."

Boshlek replied with disdain, "I distrust everything you say. Yet the Tukor and his troops would not gather up here unless we were close to finding the blue stones."

Jatuh said, "And we're still feeling those bitter auras rippling through the air. Something is brewing up here. And the Tukors must be behind it all. If you grant me leave from the regiment again tonight, I will hand the blue stone mine to you. I will not betray your trust."

"If your next clue is wrong, you will be destroyed."

Jatuh's legs trembled ever so slightly, and a little plover feather popped out of its foot. Jatuh quickly plucked and ate the feather before Boshlek saw it.

Boshlek felt desperate to beat the Tukor and said with urgency, "I just felt the strange aura again. You are right: something is brewing up here. Leave tomorrow evening.

We must move fast before the Tukors move the stones and destroy the clues. I will once again provide others with an excuse as to why you are absent."

Boshlek dismissed Jatuh, and Skarb snuck away unseen.

The next evening, just like every other night, Skarb walked away from all the Grezniks and lay down to sleep alone. But this time, Skarb only pretended to be asleep. It kept its extra eye open and attentive. Skarb waited for Jatuh to leave the encampment. After Jatuh passed Skarb and traveled quite some distance, Skarb followed Jatuh's scent all the way to the western coast of Alaska along the Chukchi Sea.

Near the Chukchi Sea, suddenly and mysteriously, Skarb could no longer trace the smell of Jatuh. Skarb searched and zigzagged like a hound, trying to recapture the scent, but it could not. Jatuh was gone.

Skarb sank down at the harsh reality that Jatuh was right after all. Skarb was too slow. Skarb could never keep up. Always too far behind. Always unimportant. Unneeded. Disposable. Worthless. Skarb flattened its body against the earth and wished to disappear.

58

CLOSE ENOUGH TO STRIKE

Fingal and the kids traveled far from the cabin. Once he was sure they were in a safer region, they stopped at a freshwater spring for a break. While resting, Fingal taught them the details of one corner of the triangle, the clue held by the deepwater yelloweye rockfish. Then he added, "The marble run is located in the Serpentine Hot Springs in the Bering Land Bridge National Preserve. We need to find their granite tors. We are headed there next."

"We're taking a tour?" asked Jovi.

"No, this is spelled T-O-R-S. Tors are large granite rocks, like natural-made cairns. They were once underground, but after many million years of erosion, they are now exposed and sticking out of the tundra landscape. The tors we're traveling to are located near beautiful, ancient hot springs. The rock structure we're looking for is shaped like a hand with its index finger pointed to the sky."

Fingal continued, "You three will lead the way on your own. I'll circle our position and keep an eye out for

Grezniks. I've scrambled the walkie-talkie signals so we can use them again, but use them sparingly. I won't be far away from you."

Fingal drove away before they even had a chance to ask any questions. The weather turned dark, cloudy, and windy, and a thick fog descended upon them. Their powerful goggles allowed them to see ahead, despite the fog. About halfway to their destination the fog cleared and revealed a beautiful blue sky. Yet their relief was short-lived.

Sandhill cranes flew toward the kids and swooped down on them. Then Fingal said on his walkie-talkie, "Three scout Grezniks are nearby. Follow the cranes!"

The kids looked up and followed the cranes, as the birds led the kids over a treacherous route. They jumped over rivers, rode up steep valleys, navigated through narrow gaps, and bounded over marshy terrain—all very difficult feats on a motorbike.

Tony was the first to speed through a narrow gap, and he scraped his shoulders on the sides. He warned Mitch and Jovi, "Watch your shoulders!"

"Can't the cranes see what they are leading us through?" said Mitch, as he, too, scraped his shoulders passing through the narrow gap.

Jovi yelled at the birds, "Hey, watch where you're going! We don't have wings!"

As they passed through the gap into an open valley, they did not see the sole scout Greznik standing up high on a mountain arête looking down at them. When Grezniks need to test if someone is a Tukor, they force the highest-numbered Greznik to stand alone and wait for the person to see it. If the Greznik explodes, the person is not a Tukor, and the other Grezniks will run far away.

Fingal saw the scout Greznik and instantly knew what was happening: if the kids looked right at the Greznik and it did not explode, other Grezniks would suddenly appear, charge down, and devour the three kids instantly. Fingal was determined to protect the kids. Before they saw the Greznik, Fingal purposely drove right toward it and made eye contact with the Greznik, then spun around. Suddenly, from out of nowhere, the kids saw Fingal racing away from them at an incredible speed.

Fingal warned the kids, "Don't look back! Keep your heads down! Go north! Fast! Go! Don't follow me!"

But it was too late. The kids had already looked behind and made eye contact with the Greznik. Immediately after, the other two scout Grezniks appeared, knowing they now had four Tukors to capture and destroy. They stood up on the ridge and launched their attack. They charged at Fingal, who was the closest.

The scout Grezniks sprinted down into the valley toward Fingal with their mouths open wide, their extra sets of fangs popped out, a far more terrifying thing to see than the kids had ever imagined. Fingal's bike was not fast enough to get away.

"We've got to help him!" said Tony.

All three turned around and sped at the Grezniks, one from every side, like prongs ready to spear the beasts— except the kids had no idea how to destroy a Greznik.

"What're we doing?" asked Jovi.

"Use our flamethrowers!" said Mitch.

They all activated their flamethrowers at full throttle, and a fifteen-foot flame shot out the back of each of each bike.

"I'll go first!" said Tony.

The forward Greznik was just a few strides from devouring Fingal. Tony sped his bike straight toward it, and when he got close enough, he spun his bike around at the last second so the flame went right into the Greznik's eyes. Momentarily blinded, the Greznik tumbled backward and tripped the Greznik behind it. The third scout kept its focus on Fingal and charged toward him. Mitch sped right at it and turned his bike at exactly the right time. Mitch's flame hit the Greznik's snout and burned the tentacles. The Greznik shook its head to stave off the pain and slowed enough for Fingal to get a strong lead.

The scouts pulled together again and initiated their next attack.

Fingal pointed up ahead and said urgently, "Get ahead of me. Cross through that gully right there, then speed directly for the mountain face. Watch for a blinking green light on your handle bar. Push it when it turns solid green! Hurry!"

"What does the button do?" asked Jovi.

"And where are you going?" asked Mitch.

But Fingal did not have time to finish the explanation.

"Don't worry about me!" said Fingal. He spun away from them and drove toward the Grezniks.

The kids obeyed and sped forward, but the Grezniks regrouped and mounted another coordinated attack on Fingal.

"We can't leave him behind!" said Mitch.

"No, we can't!" said Jovi, as all three kids spun around and repeated the same attack on the Grezniks. The Grezniks, angry at the kids' previous successful intervention, turned and chased them instead of Fingal.

To avoid the coordinated attack, the kids crisscrossed and intersected each other's paths at incredible speeds—so close to each other that Fingal thought they were going to smash into one another. Their crisscrossing patterns confused the Grezniks, causing their many eyes to go cross-eyed. The Grezniks stumbled or smashed right into each other. The scouts readjusted their attack to charge one child at a time. They went right for Jovi.

Fingal said, "Use the flip button!"

Jovi yelled, "I don't have one!"

The three Grezniks were right on her tail. Mitch and Tony sped forward to save Jovi.

Fingal answered Jovi, "It's on the tip of the left handlebar."

Jovi pushed it and her bike sprung upward and did a backflip with a half twist in the air. She landed on her wheels, facing the other way. The scouts ignored her maneuver and charged at Tony and Mitch, who were now within easy range.

Mitch and Tony flipped their bikes too and evaded the scouts, but the Grezniks came right after them again.

Fingal accelerated toward the Grezniks to stop them from devouring the boys. But the attack was too coordinated to stop it. Fingal could not get to the boys in time. The Grezniks gained on Mitch and Tony, who rode parallel to each other. The boys stood no chance.

Tony remembered what his fencing coach had said: *"You have to get close enough to strike. Make them move in so you can strike."*

Tony said to Mitch, "Remember the roadrunner! We're both roadrunners this time!"

"Beep! Beep!" said Mitch. "We got this!"

Roadrunner was code for a game they used to play at home when they were little boys. One played the roadrunner and the other the coyote. But this time they were both roadrunners, and it was all for real.

Mitch pointed to a cliff up ahead. "That one?"

"Perfect!" said Tony.

The boys accelerated up a sloping plateau with a sheer cliff at the end of it. At the highest speeds possible, they drove directly for the cliff. Jovi saw that her brothers were headed off a cliff and to their deaths.

"Turn, Mitch! Turn, Tony!" said Jovi as tears streamed down her face.

Fingal, still too far away to help the boys, warned them, "Your gliders aren't strong enough for a cliff jump like that! Don't do it!"

Tears flew off Jovi's face. She gripped the handlebars of her powerful purple-and-yellow bike, certain her brothers were rescuing her again, but this time with their lives. She believed it should be her going off that cliff—since she had the bike with the parachute-like gliders that could spin her around and float her to the ground. But there was not enough time to get up there.

At only two seconds from the cliff's edge, the Grezniks expanded their mouths like vipers and were within one stride of gulping Tony and Mitch.

Tony looked over at Mitch and said, "Beep! Beep!"

They pushed their flip buttons, and their bikes flipped backward with a half-twist. The Grezniks ran right under them and straight over the cliff, dropping like stones to the ground.

Mitch and Tony landed upright on their bikes, facing Jovi and Fingal who were riding up the slope.

Jovi and Fingal each took a deep breath of relief.

When they caught up to each other, they high-fived each other.

Fingal said, "Great job, but they'll be back up here to mount another attack. We must get out of their range—and fast."

"How can that be? Aren't they crushed like bugs?" asked a stunned Mitch.

"Grezniks can fall from great heights and not suffer much damage. If they fall from too high, they will shatter and explode. But that cliff wasn't high enough for them to shatter."

Fingal led the way down the slope, across the valley, and toward a mountain wall ahead of them.

"Do not slow down!" said Fingal.

When they got close a green light blinked on their handlebars.

Fingal said, "When the green light turns solid, push the button on your handlebars. Do not slow down."

The green light turned solid. Tony pushed the button and a mountain door opened to a long cave. They sped their bikes directly in. The door closed shut so that no one, including a Greznik, could ever see that there was an opening there.

As soon as they were all safely inside, Fingal said, "We'll stay in here until they're gone."

"Were they going to eat you?" asked a shaky and anxious Jovi.

Fingal paused and then said quietly, "Yes, they would have. I am deeply grateful. You saved me when I had no chance."

▲ ▲ ▲

The scout Grezniks ran off the cliff, dropped like rocks, and landed face-first. Their snouts squished in like accordions, their faces flattened like pieces of paper, and their legs bent like curly straws. The impact paralyzed them and they lay motionless, furious that their enemies were getting away. After some time, their claws could move ever so slightly, then their legs moved like rusty springs. They wiggled their feet and stretched their backs. For a time, they could only crawl on their curly legs. Finally, their legs straightened out, and they got up on their feet ever so slowly to hobble around a bit. Yet their snouts remained squished and their faces crumpled. And the fall had completely knocked out their sensory capabilities.

They suffered severe dizziness and motion sickness and wobbled when they walked. Their faces would eventually slowly return to their normal shapes, but it would take some time. They were furious that they had been outwitted by the Tukors.

"We must find them before they get too far away," said the lead scout.

The scouts ran to find Fingal and the kids, but their sensory capabilities were still muted by their squished-up faces. They ran right into each other and knocked themselves out again. It did not matter anyway: Fingal and the kids left no trace. There was no trail to pick up.

The three scouts growled and spit and broke into a vicious fight, each one blaming the other for not being able to find them. But none of them was to blame. They had mounted the most effective attack they could. That did not stop them from mauling each other uselessly for an hour and finally ending in a draw, their snouts still deformed from the fall.

"We should return to Eternal Commander and report that Tukors are here," said the lead scout. They staggered back to their regiment, hoping their faces would return to normal before they got back. They did not want Boshlek to find out that they were defeated by Tukors and fell off a cliff.

But as they neared their regiment, their snouts were still half-squished. They tried to pull the lead scout's snout back to shape first. The lead scout stood in the middle while one scout pulled on its snout and the other pulled on its tail, like a tug-of-war. They pulled and tugged, but the snout would not budge. Yet that did not stop them from continuing to try.

"Pull harder, you weaklings!" shouted the lead scout.

The Greznik pulling on the snout lost its grip and fell backward. But the other one still had a firm grip on the tail and tumbled backward but did not let go. As a result, it threw the lead scout's over its head and smashed it, face-first, on the ground behind him, squishing the lead scout's face again.

Meanwhile, Boshlek was pacing around the regiment when it smelled the scouts nearby. It left the regiment to follow their smell and found them trying again to pull each other's snouts back to shape.

"What are you doing?" asked Boshlek. "What happened to your faces?"

The scouts had not noticed Boshlek approach, and they jumped to attention.

"The Tukors are here," answered the lead scout. "They are potentially the most powerful ever."

The scouts expected to be peppered with questions, but instead Boshlek paced angrily in circles around them. They huddled together, waiting to be reprimanded. But Boshlek was obsessed with Jatuh's lengthy absence and asked, "Did you see or smell the circle leader 401^4 during your search?"

"No."

"I order you three to leave and find 401[4]," said Boshlek.

"Where is it?" asked the lead scout.

"I don't know. Find it. Capture it and bring it back to me."

"With whom is it traveling?"

"No one," said Boshlek.

"Why is it traveling alone?" asked the lead scout.

"*Just find it!*" ordered Boshlek, who then punched all three in the face, squishing their snouts all the way back in. "Leave now and find it!"

"Eternal Commander, we cannot travel with our faces squished in like this. We cannot sense anything around us," said the lead scout. "We cannot travel until they retake their shape."

Boshlek knew their statement to be true, but it would never admit that it made the whole situation worse by reinjuring them and delaying their departure. Boshlek walked off in a huff.

The scouts were relieved that Boshlek did not ask what had happened. They were even more relieved to have a reason to stall their departure to find Jatuh. They would rather search for a Tukor than that swaggering circle leader. They were so delighted over the needed delay that even with their slowly recovering snouts, their tails wiggled excitedly as if anticipating an upcoming party. But Grezniks never have celebrations and cannot understand joy—so the scouts could not account for their wiggling tails and assumed another part of their bodies had been damaged in the fall.

59

THE SAND HAS EARS

After losing Jatuh's trail, Skarb lay collapsed on the ground, disappointed in its inability to keep up with its circle leader. It rolled over onto its back and let the sun warm its belly—something that would otherwise have caused other Grezniks to attack. But far away, out in the open, the warmth of the sun felt good against the backdrop of defeat. Skarb pondered never going back to the regiment again. It would have the whole Earth to roam around within, never to mine for the elusive blue again.

Yet Skarb thought, *But what am I to do if there is no more search? Race across the landscapes, flit across oceans, dodge a human eye around every turn?*

It all felt so worthless. Pointless. Useless. Skarb rolled over onto its side and retracted all its eyes to shut out the world from within. But then the smell of the Chongchon River drifted over Skarb, and it jumped onto its feet again.

A faint pitter-patter of tiny feet was heard nearby. Grezniks know exactly where all animals are relative to their position, but this one snuck up on Skarb seemingly out of nowhere. Skarb sank down and slithered up a slope to get a glimpse of the little creature from a well-hidden position. Looking around, it saw one darling little bird—a delightfully feminine semipalmated plover—her dainty little feet limping westward. The plover had a numbered band around her ankle, the kind that people put on birds to track their travels across many miles. She did not know Skarb was watching her every move.

Skarb positioned its feet, ready to pounce, but it jumped back when it saw her eyes. Grezniks can see through an eye to the back of an eyeball. Skarb looked deep in the plover's eye and saw something wholly unexpected. It saw its own reflection in the back of the little bird's eye.

Grezniks' eyes are like mirrors. If a Greznik zooms in its sight on the eye of another Greznik, it will see its own reflection in the back of the eyeball. But why was this happening with a plover? Skarb crouched down, slithered backward, and kept its eyes focused on the plover.

The little bird flew away. Her wings were a bit tattered and shabby, so she flew awkwardly. Yet the vibrations of the wings were slightly different from most birds, so slight that only a Greznik could notice. It was all peculiar enough to spur Skarb to trail her from the ground. The plover landed on the coast of the Chukchi Sea to join a gathering of plovers roving the shoreline, enjoying the long sunlit days of an Arctic summer before flying south to winter on the warmer ocean coasts.

When the banded plover landed, the other plovers were scattered about, whispering and fretting over the news that Grezniks had discovered at least one of the tightly held secrets of the hidden mine. As they scampered about, the plovers hashed out dozens of scenarios to determine how a breach of such magnitude could have occurred. But every single scenario they discussed was deemed impossible. Not being able to explain the breach left them terrified and deeply worried.

The little birds scuttled across the beach in a disorderly fashion, talking to each other only briefly, constantly fearful that something might be listening. Perhaps a bug. Perhaps a bird overhead. Perhaps a sand crab. They had a new saying: "Be careful. The sand has ears."

Groups of two or three little birds would form only briefly to speculate who could have fed information to the Grezniks. But they would quickly disband and scatter away from each other again. Their skittish speculations were interrupted when the adorable new visitor landed on the shore. They all scampered over to her to welcome the pretty little one to their shoreline. Skarb had followed and was perched at distance, but close enough to hear their chatter.

One admiring plover named Paul scurried over to the lovely newcomer. "From where do you come?"

"I'm searching for my home. Last winter, I suffered awful injuries, and I no longer know my past. Do I belong here?" asked the newcomer.

"I don't think we've met before, but you can join our community. We'll welcome you. What caused your injuries?"

asked Paul, as other plovers joined to hear her story.

She answered daintily, "Last winter I was in Los Angeles. And one morning I was eating breakfast when my beak got caught in an old beach volleyball net left on shore. I tried to get my beak out, but my whole head got tangled in the mesh. Stuck in the net, the surf kept taking me in and out to sea. A young boy found me washed up on shore, barely alive. The boy and his father cut the net to free me, but I could not fly away. They took me to a bird rescue center, where I recovered. What a blessing! After I was healed, I was set free to fly north to find my home and my family, but the trauma of my injuries was so severe that I have no memory of where I came from. I've found joy in what has become a beautiful traveling adventure. Even so, I would be ever grateful if you would accept me as one of your own."

The plovers welcomed her with open wings. As others joined the gathering, they asked her to repeat her wonderful story of injury, rescue, kindness, and healing. They just loved hearing about good people in the world who would rescue a bird, and they believed her rescue to be a miracle.

Paul and his friend Rover introduced themselves and fluffed their feathers to garner her attention.

"What's your name?" asked Paul.

"Sauvee," she answered.

"That's an unusual name."

"I have no memory of my real name," said the sweet Sauvee. "That's what the little tourist, a French boy, called me when he rescued me, and I have kept it."

The plovers listened to Sauvee's story and then scattered to talk more about the broken secret—except for Paul and his friend Rover, who stayed with Sauvee. Paul and Rover were weary of talking about the security breach over and over. They took interest in the little newcomer and asked her to tell her amazing story again.

Sauvee expressed how grateful she was that their plover community took her in as their own. She asked in a sweet voice, "What's making everyone so scared? Everyone is so nervous. So jittery. I've been gone too long to know any recent news."

Rover said, "Grezniks are discovering the secrets that will lead them to the blue stones. No one can stop talking about the breach. They run around like crazy, constantly worrying. We're so sick of all their depressing talk. What's the point? The breach can't possibly jeopardize our lovely plover community. There's no way it could ever get that bad."

Paul added, "Fear—that's all plovers have now. We shouldn't be living a life of fear."

Sauvee agreed. "What's there to fear anyway? There's no possible way the Grezniks could've found all the clues to the blue stone mine."

Rover added, "You're right. Grezniks can't discover our clue unless they come very near, and they can't come close enough to us without us seeing them. We have guards that keep an eye out. And we never share our most beautiful clue with any other creature."

"Yes, ours is the most beautiful clue," added Paul. "A musk ox carving. Pointed to by a stone's shadow of an old woman smiling."

"But only by the midnight sun in July," added Rover.

Sauvee smiled at the sunlit summer sky and said, "Yes, yes. The midnight sun. A shadow. A musk ox. An old woman smiling. What a beautiful clue."

Paul said, "But I suppose we still shouldn't mention the secrets in the open like this."

Their little group of three plovers disbanded, and they each scampered away to look for something to eat.

While all the plovers meandered along the shore and fretted, none of them knew that Skarb had heard everything. Sauvee and her two admirers had unknowingly given Skarb a critical clue to the mine. Skarb was ecstatic. It would race back to the regiment and deliver the clue to Boshlek. What a cunning move against Jatuh that would be! Boshlek would finally have to acknowledge Skarb to be even more worthy than Jatuh.

60

THE JOURNEY FOLLOWS YOU

Mitch, Tony, and Jovi huddled in the pitch-dark of the cave next to Fingal. The fearful chase had left their hearts pounding like timpani drums. Fingal did not say a word, but they could sense he wanted them as silent as they could be. They stood still in the quiet darkness. It was so dark that the kids did not see a bat land on Fingal's shoulder.

Shortly after, Fingal said, "The Grezniks are gone. Let's go."

He opened the cave door and guided the kids out.

Jovi feared another Greznik attack and peeked only her head out, reluctant to leave the safety of the cave. "How do you know they aren't here?" she asked.

"I just received a message. The three Grezniks have returned to their regiment, far away from here. The regiment is already searching for the marble run, and we must beat them to it."

Tony looked around the cave, trying to figure out how Fingal could have possibly received a message.

The biting black flies were miserable in the tundra landscape. Jovi scratched a multitude of bug bites on her neck. "Will the bugs be this bad everywhere?"

"Yes, so let's hope for wind," said Fingal. "Wind but not storms."

Fingal noticed that Tony was not ready to leave again. "Tony, is everything okay?"

Tony walked over to Fingal and asked quietly, "So you are a Tukor?"

Fingal breathed slowly before answering, as though he were exhaling memories into the tundra air. He said solemnly, "Yes, and with that, your adventure is just beginning. We have no time to lose."

Mitch led the way, following the map on his bike. As they rode across the landscape, Mitch, Tony, and Jovi were silent, yet each was remembering Fingal's words on the farm: *"I'm getting too old to do this work. And I need you to take over."* The implications of their frightening day were sinking in. They had *all* looked directly at the Grezniks, and the beasts did not explode. Yet how could all three of them be Tukors already? Wouldn't the day that one becomes a Tukor be marked by a ceremony, or a graduation? Even just the idea of it left them uneasy. Yet Fingal's words were strong in their memory: *"The Journey chooses you. And it follows you until you follow it."*

After traveling a good distance at top speed, Tony pulled ahead of Mitch and flagged for everyone to stop. He had been watching the landscape and was the first to see a series of very large granite structures protruding from the barren landscape ahead of them.

Tony said, "I think I see the tor ahead of us, the one that looks like a hand with an index finger pointed to the sky."

"Good eye. It really does look like a hand," said Mitch.

"Is that the right tor?" Jovi asked Fingal.

"Sure looks like it," said Fingal as he handed Jovi a shiny yellow marble. "Here's the marble for the run. Keep it safe. You three go ahead and dismantle the run while I keep on the lookout."

The kids rode directly to the crag, and Fingal sped away to circle their position.

Tony said, "The marble starts at the top, but the top is too small for all of us to be up there."

"It's a job for Monkey Jo," said Mitch.

Jovi was excited to help with something that came naturally to her and quickly climbed to the top of the tor. While Jovi looked for the start of the run, Mitch and Tony walked around it to figure out how the marble would loop around in four figure eights.

Jovi said, "I think I found the start of the run. But it's overgrown, clogged up."

Jovi kept the sparkly yellow marble safely secured in her pocket while she cleared the marble's path.

When the run was clear and ready, Mitch and Tony positioned themselves around the tor to follow the marble as it looped around on its way down. Jovi held the marble carefully in her hand.

"Should I send it down?" asked Jovi, worried about losing the pretty little marble.

"Let it go!" said Mitch.

Jovi lay on her stomach looking down the narrow hole and counted to three. "One, two, three!"

The marble dropped down into the center of the tor, and from there the marble slowly looped outward to form the first petal shape. They were relieved each time the marble came into view as it traced the outer edges of the flower.

They breathed a huge sigh of relief when the marble successfully ran down the entire rock structure, forming eight flower petals. The marble stopped on a ledge, and they noted the GPS coordinates and put the coordinates to memory.

"Now we must ruin the run so the Grezniks cannot find it," said Jovi.

They shifted the stones of the tor like the pieces of a puzzle. When they were done, there was no way that even a Greznik could discover a marble run within the tor.

They signaled for Fingal to come back.

Mitch asked Fingal, "Why does the blue stone mine need to be marked by secret triangle corners anyway? Seems like a lot of work when someone could just mark the mine with precise GPS coordinates."

"The blue stone mine was originally marked hundreds of years ago, before there was equipment to locate precise coordinates. Kids today now assume that electricity, cell phones, and satellite communications will always be available. But if Grezniks or anyone were to destroy those systems, you'd need to be able to use manual tools and know how to rebuild what you once had. Users of tools don't win battles, the designers and maintainers of tools do.

The community that understands that will always be more likely to win a battle."

Jovi was always rather perplexed by Fingal's long explanations and said, "Your answers are always long. Our parents never have long answers."

"The only thing they answer is the phone," said Mitch.

"What's next?" asked Tony, who was anxious to finish their work and get home before their parents or Tobias got nervous about their absence.

"To find the shadow of an old woman smiling," said Fingal.

Mitch had been watching the radar on the bike's weather monitor. "The weather is turning for the worse. We should get going."

Fingal said, "Before we leave, let me explain the next corner. It's a very small carving of a musk ox, carved into a large, smooth granite rock. Near to the carving is a large rock edge that casts a shadow shaped like an old woman smiling. The shadow of her nose, the tip of her nose, points to the carving. But only by the midnight sun in July."

They traveled quietly for quite some time. Loads of rain and bitter winds ripped past them and made the ride more exhausting. Even so, they reached the next location in good time.

"The carving is very small, so you'll have to get on your knees to find it," said Fingal.

The kids lined up on one side of the smooth rock face and crawled methodically forward to look for the carving.

"I found it!" said Mitch. "Wow, look how detailed that is. Do we have to destroy such an amazing carving?"

Fingal also did not want to destroy the tiny yet beautiful carving. "Let's work on changing the shadow first."

The shadow was cast from stones jutting out from the bottom of a large rocky cliff face—massive stones that could not easily be moved.

A musk ox walked directly over to the stones that formed the shadow and used the boss of his horns to push and shift the stone that formed the shadow's nose. The unexpected shadow of a woman's face went into hiding.

"Wow, how did they know how to do that?" asked Tony.

"A good friend knows when you need a hand," answered Fingal.

"Do we really have to destroy the beautiful carving?" said Mitch, disappointed at the thought of ruining it.

The kids looked for the carving but could not find it.

"I know it was right here," said Jovi, pointing to the rocky surface near her foot.

"Jovi's right. It was here. I know it was," said Tony. "Where'd it go?"

"I think the lichen grew over it," said Fingal.

"That's impossible. Lichen grows slowly," said Mitch. "It grows about half a millimeter a year. And this has grown a couple of centimeters in just an hour!"

"The lichen must've sped up to cover it," said Fingal.

"This adventure is getting very bizarre. Is time speeding up while we're here?" asked Tony.

"Time isn't speeding up. We humans can only see one face of time. We think of time as taking equal steps along a line where every tick is one step forward, followed by a tock taking another step forward. But time isn't a straight line."

The kids did not listen well to Fingal's confusing answer. They were watching the lichen to see if they could see it growing. But they could not. It was as still and motionless as ever. The kids were extremely puzzled by the lichen's speedy burial of the carving, and saddened by the beautiful secret gone into hiding.

"Where to next?" asked Jovi, who was careful not to step on the lichen as she walked back to her bike.

"To find the echo," said Fingal.

"How does one find an echo?" asked Mitch. "There's probably thousands of places in Alaska that will echo a sound back."

"This one is marked by a nonagon-shaped stone. You must stand on that stone to hear the echo. However, the only one who can hear the echo is one who sings the C-sharp. And we cannot sing the C-sharp or the Grezniks will find us."

"Great. Finding an echo that can't be heard. This'll be easy," Tony said sarcastically.

"You're right, Tony," said Fingal. "This won't be easy. I fear it will be the most difficult of all."

61

MIRROR IN THE EYEBALL

Skarb zoomed in its vision on Sauvee and again saw its own reflection in the back of her eyes. Skarb noticed that not only did her wings have an imperceptible variance in their movement, but also her voice had a slightly different cadence—so slight it would take a Greznik ear to hear it. Skarb delayed its departure to snatch the sweet-talking Sauvee and figure out what caused these peculiar differences. Then it planned to eat the strange morsel of a bird before racing back to the regiment.

Sauvee said to her two plover friends, Paul and Rover, "You have been so kind to let me stay. But I realize now that I am meant to roam, to be a bird of adventure and distant travels. When the days get shorter, I will return to fly south with you. But until then, I must fly away again."

"We just welcomed you. You can't be leaving already!" Paul said disappointedly.

"An adventure is missed every day if you only scamper about," said Sauvee.

Paul pleaded with her. "Please stay. At least until you have recovered more. It's too dangerous otherwise."

"You are a dear friend. And yes, traveling alone can be dangerous. But while living in a cage for many months, I learned about the adventures of black-crowned night herons, eared grebes, and surf scoters. Now it's hard to be just a plain plover."

"I don't think of you as a plain ol' plover." Paul smiled flirtatiously.

"But I need to experience new things, to be free," said Sauvee dreamily. "And don't you worry. I'm careful. I'll be okay."

They said their final, reluctant goodbyes, and Sauvee flew off into the distance. Skarb followed her by ground. When far enough away from the other plovers, Sauvee landed and flapped her wings as though trying to cast dust off her wings. Skarb took a stance nearby, out of sight of Sauvee, and stood ready to pounce.

Then Sauvee's scrawny bird legs started to shake. The smell of the Chongchon became overbearing for Skarb. Her wings flapped frantically and with such speed and intensity that her feathers melted into her skin. Her body shook so violently that every bone in her body broke. Her belly bloated outward, and her shaking legs grew wider and taller as Greznik hair grew out of them. Two more legs popped out of the side of the bird, and another leg grew down from the belly. The featherless wings contorted painfully, then shrank down to a speck. The body and head distorted, and hair grew around the eyeballs and inside the bird's mouth.

Extra eyes bulged out from under the skin and then popped out. The beak turned into the vile snout of a Greznik. The process proceeded until Sauvee had fully converted to a Greznik.

Skarb crouched down, aghast as the cute little Sauvee gruesomely morphed bit by bit. Skarb smelled the definitive stench and instantly knew the Greznik was Jatuh. The surprise transformation took the air out of Skarb, but it did not dare take a deep breath for fear of exhaling its signature smell. Skarb was completely baffled and wondered, *How did Jatuh do that?*

Then Skarb recalled its time along the Chongchon River when the Voices sang to Skarb: *"When you drink the waters in, you will be the most important, most powerful Greznik. You will rule the regiment. You can become anything. And all the blue stones will be yours."*

Questions raced through Skarb's thoughts. *Did Jatuh swallow the waters, the Voices of Proznia? How else could a Greznik become an animal? And is that what the Voices meant when they said I could be anything?*

Skarb also remembered its fight with Jatuh. Perhaps Jatuh's strength came from the Voices.

None of it made sense to Skarb. *Did Jatuh drink the water, or find the blue stones, or both?*

Skarb wanted answers. Spoonbill and Bustard had told Skarb that it had defeated the Voices, but what a regret to have done so if drinking the blue stone waters gave a Greznik the power to change into any creature it wanted to! Skarb envied Jatuh's strength and now wished it had swallowed the waters.

But there was no turning back. Jatuh now had all the power and Skarb none. If Jatuh attacked now, with no other Greznik to witness the strength, Skarb would have no chance. Skarb held its breath to remain hidden. Then it softened its bones, flattened itself, and camouflaged its fur to hide from Jatuh.

Jatuh fully converted back to a Greznik and ran back to the regiment. Skarb did not dare follow immediately but waited, flattened, for a long time. Once Jatuh had a long head start, Skarb followed Jatuh's smell with no intention of catching up. Skarb took its time to return to the regiment to guarantee that Jatuh never discovered that Skarb had witnessed its transformation.

Jatuh returned to the regiment and waited for a private meeting with Boshlek. Jatuh shared the clue about the musk ox carving and added, "And it is July right now. So the regiment must find the shadow immediately."

"Do you know the location of the shadow?" asked Boshlek.

"No, the locations are not known, except perhaps to a Tukor."

"How do we know this isn't another trap?" asked Boshlek.

Jatuh risked another lie and said, "I got the previous clue by listening to a gathering of shrews who were out in the open, where anyone could hear. That one had to be a setup. Whereas this was a highly secretive conversation between two skittish, fearful king eider ducks."

Boshlek pretended to believe Jatuh's story and excused Jatuh to leave again to search for the next clue. Jatuh walked away just as Skarb was returning to the regiment. Skarb sank down, held its breath, and waited for Jatuh to pass. Then Skarb followed again, unseen.

After Jatuh left, Boshlek ordered the three scouts forward whose faces were now recovered. Boshlek said, "Follow the circle leader, 401^4. I do not trust it. I can see rebellion in its eyes. Do not let it know you are following. Find out what it is up to. Then bring it back to me, and I will toss it into the sea myself. Do you understand me?"

The scouts nodded.

"Will you obey?"

The scouts nodded again and bowed to confirm their abject obedience, then left to follow Jatuh. They despised Jatuh and relished the idea of Eternal Commander finally eliminating the circle leader. The scouts easily followed Jatuh's smell and expected their task to be an easy one. But after traveling many miles, the trail of Jatuh's scent suddenly evaporated. They ran around trying to pick up Jatuh's trail, but it was as though Jatuh had disappeared.

Alarmed at losing Jatuh's trail, the scouts scurried back along their route, hoping to pick up Jatuh's scent again. They reluctantly had to give up: Jatuh was long gone. Then the scouts felt the strong tremors again. Fearing a nearby Tukor, they dashed back toward the regiment.

When the scouts got back to the regiment, they avoided returning to Boshlek to report their failure. Instead, they wandered aimlessly while discussing what lie to tell Boshlek to explain how they lost the trail of the odious circle leader.

Skarb waited for the bewildered scouts to leave the area. Unlike the scouts, it knew exactly where to find Jatuh.

62

A SILENT FEAR FLIES BY

Fingal and the kids made good time traveling toward the echo, but not long into the journey a mountain storm descended upon them. The snow came down heavily and blew swiftly, so they could not see their path ahead.

Fingal stopped their ride and said, "In weather like this, it's too easy to get separated from each other. We need to travel by other means in these conditions."

Fingal led them to another hidden cave, and they pulled their bikes inside.

"We'll wait here for our ride to come pick us up," said Fingal.

"A ride? I don't think we can hail a taxi up here," said Mitch.

Not long after, they heard a rustling coming toward them. In the heavy snow, the kids could not see what was lurking nearby and feared the worst—Grezniks.

"What are those?" asked Jovi as she backed away.

"Caribou. And we are going to ride them. They'll be

able to guide us through the storm. And they can sense Grezniks from far away."

Four caribou came forward, and Fingal helped each kid get on one. Fingal connected their caravan with rope, but loosely enough for the caribou to move fluidly and dash off in case of an attack.

"If you need to stop for any reason, gently pull the rope to let the person ahead of you know. And if you feel someone pull your rope, send the message forward and backward. Ready?"

The kids nodded.

Fingal got on his caribou and said, "Let's go!"

Their four caribou ran quickly to catch up to the full herd. The caravan traveled for hours, seldom resting. They traveled through valleys, gullies, and treacherous mountain passes, then came upon a plateau when suddenly the herd of caribou broke into a full sprint. "Hang on tight!" said Fingal.

"Why are they running?" asked Jovi, hanging on for dear life.

Fingal said something else, but the kids could not hear over the loud pounding of the hooves. The herd of caribou darted up a rocky path and stopped. Fingal got off his caribou and lay flat against the earth, and gestured for the kids to do the same and not speak a word. The four caribou got down on the ground right next to them as the other caribou gathered around. The deep breaths of the caribou surrounded them. Danger was imminent, and the kids knew to stay quiet and ask later.

Suddenly the caribou's muscles flexed, and their hearts pounded rapidly in fear. Yet there was nothing but deadening silence across the landscape. Mitch opened his eyes and saw the regiment of Grezniks racing across the lower plateau, making not a single audible sound as they sped by. He elbowed Tony and Jovi to open their eyes. As the Grezniks ran by, a putrid green ooze slopped out of their mouths and their eyes glowed with a tortured rapaciousness. It all felt like a horrifically silent fear flying eerily by.

Even after the Grezniks were miles away, the caribou did not move. The kids knew Fingal was telling them all silently to not even move a muscle.

When the coast was clear, Fingal said, "That was too close."

"How'd the caribou know to hide?" asked Tony, who shivered from the awful scene of the Grezniks.

"Caribou, like musk oxen, can sense Grezniks from over five hundred miles away. This time, they took precautionary measures early enough. But even so, that was too close. It's all getting too dangerous. We need to finish up our business here and get home."

63

SECRETS CAN BE SUCH LONELY THINGS

The scouts were long gone when Skarb snuck up on Jatuh. But just as it neared, Jatuh started to shake violently, and Skarb smelled the Voices of the Chongchon waters again. Skarb knew this time what that intense shaking meant: Jatuh was changing into another creature. This time Jatuh's gross distortions turned the Greznik back into Tiro the Arctic lemming.

Skarb ran forward quickly and caught Tiro by the leg, throwing him high up in the air and then batting him back down. Tiro landed far away, tumbled along the rocks, and came to a stop very bruised and weakened. Skarb pounced on the lemming and held Tiro down with its front leg.

Tiro said in a terrified, squeaky voice, "Don't hurt me!"

Skarb's extra layer of teeth popped out as it growled, "You aren't afraid, you filthy liar."

Skarb picked up Tiro in his teeth and gnawed on the lemming's legs. Tiro squealed in pain. Skarb's saliva turned a rainbow of colors, and its tongue tasted something putrid—blue stone waters in Tiro's blood. Skarb spit Tiro on the ground, covered in the vile saliva.

Skarb grabbed Tiro in its claws, batted the lemming around like a toy, then opened its jaw to eat him. Tiro cowered from the large protruding teeth as he squealed, "Don't hurt me. I'm just Tiro. I'm just a lemming. I'm lost and trying to get home. Don't eat me!"

Skarb stepped on the lemming's stomach and said, "You are not a lemming. I know who you are. You're my miserable, odious circle leader. Tiro is not your name. You don't have a name. You are a number. You are 401^4."

Tiro stopped pretending to be a fearful lemming and gnarled at Skarb. "You ugly Greznik. Lopsided blight. Foul fiend. Worthless to the circle. Worthless to all."

"But I found you and figured you out, you devious little scamp," said Skarb. "And I now know your secret. I tasted it in you. They told us not to swallow blue stone waters. But you did, didn't you? That's why I smell the Chongchon River—the stench is coming from Proznia in you! I'll tell Eternal Commander you're extracting and hoarding the blue stone mine for your own power, and it will have you destroyed."

Tiro laughed. "Worthless, pathetic threats. No one can destroy me. Not now that I can change into another creature at will. You are all powerless. Meaningless. Nugatory. I can crush and pulverize any one of you, in fact, the entire regiment.

Toss them all into water. And swallow them whole like flecks of dust. As for you, specifically: Hideous. Useless. Pointless. Deformed. Better off evaporated. That's what you are. Gone. No more. Vanished you will be."

While under Skarb's foot, Tiro's lemming fur turned into Greznik fur, and its face grew. Skarb ran off, but not fast enough. Tiro converted back to Jatuh the Greznik at such an incredible pace that Skarb's nose burned from the fetid winds. Jatuh easily caught up and hit Skarb with such strength it was as though Skarb were merely a lemming.

Skarb fought back but was no contest for Jatuh. Soon Skarb was so weakened it could not defend itself anymore, and Jatuh held Skarb down with its legs.

Jatuh cackled victoriously and said, "You are finally gone. Forever."

Jatuh's mouth grew large enough to swallow Skarb. But then they heard many squeaky voices coming near. Jatuh had been focused entirely on eliminating Skarb and had not paid attention to its surroundings. Hundreds of lemmings were marching toward them, chittering and chattering. The marching lemmings were on the other side of an enormous boulder, and they were just about to round the corner and see the two Grezniks.

Jatuh said to Skarb, "Ah, there they come. The idiotic, thick-witted lemmings. I'd have eaten you right now, but what a nuisance. I'll destroy you in a more painful way. Easily. I can destroy the entire regiment whenever I want to. I will rule it all. I will destroy, shatter, obliterate everyone and everything. And even if you go back and tell anyone, they won't believe you. You, the one they cast away. The one they wish to throw away."

Skarb was utterly defeated and knew that next time, whenever Jatuh felt like it, it would rid itself of Skarb forever. Skarb had nothing to lose and said, "Even if you destroy me, the Voices control you. I know because I did not drink the waters. And because I did not take them in, I can smell the Voices every time they speak to you. And no one else can. Go ahead and eat me. Devour as you wish. But you remain a tool of Proznia. Shackled. Forceless. Enslaved. It is I who is free."

Skarb's words sent that unfamiliar foreboding ripping through Jatuh again, and it spit on Skarb. Then Jatuh hurled Skarb a great distance, smashing Skarb against a mountain cliff. Skarb fell behind a rock and lay motionless.

Jatuh had no time to spare. It hid from the lemmings as it converted back to Tiro, but this time Jatuh purposely gave its lemming disguise visible injuries and scampered away.

Hundreds of lemmings came around a rocky mound, just as Jatuh's tail shrunk down to the size of a lemming's. Tiro scurried up to them. Out of view, Skarb lay helpless and unseen.

The lemmings waited for Tiro to catch up to them and welcomed him back excitedly. Sally was excited to see the handsome Tiro return and asked him, "Where have you been? I've been worried about you."

"It's been a sad story since I went away," lied Tiro. "I finally found my cousins, and I was so happy to have found them at last—"

Sally interrupted, "What a blessing!"

"Yes, but tragedy befell us immediately. I was running toward them, by myself across an open valley, and a hawk grabbed me in its talons and lifted me into the air. But then, out of nowhere, the Grezniks came by. They were rushing by on their way to the C-sharp echo at the Grand Parapet, and they ate my cousins and their entire community as they sped through. The hawk, in fear of the Grezniks, dropped me in midair and flew away. If it weren't for the hawk, I'd have been eaten by the Grezniks. And if it weren't for the Grezniks, I'd have been eaten by the hawk. It was so awful to witness my family, everyone, gobbled up by the Grezniks," said Tiro with convincing but insincere devastation.

Sally nursed Tiro's injuries and said, "We live such perilous lives as lemmings. So brief, so vulnerable. But I hope it is okay to say that I'm glad you survived. Because I'm relieved to see you again."

"Of course it's okay. You were the first person I wanted to see," said Tiro.

"Your tragic story reminds us that at least one thing has gone right in our world."

"What do you mean?" asked Tiro.

"I know—we aren't supposed to talk about it out loud. You are right to feign innocence. But you and I are dear friends, aren't we?" whispered Sally.

"Yes, we are," said Tiro.

"Then you and I can secretly rejoice that the Grezniks fell for our trick—giving them the wrong location of the echo. What a delight!"

"Yes. Such delights!" said Tiro, who was riled that he had fallen for the lemmings' ruse. He was so angry his leg began to shake. She placed her tender paw upon his leg to calm it.

"You're shaking from the awful memories. Seeing your family disappear has traumatized you," said Sally.

Tiro saw a gathering of lemmings preparing to march again.

"Where are they marching to?" asked Tiro.

Sally whispered, "I know we aren't supposed to talk about where we're going, but secrets are such lonely things, aren't they? I'm glad to have someone to talk to."

"You can tell me anything, Sally. You know you can trust me. Where are they marching to?"

"Oskar doesn't think the traitor comes from within our community, so our team was selected to rush to a hidden mountain lemming community where the secret is protected—the instrument that echoes the C-sharp. We must get there as soon as possible to help protect it from the Grezniks."

"Terrible Grezniks," Tiro said deviously. "Sally, I will help you. I'll help all of you. I'm very strong. How can I best help?"

Sally said, "Follow me. You arrived just in time. I'll bring you to one of the lieutenants. He has an elite unit and needs strong lemmings to make the charge up the mountain."

Tiro marched with the lemmings to the source of the C-sharp echo—not to protect it, but to gain control of it.

At the exact same time, Fingal and the kids were also traveling to the echo . . . but to protect it, they would have to silence it.

64

TO MOVE AN ECHO

The close call with the Greznik regiment placed a heavy burden on Fingal's heart. Once the coast was clear, they traveled deep into treacherous terrain rarely visited by people due to lack of roads, footpaths, and air landings. They all kept a swift traveling pace, wanting to finish their work and go home. When they reached a broad valley, Fingal halted the caribou herd and pointed to a nonagon-shaped stone on the ground. "We found it. Our objective here is to silence the echo."

Mitch said, "But there's no way to silence an echo unless we change the location of the mountains."

Tony said, "We can't move mountains."

Fingal sat down and said, his smile aslant, "You're probably right. That'd take a while."

Jovi asked, "Can I sing a C-sharp to hear the echo?"

"No, the Grezniks might hear it and come," said Tony.

"Then we have a problem," said Mitch. "We can't test the echo, but we have to move it—and we can't move the echo because we can't move mountains."

"Let's think about this. Sound has to hit something for it come back to our ears in an echo," said Fingal. "That mountain over there is the only thing that could be echoing back a sound. So let's see: Sound travels at about 1,127 feet per second. The clue says if a C-sharp is played here, the echo comes back in half a second."

Mitch said, "So for sound to come back in half a second, the mountain face has to be closer than 1,127 feet. How far do you think that mountain face is from here?"

"Farther than that, I think," said Tony.

Fingal added, "We can't say for sure unless we measure it."

Mitch said, "We'll measure our steps like an old surveyor would have done."

They walked to the mountain, counted their steps, and measured the distance. When they got to the foot of the mountain, they had walked 3,001 feet.

"An echo would take more than one second to travel back to where we were standing," said Tony.

"This isn't making any sense," said Mitch.

"It is a mystery," said Fingal. "The echo seems to defy the speed of sound."

Tony studied the mountain face closely. Looking through his binoculars, he noticed an opening at a great height. "It looks like there's a cave up there."

Mitch saw it too. "And the entrance is worn down, like something has traveled in and out a lot."

Fingal said, "Perhaps that cave holds the secret to the echo."

"Can we get up there somehow?" wondered Mitch.

"It's a job for Monkey Jo, the trained climber," said Tony.

Jovi said, "Trained to climb a fake wall in New York— not a real mountain." She looked up through her binoculars at the cave and said, "I think I see little critters up there!"

The others looked too. A lemming stepped to the edge of the cliff to get a good look at them.

"Is that a lemming?" asked Tony.

"It is," said Fingal. "And lemmings have held the secret of the echo. They're probably guarding whatever creates the echo."

Tony asked Jovi, "Is there any way up?"

Jovi shook her head. "Seriously, I can't climb that."

"I'm not surprised that one of the secrets is hidden in a cave that's impossible to climb to," said Fingal. "Let's study the mountain face and just make sure there is no way up."

Fingal reviewed possible routes with them. But they all concluded that a climber could only get about a third of the way up before being met by smooth-faced rock, over-hanging cliffs, or other impossible barriers.

"Maybe we can't see the route up the mountain until we are on the mountain?" suggested Tony.

"Good point, Tony. It's worth a try," said Fingal. "I'm too old to climb. But all three of you can try."

Fingal pulled climbing gear out of the kids' packs and even more out of his own pack. The kids were surprised to see how much more weight Fingal had been carrying in his pack.

They found three possible climbing routes that could get them about one-third of the way up, and along their way they would look for routes to climb the rest of the way. Jovi also analyzed how to come back down, since descents can have different technical challenges than climbing up.

Jovi taught her brothers the basics of climbing and how to use the equipment. The kids studied the equipment very carefully, and they completed several practice climbs. They confirmed that their walkie-talkies were working so they could communicate with Fingal and each other as they climbed.

Mitch was uneasy about using the walkie-talkies. "Remember, Fingal, you said Grezniks can hear the walkie-talkies. Should we really use them?"

"There are no Grezniks reported in the area. We should be okay right now. So . . . are you three ready?" asked Fingal. "Check or hold?"

None of the kids answered.

"I'm guessing your silence means hold," said Fingal.

"It does," said Jovi. "I've never climbed a real mountain. This is too dangerous."

"You all can do this. I'm sure of it. Do not take unnecessary risks. If there's no way up, there's simply no way up. Just stop and come back down. This is an exploratory climb only. Stay safe. Check or hold?"

All three answered, "Check."

Their caribou got increasingly jittery and edgy as though dangers were approaching. The mountain made the children nervous too. As they began climbing, not even

Fingal or any of the watchful animals who protected them would ever have guessed that Jatuh, disguised as Tiro the lemming, was already inside the mountain. And Tiro was ready to destroy anyone who got in his way.

65

WHAT'S GOTTEN INTO YOU?

Sally introduced Tiro to the lieutenant whose elite unit was to rush to the top and make the fewest stops along the way. The lieutenant tested Tiro's strength, and Tiro surpassed their expectations and was immediately accepted into the unit.

The lemmings marched to the base of the highest peak and split into twenty-three separate teams. Sally was assigned to a diffcrent team than Tiro. Before they all entered the mountain, Sally ran over to him and said, "I wanted to see you before our teams separate."

"This isn't goodbye, is it?" asked Tiro. "I was hoping to see you again."

Sally smiled. "You'll reach the cave sooner than I, but when I get there, I'll come find you. Is that okay?"

Tiro nodded his head approvingly. She ran back, happy to know that her new friend would be waiting for her.

Each team entered a very tiny but different entry at the base of the mountain. As soon as the last team member entered, the entry closed behind them. And they began their journey through a complex tunneling system that wound through the interior and gradually climbed up. They all knew that they were being called into the mountain to protect the mysterious musical instrument from the Grezniks.

Each lemming was assigned unique duties to complete along their journey and for their permanent work inside the mountain. Some carried packs full of food to replenish stockpiles scattered throughout the tunnel system. Some carried construction supplies, equipment for infrastructure development, replacement parts for equipment maintenance, and so on.

Lemming towns existed inside the mountain along the main routes, with homes for each family, food stores, grooming shops, hospitals, churches, and so on. Water supplies were carefully monitored by guards who ensured safekeeping of the drinking water. There were hundreds of smaller, less-traveled tunnels that branched off from the main routes up the mountain. Hoists were available to lift supplies and lemmings more quickly. Routes, no longer needed, were abandoned and were not regularly maintained by the maintenance crews.

Tiro's elite unit hurried up the mountain to provide additional troops in case of a possible Greznik attack. Tiro's unit consisted of the strongest lemmings who could keep up a swift pace. Tiro demonstrated early in the climb that his strength and stamina far exceeded the others. He quickly developed a following of envious and admiring lemmings who wished to be just like him.

Tiro was determined to reach the mysterious instrument quickly and kept a brisker pace than the other lemmings could sustain. As they got closer to their destination, he grew increasingly obsessed, and his pace increased.

One member of Tiro's elite unit said, "Slow down, Tiro. This has never been a race to the top. Why are you rushing? Can't you see we need a rest?"

"Why should we rest?" grumbled Tiro.

"There's no point in being exhausted or injured once we get there," answered the lemming.

"Maybe you all should've trained more before making the climb. I'm not tired."

"Well, the others are."

"I'll go ahead without you if I have to," sneered Tiro.

"What's gotten into you? Look at you! You're breathing harder than the rest of us. Let's just take a break—you need it." Then the lemming dropped his voice and warned Tiro, "Besides, if you can't garner the respect of your unit, our lieutenant will deem you unfit for your assignment and send you back down."

The other lemmings admired Tiro's strength, but they began to resent his obsessive and angry manner. Tiro reluctantly stopped for a rest with the team but could not stop breathing heavily. The fast breathing was not from the climb as the other lemmings assumed. The Voices of the blue stone waters inside were surging, desperate to reach the mysterious blue stone instrument held within the mountain.

After resting, Tiro's team walked the last stretch single file through a secret, narrow tunnel. None of them asked for another break for fear of being humiliated by Tiro's strength and fiery anger. Completely exhausted from the dash to the top, they rounded the corner and entered the huge cavern where the magnificent instrument was kept.

The base of the instrument was long and rectangular. Layers of piano keys started at the floor level and moved upward in 167 staggered layers. The keys of this strange piano were thin, narrow, and short in length. The keys at the bottom were so dark blue that they appeared black. Each layer of keys going up from there was a lighter shade of blue and more iridescent. The sides of the instrument were made of crystal-clear glass that gave view to the complex insides of the instrument. The keys were attached to strings—hundreds and hundreds of strings, some with hammers like a piano and some with miniature violin bows that moved back and forth to create the sound of a violin, viola, or cello. Some keys were connected to piston-like mechanisms that blew air toward the back and into the bells of trumpets, trombones, clarinets, and oboes.

Hundreds of lemmings were working on the instrument, cleaning the mechanisms and rappelling down the sides with squeegees to ensure the glass stayed perfectly clean. Others were polishing brass and oiling valves. Some had climbed inside and were tuning the strings, repairing valves, and so on. One lemming stood on each key and tested its mechanism before stepping onto the next key. If there was a mechanical problem, lemmings stationed inside the instrument worked to repair it. There was one key that was covered with an intricately embroidered silk banner. That key had a piece of unusual volcanic rock embedded into the blue, and its mechanism was disconnected from the key.

The instrument's magnificence took Tiro's breath, as though something gripped his throat. A putrid green, thickened saliva poured forth, and he repeatedly slurped it back in to hide it and was overcome with dizziness.

"You aren't well, Tiro. You look awful," said one lemming. "I told you racing to the top was unwise. You should've listened."

Tiro was not listening to anyone. He was scheming on how to remain a deceitful lemming long enough to learn the secrets of the instrument. Once he learned how to operate it, Tiro would destroy all the lemmings and take control. But Tiro had not anticipated the strength of the Voices' desire. When Tiro gazed at the instrument, his lemming blood burned hot and feverish, like lava flowing inside. The particles in his body moved faster and collided. The Voices were seizing control in their own unbridled desperation for the mysterious instrument. Tiro's blood rushed too fast, and his insides wanted to be a Greznik again. Tiro closed his eyes to retake control of his body from the Voices.

But Tiro could not calm his insides.

He desperately needed to catch his breath and slow down his system before the other lemmings noticed something terribly wrong with him. Tiro retreated from the instrument by walking out of the cave and into the tunnel.

When he was alone in the tunnel, the Voices spoke to him. He plugged his ears, but it did no good—the Voices were speaking from inside. No one else could hear them.

The Voices said, "You, our loyal, obedient stooge. You will get control of the instrument and it will be ours. And you will return to the waters to set us free."

Tiro plugged his ears again, but the Voices grew louder and louder. Tiro gasped for air as his blood rushed faster and faster.

Alone in the tunnel, Tiro said to the Voices, "I am not yours. You burst and sank to the bottom of the muddy waters. Your claims on me are bogus. This instrument is mine! Its power will be mine and mine alone!"

The Voices laughed and laughed, rhythmically over and over with such speed that Tiro fell to the ground.

They fluttered inside him. "You chose our desire. We rule you now. The instrument is ours!"

The Voices whispered things he could not hear, then they went instantly silent. Tiro mistakenly assumed their sudden silence was his victory.

Tiro said confidently, "The Voices are gone!"

Tiro believed he had crushed the Voices and would soon control everyone, rule everything, and harness unimaginable power. Excitedly, Tiro raced back into the cave and looked out at the crowd of hardworking, loyal lemmings, salivating at what a delicious victory it would be to shatter them all.

66

LOCKED IN

At the base of the mountain, the kids wished there were another way to reach the cave other than climbing the mountain, and Fingal wished he were young enough to make the climb. He also wished they could all turn around and avoid the dangers within, but there was no choice. There was too much at stake.

But Jovi said, "Let's just try to climb it. We'll probably just have to turn around and come back down anyway."

Fingal reiterated, "Do not take any unnecessary risks. If there's no way up, there's no way up. Just turn around and come back down."

Mitch, Tony, and Jovi each had a different location to begin their climb, so they separated and hiked to their starting points. They kept in close contact with each other over their walkie-talkies. Tony climbed without problems for a while, but Mitch and Jovi ran into unexpected challenges right away, and their routes proved to be slow going.

Mitch looked up toward where Tony was headed. He saw a big chunk of ice cracking from above Tony. "Tony! Go to the right! Now! Move now!"

Tony moved just in time. The ice broke loose and fell crashing to the ground.

"Wow, that was close!" said Tony.

Even Fingal did not know that the mountain was designed to trigger dangerous events if anyone tried to reach its peak.

Jovi found herself under an overhanging ledge and unable to see whether it would be better to go right or left. She asked Fingal, "Which way should I go?"

Fingal advised, "Go toward your right."

But Tony heard some falling rock nearby and saw stones crumbling above Jovi. "Jovi, don't move! A rockslide is headed right for you. Stay there!"

The few cascading rocks escalated into many. A dangerous rockslide tumbled over Jovi's safe position under the ledge.

Jovi watched as large rocks fell over her hiding spot. Had Tony not warned her, she would have been crushed in the rockslide. After the rocks settled and stopped falling, Jovi said, "Wow, thank you, Tony. That would've killed me."

The others were relieved to hear her voice.

Mitch made good time in the next section of his climb, but he reached a point where he could not see any possible next step. Mitch said, "Fingal, unless you can see a route for me to take, this is as far as I can go. Tony, can you keep going?"

"Yes, I can go a bit farther, but not much."

Jovi said, "There's nowhere for me to go from here. I'm coming down."

Tony said, "Wait! Don't go down yet. I see steam coming out from a break in the rock."

Tony shifted sideways, moved toward the steam, looked through the crack, and saw that there was light behind the stone.

He said, "There's light coming from inside."

To Tony's surprise, a square stone slowly moved backward.

"A door is opening!" said Tony.

Tony carefully peeked over the lower edge of the door and pointed his flashlight inside. "It's a tunnel, and there is a lemming way up ahead. Should I go in?"

"No. Mitch and Jovi need to be with you," advised Fingal.

The square stone started sliding forward to close shut again. Tony asked Fingal, "The entrance is closing! Are you sure I shouldn't jump in?"

"No, please wait. It's too dangerous to go alone," insisted Fingal.

The door shut as Mitch and Jovi made their way over to Tony. When they got there, the square stone door shifted back again and opened. The one lemming was still standing far back in the tunnel.

Jovi said, "The lemming looks like it's asking us to come in. Let's try."

Mitch asked Fingal, "Should we go in?"

"Use your best judgment. If you go in, make sure that I can still hear you when you're inside. Don't travel outside the range of our walkie-talkies," said Fingal.

The kids crawled, single file, into the opening. Mitch went first, then Jovi, then Tony. The tunnel was not large enough for them to sit up, much less stand up.

Jovi checked in with Fingal on the walkie-talkie. "Can you hear us?"

"Yes, I can hear you fine," said Fingal.

"Okay, we're going to crawl ahead and see what's in front of us," said Tony.

First, they had to put their climbing gear into their packs while lying flat in the tunnel, which proved a challenge. Once everything was packed safely away, they crawled forward on their stomachs, one after another. Their headlamps lit the narrow tunnel.

But suddenly, behind them, the door shut swiftly and loudly.

Mitch tried to reach Fingal. "Can you hear us?"

No answer.

Tony tried to connect to Fingal too. "The door just shut behind us. Can you hear us?"

No answer.

Tony could not turn around in the tunnel, but he slithered backward to the door and tried to open it with his feet.

"It won't open. Even if I could use my hands. We're locked in," said Tony.

Mitch in the lead saw the one lemming at the far end of the tunnel. "There's a lemming ahead, and I don't know what else to do but to follow it."

▲ ▲ ▲

Skarb tried to follow Jatuh but was severely incapacitated from Jatuh's attack. Its legs wobbled and its eyes spun in circles, leaving Skarb miserably dizzy. Skarb dropped its head to the ground and held its middle feet over its eyes, trying to calm them down. But it was no use. Skarb just had to wait it out.

Skarb was frustrated at how long it was taking for its eyes to stop spinning and for its legs to straighten and stand. Finally, its body recovered enough for it to limp along and pick up the lemmings' scent. Skarb followed their trail to the base of the mountain, but then the scent abruptly ended as though the lemmings had disappeared.

Skarb concluded that the lemmings, with Jatuh in their midst, somehow got inside the mountain. Skarb searched methodically for an entrance, taking extreme care to avoid being seen. But it found no place that could be an entry point for hundreds of lemmings to file into the mountain.

When Skarb reached the other side of the mountain, it looked upward and was surprised to see three children climbing the mountain face. Skarb collapsed to the ground to prevent being seen and watched as all three kids crawled into a square stone door leading into the mountain. Then Skarb saw the door shut behind them. They, too, were now in the mountain with Jatuh.

Skarb muttered, "There's something important in that mountain. And I must beat them all to it."

To Skarb's luck, a dense fog moved in, and the mountain face was obscured from view. Skarb began its climb, but a challenging climb it was. The mountain's built-in triggers attacked whoever attempted to surmount the mountain, and Skarb was no exception. However, unlike Mitch, Tony, and Jovi, Skarb did not have any siblings to warn it of the dangers.

A rockslide came down upon Skarb, knocking it off the mountain and burying it under a pile of rocks at the base. Skarb crawled out of the rubble and tried again, only to be foiled by an avalanche of snow from high up on the mountain. Skarb was buried under a very deep mound of snow and again crawled its way out. Skarb made a third attempt and finally made it to the spot where the children had entered the mountain. Skarb clawed and scratched at the rock face, trying to force the stone to give way. But the entry was sealed tight, and even for a Greznik, there was no way in.

67

COME WITH US, LITTLE ONE

The kids, trapped in a dark tunnel, had nowhere to go but forward. The lemming they saw at the entrance was long gone. The kids courageously crawled for an hour and hoped they would reach an exit somehow.

"I feel like we might be crawling back to Minnesota," said Jovi.

Mitch, leading the crawl, said, "I think I see the end of the tunnel up ahead. It looks like it opens up."

Mitch was the first one to reach the opening, and he pointed his headlamp up and down into the pitch dark and said, "It's a vertical tube, like a ventilation shaft. There's a ladder attached to the wall, and it looks like the ladder goes all the way up and all the way down the shaft."

"A long way down?" asked Jovi nervously.

Mitch pointed his headlamp down to look to the bottom of the shaft. But he was absolutely spooked by the height—the ventilation shaft dropped down so far that Mitch could not even see the bottom.

"It's not too bad," Mitch said casually, so as not to alarm Tony and Jovi.

Tony said, "We have to try it. We need another way out. Are we going up or down?"

"I feel air flowing down from above," said Mitch.

"Then let's go up," said Jovi.

Mitch grabbed hold of the ladder and pulled himself out of the tunnel and onto the ladder, then started climbing upward. Tony looked down and he, too, was spooked by the depth of the shaft. He crawled onto the ladder and cleared the way for Jovi to do the same. But he warned her not to look down.

"Why not?" asked Jovi.

"Just don't. Stay focused upward," encouraged Tony.

Jovi got to the ladder and climbed on without looking down. But once she got a firm grip on the ladder she could not help herself. She said, "There's no bottom to this shaft!"

"We told you not to look!" said Mitch.

"We should mark this spot in case we need to find this tunnel again," suggested Jovi. Jovi pulled out her yellow handkerchief and tied it to the wall to mark the tunnel's entrance.

Mitch said, "The air is much better in here. At least it's moving."

Tony agreed. "The air in that tunnel was about a thousand years stale."

The climb up turned out to be much farther than it looked. Their hands were already chafed, and now blisters were forming on the palms of their hands. They put their gloves on to relieve the blistering.

Mitch said, "I'm too tired to keep going."

Suddenly, the ladder started moving upward slowly.

Tony asked, "Did you turn something on?"

"No," said Mitch.

Jovi said, "I hope Fingal turned it on."

The ladder stopped moving at an opening in the shaft.

"I guess we should get off here. At least for a rest," said Tony.

Mitch got off the ladder and stepped into the cavern. Jovi and Tony stepped off too, grateful for a rest. The cavern was large enough to stand up straight, and their legs, arms, and backs appreciated the break. They also drank some water and split a piece of pemmican.

Jovi tried her walkie-talkie again, but it still had no signal. "How are we going to get out of here? I wish we could talk to Fingal."

Mitch saw a lemming peek around the corner and said, "Look, there's the lemming we saw at the entrance. I'm pretty sure it's the same one."

"How can you tell?" asked Jovi.

"It has a black diamond spot on its back."

The lemming ran away, and the kids followed. The cavern opened into a corridor that was also tall enough for them to walk upright in. From around the corner, they heard a rustling sound. Tony peeked around and put his finger to his lips to tell Jovi and Tony, "Shh." Mitch and Jovi took turns looking around the corner. Hundreds of lemmings were coming toward them via a different tunnel. The tunnel was so full of lemmings they were almost crawling over each other.

The lemmings did not see the kids and turned and filed into another corridor. Sally was in the pack of lemmings, but the kids could not tell one lemming from another. When the last of the lemmings rounded the corner, the kids followed them quietly, unseen. They peeked around and found the lemmings gathered in a large cave, which opened to the outdoors. Then they saw the strange yet beautiful instrument and were stunned by its magnificence.

"What is *that*?" wondered Tony.

"Wow, incredible," said Mitch.

Jovi said, "How strange."

"Yet beautiful. I've never seen anything so amazing," said Tony.

"What a weird world we just walked into," said Mitch.

The kids were close enough to the cave opening so their walkie-talkies could receive a signal. Fingal was extremely worried about what had happened to the kids and had been trying to reach them every ten minutes. This time, his signal got through, and the kids' walkie-talkies went off loudly.

"Can you read me? Are you okay? Can you hear me?" asked Fingal.

His voice came through on all three walkie-talkies. When the lemmings heard Fingal's voice, they scurried over to where the sounds came from and found the three kids. Hundreds and hundreds of lemmings scampered forward, surrounded the kids' feet, and stared up at them. Tiro was in the middle of the crowd watching the kids' every move.

Tony responded, "Yes, we can hear you."

Fingal nearly collapsed in relief that they were safe. He looked up at the sky and said, "Thank you."

"We're in a cave surrounded by lemmings and an amazing instrument in front of us," said Mitch.

"Are you safe?" asked Fingal.

"Yes, it's just lemmings around us. They're so cute," said Jovi.

"The critters are all at work, like people!" exclaimed Tony.

The lemmings shuffled around the kids and chattered. To the kids, it just sounded like hundreds of lemmings squeaking and chomping their teeth. They were surrounded by lemmings, except for a narrow path leading to the instrument. From behind, the lemmings nipped at their ankles to get the kids to move forward to the instrument. The kids yelped from the bites and walked forward to avoid being nipped.

A few of the lemmings ran across the keys, playing a beautiful tune. The kids were mesmerized by the lovely music.

Fingal asked, "Any sign of what causes the echo?"

Jovi said, "There's an instrument up here. It's beautiful and sounds so pretty, like a thousand instruments."

Tony added, "I bet it can play a C-sharp. Maybe it's the echo."

"Can you bring it down with you?" asked Fingal.

Mitch circled the instrument. "No. It's way too big."

Fingal was instantly concerned, recalling a story he had heard of a powerful instrument that could pull in forces from beyond. "Can you take it apart and send it down in pieces?"

"No, it'd take years," answered Tony, "It has thousands of pieces."

The lemmings listened carefully with great concern.

Fingal was quiet and did not respond.

"You still there?" Jovi asked Fingal.

"Yes, yes. I think you need to come down right away."

"We wish you could see this instrument. It's so pretty," said Jovi.

"It's incredible," said Tony.

"The instrument is very powerful and can be dangerous in the wrong hands. Grezniks will wish to seize it," said Fingal. "We may need to come back and get it later. Right now, I want you to come down. Can you climb down from there?"

The kids looked out from the cave's edge and down the cliff wall. They analyzed whether they could find a place to secure their climbing equipment and descend safely. But it was an impossible descent.

"No, we can't. We'll need to retrace our steps," said Mitch.

"Come back down right away. Be careful, and do not get diverted. Move quickly," said Fingal, whose voice sounded more worried than ever before.

The kids looked at each other, dreading that long climb down the vertical shaft. Not to mention they had no idea how to get out of the mountain.

"The problem is, we don't really know how to get out of the mountain. The entrance we came through locked behind us," said Mitch.

"The lemmings must've opened the mountain for you to enter," said Fingal. "Trust them to open an exit for you."

"Got it. We're on our way," said Tony. "But as soon as we enter the tunnels you won't be able to hear us anymore. We'll make contact as soon as we can."

"Okay, I'll wait to hear from you. Have courage," said Fingal.

Mitch and Jovi started to leave out the cave's back corridor.

Tony said, "Wait. We should memorize the details of this instrument so we can explain it to Fingal."

The kids walked around the perimeter of the instrument and took detailed mental photographs. They took careful note of everything they possibly could about the instrument—size, structure, and components—and they watched the lemmings work inside. Jovi had no idea she was followed by Tiro, right at her ankles, as she rounded the instrument.

There was no way Tiro was going to let these humans take the instrument away. After hearing what Fingal said, he knew the instrument could harness the unimaginably powerful forces from the far beyond. And he was determined take control of it.

Tiro felt a surging urge to take a big bite out of Jovi's ankle. Instead, he followed Mitch, Tony, and Jovi and schemed to ensure they failed catastrophically.

"Okay, let's go," said Mitch.

The kids walked out of the cave to retrace their steps back to the shaft and find their way out.

Tiro maneuvered slyly through the lemming crowd and followed the kids. Jovi looked behind her and saw Tiro following them.

"One of the cute little lemmings is following us. Probably making sure we get out okay," said Jovi, waving at Tiro. "Come with us, little one!"

68

NO MORE AIR

Once the kids exited the cave, the lemmings murmured to each other.

"Who were those children?"

"How did they get up here?"

"Who let them in?"

"Was that the voice of a Tukor?"

"How did they know about our mountain?"

"Did you hear what they said? They're thinking of taking the instrument!"

None of them saw Tiro sneak away from their crowd and follow the kids, except for Oskar—the lemming with the black diamond spot of fur on his back. Oskar hoped to help the children get out of the mountain just as he had helped them get in. But he was worried as to why Tiro would follow the children.

Oskar followed Tiro and asked him, "Where are you going?"

Tiro turned around abruptly, surprised to hear that someone had followed him. But he saw that it was just that old lemming again. "Someone must follow those kids," said Tiro. "They can't just come in here, expect us to trust them, and take our instrument!"

"They're with the Tukor. We can trust them. Let them go on their way," said Oskar.

Tiro ignored Oskar and ran off. He easily ditched the old lemming and sprinted toward the kids, determined to ensure they never left the mountain alive.

Tiro neared the shaft after Mitch and Tony were already on the ladder and climbing down it.

"Hurry up, Jovi! Get on the ladder," said Tony.

Jovi was just about to get on the ladder when she saw Tiro round the corner and run toward her.

Jovi said, "I'm waiting for the lemming to catch up. Maybe he wants to come with us. Can I put him in my pocket and keep him?" Jovi said to Tiro, "Run faster, little lemming. We're in a hurry!"

Tiro raced to reach Jovi.

Mitch said, "We can't take care of a lemming, Jovi. Hurry and catch up to us. We need to get out of here fast."

"Fine. I suppose you're right. Bye-bye, lemming! It was nice meeting you!" said Jovi as she waved goodbye to Tiro and got on the ladder.

She said to her brothers, "The lemming was so cute. Do you think lemmings make good pets, like hamsters?"

"I've never heard of a pet lemming," said Tony, climbing down.

"I wanted to see if he would let me pick him up," said Jovi.

"Come on, hurry up! You're falling behind," said Mitch.

"I'm right here. It's you who's going slow. If I was going down first, you'd be hurrying to catch up to me."

"No way," said Mitch.

Jovi looked up and saw the lemming with its head over the ledge.

"See, he wants to help! He's waiting to make sure we get out," said Jovi.

Tiro knew that the fastest way to stop the three youthful irritants would be to wrench the ladder loose from the wall and shake it until the kids lost their grip and fell down the shaft to their deaths. But as a lemming, Tiro was too small to do that. And he did not want to change back to a Greznik since the mountain was riddled with traps to destroy Grezniks. Then Tiro noticed two buttons next to the shaft.

Tiro pushed the first button. The exit below the kids slammed shut and locked, and the sound echoed throughout the shaft.

"I hope that wasn't the exit slamming shut," said Mitch.

Then the remaining doors slammed shut in rapid succession from the top of the shaft all the way down to the bottom.

"Not good," said Tony.

"We're locked in. Definitely not good," said Mitch.

Tiro hit the other button, and all the air vents slammed shut.

"And the air stopped flowing," said Tony.

Mitch said, "Now the air is being pumped out."

"Let's go fast. We have to get out of here," said Jovi.

After locking them in and cutting off their air supply, Tiro destroyed both buttons and the electrical wiring. No one would be able to reopen the shaft.

Tiro walked triumphantly back to the lemmings, knowing the Tukor's fellow travelers would die soon.

Oskar was walking toward the shaft when he heard Tiro running back to return to the cave. Oskar ducked quickly behind a wall and hid. After Tiro passed his hiding spot, Oskar went directly to the shaft to check on the kids. He found the shaft locked shut, and when he reached up to hit the buttons to open the shaft, the buttons had been thoroughly destroyed. He knew the kids were trapped inside, and if they did not get out soon, they would run out of oxygen.

69

A MEMORY OF SEVENS

Oskar had no time to lose. He walked back to the main cave but carefully entered to remain unseen. He snuck along the back wall, hoping no one would notice, especially Tiro. He scurried to reach the opposite side, ducked into a corridor, and ran as fast as his old legs could take him. After some distance, he took a sharp right turn into an abandoned, dilapidated corridor. Then he took another left, another left, three rights, two lefts, and a right. The pathway got narrower and darker at every turn until he reached a long dead-end corridor that was covered in years of dust. No one had walked along it in years.

He walked halfway down that corridor, looking skittishly behind him. When he was sure the coast was clear, he dusted off a rough-edged stone jutting out from the wall. He twisted that stone and pushed it in. A small door opened, and he crawled carefully through, swinging shut the door and being careful not to lock himself in.

Oskar entered a very large electrical room with hundreds of circuits, wires, switches, breakers, control panels, and a long wall of oddly shaped cabinets. Oskar was one of only a few lemmings who knew the room existed. He walked the length of the long room, wishing he could remember what he was taught years ago.

When Oskar was young, his grandpa had told him how the old electrical controls in the mountain worked, but back then Oskar was bored with his grandpa's technical talk. Now he desperately needed to remember what his grandpa had told him and regretted that he had not listened more carefully. He wished his loving grandpa was still right there with him.

Facing a panel of switches, he talked to himself. "Grandpa, I know you taught this to me long ago. Now I, too, am old, as you were then. I need to remember what you said. The traitor Tiro trapped three children inside the old shaft. They will die unless I remember which switch opens the shaft."

Oskar walked the length of the room, hoping something would trigger a memory. All the cabinets were differently shaped polygons. At the end of the wall, he came upon a heptagonal cabinet locked shut with a combination lock—and the seven-sided polygon was the memory trigger he needed. He remembered that his grandpa had set the combination to Grandma's birth year times the number of children they had—seven. Oskar unlocked the cabinet.

The door opened to a large library with stacks and stacks of books—3,767 in total. The books documented every detail of the 3,767 tunnel systems inside the mountain. Oskar did not have time to read all the books to find the one page he needed, so he scanned the spines, hoping a clue would emerge to tell him which book had the right information. He randomly picked one book and pulled it off the shelf. He scanned through it but did not find what he was looking for.

"I don't have time to look through every book," said Oskar, frustrated. "I must remember!"

Meanwhile, the kids climbed down the ladder, shining their headlamps along the walls and running their hands against the surface, looking and feeling for an exit. They were scared and felt claustrophobic as the air grew increasingly stale and breathing became more difficult. But they did not dare voice their fears. They wanted to be strong for each other.

Oskar remembered that, in addition to loving his seven children, his grandpa loved prime numbers. Then it all came back to him. The switches for the old shaft and tunnels were labeled with the first seven prime numbers starting with the number seven—7, 71, 73, 79, 701, 709, 719.

Oskar said out loud, "Kids, I hope you're hanging on tight."

Then he flipped those seven circuits. He breathed a sigh of relief when the circuits turned on and blinked green. He had successfully activated electrical circuits in the old mine shafts that had been dormant for years.

He said with great relief, "Thank you, Grandpa."

But Oskar also knew the circuits stayed on for only seventy-one minutes, and he hoped the children were moving fast enough to get out.

When lights came on in the shaft, the kids cheered. Yet the old electrical system had deteriorated over the years, so when the circuits went on, sparks and flames flew forth and crackled up and down the shaft. Then the ladder dropped abruptly downward, about five feet. The kids all lost their grip and fell off the ladder.

Wisely, they had secured themselves to the ladder with their climbing equipment and were saved from plummeting.

"Are you okay?" asked Tony as he got his firm footing again.

Before Jovi and Mitch could answer, the ladder moved upward, like a rickety vertical conveyer.

"It better not drop again," said Jovi, her voice shaking.

"I'm hanging on tighter this time," said Mitch.

The ladder moved upward slowly, clanking loudly the entire way. Then it stopped abruptly, and a tunnel opened right in front of them.

"Do we dare go through that?" asked Tony.

"I don't think we have a choice. There's nowhere else to go," said Mitch.

"And I want off this ladder. So let's go," said Jovi.

Jovi was the closest to the tunnel and got off the ladder first. She crawled forward to make way for Tony and Mitch. They were relieved that the path ahead of them was lit with floor lights along its edges. But little did they know that they did not have long before the passageways ahead of them would lock down again.

They crawled on their stomachs as the tunnel wound around in the shape of a slithering snake. Then it turned sharply to the right and opened to a tunnel that was tall enough for the kids to stand up in. They stood and stretched, weary from the ladder climb and achy from crawling.

A green light blinked a good distance ahead of them and they ran to it. Jovi pushed the button and the mountain wall opened upward like a garage door to the outside. Tony pulled out his walkie-talkie.

Mitch said, "Fingal, can you hear us?"

Fingal was so happy to hear his voice and said, "Yes, I can hear you. Where are you? I can't see you."

"We're in the mountain, but I don't know where we are. Something trapped us in a tunnel. Too long to explain. Can you see us?" asked Tony.

Fingal said, "Too much fog. I can't see the mountain at all. But can you get down from where you are?"

Jovi responded, "It's a tough climb down. I think we're on a different side of the mountain."

A light on the door blinked yellow, and they heard gears getting ready to shut the door again.

"The door is shutting. We've got to get out of here!" said Mitch.

The kids wasted no time and hastily unloaded their climbing gear from their packs.

Fingal said, "Hello! Hello? Are you there?"

A loud warning clanged and the door began to shut.

Mitch answered, "We've got to go! The exit is shutting on us!"

Tony was closest to the edge, so he got out first and started down the steep mountain face. The door was half-way down when Jovi got through, and Mitch squeezed through the door just before it closed completely. He slipped his fingertips out from under the door just in time.

Up in the electrical room, Oskar saw the circuits go dark again. He closed his eyes, placed one paw over the other, and said, "I hope you all got out of the mountain in time. Be careful, my friends. It's difficult to make it down the mountain alive. No matter how tired you are, do not give up or the mountain's power will swallow you up."

Oskar left the library, then closed and locked the heptagon cabinet door. He exited the electrical room and walked back to where the instrument was located. When he saw all his fellow lemmings again, he never said a word about the children. He was looking only for Tiro.

70

RAADSEL

Luckily, Mitch, Tony, and Jovi exited the mountain door fast enough and began their descent. Tony had gotten out first and descended ahead of Mitch and Jovi, but he soon ran into trouble. He found a safe place to get his footing and pulled out his walkie-talkie. "Jovi, Mitch, don't follow me. It's too difficult here."

Mitch's route also proved too treacherous. Jovi's was not any easier. No matter which way they went, the climb was unyielding. Tony reached a ledge and could not go any farther.

Tony said over the walkie-talkie, "I'm stuck. There's no way to maneuver out of here. There's nothing to grab onto."

Mitch and Jovi were in the same predicament as Tony, with nowhere to go next. The fog that had enveloped the mountain turned into rain, followed by freezing sleet.

Fingal listened to their conversations over the walkie-talkies and heard fatigue in their voices. The weather conditions were devastating. There were no options but to hope that they could hang on. But even for Fingal, hope in these circumstances was difficult to muster. With the sleet, Fingal knew they needed to be rescued quickly. The storm worsened, and he could not see ten feet in front of him, much less the mountain face. The caribou huddled around Fingal to help keep him warm. He repeatedly tried to communicate with the kids, but they did not answer.

A tremendously large eagle with a nine-foot wingspan dove down toward Fingal, his long, sharp claws facing him as he landed. The storm raged too strongly for Fingal to see the eagle approach until it was too late. The landing startled the caribou, and they darted away, leaving Fingal exposed. He dove to the ground and hid behind a large stone, and the caribou bravely came back in front of him to protect him.

The eagle landed threateningly but did not attack. He towered over Fingal and said, "I know you to be a Tukor. I assume you know, or you wouldn't be here, that the Grezniks have discovered the clues to the blue stone mine. The breach is severe."

Fingal stood up carefully, still fearing whether this large eagle was friend or foe. He was puzzled by its size and features. "Are you a Haast's eagle?" he asked.

The enormous eagle nodded.

"But your species has been extinct for over six hundred years. How can you be here?" asked Fingal.

"They call me Raadsel. You need not know more. The Grezniks will soon put all the clues together and find the blue stone mine. We are all in grave danger. I have come to you to seek help in preventing a terrible battle."

"How do I know that you are not the creature who betrayed us?" asked Fingal.

Raadsel paused and flapped its broad eagle wings. The draft from the wings created a wind that nearly knocked Fingal over.

Raadsel said, "You do not know. And I cannot prove it to you. The mountain holds an instrument that has been hidden for centuries. A strangely shaped Greznik has been climbing the mountain trying to get in. It is extraordinarily sly and hard to keep an eye on. It is only a matter of time before Grezniks seize the instrument. We need your help."

Fingal made a calculated decision to trust Raadsel and said, "I received a message from Geduld, a shark from the waters of Papua New Guinea. Last century, a Greznik drank of the blue stone waters and chose the Voices within. The danger has been brewing for quite some time. Not long after his visit, I received word that Grezniks had discovered clues to the mine."

Raadsel asked, "The odd Greznik must be the one who drank of the waters. Why else would it have seven legs?"

"Yes, it must be. I'm here to help, but I have three children traveling with me. And we need them. They're on the cliff in this terrible storm, and they can't hang on much longer."

Raadsel did not acknowledge Fingal's concern for the children but said, "The Grezniks will soon find the blue stone instrument, so we must move it. We're closing all entrances and tunnels to the mountain as soon as we can. The instrument was built in this location and has never been moved. It's large and very fragile and will be extraordinarily difficult to relocate without damaging it. Earlier this summer, I saw your three young travelers flying over this region in your aircraft, and I believe the instrument can fit inside it. That is our best option."

"I can fly back here and load the instrument in the aircraft. But I need those children off the mountain safely," said Fingal, desperately hoping his intuition was right and that Raadsel was a trustworthy ally.

Raadsel did not respond and flew back into the storm so coldly and abruptly that Fingal worried that his intuition about Raadsel was wrong. Years ago Fingal was betrayed in battle by those he had mistakenly trusted, and those memories flashed before his eyes. He feared that Raadsel would not help the kids, or worse yet would report their whereabouts to the Grezniks.

Fingal tried to reach the kids. "Tony. Mitch. Jovi. Can you hear me? Anyone?" There was no response. Fingal kept a calm voice, hoping they could hear him as he spoke words of encouragement. "Do not give in. Do not give up. You have more strength than you realize. Stay strong. Hold on. Believe."

Back on the cliff, the kids each heard Fingal's voice on their walkie-talkies, but they were hanging on for dear life and could not free one hand to answer him. Each one hoped to hear their siblings' voices, but no one replied to Fingal.

They cried out for each other.

"Tony!"

"Jovi!"

"Mitch!"

"Can you hear me? Anybody?"

Mitch hoped they could hear his encouragement. "Jovi! Tony! Hang on!"

But the storm was too wickedly loud, and none of them could hear each other. Tony hung on with both hands and struggled to keep his feet firmly planted on a rock that jutted from the cliff, but more and more ice was building up on every surface. His feet slipped repeatedly, and he prevented a fall by the strength of his hands. The fatigue from the unrelenting effort was punishing. He was losing his grip, and it was impossible for his feet to retain their firm footing. He looked below and could not see the ground through the storm. He wished it was not a long way to fall, but he was sure it was.

Jovi and Mitch ran into the same problems. The rocks were coated in a sheet of ice, and there was nothing secure to hang onto. But Tony's route had been more difficult, and his grip could no longer hold his weight. His fingertips slipped off and he dropped into a free fall. He cried out, "Mitch! Jovi!"

He reached out his hands as he fell, hoping he could grab hold of something on his way down, but all he felt was the stormy air hitting his face. The wind was strong enough to toss him about in the air. He shouted, "Don't give up!" as his final encouragement for his brother and sister and closed his eyes, expecting to crash to the ground.

Out of nowhere, Raadsel swooped down and caught Tony in midair, his talons grabbing the boy on each side of his waist. The eagle flew him higher and higher. Tony did not know if the eagle was friend or foe. Attempting an escape was useless anyway, since Tony would plummet to his death—so he let his legs and arms dangle as he was flown through the storm.

The eagle flew faster, and particles of ice pinged Tony's face like sharp, stinging needles. He tried to cover his face with his hands, but the speed at which they were flying prevented him from being able to control his arms. It was impossible to see the mountain face, much less Jovi and Mitch. He called out to them anyway, hoping they could hear him despite the impossible conditions.

Raadsel dove sharply downward and dropped Tony on the ground. The landing was rough, and Tony tumbled. Despite his exhaustion and painful landing, Tony stood up strong, fearful the huge eagle would attack. But the eagle flew off, leaving Tony by himself. He looked around to determine which way to go to rescue his brother and sister, but the storm was blinding and the wind whipped by him. There was no way to even know where to look.

Jovi's strength was breaking down as wind gusts whipped her from the side. A chunk of snow fell on her from above and pushed her off her perch. She dropped fast and hard but was relieved to land safely on a rocky ledge that jutted out right below. But the rocky ledge was slanted downward and covered in ice. As soon as she landed, Jovi slid dangerously toward the edge. She caught herself and crawled on her stomach back up the slant. But there was nothing to hang on to, and she slid back downward again. She repeated this several times.

By the fourth time, Jovi was too exhausted and could not keep herself away from the edge any longer. Her legs went over the edge and she tried to hang on by her fingertips, but her hands slipped too and she fell.

She closed her eyes and cried for Mitch and Tony as the wind spun her in a free fall. Raadsel swooped down and grabbed her arms tightly in his strong feet and flew her away from the mountain. But Jovi's jacket was loose, and she slipped out of the jacket and out of Raadsel's grip. Raadsel let go of the jacket, and the wind blew it upward and away. He nose-dived and caught Jovi just before she hit the ground. He flew her back up into the sky, then set her down near Tony and flew away. Jovi landed hard and tumbled.

Tony and Jovi were so relieved to see each other, but the relief was short-lived when they realized that Mitch was not with them.

Jovi yelled, "Mitch! Where are you, Mitch?"

"Don't give up! Hang on!" said Tony.

They looked around, but the storm raged too hard to even see the mountain.

"Were you carried by that eagle too?" asked Jovi.

"Yes, but he'll get Mitch too, right?" Tony said in desperation.

"We can't leave Mitch up there!" Jovi cried. She grabbed Tony's hand and pulled him to run and look for Mitch.

With crushing sadness, Tony said, "Jovi, we can't go anywhere. We can't see a thing. We might end up running away from him."

She could hardly hear Tony through the winds, but she gave in to the reality that there was no way of knowing which way to go to find Mitch.

Tony said, "We can pray that Mitch hears us somehow."

She screamed frantically, "Don't give up! Hang on, Mitch Bosonataski-Fishengardet!"

Mitch heard nothing and did not even know he was on the cliff all by himself. He hung on for dear life and said, "Tony! Jovi! Are you okay?"

His fingers were raw from gripping a jagged stone and so terribly cold. He carefully made his way over to a ledge that was more stable. Yet it was so small and narrow that his feet could barely fit. He stood straight as a board. If he leaned even slightly to the left or right, he would slip and plummet downward. He carefully pulled out his walkie-talkie. "Can you hear me? Anyone?" But the battery was dead.

Mitch shouted words of encouragement to Tony and Jovi again and hoped they were safer than he was. The wind gusts strengthened. He looked below, using only his eyeballs to look downward. Even the slightest tip of his head might be enough to throw off his balance. He saw a rock ledge not too far below and thought of leaping, but the ledge was sure to be covered in ice. But he could not stay where he was either. He decided he would leap and would do so on the count of three. He counted as he carefully aimed for his landing spot. "One, two . . ." But before he was ready, the strongest gust of wind yet whipped around the mountain and shoved him off. He completely missed the ledge. The wind blew him upward, whirled him about, then plunged him downward.

The next thing Mitch saw was Raadsel tipped backward with sharp claws pointing at him. Mitch closed his eyes, bracing for the ginormous eagle's attack. Raadsel caught Mitch in midair, at his waist, and flew him away from the mountain. Raadsel set Mitch down but took off immediately. Mitch was alone on the ground. "Jovi! Tony! Where are you? Are you okay?"

Mitch feared the worst—that they had fallen off—and he was afraid to think of it. He could not see more than a few feet in front of him but, desperate to find them, he pulled out his compass . . . but an arrow pointing north means nothing if where you need to be could be anywhere. He put the compass back in his pocket and pleaded to the sky. "Keep them safe. Please. Be strong, Jovi and Tony."

Raadsel swooped down again toward Mitch and dropped Jovi's jacket at his feet, then flew off again. Mitch grabbed the jacket and broke into tears. It was torn to shreds from the eagle's talons, soaking wet from rain and sleet, and it had drops of blood on it.

Mitch cried out to Raadsel, "Where is Jovi? What did you do to her?"

Raadsel was out of sight as Mitch collapsed on the ground and cried. Mitch did not see Raadsel swoop over him and then circle back. Suddenly Mitch was in his talons again and flying away. Mitch hung onto Jovi's jacket through the winds. Raadsel flew him across the mountainous landscape. Unexpectedly Raadsel dove down as if to attack something on the ground, but then he flew upward again and away.

Even though Mitch could see nothing through the storm and clouds, he knew the Haast's eagle was flying him higher and higher into the sky. Suddenly, Raadsel pulled in his wings for a straight drop downward. The speed of the fall was terrifying, and Mitch felt Raadsel's talons clamping down even harder to keep Mitch in his grip. Raadsel stretched out his wings to break the rapid descent, swooped down next to Jovi and Tony, and set Mitch down. Raadsel pushed them with his beak to huddle them together. The kids knew from the look of intensity in his eyes that the strange bird could maul them to bits.

The storm had moved from rain to sleet to a heavy snowfall. The kids—freezing, exhausted, and shivering—stood straight as boards, crunched together, shoulder to shoulder, fearful of the eagle. Afraid to speak. Afraid to move. The eagle put his giant beak right up to Jovi's nose and glared into her eyes. Jovi cringed, believing he intended to eat her head in one bite. But Raadsel stepped aside to stand before Mitch and stared right into his eyes too. Raadsel moved to stand before Tony then suddenly flew off.

They hugged each other, so relieved to be safely off the mountain and back together again.

"I thought he was going to eat my head," said Jovi.

"And me for the full meal," said Tony.

"He could've eaten all of us," said Mitch, noticing his hands were bleeding from the climb.

Tony took out his walkie-talkie and said, "Fingal, can you hear us? Fingal?"

Fingal answered, "Where are you? Are you okay?"

"We're on the ground. We were saved by some huge bird—like an eagle but way, way too big. We don't know where we are, or where to go," answered Tony.

Fingal looked up and into the storm and said, "Thank you. Thank you." Then Fingal said to the kids, "You have no idea how happy I am to hear your voice. Let me hear all of you."

To Fingal's great relief, he heard all their voices and said, "So grateful to hear you. So very grateful. It's extremely dangerous weather. Is there a place for you to protect yourselves from the storm?"

Tony said, "We'll look for one. Jovi and I don't have much battery left on the walkie-talkies. Mitch's battery is dead. We'll connect after the storm is over, unless there is an emergency."

Fingal said, "There is a Greznik in the area. Communicate only in an emergency."

The kids walked toward some large boulders jutting out from the base of the mountain. They got behind the boulders and found an entrance to a small, hidden cavern at the mountain's edge where the snow had not yet blown in. They crawled inside. They were hungry and thirsty but only had a little bit of pemmican left to eat. They melted snow for water to drink.

To get some rest, two slept while the other one stood guard, trading places every two hours. Whoever was awake and on duty worked to keep the entrance clear of snow, but the snow fell fast and hard, and their fatigue made it difficult to keep up with the clearing of the snow.

Fingal found shelter between the warmth of the caribou, but he could not sleep a wink, fearing that the kids were not safe. Throughout his life, Fingal had journeyed through so much—amazingly wonderful experiences and yet terrible battles too. But a powerful, extinct eagle guarding this mountain was wholly unexpected. It meant that the battle was bigger than even he understood, involving dimensions unseen. And this strange instrument was somehow intertwined with the defense of the blue stones—but how, exactly, Fingal had no idea. If only he had received the Story, he might know just what it was. He never learned exactly what happened to the Story, other than it never arrived. One day he found a note clipped to his front porch swing that said only:

With deep regret, we report that we cannot deliver the Story. The last copy of the Story is gone. It blew away like confetti.

Mitch had the third night-watch duty. Tony and Jovi slept soundly while Mitch kept busy clearing the blowing snow, trying to prevent it from barricading them in. In between clearing efforts, he monitored the entrance to their hiding spot carefully. To help himself stay awake, he reviewed in his head the memorized instructions for the flying tractor combine.

▲ ▲ ▲

Up on the mountain, Skarb tried to break into the square
door entrance the kids had originally crawled into, but there
was no way in. Skarb was determined to get inside to find
out what Jatuh and the three kids were after. It crawled back
down to the base of the mountain and started a new ascent.
But this time, Skarb spiraled up the mountain methodically
to find any other way to get inside. But the triggers to prevent anyone from reaching the top were unrelenting. Skarb
was repeatedly knocked back down to the bottom.

Skarb tried again and again at different sections of
the mountain and failed each time. Then fog moved into
rain, then sleet, then snow. Skarb tried one more time,
climbed up high, and clung to the mountain face. Even for
a Greznik who could normally scale walls like a spider, the
conditions were unforgiving. Skarb could not see or sense
anything on the mountain. Yet this time, it heard children's
voices not too far from its position.

"Mitch!"

"Jovi!"

"Where are you?"

"I can't see you! Where are you?"

Then Skarb heard another unknown voice, Fingal's,
over their walkie-talkies: "Do not give in. Do not give up.
You have more strength than you realize. Stay strong. Hold
on. Believe."

Skarb mocked the encouragement. "Believe what? It's
impossible up here! I can't even stay on!"

The storm was too wickedly strong, even for Skarb. Thus, Skarb did not see Raadsel rescue Tony and Jovi in midair. But Skarb did notice that in the end there was only one voice yelling out—Mitch's. Skarb assumed the other two had fallen to their deaths.

Skarb heard Mitch calling for his brother and sister. "Jovi! Tony! Are you okay?"

This time Mitch's voice was dangerously near to Skarb's position. Skarb had no idea if the voices were those of Tukors, and it retreated quickly to avoid the risk of being seen. But Skarb moved too quickly, and one of its extra legs snagged on the cliff wall, causing Skarb to lose its balance and slip off its perch. Skarb fell hard and fast onto a ledge below. When it landed, it bounced off and fell downward again. It caught itself on a rock jutting out, but the rock was too slippery even for a Greznik. Skarb slipped off and landed headfirst on a slanted rock face below and bounced off into yet another free fall. This waterfall of wipeouts continued all the way down. In the final fall, Skarb rolled like tumbleweed down a steep scree and landed in a deep, cold puddle at the base of the mountain.

71

CALL THE MURKY FOG IN

Raadsel left the kids alone in the punishing storm and flew back to the mountain. He circled to find the seven-legged Greznik but was unsuccessful. So he flew high up the mountain to his hidden nest and grabbed some very heavy rope. Then he circled back around to the other side of the mountain to the lemmings' cave. He landed on a perch just below the cave so he could see directly in. Then he carefully placed the rope into the cave. Although eagles are a dangerous enemy of lemmings, Raadsel was their trusted protector who had, over many centuries, saved thousands of their lives in battles to protect the stones.

Tiro was alarmed to see a Haast's eagle, the predator from New Zealand that had gone extinct so long ago. He had no idea how one could still be alive, but he knew that the bird's arrival complicated his plan to hijack the instrument.

Tiro slyly moved to the back of the crowd to ensure that Raadsel did not see his eyes, fearing the mysterious eagle could perceive the devious secret that Tiro was a Greznik.

Raadsel said to the crowd of faithful lemmings, "Our secrets have been betrayed. An oddly shaped Greznik has come to our mountain alone. This Greznik is like none other. It has too many legs and an extra eye and is extremely fast and sly. It has tried repeatedly to get inside the mountain, but the mountain's defensive triggers have succeeded in keeping it off. But this Greznik will never give up. It is believed that this strange Greznik has discovered the clues to the mine and is seeking the instrument. The instrument must leave here at once."

The lemmings were dumbfounded, and their hearts sank from the news. They had safely protected and cared for the instrument for many years and took great pride in doing so in their beloved mountain home. Their whole lives, their purpose, and every ounce of their energy was dedicated to protecting the instrument. They did not want to let it go. Worries raced through their thoughts as they reflected on their peaceful world changing so suddenly.

Oskar said to Raadsel, "We are deeply saddened by your news. Yet we trust your wisdom. It has always guided our hearts. We will prepare the instrument to leave."

Raadsel said, "There is a Tukor nearby who is traveling with the three children who entered your mountain. He will arrive here by aircraft to load and remove the instrument from the mountain and fly it away. I do not know how you can move it safely, but you must try. Use the rope I gave you to create a pulley system for it, if possible. Move quickly and be ever wary of the oddly shaped Greznik who is trying to reach you and steal it."

Tiro surged with anger that the wretched seven-legger had recovered from their fight and was interfering with his plan. Tiro was overcome with that same unsettling agitation he felt anytime he came face-to-face with Skarb. Tiro refused to acknowledge that those feelings were a warning, like the blinking signal of a lighthouse.

Instead, Tiro believed a powerful destiny was ready for the taking. He seethed within, and his muscles clenched as the desires of Proznia came upon him like a thick fog surging within his soul. One cannot take hold of the fog within one's own hands. One cannot fight it like one can a thug. It envelops you. Chills you to the bone. And if you do not lead your journey into the sunlight, the fog will blind your path ahead and trap you inside. But Tiro did not change his journey. Instead, Tiro moved to the front of the crowd of lemmings, stood on his hind legs, swooshed his front legs from side to side, and clapped his little feet to get everyone's attention in the cave. When he did, he called the murky fog in and set a heavy curtain down upon the sun.

72

LET IT BE. LET IT GO.

Raadsel flew off the mountain ledge, leaving the lemmings stunned and dismayed at the alarming development—a Greznik lurking on their mountain. But they had no time to grieve the troubling news. They went to work right away to design a pulley system to transfer the instrument out of the cave. With so little time to design something so complex, they pulled their best engineers together and asked Tiro to lend his tremendous physical strength to the project.

Tiro feigned enthusiasm and agreed to help, but worked sloppily, purposely made errors, and took frequent breaks, all to slow down and sabotage their efforts. As he watched them all busily working, he could not solve his predicament. He needed to hijack the instrument as soon as possible, but there was no value in gaining control of the instrument unless he knew how to operate it.

Tiro walked the perimeter several times, listening to the workers and observing everything they were doing, but he could not figure out what made the instrument so powerful. The elusive capabilities were not easily discovered unless one had the trust and guidance of the lemmings. Tiro knew it might take years to accomplish that. There was simply not enough time. Tiro could not just turn back into a Greznik and seize control, since the mountain was riddled with security controls to ensnare Grezniks. He made a split-second decision to seize control of the instrument anyway, believing he could learn to harness the power of the instrument without the lemmings.

Tiro stepped out from the crowd of lemmings, stood on his hind legs, clapped his feet together, and said, "Why are we letting the eagle command us? We are the instrument's protectors, not him. Let's believe in our own power. We can protect this instrument and keep it right here. We have for centuries, and we can for centuries more. The world might think us small and defenseless creatures, but we are not. We have built this mountain into a towering display of lemming ingenuity and engineering prowess— the complex tunnels, the lovely neighborhoods where you raise your families, the successful businesses you run to support our important work."

Many lemmings stopped their tasks to listen to Tiro, and the more he talked, the more they liked what he said. But not Gwilim.

"Yet we don't need to live our lives stuck in a mountain," Tiro continued. "That's not an inheritance worthy of keeping. Such unnecessary traditions. We can both keep the instrument and live our life out in the world. We must be free!"

Enraptured by Tiro's inspirational call, the lemmings crowded close together and stepped forward to get a better view of Tiro.

Gwilim squeezed through the crowd to stand eye to eye with Tiro and said, "We are already free. Let us not throw away wisdom grown and cherished over many lemming lifetimes." Then Gwilim stepped in front of Tiro and turned around to face the crowd. "Raadsel reminds us that we are called to protect. A Greznik is nearby, and we must heed Raadsel's call. We have worked for centuries to build the skills and heritage to defend against conniving and slithery forces like Grezniks. Remember how hard it was and how long it took to build our community, our traditions, our faith in each other—everything we are willing to defend and to sacrifice for. We give of ourselves to our fellow lemmings."

Gwilim's words inspired many lemmings to recall with fondness their sense of duty, their loyalty, and their hard work in protecting the power of the instrument. Tiro was losing his grip on the crowd. No way would he let a measly weakling creature control his audience.

Tiro put his front leg around Gwilim's shoulder and spoke loudly to drown out Gwilim's voice. "This little lemming means well but is but a pipsqueak and speaks the jargon of those who fear change. I am the voice for all lemmings."

Tiro butted Gwilim to the side and continued. "But listen here, friends. Right now, we are not free. We are enslaved to the past. Why carry on traditions of those who live in a tunnel, live tedious lives of polishing and tuning an old instrument? In the eyes of Raadsel, you're only a measly string tuner. Or just a bell polisher. Or a key pusher! You study and study many minute technical details—but why? Don't conform to this madness like your parents did. Let it be. Let it go. Let yourselves fly free of formalities. We're the voice of a new generation! We know there is a traitor in our ranks. The traitor is Raadsel, who comes to take away what we have the power to keep for ourselves. What if he decides to fly the instrument directly into the hands of the enemy, the army of Grezniks? What if, folks? That will be the end!"

"Raadsel would not betray us," said Gwilim, but even his loudest voice could not overcome Tiro's booming voice and the murmurings of the many excited lemmings. Gwilim continued anyway. "Raadsel is our trusted friend. He protects us. Don't listen to Tiro. He's manipulating everyone, but to what end? For his own power over you!"

Even Gwilim's good friend Sally was enamored by Tiro's rallying words and pulled Gwilim to the side and said, "Why must you worry so? Tiro will set it all straight. He understands us. Times are changing."

"Can't you see what he is doing? He's unraveling us. He hates everything we do. Everything."

Sally said, "But look at the energy he's given us." Then she squeezed through the crowd to get closer to her handsome hero, leaving her good friend Gwilim alone.

One concerned lemming asked Tiro, "Shouldn't we move the instrument away from the Greznik with too many legs? The one trying to get in?"

Tiro shrugged and said, "The existence of a Greznik with too many eyes and legs wandering around the base of our beautiful mountain is a fearmongering lie. Raadsel never saw such a thing. Grezniks never travel alone. And Grezniks all look the same. There's no such thing as a Greznik with too many legs and eyes! Lies! You know that. Raadsel is just an illusion anyway. We don't listen to what comes from beyond!"

The youthful lemmings were especially energized to a fervor by Tiro's excitement.

One excited lemming said, "Raadsel must be the traitor!"

Another one agreed. "The traitor is Raadsel. Because there are no traitors among friends, ever. Right, Tiro?"

"There's never a traitor among friends, and I'm your friend, speaking for you, fighting for you," said Tiro.

Tiro faced the crowd. By then the storm had calmed, so he was backlit by the beautiful view of the world beyond the cave. The sun lit colorful clouds behind him. "The storm has subsided, and the horizon invites you. Isn't it beautiful? Don't you want to be out there in the world? Don't you want to be free?"

Some older lemmings urged the younger ones to pause and think carefully about the value of their work. "You'll come to know the value of protecting this instrument of our freedom, of Life itself. And you'll come to understand the guidance, care, and the love of Raadsel."

But their older voices were weak and their pace slow compared to the energy of Tiro, and their ideas and methods felt faded and long past their prime. The younger lemmings sneered and chuckled at the elder lemmings, talked back at them, and shouted at the same time.

"This isn't freedom! It's just an instrument!"

"The world has changed. We must change and end the injustices up here!"

"We don't need to listen to you. You're a generation gone by!"

"Your old procedures and structures and rules don't work for us anymore!"

"Gone with the rules!"

"Change with the times!"

"We are about the future! Freedoms for ourselves!"

The excited lemmings, young and old, gathered around Tiro and pushed and jockeyed to get as close to him as possible. They had always been a community that respected one another, even when they differed, standing in lines, obeying rules of order in their little mountain neighborhoods, giving each other polite courtesies at the shops and in the tunnels, and supporting each other in hard times. But that disappeared with sudden reckless abandon. They shoved, pushed, and shouted down those who wanted to be heard. Amid all the pushing, some lemmings were shoved off the ledge and fell to their death. Tiro saw it, but he kept the fervor high so no one else took notice.

Sally waved and winked at Tiro admiringly, while Gwilim got shoved and trampled upon as others pushed their way forward.

Gwilim tried to shout over the noise of the crowd. "Sally! Sally!"

Sally heard his voice and turned to see him but could not find him in the crowd. She turned back to cheer Tiro.

Excited by the energy of the rally, some lemmings jumped up on the instrument and played it wildly. Other lemmings urged them to stop. "You don't know what you are unleashing! You haven't learned how to play this. Please stop. You must! Please!"

But more lemmings followed the others, and they, too, jumped on the instrument and played with greater recklessness.

Others watched in horror and pleaded with them. Their voices trembled with dismay as they begged the reckless to pause, to think, and to heed the warnings they were taught so long ago.

One elder climbed up the instrument and warned those who were playing fast and loose with its powers. "You shouldn't do that. You need to think about this. It's not that simple! You don't know what you are doing!"

"We do know what we are doing!" said the lemmings playing the instrument. "We're unleashing expression. Our voices. New voices! Fresh voices! New sounds! We are boundless!"

Some laughed at their elders and said, "You didn't know the instrument could make these sounds, did you?"

"Of course we did," said Oskar, stepping forward confi-dently. "But you never bothered to listen. And to learn. You never bothered to show up to play."

73

CLOSING THE MOUNTAIN

Mitch, Tony, and Jovi slept inside their hiding spot to wait out the storm. On watch duty, Mitch cleared the snow from the entrance as the storm raged outside their cave throughout the night. But the snow was falling more quickly and he was having difficulty keeping up with it. His hands got miserably cold so he stopped for a short break. He tucked his hands inside his jacket to warm them but he was startled when six blinking eyes peeked out of the snowdrift. Jovi was asleep on his left side and Tony on his right, and he shook them both to wake them up. Jovi and Tony shot up.

"Shh!" whispered Mitch as he pointed, just as the eyes disappeared. "Something's in the snowbank. It has six eyes."

Jovi jumped up. "A Greznik?"

"Where?" whispered Tony.

Mitch pointed just as three white-as-snow ermines popped out of the snowbank, stood up on their hind legs, looked at the kids, and then jumped back in.

"Ermines!" exclaimed Tony, relieved to see the adorable creatures.

The ermines jumped out of the snow again, and each grabbed a pant leg of one of the kids and pulled on it.

"Are they trying to pull us out?" wondered Jovi.

The ermines jumped up and down frantically, as if they wanted to say something. They pointed their noses toward the cave entrance, then pulled on the kids' pant legs again.

"Maybe they want us to leave," said Tony.

Mitch added, "We're getting snowed in anyway. We have to get out."

The kids tunneled through the snow and got out of their hiding spot. Right after they did, a massive landslide of stones tumbled down the mountain and blocked the entrance to where they had been resting. Raadsel was closing up the mountain.

▲ ▲ ▲

If Skarb had not landed in a freezing puddle, it would have just lain there and maybe even given up. Instead, it got out of the icy water and listened carefully to locate the children's voices again. But their voices had gone silent. Skarb knew that if a Greznik could not withstand the mountain's conditions, there was no way those three children could. It crawled along the base of the mountain face expecting to find three children who had fallen to their deaths. But the children were not there.

How could they have gotten off the mountain? They must have gone back inside, but how? wondered Skarb.

Skarb was determined to find a way in but reluctantly concluded it had to wait out the storm before trying again. It found a deep crevice at the base of the mountain and crawled in to wait.

All night long, Raadsel closed the mountain by triggering events to block all entries and hiding places. There was no one who would wish to save Skarb. Without warning, a big boulder fell in front of Skarb's hiding place—there was no way out. Skarb awoke to the crashing sound of the boulder. A defeated silence surrounded Skarb, and it said, "They know I'm here."

▲ ▲ ▲

Outside in the storm, the kids looked back at all the stones that now blocked their resting spot.

"What if we were still in there?" wondered Jovi.

The relentless danger of their adventure was undeniable and daunting.

Mitch repeated Fingal's words quietly, "*Adventures in faraway lands. Complex missions. Pushed in directions you do not want to go.*"

"I don't want to go. I want to go home," said Jovi.

The wind picked up strength, and snow came down like slush, worsening the miserable conditions. The ermines scampered in circles around their feet and appeared to be directing the kids forward.

"I think we should follow them. There's nothing around here to protect us, and it's freezing out here. We've got to keep moving, or we'll end up with hypothermia," said Tony.

"The ermines saved us once. Let's assume they'll do it again," said Mitch.

As the kids followed the ermines, Mitch kept track of their journey by measuring the distance of their steps and watching the direction on the compass so if they needed to backtrack they would be able to.

They had walked for about two hours when the ermines stopped, stood on their hind legs, and sniffed in the air. One ermine ran forward like a scout, while the other two scampered around their feet as though they feared a danger nearby and wanted the kids to stay put.

By then it was dawn and the storm was letting up. The skies cleared on the eastern horizon to unveil a full blue sky. But even with a clear sky, the kids had no idea which direction Fingal would be.

Suddenly, piercing, stinging sounds ripped through the air, and the kids dove to the ground.

"What is that?" cried Tony, covering his ears.

Mitch and Jovi also covered their ears as they huddled on the ground. The harsh noises felt like thorns ripping their ears to shreds.

Jovi said, "It's coming from up in the mountain."

"Could it be noise from the instrument?" asked Mitch.

"But the music the instrument made was so beautiful. These sounds are like screeching urchins," said Tony.

"It can't be the same instrument," insisted Jovi. "Fingal! Where are you?"

One frightened little ermine curled up right next to Jovi, and she held the ermine close. She closed her eyes and hoped the adventure would end soon. Another ermine scampered around them, keeping a lookout. The third ermine ran off as fast as she could and said to the sky, "Please help me find him. Please guide my way."

▲ ▲ ▲

The massive boulder trapped Skarb in its hiding spot. It had no choice but to claw away at the rock and make its escape, but the effort was difficult and the progress was frustratingly slow.

Suddenly, distressing sounds rumbled through the mountain and startled Skarb so severely that it jumped, hit its head on the rock above, and crashed back down. The awful sounds vibrated through the entire mountain, shaking the boulder and destroying all the progress Skarb had made.

Even for a Greznik, the noises were unbearable. Skarb had no idea that far above, many lemmings were running over the keys of the instrument with reckless abandon. Tiro's willing toadies were triggering thousands of sounds, spewing forth dissonant noises all the way down to Skarb and the three children who huddled together. Just a day earlier, those lemmings would never have trampled over what they took care of so wonderfully. But now, Oskar and other wiser lemmings stood aghast and witnessed how quickly foolish and fawning lemmings could devour the heart and soul of their little hamlet up in the mountain.

Skarb had no idea what was making the noise, and it never would have imagined an instrument with a bunch of little creatures running across the beautiful keys.

"What is that sound?" screeched Skarb as it put its feet over its head. Yet nothing could block the dreadful noise that ripped through the mountain's granite. Then it smelled the Chongchon River.

Skarb hollered as it thrashed in misery. "What has my circle leader found? Stop, you fool! The Voices of Proznia are unleashing. Proznia will take us all back!"

74

NO RULES FOR ME

Tiro's rallying cry excited many lemmings, and word spread throughout the mountain. Lemmings stationed at other work sites climbed to the cave and crammed into the space to hear Tiro's electrifying speech. Feverish with the thrill of unleashing their duties, many more in the crowd climbed upon the instrument, crawled through its insides, and jumped all over the keys. Others danced with Tiro to the raucous sounds they made.

Skarb was right; the Voices of Proznia were unleashing, and more powerfully than Tiro anticipated. The Voices feverishly pulsated Tiro's insides with such vehemence his eyeballs bulged and his legs struggled to keep balance as he climbed up a tall podium. He knew he had to move quickly. Tiro towered over the throngs of lemmings and raised their intensity and zeal.

"The battles are over!" said Tiro. "We are safe in our mountain home. We are free from the strife of fighting."

One lemming joined Tiro at his side and said, "Tiro is right! Why do we do this tedious work? We can let it go!"

The crowd cheered. Others danced and sang, "Let it be, no boundaries, no rules for me—break 'em, crush 'em, quash 'em down!"

Tiro cheered them on. "Why should we be trapped in a cave, just to avoid Grezniks getting this here glorified piano? We could be roaming the lands living the lives we want to live! Battles are things of the past. Who's the fool who thinks battles solve things? Outlaw battles! What were they fighting over anyway? This instrument? Play it! Have fun! Peace is ours!"

Tiro had the crowd right where he needed them. After every sentence, the crowd broke into thunderous praise. Oskar stepped out from the crowd to speak, but his voice was drowned out by the noisy fervor. Yet some of the lemmings wanted to hear what Oskar had to say and managed to quiet the crowd. Many willingly turned away from Tiro to listen to their wise, old, beloved leader who had guided them through many hardships.

Oskar spoke as loud as he could. "Hold on, hold on. Let's be careful. We have much to lose. We can trust Raadsel, our protector. If we had not trusted him, our community would've been destroyed and we would've been dead many times over. We can take pride in our work. Yes, it is sometimes tedious, but the instrument needs our careful and protective hand. Our steadfast sacrifice gives us strength to secure the good things we need to live peacefully. And who is this Tiro? Why should we trust him? We shouldn't. He followed the children who travel with the Tukor. He locked them in the shaft to suffocate them—"

Tiro interrupted, shook his head, stood on his hind legs, flailed his front legs, and drowned out Oskar's voice, saying, "Lies! Lies! Lies!"

Oskar continued, but too few listened. "The Tukor is here because we are in danger. A menace lurks in our mountain home, and a Greznik is on our mountain trying to get in. Grezniks are in our midst. Make no mistake: Grezniks are our enemy. They want everything about your life destroyed. And Tiro is not our friend. He left those children to die. *Tiro is the traitor!*"

Tiro thought, *I'm not going to let this old nobody turn the crowd against me.* And he had no time to lose. Tiro walked to the edge of the cave and pointed to the view outside. "Now, now, everyone. Let's not get distracted by the voices of the old and established. Sometimes we must shatter our world to seize the life we want for ourselves! Come alongside me. Line up beside me. I'm going to jump. Yes, jump! A jump to freedom! You think you'll die if you jump, but that's a lie." Tiro soothed his voice and said, "We can jump. We can fly. We can leap to the sky and float safely to the ground! Watch me glide softly through the air. We can be like birds, yet no one told you this!"

The lemmings gasped at the idea but got so excited about the possibilities that they believed him. Trusted him. They lined up beside Tiro. Those that could not fit alongside Tiro lined up behind him.

"Don't follow him! Don't do it!" warned Oskar. "Turn around! Save yourselves!"

Some lemmings laughed at Oskar, cornered him in the back of the cave, and sneered at him.

"You don't understand our generation. You're of a bygone era."

"We see how we have been brainwashed about there being purpose in all this."

"How could there be purpose in protecting an instrument? It's not an instrument of freedom. It's a chain around our lives. We can fly away!"

Oskar said sorrowfully, "You'll die before you find out you're wrong."

The lemmings walked away, mocking Oskar.

"He's just part of the old mountain institution," said one.

"He's just afraid of losing his position," sneered another.

Oskar knew it was too late to change their minds. With sadness, he moved through the crowd and exited the cave to find an old path he had taken many times over the years. Despite his fading memory, he followed the curves of the corridors to get to a distant, rarely used section. The winding path burrowed deep into the mountain and led to his favorite lookout.

His legs were weak and crooked from arthritis, so he could not easily make the trek anymore. His older, yellowed eyes struggled to see as he walked the dark corridors. He grew weary and out of breath, and he worried that he could not make it.

He remembered his younger days when he and his wife could easily run to the lookout on a restful evening. After she had died, he missed her terribly and would still make the trek to the lookout to remember her gentle presence by his side. As he got older, the hike grew more difficult, and it was now nearly out of reach of his aging heart.

But this trek was not for sentimental reasons. He traveled there to find Raadsel without anyone else knowing. Raadsel's hidden nest was on the far west side of the mountain and Oskar hoped that he could secretly summon Raadsel from his favorite lookout. He sighed in relief when he finally turned the last corner and saw a glimpse of daylight. The beautiful mountain lookout was just ahead.

He stepped to the edge and called out as loud as he could, "Raadsel! Raadsel! Raadsel!" But his voice was too weak. He sat back, breathing heavily and weary from his hike. He fretted that Raadsel would not hear his calls. And it seemed Raadsel had not. The eagle was nowhere to be seen, and Oskar crawled away from the edge and hunkered down to rest.

A few minutes later, Raadsel swooped down and landed on a nearby rock shelf. He looked in the little opening but did not see Oskar.

The wind from Raadsel's wings woke up Oskar and he walked back toward the edge, limping and barely able to move. The climb had been too difficult.

Oskar said, "I'm here, Raadsel. Over here. I'll be right there. It is a sad day. Tiro is our traitor. I never thought I would say this in my lifetime, but you need to attack one of our own. Tiro."

"Are you sure?" asked Raadsel.

"Yes. His end game is to take control of the instrument. I'm sure of it. Tiro is the traitor. He has some kind of trick planned to leap into the sky. And he has them stirred up to such a foolish fervor they'll follow him and jump to their deaths."

"From where did his betrayal begin?"

"I don't know. But it is thorough. He locked the Tukor's travelers in an old shaft to suffocate them. I opened the old escape tunnels, but it's unlikely they got out quickly enough. I fear they fell to their deaths. Why, why, why? Why would a fellow lemming do this?"

"All three children got out, but barely. It was dangerously close," said Raadsel.

"Such wonderful news. Such good, good news. But I never thought we'd see this battle return in my lifetime. You need to hurry and attack Tiro. It's probably too late— I'm not young anymore, and it took me too long to get down here."

Raadsel said, "That strange, seven-legged Greznik is trying to get in the mountain and will not give up. The Greznik must know the secret of the instrument. Tiro the traitor must be working with that seven-legger. Thank you for your courage and for traveling so far to tell me. How will I know which one is Tiro?"

"You'll know. He's unmistakable. They're fawning over him."

Raadsel flew away as Oskar tried to climb back to the instrument, but he only took a few steps before he knew he could not make it. He lay down and closed his eyes, remembering his lifetime in the mountain, the many messy, imperfect days of the arduous yet rewarding work. He remembered how after every long day, even the discouraging ones, he went home to his wife. Her love and encouragement made it all worth the journey. He smiled and closed his eyes.

75

RAW AND BLEEDING

Skarb writhed in pain from the excruciating noise com-ing from the mountain cave high above.

"Proznia is unveiling its power," said Skarb.

Skarb could not stand the terrible sounds any longer. It wanted to flee far away. But the fallen boulder still blocked its exit. Determined to escape, Skarb's tail began to vibrate and spin with such an unexpected, ferocious intensity that its tail drilled into the boulder. The rock crumbled to the ground, and the pile of rubble smoked from the intensity of the drilling. Skarb stood stunned, not knowing its tail could do that. But there was no relief from the wicked sounds tearing through the air. Skarb crouched down behind the rubble, fearing Proznia's power and hoping the noise would subside.

The horrible racket gradually faded into silence. Skarb cautiously slithered out of its hiding spot. It smelled both the herd of caribou and Fingal nearby and crawled carefully toward them. They had no idea Skarb was so dangerously near.

Meanwhile, an ermine ran toward Fingal, completely out of breath from running a long distance. Then it jumped up and down to catch Fingal's eye. Fingal picked up the weary creature, put it in his jacket, and got on his caribou and rode away. Skarb followed.

The ermine led Fingal by pointing her paw in the direction she wanted Fingal to go. Fingal saw Mitch, Tony, and Jovi ahead at last, raised his arms in delight, and hurried his caribou forward.

Fingal got off his caribou and greeted the kids with relieved and grateful joy. The familiar comfort of Fingal's gentle presence calmed Mitch, Tony, and Jovi. Skarb recalled having witnessed such a warm greeting once before when the boy Bogdan was welcomed home, many valleys away from his own by the sheltering arms of his grandparents.

Watching Fingal welcome the three forlorn children made Skarb's wiry hair stand on end as though lightning were about to strike. Skarb remembered a similar feeling centuries earlier when a defense tower in the Caucasus Mountains had become the boy's brutal cage. And an unhinged Skarb buried three goats and set free the tower's farm animals.

But this time a surge of warm waves paralyzed Skarb, and it fell to the ground helplessly as though its body were ice melting into a puddle. Unable to move. Skarb hoped the travelers would not find it lying paralyzed there.

Fingal said to the kids, "We're forever indebted to those ermines for our finding each other again. I was worried sick about you . . . That you might not be able to get out of the mountain. That you wouldn't get off the cliff. That I might not be able to find you after the storm. But the worries were all for naught! What a wonderful surprise and an incredible joy to see you safe."

Jovi held out her hands for Fingal to see. Climbing the mountain, gripping the ladder in the shaft, and crawling through the mountain tunnels left their hands blistered, raw, and bleeding. Fingal was sorry to see how difficult the journey had been. He pulled bandages out of his pack, put ointment on Jovi's hands, and wrapped them carefully. Then he attended to Mitch and Tony's hands too.

The kids were still chilled from the fearful sounds they heard only moments before. Jovi asked Fingal, "Did you hear those awful noises?"

"Yes, I did. The sounds were wickedly dissonant, and if . . ." Fingal did not finish the sentence. He despaired that something far graver was happening in the mountain and did not want to burden the children. But Fingal himself was gripped by a surge of dread. The instrument, in the hands of the enemy, was unleashing its darkness.

The caribou herd gathered protectively around them. Fingal encouraged them to get back on their caribou and move onward again. The kids all took a deep breath and summoned the courage to keep going.

Fingal and the kids began their journey back to their bikes, but Skarb was overcome with weakness and could not follow. It lay down to rest. Not long after, Skarb was hit with the sudden sensation of an electrical shock. It looked up at the mountain and saw Tiro on the edge, surrounded by lemmings, getting ready to jump.

76

SHALL WE GO?

The lemmings crowded alongside Tiro's left and right, shoving and pushing each other to get as close to their hero as possible.

Tiro hushed the crowd and said quietly, "Watch this step to freedom. Watch me glide safely and follow me! Let's all jump together! To fly is to be alive—shall we go?"

"Yes!" yelled the crowd.

The lemmings chattered with excitement to take their first flight with Tiro. They looked out at the horizon and believed that the lightness of their bodies could float like a parachute and land safely, just as Tiro had said.

Tiro said calmly, "Look at that world beyond! It's yours for the taking! Are you ready to fly?"

"Yes!" responded the lemmings excitedly.

Tiro turned around and faced the open horizon and jumped. The lemmings gasped at his courage. Tiro quickly grew clear, insect-like wings, which the lemmings could not see. He coasted gracefully. Tiro spread his arms and legs and encouraged the lemmings gleefully. "Come and see how wonderful this is! Follow me! You'll love the ride! You'll love the glide!"

"He's really flying!" said one eager lemming.

"Lemmings can fly!" said another excitedly.

"What fun we never knew!"

From the ground, Tony looked back at the mountain at just the right time and said, "One of the lemmings jumped! And it's flying!"

Tiro glided softly, slowly, and gently across the sky like a soaring eagle. The lemmings were so delighted to discover that what they had been told all their lives—that lemmings could not fly—was a wicked lie. The thrill of possibilities called more lemmings forward who were excited to jump and float gracefully across the sky. But they immediately fought over who should follow Tiro first and take the inaugural flight down. Should it be the young or old? Higher or lower ranks?

Tiro was frustrated that the crowd of lemmings did not immediately follow and jump with him. He glided over to them then said with devious encouragement, "No need to bicker. No one needs to be first. You can all fly! Jump! Come join me! Come see the beautiful view!"

Tiro encouraged the lemmings who were far back in the crowd to push their way forward. As they pushed, more lemmings on the edge fell to their death below just as Tiro had hoped. But, once again, in the flurry of excitement, no one else noticed.

Skarb followed Tiro's flight path from the ground, knowing the devious lemming was Tiro. Tiro glimpsed downward and was shocked to see his enemy following below. Tiro yelled down to Skarb in a pitch that no other creature could hear, "You filthy, disgusting fiend!"

Fixating on Skarb, Tiro never saw Raadsel coming. Raadsel dove down from above, unseen, and grabbed the gliding Tiro in his talons. The lemmings in the cave shrieked in horror and fear.

"Raadsel will kill Tiro!"

"He'll kill all of us!"

"Raadsel is the traitor!"

"Tiro was right! The eagle is our enemy!"

Tiro said to Raadsel, making sure all the lemmings could hear his words, "Thank you, but I didn't need saving—lemmings can fly! Let me go, and let me soar!" Then Tiro encouraged the lemmings on the ledge, "Jump, everyone, jump!"

"I did not catch you to save you. You are the traitor," said Raadsel.

Tiro said, "I'm not the traitor. You are! Don't kill me! Everyone, jump, fly, set yourselves free!"

"Raadsel is the evil traitor!" said many lemmings in the cave.

"What a delusion Raadsel is!" said others.

From the ground, Skarb was astonished to see an extinct Haast's eagle. Skarb felt those same feelings again, the same ones that centuries earlier had caused him to bury the goats and set the animals free. Skarb hollered up to Tiro, "You speck of filth Greznik. You took in the blue waters of Proznia!"

Tiro yelled back, "You blundering, botched-up beast! I will never lose! I am the master now. The supreme power over all!"

Raadsel choked Tiro. The lemmings gasped and cringed at the fierceness of Raadsel's attack. Tiro's body shook as his lemming body began morphing into a Haast's eagle. Tiro's vibrating movements were so violent that Raadsel could not keep his balance in flight.

Tiro desperately tried to become a Haast's eagle but was enraged to discover that its body could not become an extinct creature. Tiro instantly altered his transformation to become a Steller's sea eagle instead, and he grew wings, feathers, talons, and an eagle head.

Raadsel clenched his talons harder on Tiro's throat, as he realized that Tiro was a Greznik with blue stone waters surging within. But Raadsel was losing altitude quickly.

Raadsel said quietly, "You are in deeper than you know. Proznia is plunging you down. And trust me, you do not want to fall into its shaft. Do answer me. Who do you choose?"

Jatuh answered, "Trust you? Never! I choose to destroy you."

Raadsel plummeted toward the ground and could not hold Tiro any longer. He let go, hoping Tiro would fall to his death below. But Tiro did not. Instead, Tiro the lemming was no more. Jatuh had successfully and quickly become a Steller's sea eagle.

Although a Steller's sea eagle has a much smaller wing-span than a Haast's eagle has, it is nonetheless a highly skilled fighter. Jatuh flew at breakneck speed to pierce Raadsel's eyes with its beak. But just in time, Raadsel pulled his wings in, spun, and avoided the attack. The intense aerial combat spurred harrying dives, vicious strikes, and dizzying spins.

Raadsel's larger wingspan and talons gave him a decisive advantage in the battle. But as the fight wore on, Raadsel's energy began to fail as Jatuh grew stronger from the Voices of Proznia inside. Jatuh gained control of the fight and darted forward, aggressively attacking Raadsel and severely damaging one wing. Raadsel was imbalanced and could no longer glide or spin to dodge an attack. He could only fly angled upward. Raadsel flew higher and higher as Jatuh followed.

Skarb watched the exhausted Raadsel flying so far upward. "Why bother flying so high?" mumbled Skarb. "You have no chance against my circle leader."

Jatuh was confident that Raadsel's attempt to fly at such a high altitude was a hopeless, last-ditch effort to flee. Jatuh followed him lazily upward, waiting for the moment when Raadsel collapsed his wings from exhaustion and fell to the ground. Jatuh wanted the lemmings to witness the long, drawn-out, disgracing decline of their hero, Raadsel. Jatuh, not tired at all, followed mockingly at a good distance, knowing it could easily catch up and destroy Raadsel for good.

Jatuh was right. Flying higher was Raadsel's last-ditch effort to seize a victory out of an otherwise impossible battle. Yet as Jatuh arrogantly followed Raadsel upward,

Raadsel had flown Jatuh over a very small quarry of unusual stones that no one except Raadsel knew existed. From the ground, the stones were merely a small, scattered patch of granite gravel. But by Raadsel's eagle eye, flying high, they dazzled blue. He desperately hoped that a Greznik who drank the Voices of Proznia could also see the shimmering blue stones from the sky and be unable to resist seizing them.

When Raadsel was directly over the stones, he pulled in his wings, dove straight downward like a bullet, caught Jatuh harshly in his talons, and said, "Look below you."

Jatuh looked down and saw the unexpected patch of blue stones. Putrid green slime of desire poured out like rain from its eyes.

"You swallowed in the waters of blue, didn't you?" asked Raadsel.

"The stones will be mine! I have power over all!" shouted Jatuh.

The lure of the stones was more powerful than Jatuh, as the desperation of Proznia overtook Jatuh's insides and tore through it like cockleburs. Jatuh's body started converting back to Jatuh the Greznik at an incredible speed.

The Voices inside Jatuh screeched, and Jatuh writhed. Then the Voices said, "Go to the stones! Get those stones! Give them to us now!"

Jatuh shouted back at the Voices as its own eagle wings began shrinking. "Stop! Don't take my wings! Don't make me a Greznik. Stop!" Two Greznik legs popped out of its belly, and its eagle feathers started melting into Greznik skin. "Don't do this. Look how high we are. I cannot fly as a Greznik. Raadsel will drop me, and I will shatter. Stop!"

Raadsel hung on to the desperate Greznik as the Voices ripped through Jatuh so harshly they felt like bits of broken glass flowing within its morphing body.

Jatuh wailed in anguish. "Leave me alone! You wicked Voices. What did I ever do to you?"

The Voices said in a horribly searing pitch, "You made us your master!"

"Never will I answer to you, Proznia!" replied Jatuh.

"Right!" said Raadsel to Jatuh. "You do not have to answer. You must never answer! Do not fall for Proznia's trickery. Will you forgo its false promises?"

"I do not need to! Proznia has no power over me," insisted Jatuh.

"If you do not reject the Voices, you choose them," said Raadsel. "Tell me, will you turn away? Refuse, spurn Proznia, and I will lead you away!"

"Never will I follow you. I listen to no one but me!"

The Voices laughed triumphantly.

Jatuh, now half eagle, half Greznik, asked the Voices, "Why are you laughing?"

Raadsel said as the Voices laughed wickedly, "Because you fell for their ruse."

"No! I did not!"

"Yes, you have fallen. They tricked you to believe the power can be yours. Will you follow me and—"

"Never. I am my own master!" shouted Jatuh.

Suddenly an agonizing screech tore through the air

and Skarb was struck with a painful shock. Skarb bellowed and fell, stricken, to the ground. Its circle leader, the same number raised to a different power, had chosen Proznia. Skarb knew the end was nigh.

Jatuh looked down and saw the limp and helpless Skarb and was overcome by a strange longing. A heavy weariness weighed down upon Jatuh. Yet even so, Jatuh rejected Raadsel's plea, and the speed and violence of its change back into a Greznik increased. Jatuh's two eagle wings shrank to the size of a sparrow's. Two spindly bird legs shriveled to nothing as two more Greznik legs expanded to full length. A snout grotesquely grew out from the inside of the beak, and eyeballs popped out from under the molting feathers.

The violence of the change made it difficult for Raadsel to maintain his grip and stay in flight. Raadsel held on to Jatuh with the last bit of strength he had left. With only enough strength for a few more minutes of flight, Raadsel flew crookedly and awkwardly beyond the small patch of blue stones and over a wide and deep lake, very near to where Fingal huddled with the kids.

Jatuh looked down, longing to see the shimmering blue stone quarry again, but the quarry was out of sight. All Jatuh could see was water below—and if Raadsel dropped Jatuh now, Jatuh no longer had wings to fly and would both drown and dissolve as part eagle, part Greznik. Jatuh began morphing into a fish to survive the fall. Inside the grip of Raadsel's talons, Jatuh's mixture of fur and feathers started turning into fish scales and its Greznik tail into a fishtail.

Raadsel seized the moment and nose-dived toward the water with Jatuh in his grip. Jatuh let out a woeful moan. The anguished lament was heard for miles and echoed off mountains near and far. Raadsel plunged into the water and submerged a fighting Jatuh, who hit the water as part Greznik, part bird, part fish—coated in a mixture of feathers, hair, and scales. The two fighting warriors thrashed and splashed in the waters but then dropped like stones and sank far below.

Underwater, Jatuh's Greznik body dissolved and was gone forever. A fishtail floated to the surface of the water, followed by Jatuh's two stubby wings and a bloody eagle's beak. The bits floated away from each other before melting into the water. Complete silence fell across the landscape, as though air itself was a heavy blanket set upon the land to hold everything still. The ripples in the lake faded, and the sky's mirror fell still and turned a hazy blue.

From the edge of the cave, the lemmings wailed in despair at the disappearance of their dear friend—the mysterious, extinct Raadsel. Then they stood in shocked silence. They backed carefully away from the ledge, embarrassed they had believed that they could reach the horizon and glide away from their duty.

Fingal and his three travelers witnessed the dreadfully grotesque battle in horror and silence. Mitch, Tony, and Jovi huddled up close to Fingal and sometimes turned their gaze away as the scenes fell heavily upon them. Jovi gripped Mitch's hand so tight his fingers turned white. Fingal held his arms around their shoulders to shelter them. Yet after so many battles during his long lifetime, he knew children cannot always be sheltered from what the world sometimes cruelly foists upon their eyes and hearts.

Raadsel hit the water and never came up for air. Mitch choked back a sadness breaking within. Raadsel had saved them from death only moments earlier, and now the majestic eagle was gone. Jovi ran toward the edge of the water and tossed in a stone, as if stirring the stillness could bring Raadsel back. Tony closed his eyes, listening and hoping for the sound of an eagle breaking through the water and flying away. But hearing nothing, he felt as though a deadening, silent despair lurked behind every sound.

▲ ▲ ▲

During the battle, the memories and smell of the Chongchon River dropped swiftly down on Skarb like a rapid change in air pressure. As the fight intensified, its skin felt intense heat as though the sun were moving closer in. Skarb's snout burned, and its skin throbbed. Skarb never heard anything so fiercely stabbing in its ears as Jatuh's defeated howl as it plunged toward the water. But afterward, the smell was gone and the burning was relieved. Skarb looked out at the still waters, wondering what happened to the Voices of Jatuh's demise.

▲ ▲ ▲

The lemmings froze with regret, unable to speak, stunned by their own delusion. They had nearly followed a Greznik and jumped to their deaths. Many were overwhelmed with gratitude for the strength of their beloved friend Raadsel.

Some looked down from the ledge at what would have been the place of their death only moments before. They were shocked to see that some of their friends had fallen to their end in the excitement of Tiro's rally. Many cried and ran down the mountain to find their lost below. Others collapsed in anguish and shed the bitter tears of shame and loss.

Ashamed of their mistake, many lemmings looked for Oskar in the crowd, but he was nowhere to be found. They hushed everyone and called out to him, but there was no response.

"We should've listened to him."

"Yes, we should've."

"We need to find him."

"And apologize," said Gwilim.

The lemmings gathered around one another and devised a search plan. Some of them were to stay with the instrument to prepare for its departure. Others were to stand guard against the strangely shaped Greznik. The rest were to form teams of three and search the mountain in every tunnel, corridor, neighborhood, work site, shop, school, and community for their quiet, wise old leader. Gwilim volunteered to help find Oskar.

Sally walked up to Gwilim and said, "I didn't think it would end this way."

"You would not hear the truth earlier," said Gwilim.

"I didn't understand what would happen," said Sally.

"There was not much to understand. Tiro promised a new world, an easier world. But the world was not his to give, was it? But it's too late now. Our cherished world here will go away."

"Will you ever forgive me?" asked Sally, who thought Gwilim looked so much stronger now.

Gwilim was not sure what to say. He had always admired Sally and dreamed that someday he would marry her, but she had never noticed him much, no matter how hard he tried. That all seemed so long ago now.

Gwilim answered, "Forgiveness calls out to us, and we must choose it. For you. And for me."

"So we are still friends?" asked Sally.

Gwilim answered with sorrow, "We are on different journeys, you and I. There is work to do right now to prepare the instrument to leave our care. Your hero left much damage in his wake."

"He's not my hero," said Sally.

"But he was your hero. Even if only briefly. False heroes bear a heavy cost."

Gwilim's search crew was ready to leave to find Oskar, and they called for him to hurry. Gwilim said to Sally, "I must go now."

Gwilim dashed off to join the search and Sally's heart ached with the sting of regret. She went to work to help prepare the instrument, yet she could not shake the sorrow and wanted to make amends with her dear friend. She never expected as she watched Gwilim leave the cave that he would be leaving their mountain home forever to do a hero's hidden work. She would later mourn that she never had the chance to say goodbye to a friend who had always been a friend to everyone. The regret fell heavily on her heart, and remorse dripped on her soul like rain.

77

DO NOT SLEEP YET

The instrument stood silent in the cave as lemmings prepared for its departure. A somber quiet blanketed their effort. The search teams left the cave and worked methodically for hours to find Oskar, calling his name everywhere, desperately hoping to hear a response. But Oskar did not hear any of them. He was sleeping, curled up in his faraway lookout, as his heartbeat slowed.

One by one, search teams returned to the main cave to report their failure. Gwilim's team came back unsuccessful too. They soon all lost hope that their wise leader had survived, and they could not bear to think what Tiro might have done to him. Despairing of their error, they sang a mourning song for their dear old friend. The quiet melancholy song flowed through the mountain tunnels as tears drained from their eyes. In Oskar's last moments, they had followed a Greznik and not the wisdom of their wise and loving guide.

As they sang, Gwilim did not want to give up. Without telling anyone, he left everyone to run alone to the mountain's far west side, which had been long abandoned. He knew Oskar and his wife had often hiked to a secret, unknown lookout to watch the sunset and northern lights.

Finding Oskar's favorite lookout was a long shot. Gwilim did not know where it was, except that it was on the far west side, which was riddled with old, intricate, and complex tunnel structures—all abandoned years earlier due to the inefficient and outdated infrastructure. He tried to methodically search the messy tunnel system, but he wound around so many bends and curves that it was difficult for him to keep his bearings. Gwilim ran so far into the maze that he was no longer sure he was even still on the far west side.

Gwilim looked for Oskar in dozens of hidden corridors but found not a trace. He approached another crooked tunnel that he doubted would lead to a lookout. Exhausted, he did not run to it as he had the others. He walked forward without hope, simply to rest there for a bit, then give up and go back.

Gwilim walked down the passageway, disappointed to realize it was a dead end. But he noticed another narrow turnoff that was more like a fissure in the rock than a passageway for lemmings. He decided not to explore it, but to rest and quench his thirst before making the hike back, defeated. He drank from his canteen and leaned against the wall, breathing heavily from his arduous search.

He caught his breath and rested in the silence. But then he thought he heard raspy breathing coming from inside the fissure. He sat perfectly still and heard it again.

He walked into the fissure, and as he rounded a bend, he saw some light faintly shining ahead.

Gwilim walked farther down, turned slightly, and saw Oskar at the end of a long passageway that opened to a beautiful view.

He ran forward and joined him at his side. Every breath Oskar took was labored. Gwilim gave him all the water he had left in his own canteen, but it was not enough.

"Is there a water source on this side of the mountain?" asked Gwilim.

Oskar told him how to find a small internal waterfall nearby, where melted snows from the mountain's peak leaked down through the interior. The springwater was fresh and clean and perfect for refilling their water supply. He also told him about a secret stash of emergency food supplies. Gwilim ran off and came back with more water and food to help Oskar recover.

Gwilim said, "I can't believe I finally found you. I almost gave up. All the lemmings have been looking for you."

"Did Raadsel get Tiro?" asked Oskar with a weak voice.

"He did. Tiro is gone."

"Are you sure?"

Gwilim told the story of Tiro's final demise.

"So Tiro was a Greznik?" asked Oskar.

"Yes, but it could change into any animal it wanted to. How can that be?"

"That means it took in the Voices of Proznia."

"The blue stone waters of the legends we were taught as kids?" asked Gwilim.

"Yes."

"Then we were horribly betrayed," said Gwilim.

"Yes, we were. But how could I have missed that he was a Greznik and not a lemming?" said Oskar, disappointed in himself.

"You didn't miss it. You knew all along something wasn't right with Tiro. We should've listened to you. We were fools. Not you, Oskar. The rest of us were the fools."

"We can easily be betrayed when the betrayer says what we want to believe. Our dear friends wanted to believe that freedom from duty could be theirs. And that battles could be forever over if only we stop battling. But the force of the Grezniks is a battle that renews every generation. And the call to duty never subsides. The insatiable darkness strives to seep into your heart. It often slithers into our world. It will hide in words we like to hear, in alluring packages wrapped beautifully. Or is delivered by our own spurious and beguiling heroes of our time. Like Tiro's words, they all sounded so right, so obvious, so easy, so fun, and yet it was so wrong for everyone."

"I'm sorry, so very sorry we didn't listen to you."

"You listened, but the others did not. But I have often been like them. Throughout my life, I wished to let it go, to fly away, to roam, to let it all be, but that's not possible. My wife and I often dreamed of escaping the challenges of the mountain. We dreamed of running away into the sunset to find a less burdened life. But we're called to fight against the darkness and sometimes to go right into it and pull light out. And sometimes it's an unglamorous job, like cleaning the oily valves—that was my first job, crawling inside the instrument to clean it. My fur was always filthy when I got home. It took two shampoos every day, and even then, I couldn't get clean. Then I got a job squeegeeing the glass walls of the instrument to keep them shiny. I loved scaling down the side of the instrument. I was so proud of that job. Anyway, life calls us to goodness in every little task we do. You find your freedom by answering the call."

Oskar was out of breath and could not talk anymore. He tried to keep his eyes open to watch the beautiful sky.

He regained some strength and said, "I need you to do something."

"Yes, what is it?"

"There's a manual for the instrument hidden nearby. Can you retrieve it for me?"

"Yes. Where is it?"

"Follow this corridor back toward where you came. Take the first turn to the left, then the second turn to the right. That corridor has a ledge that runs the full length of the corridor. Climb up it and follow it to the end to find a smooth, round stone built into the wall. The stone is a granite dial. Turn it a full circle three times to the right, once to the left and back a full circle to the right again. When you do that, a cupboard will open in the wall below. Jump down from the ledge and crawl in. The cupboard is large, and you will find a lot of books inside. Remove the books stored on the center shelf. Behind them you will find a pressed-metal box. The manual is hidden inside that box."

Gwilim followed the directions and found the box with a large, beautiful book inside. He locked up the cupboard again and carried the box to Oskar and opened it for him.

"Yes, that's it. The Tukor must have that book if they take the instrument. They'll not know what the instrument can do without it. Please take it to them," said Oskar as his eyelids flickered from fatigue. "I'm too tired to walk, so you must hurry."

Oskar's eyes closed, and Gwilim gently shook him to keep him awake.

"Please do not fall asleep yet. The night is young," said Gwilim.

"I'm very tired, very tired. You must rush back, get that book to them."

The book had tiny pages and even tinier print. The pages were gold leaf and written in the ornate, colorful letters of the ancient lemming language. "I don't know how to read the ancient language."

"You'll figure it out," said Oskar.

"I don't think I can. Can you teach me?"

"Yes, but I'm so very tired. You can persevere. I believe you can do it," said Oskar in his fading voice.

"Does anyone else know the ancient language?"

"I don't know . . . I don't think so. But the instrument is leaving, and the book must absolutely travel with the instrument. I believe and trust the Tukor and the young travelers to figure out our ancient language. The instrument is beautiful and can do some amazing things, but it can be wickedly dangerous. They need the book for their own safety. Please run and deliver it to them," said Oskar, speaking slowly as he labored for every breath.

Gwilim feared Oskar's failing strength. "You're not well. I can't leave you."

"You can and you must. The work is urgent. Once you've delivered the manual, you can always come back to help me."

"I was trained to never leave a lemming behind. Ever," insisted Gwilim.

"You have to this time. You must get that to them."

Gwilim put the book back inside the box, put it in his pack, and then left on his mission. The route back wound around many twists and turns, and he was making good time. Yet he felt the heavy weight of regret. He turned around and ran back to where Oskar was lying and found him watching the glow in the sky, as if it were a burning candle whose light will not always shine.

"You came back," said Oskar.

"I cannot leave a fellow warrior behind," said Gwilim.

Gwilim picked up Oskar to carry him back to the top. He only took a few steps before he realized that carrying Oskar the entire way would be impossible given the difficulty of the climb.

"It's all right, son. It's okay. Thank you for trying."

Gwilim stayed with Oskar to admire the midnight sun's hazy repose on the tip of the horizon. When the sky's lightshow was over, Oskar said, "I would wish for there to be northern lights tonight, but the sun isn't willing to part this evening."

"When winter comes, you and I can come down here and see the northern lights," said Gwilim, hoping for the days ahead.

"I believe in you," Oskar said quietly. "Now it's time for me to be carried Home."

Gwilim brushed Oskar's back for comfort, smoothed his fur, and made the resting spot softer with bird feathers that had blown into the entrance.

Gwilim walked back to a small cubbyhole where Oskar kept supplies for his visits to the secret lookout. He found the feather thread blanket that Oskar's wife had made and covered Oskar with it.

"Thank you," said Oskar, curling up in the beautiful blanket. "It makes me feel as if she is still here with me. I miss her so." Oskar was so weak his voice was barely audible. "You are a son to me, a son to both of us. You are deeply loved. Never forget that, no matter what others say. You're a special one. Don't let the world make you think you are small at heart."

"But I was too small to stop what happened today. I tried to speak, but they shouted me down. They'll never listen to me as they do to you. I get trampled on."

"They didn't shout at you. They were shouting down the rumblings of their own hearts. After you deliver the manual, please return and lead the lemmings. And always remember that sometimes we must shout over the voices, and other times we lead by quietly not doing what everyone else is doing. We must be careful not to switch them at the wrong times. Grezniks act in their self-interest. Fighting our self-interest is fighting the Grezniks."

Gwilim shifted the blanket a little and gave Oskar some water.

"Thank you, son. Thank you," said Oskar.

Oskar closed his eyes forever. The brilliant colors of the skies put their curtain down.

Gwilim put his paws upon his own eyes and cried. It was too soon. He brushed Oskar's fur, wishing he could bring him back. He drifted into memories of the many times that Oskar had been a father to him when his own father was not. Early in Gwilim's life, Oskar had given the young, lost, and forlorn Gwilim a chance, an unwavering guiding hand. Gwilim kneeled and said a prayer which Oskar had taught him when he was young. Reciting the prayer reminded him of Oskar's kind and reassuring presence throughout his life. He held the manual tight as the fading light of a midnight summer sun gave him strength. Gwilim's soul felt the voice of the Father assure his broken heart that the lost little rascal he once was now had a determined heart ready for the battle ahead. Burdened with sorrow yet full of gratitude to Oskar, he kissed his father's forehead in a goodbye and prepared for the journey.

78

WITHERING IN THE SUN

Jatuh's aerial battle had been witnessed by creatures on the ground who took cover and did not dare emerge afterward, fearing that more Grezniks could be nearby. The wind was still, the water calm as glass, and nothing stirred. The silence was so quiet it felt like fear itself echoed across the land.

The barren land stretched out before Mitch, Tony, and Jovi, and the midnight sun drooped toward the horizon like a fading stage light. Black flies came out in a fury and bit the kids. The kids put their bug nets on, as their home-sickness rose from their hearts like smoke. The grotesque demise of Jatuh disturbed their thoughts, and they were afraid to ask of its implications.

"I want to be home," said Jovi.

Mitch said, "Me too."

"And I do too," said Fingal.

"I'm not sure where or what *home* is anymore. I just want to sleep on my bed on the farm," said Tony.

"And check on José, Joker, and Max," added Jovi.

"Let's get on our way, but be sure not to speak of what we just saw until we get to safety, and we must move as fast as we can," said Fingal.

Fingal and the kids rode their caribou back to their bikes. It was a fast but quiet ride as they fell into deep thought.

Tony asked Mitch and Jovi, "Do you wonder what Tobias is doing?"

Jovi said confidently, "There's one good thing: You don't need to worry about me keeping this a secret. From him. Or anyone. No one would believe me. And I'd have no idea even how to tell it."

"He's probably watching TV," Mitch speculated.

Tobias, back home, was in fact doing not much. He moped around the house, fretted about this and that, slept most of the day, complained of his headaches, and talked on the phone with his friends about how hard life is. He hardly thought of the kids, except to assume they were swimming and playing games at camp. But then he got a call from their parents.

As the kids neared their bikes' hiding spot, their walkie-talkies rang with an inbound call.

"Uh-oh, it's Tobias calling us," said Jovi. "Mitch, you answer it."

"But what am I going to say?" asked Mitch.

Tony said, "Tell him that we've been on a great camping adventure. And that we'll be home soon. That's all true."

Mitch answered. "Hello, Tobias. How are you? We were just talking about you."

Tobias was very worried. "I spoke to your parents today, and they were surprised to hear you were at camp. They said you weren't signed up for camp. I didn't pay attention to where you went, because I thought they knew. Where are you?"

"We're coming home soon. It was awesome. Climbing. Riding. Camping. Hiking. Everything. How are you? Did you remember to irrigate the basil field?"

Tobias had not remembered. He jumped up from the couch and panicked. "No, I *forgot*!" He ran around the room frantically. "I forgot. I forgot. And it's been really hot. I mean, like, record-breaking hot. Desert hot. It'll all be dead! I've got to go!"

Tobias hung up and ran outside and down the road to the basil crop and found all the specialty basil plants dead. He had not irrigated them and there had been consecutive days of dry, intense heat. Caroline and Darrell's basil business venture was wilted under the hot summer sun.

Tobias panicked. How could he ever tell his sister that he killed her entire basil crop and ruined her business plan? After Caroline's father Neil stole her money, she had very little left, and she and Darrell had put nearly all of it into their new herbal venture. That venture was now withered in the fields. Caroline would tell Tobias—once again, as she always did—that his judgment was horrible and he messed everything up.

To avoid telling his sister of his mistake, he had to somehow replace the plants before she returned to the farm. That way, she would never know. And he and her business plan could come out unscathed.

Tobias had never let his father manage his money, so unlike Caroline, Tobias still had loads of it left. Tobias decided to order replacement plants and new seed. He called his broker and said, "I'm investing in a new commodity. Basil. I need to buy as much basil as I possibly can."

The broker asked Tobias, "Why? What's happening in the basil market? Are hedge funds buying it up?"

"No, I don't want to buy hedges. The farm already has a healthy hedge going around the house. Lilacs or something. Never mind. I just need basil. Basil. Basil."

"Basil isn't like gold. You can't put it in a safe and hope it holds its value."

"But you can plant it and harvest," said Tobias.

The broker thought Tobias's plan was ill-advised and told him so. "Do you really want to put all your eggs in one basket?"

"I'm not buying eggs."

"I mean all your herbs in one bunch then? That's a very, very concentrated investment strategy. Diversify. Diversify."

"But I have to do this," Tobias said with desperation.

"Is this about your dad? Did he ask you to do this? This is something he would do. It's not good to follow in your dad's footsteps."

"It isn't about my dad. I promise you. It's an emergency. But never mind," said Tobias.

Tobias hung up and decided to just order the basil himself, but he had no idea how much. Tobias tried to calculate how much but he struggled. He felt something was not quite right with his numbers, so he redid them all, over and over again, until scrap papers were scattered all over the floor. He admitted to himself that he simply did not understand how to calculate quantities and decided it was just better to buy it all—an unfortunate conclusion because his very first calculation was actually accurate.

Tobias spent the rest of the day calling basil farms ordering fully grown basil plants to be shipped to their farm. He called seed companies and had every basil seed packet sent to the farm. He even called European farms and suppliers based all over Asia and arranged for their inventory to be flown in and shipped directly to the farm.

He figured if he bought everything, he would have plenty to plant. And on the chance those died, he would plant seedlings in pots and replace them if needed. Ordering all of it would ensure that he would not have to tell his sister about killing the basil crop.

Tobias bought out the entire supply of basil plants and seeds headed for every home and garden shop in the country, and for all the restaurants on each coast and every city in between—not realizing how much basil that was. Once he was done calling and ordering, he laid down to rest and waited for the shipments to come in. "They'll probably arrive right when the kids get home from camp, so they can help me plant it."

He smiled, flopped down on the couch, turned on the television, and relaxed as he watched a British cooking show about baking pretty pastries for the Queen of England.

79

A BROKEN ECHO

The caribou led Fingal and the kids back to their bikes, and they were all relieved to find them unharmed. The caribou had become like long-trusted friends, and the kids were sad to part from them. But they had to keep going and quickly. The kids patted their caribou and scratched their necks as a final goodbye. Then they got on their bikes and started the engines.

Fingal said, "Our next stop is the cabin marked with the anchored cross doorknocker."

"And a star-shaped doorknob," added Jovi.

"When we get close enough, you'll all see the maple leaf on your screen, marking the location of the cabin."

"It seems we were there years ago now," said Tony.

"It does," said Mitch. "Like another lifetime."

Fingal and the kids waved goodbye to the caribou and sped off. After several hours of traveling a convoluted route through Alaska, they ended up back at the Kigluaik Mountains. When they were still far beyond visual range of the cabin, unbeknownst to the kids, Fingal pushed a button on his bike. Far away, the ground where the cabin once stood opened up, and the cabin popped out and took shape. The maple leaf blinked on the bikes' mapping system.

"I see the maple leaf," said Mitch.

"Lead the way there," said Fingal.

Approaching the cabin from the other direction this time, they searched a long while and found a hidden path that looked impossibly treacherous from a distance, but it was navigable once they started along the journey. They found the cabin and pulled up alongside it. Fingal pulled his bike into the cabin and gestured for the kids to do the same with theirs.

Fingal opened the floorboards and unlocked the puzzle box entrance to expose the rickety steps again. But this time, instead of climbing down the steps, he collapsed them and lifted them into the cabin. Fingal slid another floor panel sideways, exposing an electrical switch, and said, "Make sure you have firm footing. The floor is going to move."

He flipped on the switch and the floor jerked downward. The kids grabbed each other to steady themselves as the cabin floor lowered. After dropping down several stories, the floor stopped moving. The space underground was lit only by the natural light coming from above them.

Fingal pulled his bike off the lift and parked it against an underground wall. He instructed the kids to do the same then said, "Mitch, pull that lever on the wall next to you."

Mitch pulled the lever, and the cabin above them folded down and the ground above them sealed tight. From outside, no one would ever know there had been a cabin there.

It was now as dark as the bottom of an iron mine. The kids held on to each other's arms to keep their bearings. They turned on their headlamps and lit a very long and narrow corridor ahead of them.

"We're going to ride our bikes down this corridor to find a surprise at the end of it," said Fingal.

They biked a long distance through the dark tunnel, then as they slowed around a corner, lights turned on and lit a large underground hangar. The aerial tractor combine stood before them in its flying configuration.

"Wow, how'd that get down here?" asked Mitch.

"I flew it up here. Let's load our bikes and gear into the cargo hold," said Fingal.

As they loaded their gear, Fingal said, "Now climb in and get buckled in."

Fingal got in after them and started the combine engine.

"Do you all remember how to fly this thing?" said Fingal.

The kids nodded.

"But we're underground, with a wall ahead of us," said Mitch.

Tony added, "We didn't learn how to fly a plane underground and into a wall."

Fingal smiled. "Check or hold?"

"Hold," they all said at the same time.

"There's nowhere to fly underground," said Jovi, wondering if Fingal was okay.

Fingal asked, "If we weren't underground, would you say 'check'?"

"That's a rather theoretical question, isn't it?" asked Mitch.

"Yes, it is. But if you weren't underground, would it be 'check' or 'hold'?"

They answered feebly, "Check."

Fingal accelerated the combine down the long, dark runway. The kids gripped each other's hands. The runway lights lit up along the underground runway. There was nothing ahead of them except a wall, and the combine was approaching it at a speed that would make it impossible to stop in time.

As it sped down the runway, the wing snapped a taut cord that hung vertically along the wall. When the cord snapped, it triggered a door in the wall to drop fast into the floor, opening the runway tunnel to the outdoors ahead of them. The door opened just in time. The combine flew out and above a river, but instead of flying strongly ahead, it started descending into the raging river below.

Mitch quickly adjusted the flight controls. The aircraft stopped descending but was now spinning in spirals, like a destabilized helicopter. The canyon wall was straight ahead, and the aircraft careened directly toward it.

Tony speedily pushed buttons on the cockpit's ceiling, stopped the spinning, and saved them from crashing into the canyon wall. Although the aircraft was no longer spinning uncontrollably, it was now flying directly for the canyon wall on the other side.

Jovi looked back at the wings and saw that they were not fully locked in, so she completed the steps to secure the wings in their flying position. They coordinated with each to other as they executed various steps and finally got the plane stabilized.

"Sorry about that, kids. I'm more exhausted than I realize. Must've missed some steps in the takeoff sequence," said Fingal. "Tony, push that blinking purple button."

Tony pushed it, and the canyon door they had just flown through closed instantly. Once closed, there was no evidence a door was ever there.

They flew through the river canyon, then swiftly increased their altitude, and headed straight for the instrument's mountain home. Once they were near the lemmings' cave, they descended rapidly until the cave entrance was straight ahead. Mitch and Tony then converted the plane to a helicopter, just like their first combine adventure when they went fishing from the sky. As her brothers maneuvered the helicopter closer to the cave, Jovi went back to the cargo hold to prepare it for loading the instrument.

In preparation for Fingal's arrival, the lemmings had successfully engineered a pulley system to move the instrument forward to the edge of the cave. The lemmings also built a ramp to transfer the instrument from the cave onto the aircraft and into the cargo hold.

Fingal took over the controls as Mitch and Tony joined Jovi in the back. Fingal hovered the rear of the aircraft so it lined up to the entrance to the cave. The lemmings slid the ramp forward so it reached from the cave to the cargo hold. The kids took hold of the ropes that were tied to the instrument. Tony and Mitch guided the instrument in while Jovi stood in the back to pull the instrument along the ramp and into the cargo hold.

The instrument was almost fully transferred when

suddenly the aircraft shifted downward abruptly. The kids lost their balance, fell to their knees, and grabbed the side, but the instrument jostled and many parts broke off and slid to the edge. Mitch and Tony caught many pieces. But too many plunged far below, including the piano key with the volcanic nugget and the silk banner draped over it.

Fingal asked, "Are you okay back there?"

"Yes!" said Mitch.

Fingal got the aircraft repositioned, and the kids pulled the damaged instrument inside and secured it. The ramps were pulled back into the cave. The lemmings stood on the edge, sad to see the beautiful instrument leave their care. The kids saluted the lemmings and waved goodbye.

The kids raised the back door of the craft and shut it tight.

Fingal asked, "Is everything secured? Door closed tightly?"

"Yes," said Tony.

Fingal flew off quickly. The kids ensured the instrument was fully secured, disappointed that it had been significantly damaged on its way in. Jovi put the broken pieces into a safe compartment. The kids got situated in the front and waved goodbye to the lemmings on the ledge, but in a flash they were too far away to see them.

Tony said nervously, "Fingal, the instrument was too fragile. It got quite damaged as we loaded it in."

"Broken?" asked Fingal.

"Yes. And some pieces fell down the mountain," said Mitch.

Fingal was very quiet. The kids looked out the window and down at the terrain that they had traveled over by bike just days earlier. It seemed so long ago. Fingal's old hands clenched the gears, and his face drooped with seriousness.

"I'm sorry. I didn't mean to break the instrument," said Mitch.

"Me neither," said Tony. "I'm sorry."

Jovi asked Fingal, "Are you upset with us?"

"No, I'm not upset with you. We're lucky to have transferred the instrument without it plunging down the cliff. I'm just deep in thought. The battle is broader and more complicated than I understood, even after all my years. And I don't know what that means for us. For you three in particular. There was once a book called nothing more than the 'Story.' I never saw it, but I was told of it. The Story guided the mission. It shared details of the Grezniks and Tukors and the many battles over the centuries. When I was younger, I heard that the Story described the power and might of a magnificent instrument. But one day, the last copy of the Story blew away. Drifted away in the winds. Knowing what we should do next would be easier if we had the Story. But we don't. There's nothing easy about protecting something. But I believe we are called to try. The messy imperfect journey of trying."

80

TOO SMALL, TOO FAR

Gwilim sat near the edge of Oskar's faraway lookout and was overwhelmed by the expansive view of the world beyond the mountain. He had a long journey ahead, and he had no idea where to even start. Gwilim reluctantly grabbed his pack with the book inside. The load felt even heavier, a burden he was too small to bear. Yet he knew he had to try. He put the pack on, took a deep breath, and stepped forward to begin.

Suddenly a gust of wind came in from outside and knocked Gwilim over. He looked out to see what caused the sudden wind but saw nothing. He turned around to start his journey again, but then another blast of wind blew in. When he looked out this time, he saw Raadsel flying every which way, searching high and low across the mountain face for the oddly shaped Greznik.

Gwilim thought he might be hallucinating. He had witnessed Raadsel plunging into the lake with Tiro in his grip and dying. But Gwilim watched the eagle soaring above and knew it had to be true: Raadsel was not dead.

Gwilim called out, "Over here!"

Raadsel swooped down and perched near Gwilim.

Gwilim was dumbfounded and asked, "How are you here? I saw you die."

"There is no language for where I am," said Raadsel. "The instrument has left the mountain. But another Greznik is somewhere nearby. I cannot find it, but I know it is here somewhere."

Raadsel looked in and saw his beloved friend, Oskar, departed from this world. "So sad to lose a great friend. We still need him."

Gwilim agreed. "Oskar gave me one more mission before he left this world but I failed. He wanted me to run back to the cave and deliver a book, the instrument's manual, to the Tukor. He said it was urgent. But I just couldn't leave Oskar alone. I stayed with him instead."

"It was good of you to stay by his side."

"But he gave me that one last task, and I didn't get it done." Gwilim pulled the heavy book out of his pack. "Can you fly the manual to the Tukor?"

"No, I am sorry. I cannot. The instrument has left, and they're long gone by now. I cannot fly that far beyond this mountain. I can carry you as far as I can, but after that, you'll need to take it the rest of the way. It's a long way, several thousand miles."

"I don't know how I can do this, but I'll try," said Gwilim. He put the book inside his pack again. "But I can't leave yet. We must bury our good friend first. Can we bring him back to our friends for a proper burial?"

"If I bring him back, I fear the lemmings will believe I killed him," said Raadsel.

"They couldn't distrust you anymore. After all that happened with Tiro, they must understand their mistakes now," said Gwilim.

"Too many creatures prefer to believe falsehoods about a friend than admit to their own mistakes. They will one day learn what happened to their wise Oskar."

Raadsel plucked some of his own feathers and gently covered Oskar with them. "I will ensure that he is buried alongside his beloved wife. Until then, light will shine on his resting place and keep it safe. What a deeply good soul he was."

"I have one more problem. The book is written in the ancient lemming language. Oskar was likely the last one who knew how to read the ancient language. I don't know anyone who knows it."

"Trust that you'll be able to figure it out. Tell no one about the book. No one can know the manual exists, especially the Grezniks. I don't think Tiro collaborated with other lemmings, but we don't know for sure. Are you ready to go?"

Gwilim was not ready to go, and Raadsel sensed his hesitation. Without notice, Raadsel grabbed Gwilim carefully in his talons and flew him as far as he could from the mountain, believing that when he set him down again, Gwilim would somehow find his way.

As they flew, worries weighed heavily on their minds, but they were unaware of a far greater concern nearby. Skarb had slithered up the far west side unseen and had been hiding in a crevice not too far from Oskar's favorite lookout. Skarb had heard everything. After Raadsel flew away with Gwilim, Skarb climbed quickly down and followed Raadsel's flight from the ground, wholly undetected.

Up high, where even Skarb could not hear, Raadsel told Gwilim, "The Tukor lives on a farm near a small town named Dunnell, much farther south, where corn grows strong. I do not know where that is, but search for allies along the way who can help you get there."

When Raadsel had flown as far as he could from the mountain, he swooped down and set Gwilim carefully on the ground.

"Good luck," said Raadsel. "I wish I could take you all the way."

"I understand," said Gwilim. "But it's such a long way. And look at me. I'm just a lemming. I'm not meant to migrate such distances."

"Have faith," said Raadsel.

Gwilim secured his pack on tight with the heavy book inside and started his long journey. His tiny little feet would have to carry that book thousands of miles, and he had no idea how he would ever make it.

Every step, Gwilim said to himself, "I can do this. Just one step at a time."

After several days, his feet were blistered, his muscles were exhausted, and he needed to stop more often to rest. He did not know that every time he rested, so did Skarb—who was traveling a good distance behind to remain unnoticed.

Skarb grew severely irritated with the critter's slow, pathetic plod. The speed was so boring that Skarb would sometimes fall asleep standing up and tip over. Skarb wanted to just eat the plodding critter and steal the manual. But Skarb needed Gwilim alive: Gwilim knew where the instrument was and Skarb did not. And without knowing where the instrument was, the manual was useless. Skarb was painfully aware that the two of them had no means by which to communicate. Like all Grezniks, Skarb could understand all languages but could speak and write none.

It did not take long before Gwilim was faltering. He had tried to find a speedier friend to carry him along the journey, but none surfaced. Some ran by and never saw him. Others had no interest in helping. He rested, ate a snack, and took a nap. His feet were raw, so he bandaged them as best he could. Before starting again, he took a deep breath to summon the courage to walk more before night-fall. He walked for an hour, lost his way, then collapsed suddenly from a muscle cramp in his leg. He cried up to the sky, "What am I to do? I don't know which way to go. And there's no one to help me."

Skarb had had enough. "This is ridiculous. Where does this floundering critter think he's going?"

Skarb, trailing a long distance back, zoomed its eyes in and got a good look at Gwilim's feet. There was no way that lemming could walk much more. Skarb ran ahead.

Before Gwilim even knew anything was there, Skarb had snatched him and stuffed him in his mouth alongside its cheek, and ran off as fast as it could.

Gwilim, holding his pack tightly, jostled around inside Skarb's cheek and was overcome with anguish. The manual had been captured by a Greznik. He was sure the Greznik would steal the book and then swallow him whole. He wept inside Skarb's mouth. "I'm so sorry, Oskar. I let you down. I failed again!"

Gwilim was soaking in Skarb's phlegm and could barely breathe. All crumpled up and jammed inside the mouth, he still prayed that the book would somehow survive without damage and get to the Tukor safely.

81

WHERE?

The kids and Fingal flew at a very high altitude, unde-tected, far above all other aircraft in the sky. Exhausted and anxious to get back, it was a quiet, solemn flight home. In the middle of the night, they approached the farm for a landing, and when the coast was clear, they landed on the dirt road in front of Fingal's farm. They converted the aircraft back to a tractor combine and drove it right into his barn.

When the kids stepped out of the combine, the safety of familiar ground allowed their exhaustion to fully take hold. They flopped down on some bales of hay.

Fingal said, "We made it. We dismantled the clues and kept the mine hidden. An amazing accomplishment. And I would never have succeeded on my own. The mission needed your willingness to take the journey. Your desire to help. Your determination to try."

Fingal mixed them some ice-cold chocolate milk and pulled some snacks out of his icebox. They drank the delicious chocolate milk in an exhausted haze, not noticing how strange it was that Fingal had a fresh supply of milk and chocolate syrup in his ice box after so long a journey.

"What're we going to do with the instrument?" said Tony.

"We can talk about that later. Right now, it's time for you to get a good night's rest," said Fingal.

"What if the Grezniks come here?" asked Jovi.

"The mice are on high alert and will guard it," said Fingal.

"Mice?" said Tony doubtfully.

"Yes, mice. The mice on this farm play a critical role in protecting the blue stones from capture. Invisible to the untrained eye, the mice have many security systems in place here on the farm. If a Greznik should enter this barn, the mice will drop traps from the rafters. In some places, the floor breaks open to drop a Greznik into a pool of water to be dissolved."

Fingal showed them one of the snares, and the kids were amazed. All the times they had been in the barn, they had never seen the hidden traps.

Fingal continued, "There are many camouflaged traps around and near the farm. Later, I'll show you others scattered around."

One of the mice ran out of hiding and up Fingal's leg, then dropped a note in his front shirt pocket. Fingal pulled the note out and said, "The mice want to welcome you and are excited to have you on board."

"Am I awake? This is all so strange, it has to be a dream." said Jovi.

Fingal said, "For now, you can go on home and rest assured that the stones and the instrument will be safe. The mice have it fully under control. I'll let you know when our work is ready to start up again. We'll put the instrument deep into hiding again. But for now, we rejoice that we are together and safely at home."

"I really want to sleep in my own bed, but I don't think we should go back now and wake up Tobias," said Mitch.

"And how would we explain why we got back from camp at one in the morning?" said Jovi.

Tony sat back down on a big bale of hay and asked, "Is it okay if we stay here until morning?"

Fingal pulled out some blankets, and the kids curled up on the bales and fell into a deep sleep. While they were sound asleep, Fingal wrote some notes in a journal, then locked the journal in a hidden cabinet. Then he, too, curled up under a blanket, lying on a long, cushioned bench against the wall and fell sound asleep.

They woke to Fingal making his egg coffee. Mitch, Tony, and Jovi stepped out of the barn as the sun tipped over the horizon to greet them with a welcoming sunrise. They looked toward their farm but were surprised to see many semitrucks lined up waiting to deliver goods to their farm. And many more were still arriving. The lineup of trucks started at their farm and extended several miles down the road and around a corner.

"What on earth is happening over there?" asked Fingal.

Tony looked through his binoculars to see what the

first truck in line was unloading. He saw green potted plants lined up alongside the truck and said, "Basil!"

▲ ▲ ▲

Skarb, with Gwilim in its mouth, ran far away from anything that would be familiar to Gwilim and far from any creature who could help him. It stopped running and pulled Gwilim out of its mouth, dripping in Skarb's disgusting saliva. Gwilim tried to run away, but Skarb easily snatched him, lifted him to its face, and asked, "Where were you going with your valuable little pack?"

Gwilim answered truthfully. "I have no idea what you are saying. No one can understand the Greznik language."

Skarb squeezed Gwilim's neck and said, "Tell me where you are going! Tell me where the Tukor is!"

"I can't understand you!" said Gwilim, choking.

Skarb shoved Gwilim and his pack in its mouth again and ran off, not really knowing where to go. Deep in Alaska on the outskirts of a deserted town, Skarb found an old, abandoned, one-room schoolhouse and entered through its collapsing roof. The classroom's wooden floors were rotted from years of rain and snow coming in through broken windows, cracks in the walls, and a collapsing roof. Old desks left behind were tipped over and broken. A bookshelf stood empty against a weather-stained wall. Its books were scattered on the floor with frayed covers and rippled pages. Abandoned bird nests perched high in the eaves. Yet the slate chalkboard still hung strong, ready for new lessons. A few broken chalk pieces lay inside a fallen desk.

Skarb pulled Gwilim out of its mouth and placed him on the floor. Gwilim tried to run away, but Skarb lightly stepped on him and held him back. Skarb could read any language but could write none. But it had to somehow communicate with the furry little critter.

"Where are Spoonbill and Bustard when I need them? They can talk to me," Skarb mumbled.

Skarb grabbed a piece of chalk and placed it in front of Gwilim. Gwilim grabbed it, and Skarb picked him up and held him in front of the chalkboard.

"Write where you are going," ordered Skarb.

"I told you, I can't understand you!" said Gwilim.

Skarb barked more angrily, "Where you are going?"

Gwilim wrote in the tiny lettering of a lemming: "I don't know what you are saying!!!!!"

Skarb grumbled.

Gwilim wrote: "WRITE WHAT YOU WANT TO SAY!!!!!"

"Grezniks can't write," gnarled Skarb. In frustration, Skarb took the piece of chalk away from Gwilim, threw it on the floor, and crushed it.

Skarb set Gwilim on the ground, and Gwilim bolted for an escape. Skarb let Gwilim run but just as he was about to get away, Skarb leisurely grabbed Gwilim with one of its extra legs and walked out of the schoolhouse. Skarb looked all around but had no idea which direction to go. Skarb sat down on the school's broken steps, curled up its tail, and set Gwilim down within the coil. Gwilim tried to run away dozens of times, but Skarb's tail simply grabbed Gwilim and set him down again. Gwilim, hungry and thirsty, got too tired to try anymore.

The two lost creatures sat next to each other in silence. The tundra sun tipped down to the horizon and lit the clouds a brilliant red like the blushing red cheeks and a dropping glance of a bashful girl. Skarb was oblivious to the quiet end of the day, but Gwilim was grateful to see the beautiful red sky after being stuck in the pitch-dark of the Greznik's disgusting mouth. By midnight, the clouds billowed together and faded to gray.

Gwilim fell asleep, surrounded by Skarb's coiled tail.

Skarb whispered, "You will tell me. Yes, you will, little lemming. You will tell me where that instrument is."

JEANNINE KELLOGG loves a grand adventure and a great story. But she enjoys nothing more than encouraging kids to seize life's wonderful adventure and take the lead in their own powerful journey. You can visit Jeannine and get updates on book two in The Tukor's Journey series at www.JeannineKellogg.com

Stay tuned...the adventure continues in

THE TUKOR'S JOURNEY BOOK TWO